WAR OF THE RAVEN QUEEN

THE GODDESS PROPHECIES

BOOK  SIX

ARAYA EVERMORE

WAR OF THE RAVEN QUEEN

Cover art by Deranged Doctor Design

www.arayaevermore.com
www.joannastarr.com

StarFire

Published by Starfire Epic Fantasy

Paperback First Edition
ISBN-13: 978-99957-917-4-2

Also by Araya Evermore:

The Goddess Prophecies:

Night Goddess

The Fall of Celene

Storm Holt

Demon Spear

Dragons of the Dawn Bringer

War of the Raven

Acknowledgements

Thank you to Jon for his unending support and patience. Thanks to Ian for all his help, ideas and encouragement. Thank you to Jill for her excellent editorial work.

A special thank you to Dan and all my Beta Readers (you know who you are) who made this work that much more epic. Thank you to my precious Reader Team who make this work especially fun, and to all the great people on the Raven Guild Facebook group who never fail to make my day.

Thanks to Milo and the Deranged Doctor Design team for their wonderful cover art. Thanks to the Cosmos for making this work possible. I would also like to thank you, the reader, for continuing the adventure.

For That Which Is Eternal

MAIORIA
THE KNOWN WORLD

MUNLAND

LANS HIMAY

TERAMIDES

INTOLANA

Leottlde Mountains

DAVONO

REDBEN

JUNOS

ATALANPH

MAPHRAX

Mountians
of Maphrax

ISLES
OF
TIRRY

Myrn

HALLABSTAR-IX

OSTASIA

TARVALASTONE

VENOSIA

N
W   E
S

Ocean Kingdom

CHAPTER 1

White Raven

DARK thoughts crowded Issa's mind as she lay on her bed in the cramped cabin.

Their warship, one of hundreds, sailed the dangerous and unpredictable waters between Davono and Venosia on a voyage that could well be their last. Struggling to sleep, she stared into the dark, the creaking and swaying of the ship both strangely relaxing and foreboding at the same time. Was her floating home carrying her to her death?

She imagined the sea, endless and dark beneath her, waves crashing white against the ship as it moved through the inky blackness. Above, a clouded sky made their passage even darker, and that hot, arid wind from Atalanph blew. Ahead, the coast of Venosia and the impending battle against Baelthrom's hordes drew closer.

She closed her eyes for the tenth time only to see the black claws of the Devil's Horns rising up before her, eager to smash into the pathetic hulls of their feeble wooden homes.

Where was Asaph? Where was Freydel? Had they left her in her darkest hour? *No, Asaph will come to me, I know it. And Freydel? …I can but pray.*

How long until they reached the Devil's Horns? And how would they overcome them? Between now and when they reached them, she hoped the wizards would come up with a plan. Destroying them with magic would exhaust the wizards, and they needed every ounce of strength for the battle itself – and the use of magic would also alert the enemy.

If only Freydel were with them with his orb, he'd certainly figure something out, but he wasn't here when he was needed the most. Had she pinned too much on hope? Was starting this war the most foolish thing she'd ever done? Was she about to send thousands of people, including herself, to their deaths?

With a long, exhausted sigh, an uneasy slumber stole over her.

Ahead, row upon row of jagged black spikes speared out of the ocean. Beyond them crawled the dark mass of Venosia. The wind blew harder until it screamed through the rigging and churned the sea. Gripping a rope around the mast, Issa spread her feet wide as the ship swayed drunkenly. Above, the clouds crowded thickly, turbulent and red-tinged.

In the Abyss the sky had been red—red, like blood and rage.

The Under Flow surged towards her, a loud din in her head, a cacophony of dark power hunting for her, stalking its prey. She reached for the Flow before it was smothered and formed a shield around herself. The Under Flow withdrew, its prey now unattainable.

Issa let go of her held breath and passed a hand over her forehead. It came away wet with sweat. Thunder cracked and a thick bolt of red lightning split the sky. She screamed as it smashed into a spike directly before the bow, illuminating the others around it.

A terrible groaning wailed through the air, the same tortured sound she had heard in the Dark Rift. Fear clenched her stomach, her heart thundered and the air turned too thick to breathe. The noise, the storm, the Under Flow, everything crushed down upon her. She collapsed onto the deck sweating, trembling.

She stared up, the sky was so close she could touch it. The clouds darkened and clustered together into familiar, looming shapes and an utterly helpless feeling assaulted her body, paralysing her in terror.

The Light Eaters, massive beyond comprehension, groaned and crowded above her, three hooded, faceless shapes looking down from their thrones in the sky. She was nothing. No magic could withstand their power. Hands made of dark clouds reached towards her, fingers opened wide, and from their clutches, four smaller shapes galloped.

She clung to the mast and stared, unable to look away, her body shivering and shaking. Sweat soaked her back despite the agonising cold that ate into her bones.

The horsemen grew large, hooves thundering on air. A shadow horse threw back its head and neighed, its scream cutting through the torturous moaning of the Eaters.

A raucous cawing joined it. A raven flew between her and the horsemen, but not a raven she knew. This one was pure white. She tried to reach it but there was nothing, as if the bird were a ghost, a figment of her imagination. Why was it white? Why did it not come to her?

Fear trickled like ice down her back. She inhaled sharply, more afraid of the raven than any of the horrors beyond it. The raven wheeled and dived, seeking neither to protect her nor fight her enemies.

'You've come to warn me,' she stated in a whisper.

The raven cawed, a long and mournful sound that brought with it all the desperate sorrow and emptiness she had known in the Shadowlands. Issa sobbed and clutched at the neck of her nightclothes.

The raven turned and flew straight at her. She raised her hands to ward it off and screamed.

Issa jerked awake, her eyes wildly hunting the darkness of her cabin.

Clutching her sweat-soaked nightshirt, she swung her legs over the side of the bed and, breathing hard, smoothed back her hair with shaking hands as she grappled for reality. It was still pitch black outside the porthole and the ship swayed and creaked rhythmically.

It was just a nightmare, she told herself, though she really didn't feel it was. There was more to it than just a bad dream; a prophetic message she wasn't ready to learn.

Someone knocked on the door. Softly at first, then more urgently and louder when she did not respond.

'Lady Issa?' Velonorian's voice was tinged with worry. The young elf opened the door a crack and held his lantern high. Seeing her dishevelled, distraught look, he hurried into the room.

'Lady Issa, are you sick? You're as pale as a wraith and drenched! Has some evil magic befallen you? I was passing your door and I thought I heard crying.'

Issa could barely find the words to speak. She took the water he poured for her from the pitcher beside her bed, and gratefully drank, trying to still her shaking hands.

'Some war commander I am. I'm in no fit state to lead this offensive,' her voice was hoarse and ragged.

Velonorian sank down onto his heels to bring his head level with hers, interweaving his fingers and resting his elbows on his knees. 'You won't be leading it, the well-seasoned military commanders will. You're the spark but they're the drivers. There's nothing to fear. You had a dream, a vision. I can see it in your aura. Even your eyes are blue with the Sight.'

Issa nodded. 'I saw those things in the Dark Rift. And I saw the Shadow Knights who hunt me.' Her stomach twisted into knots as she recalled the four horsemen, their forms emerging from shadow and smoke.

She let go a long silent breath and tried to sit up straighter. 'But worse than that, I saw a white raven...'

Why had she seen a white raven? Had it been sent to her by Zanufey as a warning? Was she doing something wrong?

'What is its meaning?' asked Velonorian.

Issa looked away. She didn't want to say. She didn't want to speak aloud what she knew to be the truth. She took a deep breath and met his violet eyes. 'The white raven is warning me of my death. What else can it mean? I don't know if it was sent by Zanufey. I don't know why it should come to me now. Could it be I'm taking the wrong course of action? Yet, of everything else I think of, this is the only action to take. There's nothing else for me to do.' She chewed a fingernail.

'It's a warning, a message to be cautious and nothing more,' said Velonorian, squeezing her shoulder gently. She swallowed and nodded, wanting to believe him. 'Now, why don't you try to get some restful sleep? My room is just down the hall. I've already placed a simple ward on your door, it's not much and not strong like a true wizard could cast, but it's Elven, and will hold until dawn.'

'Thank you, Velonorian,' she said, touched at the gesture though knowing nothing could stop the horsemen. She slowly laid back down, but could tell from his frown that he was deeply worried as he shut the door behind him.

She watched the creeping light from his lantern fade away beneath the door and darkness enveloped her once more. After a moment blinking into the black, she reached over the side of the bed and grabbed the orb and raven talisman. She held one in each hand protectively. *No Shadow Knight can attack me now.*

Forcing her mind to focus only upon the gentle rocking of the ship, she drifted back to sleep.

The darkness brightened slowly into a pale, grey-blue light.

She held up her talisman and orb but there was no danger, only quiet, calm, and blue fog swirling thickly around her, a fog which thickened until it took on a liquid quality. Soon she was suspended in beautiful aqua-blue water, but strangely, she could still breathe. She took a deep slow breath and let it go, watching fascinated as her exhalation emerged as bubbles. The foreboding that had gripped her for days disappeared completely. Instead she felt a playful joy.

'Issa,' a voice said softly in her head.

She looked around.

'Issa,' the voice said again, closer.

She saw the flash of purple and silver.

'Wykiry?' she answered back.

Three Wykiry appeared, their wing-like fins splaying out beautifully around them as they began to circle and dance around her.

'In the ocean, we are always close. The Undead Knights hunt you. Nowhere is safe. Be careful of your dreams.' The Wykiry spoke as one, their mellow voices barely whispers in her mind. *'There are other dangers. All the power of Maioria cannot stand against that of the Dark Rift. Do not fight the Light Eaters. Run.'*

'I try but they find me and I can't escape,' Issa said, using her Daluni talents.

'It's because the fallen out-lander has found you.'

'Who? The woman with the black eyes?' Issa saw in her mind the beautiful but cruel face of Lona and shivered.

'Yes,' said the Wykiry.

'But how are we to free Maioria if we cannot fight the Dark Rift?' Issa asked.

'We do not know. But if you fight them now, you will fail.'

Issa chewed her lip. *'Then it's hopeless. This battle will be to our deaths.'*

'*No. The more lands that are freed, the more power returns to Maioria, the stronger she becomes.*'

It seemed of little comfort.

'*And there is always hope.*' The Wykiry pressed.

Issa gave a bitter laugh. The Wykiry sensed her futility and slowed their circling. She felt warmth and comfort exude from them. They did not know everything, she reminded herself. They were not gods. *Fate will not control my destiny,* she vowed.

'*Yes,*' they said, reading her thoughts, and nodding their smooth round snouts. '*Be the Raven Queen. Chart the destiny of your people. Come.*' Their voices faded as they began to disappear into the blue.

She didn't want them to go. A thought that had been on her mind for a long time came to the fore and she took out the Orb of Water.

'*Why did you give this to me rather than take it back after Keteth? You can use it to do far greater things than I can,*' she said.

'*Because only you can set us free,*' a voice said from inside the blue.

'*What do you mean, set you free? From the ocean?*'

'*From our curse; from the Immortals and from the sea to which we are bound.*'

'*How do I do that? I barely know how to use it.*'

'*We do not know, only that you can and you will. Through the orb you can reach us if you need. Call for us and we will come,*' the voice said.

The water turned cooler and darker as the Wykiry retreated and the dream darkened. The surface found her, and she inhaled but the air felt dank and polluted after the light water she had been breathing.

A dark red sky clouded above and a heavy ominous feeling fell. The Devil's Horns rose out of the ocean before her. Yelping, she turned and tried to swim away but an unseen force pushed her forwards.

'*Don't be afraid of what you see. Remember the orb,*' the Wykiry whispered in her mind from far away.

She closed her eyes and gripped the orb, focussing her mind on it, drawing on the Flow. She poured it into the orb.

There was a strange subtle switch in the magical energy as the orb and her mind connected. She was still in the Flow but it was oddly different, lesser in scope and yet purer. *It's pure magic!* she realised with a start. Pure elemental water power unmixed with the other elements of fire, air or earth.

She let the orb's power fill her, and with it came deep understanding of the elemental. Rivers and tides weren't things and processes; they were beings in their own right. She understood the way the tiny unseen particles of water bonded together, how water froze and why it turned to mist or fog.

As understanding filled her, she became ever one with it until she felt herself melding with the ocean itself. In a rush, the immense elemental power of the sea became her power.

She spread her arms wide, holding the orb high. At her command, the sea surged, lifting her up. Higher and higher the sea rose, a great expanse of ocean reaching up into the sky. Issa looked down and laughed at the incredible sight. The ocean carried her on the crest of a great wave. Fifty feet below, the Devil's Horns were no more than harmless splinters that simply vanished as the ocean surged over them.

'*You cannot learn the power of an orb, you can only be shown what it can do,*' said the Wykiry, their voices barely audible over the tremendous roar of the surf.

The great wave slowed and Issa felt herself sinking down gently into the sea and into a place where there were no dreams.

Asaph angled his wings and looked down upon the immense gold dragon statue of Feygriene dominating the centre of the lake.

The spring sunlight gleamed brightly off the magnificent effigy and an incredible feeling of awe bloomed deep in his chest.

He roared and listened as the sound echoed around the mountains and was soon joined by three more. He glanced back at the other dragons also circling the skies: Garna, the slender red female; and the two big males, Rust the red and Pennarc the green—those who had joined him in his attack on Avernayis. Only to the three by his side had he proven himself, had he shown that they could trust him, and so they had been bonded more closely.

Whilst he had been gone, the dragons had built the statue with the gold they'd kept hidden deep in their lairs. They must have hoarded mountains of the stuff to create the life-sized dragon, thought Asaph.

Using dragon magic, they had built up the base of the lake with rock and moulded the gold on top of it into the image of their goddess. With their combined powers it had taken them mere days, whereas any human endeavour of a similar scale would have taken years.

Asaph took in the sight of the towering mountains with their snow tips set against a deep blue sky, the glistening crystal-clear lake below surrounded by rich green meadow, and he nodded his head: this was the place of their magnificent rebirth.

The dragons had told him that, long ago, in Arc's time, this place had been called Arc-Ralan, after the mighty wizard Ralan Afisius and the great dragon, Arc.

Now, the dragons called it Yis, meaning "dragon heart" in Dragon Speech. Here, the dragons had been reborn. Now was their time to live again. The Dragon Dream had gone but in its place they would have their sacred haven on Maioria.

Faelsun would be proud, he thought.

With another body shaking roar, he turned south, and the others followed.

Far below, at the base of the mountains, eight more dragons were visible. They would not come with him despite how he'd tried to convince them all to join the mighty battle—and what could be more glorious than a legion of dragons to make the Immortal Lord tremble? But the dragon race was still weak, and it was true that they were needed here to gather the others.

Asaph still sensed reluctance and distrust within those who had not fought alongside him at Avernayis. And why should they trust him? He, a Dragon Lord, the very same as those who had become Dromoorai and turned upon and destroyed their own kind.

Morhork had not been seen since their fight. He'd given up trusting the wingless dragon.

The green oasis of Yis disappeared behind him and the world turned into frigid ice sheets and towering mountains of snow. He felt the minds of Garna, Pennarc and Rust linked to his own. Just having the connection was teaching him many things—things a Dragon Lord should have known decades ago.

The wind itself carried messages, such as how far away winter or summer was, or when the next snow fall would come. He now instinctively knew how high he was, how far ahead the ocean lay, and a hundred minor things that had become second nature to him.

He sighed, feeling a deep sense of belonging for the first time in his life. If only Coronos were with him to share in that feeling. As soon as Issa was by his side, there remained only one thing left for him to do: retake Drax. Fire rumbled in his belly.

Like the great Dragon Legions of old, we will descend upon Drax and wrench it from the Immortal Lord's grasp!

CHAPTER 2

Myth of Myths

JARLAIN paused and looked back over her shoulder for the hundredth time.

It had only taken a day to get to The Centre on Fenn's back, but now the elderly, the young, and the injured made it painfully slow going on the return journey. The night was also overcast and very dark to make matters even worse.

Already, Shufen's arrows and Tarn's knife had taken down two death hounds that had ambushed them in the dark; they were easy prey with their torch beacons in the forest. There had been a third, but it had escaped and run off into the forest.

Jarlain noted the odd behaviour. Usually they fought to the death, they never fled. No one spoke aloud what they all felt—that it had run off to get others. Everyone was tired, uneasy, and jumpy, but she refused them rest.

Fenn gave a low growl. He was sick of the slow speed too.

'It's a wonder you humans survive anything,' was all he said when they stopped yet again to wait for everyone to catch up. Jarlain pursed her lips and adjusted her helmet. At least the night gave respite from the heat of the sun, though she was still sweating under her armour. She decided to stop here and wait for daybreak.

Hours later, dawn broke; thick golden rays burst through the rich green canopy of the jungle. Her vantage point on a rocky hill looked out over the vastness of the forest—her home. She sighed, wishing she were here for good. Apart from the swathes of blackened, destroyed earth along the coast, the enemy had ultimately done little to hurt this endless land. She did not allow herself to hope though. It would not stay that way. Larger countries than hers had fallen to the Immortals.

She arched her back and stretched her sore muscles. They had made it through the night alive, and for that she gave thanks to Woela. Behind her, the others wearily stirred from their far too brief sleep.

'How long, Fenn?' Jarlain asked the bear as he returned from the stream.

He sniffed the air, finding his answers there before speaking. *'An hour, maybe more if we stop.'*

'We cannot stop. I have the awful feeling we're not going to get out of here without a fight,' she said.

He growled.

Their journey became easier as Fenn led them downhill along a gentle slope. Jarlain glanced behind. The long line of people, all of whom were carrying weapons, looked tired, but there was a determined set to their expressions.

Soon they heard the sound of the sea rushing against the shore. Hushed cheers spread, and relief washed over Jarlain. She hurried forwards but as she ran the ground shifted beneath her feet, making her stumble. Everything fell silent and an odd sensation filled the air. Fenn pushed his nose into her hand but she could barely feel or see him as numbness spread over her. He was coming to recognise when the Hidden Ones brought her visions.

She tried to control herself by sitting before she fell, but reality had already shifted. She heard that awful scream in her mind, the one that nearly made her lose control of her bladder. Her breathing came fast and shallow as the ground tumbled then righted itself. Great black shadows passed overhead. She looked up; many black dragons turned to her and roared torrents of flame.

'Hurry,' she screamed, her voice coming from far away. 'They're coming!'

Jarlain found herself slumped over Fenn's back, her arm gripped gently in his mouth. The bear was desperately trying to keep her on his back as he rushed through the forest. She came around and hugged his neck, clinging on as the pounding in her head receded and her senses returned.

'Too many to fight,' said Fenn.

Blearily, she glanced behind her to see all the people running, terror on their faces. She didn't dare look up. The dragon fear would take her when it came. The black dragons weren't here yet, but even Fenn could feel them.

He came to a jolting stop just before they reached the exposed beach, staying under the cover of the trees. But trees were not going to protect them. Jarlain swung her legs off his back and stumbled to the ocean's edge. A gust of wind and great screech coming from behind made her stagger. The boatman's name was on her lips only to be ripped away by the dragon fear that coursed through her. Her legs shook and her bladder let go as she collapsed onto her knees.

Fenn roared. The bear's dragon fear made her own more potent. Flames and immense heat burst in front of her and sprayed the trees. She couldn't run or even turn her head to look back.

Call the boatman! Her mind yelled at her. The screams of her people cut through the grip of dragon fear. Kneeling on the wet sand she held her hands high and forced the words out.

'Murlonius!' she screamed three times.

Her whole body trembled as she pushed herself onto one knee, then the next, and finally to a standing position. She reached behind her back and pulled her spear free. It seemed to take an age. She turned in time to see the jungle become engulfed in thick orange flames. Fenn was locked in a struggle with a Foltoy, the undead beast's fur already slick with black blood.

A howl of battle rage escaped her throat and she forgot about the thickening mist spreading over the ocean behind her as she lunged to help Fenn.

The Foltoy slid off her spear and Fenn whirled to face the next. Huge black shapes passed overhead, darkening the ground, and the jungle was alive with the howls of Foltoy and death hounds.

Something hard slammed into her, hurling her several feet into the air. Dazed and winded, she rolled out of instinct, narrowly missing the black axe that smacked into the white sand just in front of her face.

Jarlain jumped up, flinching at the contorted, ugly, grey face of her attacker. She dodged its blade again and slammed her spear straight through its pale eye. It howled and sunk to its knees, black blood oozing down its face.

Panting heavily, she wrenched her weapon free and took in the impossible sight before her. The forest was alive with the enemy and at least four Dread Dragons flew overhead. There was no hope.

She glanced to the ocean and was struck by the picture of calm. Standing in his boat was Murlonius with Yisufalni just behind him. The sky beyond had turned orange with the sunrise and the glass-like sea mirrored the boat and boatman perfectly. Around them drifted a glowing pale mist. Neither of the Ancients moved, they seemed like statues, an island of serenity in the bloody chaos of battle. Then, he beckoned.

'Get to the boat!' Jarlain screamed.

Fenn heard. He crunched his jaws, finishing off the death hound and tossed the body aside. Standing on his hind legs, he gave a mighty roar.

Jarlain ran towards him, screaming again and again, 'Everyone, get to the boat!'

A moment passed where nothing happened other than the sounds of screams and clash of weapons, then waves of wounded, panicking people hurtled out of the forest towards the ocean. They splashed and fell, frantic to reach the boat.

A death hound bounded out of a bush and clamped its jaws down on Jarlain's spear arm. Her metal bracers creaked between its powerful jaws as it yanked left and right. She pulled her knife free and plunged it into the base of its skull. The undead dog shivered and fell.

She looked ahead and laughed. Murlonius' boat had expanded to fit the hundred or so people already in it. Yisufalni constantly lifted her arms and an unseen power lifted people from the ocean.

Jarlain glanced back. Bloodied bodies floated in the water and were scattered on the beach. Red blood on white sand. Still, people streamed out of the flaming forest, some on fire, all harried by death hounds and Maphraxies. Not everybody was going to make it. What if the Immortals attacked the boat? The thought made her stomach turn. She couldn't let that happen.

The Maphraxies hesitated at the water's edge as if they did not want to get a foot wet. Jarlain watched, curious.

'Get to the water!' Murlonius screamed. 'They won't follow you into the sea!'

She glanced back at Yisufalni. The Ancient held out her six-fingered hands, palms down, her eyes glowing vivid blue.

A dark shadow covered the sun as a Dread Dragon swooped low over the water. Not five yards away from her the giant jaws of a Dread Dragon clamped down upon those in the water. She stared at its huge, blood-red eye that was larger than her head, the slit of its pupil narrowing as it focussed on her, and her heart skipped a beat. The muffled screams of people came from inside its mouth. The dragon clenched its jaw, silencing the howls within, and lifted into the air. Jarlain shook uncontrollably.

Something clanged loudly against her helmet, then she felt an intense pain and fell forwards into the water.

Yisufalni's strength drained quickly. It took all of her power and concentration to keep their presence at once hidden from the Maphraxies yet still visible to the people they were trying to rescue. Murlonius could not assist her, consumed as he was with keeping the connection to Maioria open, the boat steady, and the sea calm. She sensed this was the most dangerous mission he had so far conducted. She couldn't imagine it being any worse.

The doomed people were surrounded on all sides by Immortals. Their only hope was the sea, and Yisufalni poured the Flow into it. Maphraxies hated water, something to do with energy of the substance. To them it was toxic. The purity of the Flow was also toxic to them, its high frequency poisonous to those who existed in the low, dark frequencies. The enemy would not go into the water unless they were pushed. And there they would die.

But she could not protect them from the Dread Dragons. They swooped and attacked with ease, picking up people in their jaws and claws. Yisufalni looked at one, its dead eyes filled with hunger, whilst its rider's gaze blazed within a metal face. She tried not to give in to hate, not now whilst she held the Flow. Hate would weaken her and muddy the pure energy she channelled.

Some people reached the boat and she lifted them in with her magic.

They collapsed in the hull in exhaustion. The boat stretched to accommodate them as each one entered.

Yisufalni glimpsed Jarlain fighting alongside Fenn. She held her spear up and was screaming at the people. The brave Navadin had come last, commanding strength and power like the people of old. She already was a leader, Yisufalni smiled. The Flow jerked, and her smile dropped.

Emerging from the trees walked a man. A normal, human man—only dark, inhuman, power surrounded him. He was not a Maphraxie but he had the black aura of one who has tasted Sirin Derenax; one who had lost his humanity long ago. His piercing eyes spoke of intelligence without empathy. His grey hair was smoothed back, accentuating deep widow's peaks and his face was long and gaunt. He moved slowly, completely controlled in a world of chaos.

Yisufalni held her breath as he looked straight at her. She froze. *He can't see me, he can't!* But the man looked on and then slowly, deliberately, raised his arm. Something glinted in his hand. Danger prickled her back. To do anything to protect herself from a direct attack—or to attack back—would immediately drop their cover.

Fenn moved fast. The bear's jaws closed upon the man's arm just as something fired from the device. A metal dart shot forth, she saw it clearly. The dart was off course; it would not hit her. But it was on course for another. Yisufalni stared at the trajectory towards Jarlain. The Navadin did not see it and there was no time for warning—to help her would reveal themselves fully and risk all the people they had saved.

Yisufalni raised her hand, formed the will to command the magic, and flicked her fingers forwards. A solid knot of shimmering air burst from her fingers and slammed into Jarlain. It knocked her into the water and continued straight into the grey man. The force tore him from Fenn's grasp, leaving the man's leather bracer in the bear's mouth. Their shield was gone. The next moments became a whir of chaos.

Fenn spat out the man's bracer and bounded into the water to where Jarlain had sunk under the weight of her armour. The Dread Dragons above turned to their new enemy. People still poured out of the jungle.

'Oh, woe,' she heard Murlonius whisper.

Yisufalni closed her eyes and focused the mass of energy that was the Flow.

The Maphraxies were black shapes moving through the living green of the forest. The red spots fleeing between them were the auras of terrified people. Energy gathered around the grey man getting onto his feet and the Flow avoided him. Fenn was a large ball of copper light and Jarlain's aura was faint beside him.

Yisufalni lifted her hands and drew large shapes of power in the air. With a word, the Flow exploded outwards. Dread Dragons scattered, Maphraxie hordes and their death hounds sprawled. Only the people remained unaffected.

Yisufalni drew her arms together, shouting words in the Ancient Tongue. The Flow obeyed and the magic she had thrown out now rushed back towards her, picking up and carrying all the people who still had an aura.

Murlonius entered the Flow, a beautiful aura of purple in her maelstrom of magic. He lifted them all and she felt herself withdrawing from Maioria. The black shapes disappeared and the taint of the Under Flow vanished. Yisufalni let go of the Flow, feeling as if she floated back down into the boat. Exhausted, she let herself drift in a sea of magical energy.

Jarlain awoke to a large, wet tongue draping over her face. It gave a long lick from cheek to cheek.

'Fenn, stop!' she tried to sound annoyed but her voice was a rasp.

The bear stopped and dunked his snout into a bucket of water where he proceeded to drink noisily. He was caked in blood, both black and red, and his ear was ripped and oozing. Jarlain tried to sit up but slumped back instead. A middle-aged woman with lighter skin and hair than her own people took a cloth to the bear and inspected the ear. Jarlain wondered if she was Kuapoh but didn't want to rasp again. Fenn flinched at the woman's touch, then got into the idea and relaxed.

Jarlain tried to get her bearings, though she couldn't see much past Fenn and the woman. She lay in the bottom of a huge boat that rocked gently and was surrounded by sleeping people. Above, the sky was a strange blanket of white though there was no sun that she could see. She rubbed her face and her hand came away bloody. Her fingers found the rough fabric of a bandage around her head.

'The bleeding has mostly stopped. Your bear was just cleaning you,' a familiar old woman's voice said then chuckled.

'Sharnu?' *Could it really be the Elder?* Jarlain tried to sit again but her battered body protested. 'Is it really you?'

The brown, wrinkled face of the old woman smiled down at her. Jarlain realised then that her head was cradled in the Elder's lap. Tears filled both their eyes and the old woman bent to hug her.

For a long moment they stayed like that. There was nothing to say, each knew everything that had come to pass and all that had been lost.

'Tarn's gone,' whispered Sharnu gently after a time.

Jarlain took a breath and swallowed against the pain of losing her half-brother. She hugged the Elder closer. So much pain, so many had been lost. She dedicated herself to protecting those who remained. Those around her in the boat.

It was the soft groaning growl from Fenn that drew them apart.

'Now stop it you big wuss,' said the pale woman tending his ear. She had a needle and thread and was attempting to sew up his wound. 'The lotion will numb the area and you won't feel a thing.'

'It's all right, Fenn,' Jarlain said.

'It hurts. The lotion doesn't work,' he growled.

'Ah, Jarlain, you have awoken in us the gift of the Navadin. You are the first but the gift will spread and awaken within us all.' Sharnu spoke telepathically, startling both Jarlain and the bear.

'You can hear us?' Jarlain forced herself to a seated position and looked at the Elder. Tears streaked the older woman's face but they were tears of wonder as she looked at the bear.

'So many ancient memories are returning to me,' she said, her voice barely a whisper. Her eyes looked far away and began to glow subtly with the blue of the Sight. 'When Hai left us, hope left my heart, despite what he said. Now hope fills it once more. I see a bright future before us but on far different shores, and the path to it is dark, many will not survive.

'Now our people are so few in number. Look at them, we're all that remain of the once great peoples of Unafey. But ahead, if we dare to reach for it, a new world dawns.'

'A new world,' Jarlain echoed, catching the feeling of hope.

'A world like nothing we have seen before.' Sharnu nodded. 'But between us and it the black chasm of Oblivion yawns.'

Jarlain shivered. 'We must leap across it.'

Sharnu's eyes lost their faraway look. Smiling, she squeezed the younger woman's hand.

Jarlain ate Tallen fruit whilst Sharnu and Fenn slept. Fighting back tiredness, she looked at the giant boat filled with the slumbering people of all the tribes of the Uncharted Lands. She had never seen so many people in one place; there were at least a thousand of them, many of them wounded, some seriously. Her eyes lingered briefly on those whose chests no longer rose or fell and her heart became heavy.

'They did not die in pain,' Murlonius spoke softly. 'In this place, their souls are easily found by Zanufey.'

Jarlain turned to the boatman. He stood at the prow with his back to her. He was not rowing but wading with his oar. It seemed impossible that he could manoeuvre this massive boat filled with thousands in this manner, but this was the Sea of Opportunity and anything was possible.

Yisufalni sat beside him, staring straight ahead. The Ancient looked exhausted as she gripped the side of the boat. The pale, strained face and distant look in Yisufalni's eyes made her realise the Ancient was deep in concentration. Murlonius' face was set in a grim expression and there was a sheen of perspiration on his brow.

Jarlain made her way over the sleeping bodies towards them.

'Something hit me on the head but...we made it out, didn't we?' asked Jarlain.

Yisufalni spoke without looking at her. 'He's seen us. He knows. They're hunting for us at this moment. I'm doing all I can to conceal our passage.' She passed something shiny to her.

Jarlain took the strange metal dart with a vicious tip. Inside was a tiny vial of green liquid.

'Venosian saran poison,' said Yisufalni. 'Deadly. A special tool of Baelthrom's second-hand man, Hameka. He saw Murlonius and I together, clear as day. Now, Baelthrom hunts us. He knows we meddle in the affairs of Maioria against him. Despite our curse he has seen what we can do. He will not let us live.'

Murlonius spoke. 'That dart was meant for you. To save you, and thus the Navadin, Yisufalni had to expose us.'

'I'm sorry,' said Jarlain. Had she jeopardised the lives of the very people who had saved her and her peoples? The thought made her feel sick.

'Do not be,' Yisufalni smiled. 'I made the choice. Responsibility rests with me.'

'You can't have known,' added Murlonius.

There was no hint of accusation in either of their voices. They accepted all that happened, without question or judgement. Humbled, Jarlain was awestruck by these beautiful beings, the ancestors of the Elves. Wisdom, grace and sorrow radiated from them.

'The lives of the Navadin are now far more important than our own,' said Yisufalni.

Jarlain frowned.

Yisufalni continued. 'There's only one last task left for us to do before our time is complete.'

Jarlain saw the frown of pain pass across Murlonius' face, though he said nothing.

'What?' Jarlain asked. What was this thing they had to do that caused him pain? But they did not answer. She tried formulating another question but found her mind drifting and a deep sleep stole over her.

The sound of waves slapping the side of the boat awoke her. Jarlain opened her eyes and shivered in the cold. The sea rocked more than usual and a thick, damp fog had replaced the soft mist. She sat up at last, thankful she wore her armour to fight the chill.

Fenn was already awake, his snout lifted and twitching as he smelled the air. The fog cleared revealing craggy grey rocks and a thick forest of evergreen trees clustering down to the water's edge on either side of the boat.

'Where are we?' asked Jarlain, her voice hushed so as not to wake the others.

'Brackish water. We travel upstream along one of the many rivers flowing down from the central Everridge Mountains between Davono and Lans Himay,' said Yisufalni, her eyes scanning the fog-covered land.

'The boat has arrived at the destination of the one who wanted it the most,' said Murlonius.

'Marakon is here, then?' Jarlain tried to see if there were any soldiers or knights moving through the forest but there was nothing.

Murlonius turned and smiled at her. 'Not you, the bear.' He nodded to Fenn.

The bear twitched his ears.

'You chose here, why? What is here?' she telepathed to him.

'We call the bears. Woo has not much time. I smell Oodabans here, they can help you humans. Otherwise they will die of cold. They have no fur.'

'Wait, who is Woo? What are Oodabans.' Jarlain frowned.

'*Great Woo of the Forest. Ood is her mate. Oodabans, deer people.'*

Jarlain blinked in surprise. Woo was Woetala in bear speak, but did he really mean the Karalanths Marakon had told her about?

Murlonius and Yisufalni stood up. Jarlain squinted to where they pointed and was startled by what she saw.

Antlers appeared through the fog, then the heads and bodies of the people they were attached to. These people had antlers on their heads but were otherwise human down to the abdomen and then animal for the rest. They looked like the three-prongs from her Gurlanka homelands, only much bigger. She realised her mouth was open and closed it. All of the people were now awake and staring at the Karalanths in silence.

Only when they lowered their drawn bows did Jarlain realise they had weapons pointed at them. There were five deer-people, four males and a female, clustered on the stony-bank at the waters' edge. They stared in equal measure back at the two Ancients and the enormous boat filled with refugees. Looks of awe spread across the Karalanths' faces and their white tails flicked nervously back and forth.

Some dropped their gaze respectfully, reminding Jarlain of the power and authority the Ancients might once have commanded. These two before her were the last of their race, just as the boat-load of refugees she sat amongst were the last of her race. She swallowed painfully.

The boat ground gently on to the pebbles and Fenn jumped out. The Karalanths looked at the bear, their surprise deepening as he padded fearlessly towards them. It struck Jarlain that they weren't in the least bit afraid of the bear, when most humans would have run.

The nearest Karalanth, a man with long, greying hair and fur, put away his bow and arrow and spoke in a clipped language to the bear. He raised his hand and touched Fenn's fur, stroking his great head down to his neck. Fenn seemed to accept this as some kind of greeting. The bear turned and looked at Jarlain as if wondering where she was.

Hesitantly, Jarlain stepped over the side of the boat and walked towards them. She laid a hand on Fenn's neck as the Karalanths eyed her up and down. The male Karalanth said something over his shoulder to the others, who replied and nodded their heads.

'You are dressed as a soldier of the Feylint Halanoi, and yet your race is not one of them. You are of those people,' he nodded to the refugees, 'but they are not dressed as you. Who are you to be bear companion?' the man spoke perfect Frayonesse like Marakon, with only the barest hint of an accent.

'I am Jarlain of the Gurlanka. These are some of my clan, the others are other clans. Cousins. We are all that remain of the peoples of the Uncharted Lands. The Immortal Lord came, with his Dread Dragons.'

The Karalanth nodded and took a deep breath. 'I am Triest'anth, and we Karalanths are also few in number, but not so few as these two Ancient Ones before us.'

He turned from Jarlain and walked gracefully towards Murlonius and Yisufalni. The other Karalanths followed.

'I have heard of your kind but never seen them,' said Triest'anth. 'You are but a myth of myths and yet here you stand. Are you truly the last?'

'We are, Brave One. The world is changing and our time is nearly done. We bring with us the last of a mighty race, also a myth of myths and possibly older. Here stands before you the first of the Navadin.' He nodded towards Jarlain.

The Karalanth looked shocked. He glanced back at Jarlain.

'Great Doonis came to me,' she said quietly. 'I was close to death. He returned to me two things, memory and speech. Memory of what we once were and the language of the bear. This is so my people might live. But we are weak and battle weary, and we do not know how to survive in this new world. Will you help us?' She caught Sharnu smiling at her from the boat, a look of pride on her face. There were warriors, Elders, chiefs and Leaders of the Hunt amongst the refugees, and yet it would be she who would lead her people.

Triest'anth studied her face, as if weighing up the responsibility of what she asked of him.

'Woo has not much time,' repeated Fenn.

The Karalanth looked at the bear, clearly able to hear him.

'I do not feel I have a choice,' said Triest'anth. 'But the bear is right, Woetala is dying. There is not much time. Because Doon has graced you, we will help you live.'

'Thank you,' Jarlain bowed deeply. 'Come.' She motioned to her people.

With everybody's help, including the Karalanths, the tribes of the Uncharted Lands climbed out of the boat, helping the injured.

'Danger draws near, our time is done here,' said Murlonius. Jarlain watched as he replaced the curious hourglass back into the sack at his feet. 'In the astral planes, others come.'

'Thank you, Murlonius,' said Jarlain.

Both he and Yisufalni nodded.

The boat, now back to its normal small size, ground off the stones and back into the water of its own accord. Glimmering mist formed in the fog.

CHAPTER 3

Dwarves, Demons and Karalanths

MARAKON waited by the entrance as soldiers and horses filed into the demon tunnel, faces pale, weapons drawn.

The stone door ground shut, sealing them in thick blackness as the torches all went out. Knowing what was going to happen didn't lessen the carnal fear that knotted itself in Marakon's stomach.

'Demon doors always shut after something has passed through them, and all light is extinguished. Somehow they know,' he said loudly, forcing his voice to sound almost bored. 'Look, Velistor glows only dully. There's nothing here for us to fear. Try lighting the torches again.'

Soldiers rummaged in packs looking for flint and tinder. Sparks lit up the cavern and torches flared back into life. The relief was palpable.

'There's not enough air here to feed the flames and us,' Eiretonne growled, his gravelly voice somehow booming although he had spoken quietly.

Someone took a few steps and then paused when they heard a loud crunch.

A torch was held low.

'Bones,' a voice said with a tremor.

The horror of a demon skull assaulted Marakon's eye. Its thick cranium and large, empty eye sockets bore into his own as if it saw and hated him again. Its skeleton lay in broken bits around it.

'Decapitated after its death. It must have been killed by magic that prevented it exploding,' said Marakon.

'Why only one?' asked Justenin.

'Mortally wounded Shadow Demons fade into the shadow taking their victims with them before they die. They leave no trace of themselves or their prey. But the others, the Grazen, they explode when killed,' said Marakon.

He scanned the tunnel and passed his hand over the wall. It came away black. 'Look, see? I thought these walls were black but they're grey beneath. The rock is blackened with soot and heat. This place is thick with dead demons only we can't see most of them.'

His explanation was intended to reassure but he found it unnerved everyone even more, including himself. Demon wraiths were the last thing they needed. Thoughts about demon battles eons past crowded his mind. Had he fought here? There had been so many battles in so many places, he most probably had.

He shook his head. They had to get moving. 'Bokaard?'

'Sir?' said the Atalanph captain, his blue eyes shining in the dark.

'You bring up the rear. You can see in the dark if anything is following us.'

The Atalanph nodded and made his way to the back.

'Eiretonne?'

'Yes, Commander?' The dwarf stepped closer, a determined look in his eyes.

'Stay by my side,' Marakon commanded. 'You can also see well in the dark in these tunnels. I'm hoping you'll have a better dwarven feel for underground caverns than I do. Where are the wizards you were bringing?'

The dwarf motioned with his hand and an unlikely slender dwarf female came forward. Brown freckles covered her nose and cheeks in an attractive manner and her long braid hung over one shoulder to her waist. She looked frightened, her large brown eyes wide and her helmet askew. She also looked completely uncomfortable in her ill-fitting armour that hung about her frame. She held her short sword too limply and Marakon quickly worried she'd do more damage to herself than the enemy.

He held back a sigh. Wizards never made good warriors. This one looked no good for battle, but the Feylint Halanoi had only allowed him two wizards of the ten he'd requested. If this was the best of them he worried what the second one was like. He remembered another dwarven female, an accomplished warrior who had been impaled upon the deck of his ship many months ago. Would this one share a similar fate? He prayed not.

'She's not a warrior, Commander, but what she lacks in strength she doubles in battle magic,' said Eiretonne, guessing his thoughts. 'That's the reason the Feylint Halanoi hired her. She is not a witch or seer but a *wizard*. They say some women are finding the power again; they say it's because of the Raven Queen.'

'I can believe that.' Marakon gave a nod, relieved somewhat. He turned to the dwarven woman whose cheeks had begun to colour under the scrutiny.

'Name?' he asked.

'Shelley, Sir,' she said.

Her voice was quiet but at least it didn't tremble.

'Shelley, when it darkens cast a low light but not so much it drains your energy. Beware of demon wraiths, they move in the shadows. Are you familiar with demon magic? Good. At this point in time, any we encounter should be our friends, but be wary.'

'Yes, Sir,' said Shelley, bowing awkwardly. She hurried away.

He turned back to Eiretonne. 'And where is the other wizard?'

'Er, well, I bargained for her over two other wizards,' said Eiretonne, standing straighter and confident in his choice. 'You see, well, the other one was really two—twins, you see, Sir. They could not be separated. Looks can be deceiving, but I know a good battle wizard when I see one. She has more ability than the other two combined. I was so impressed, it made me believe that the power is finally returning to our women folk with the rise of this, er, Raven Queen.'

Marakon took a deep breath and let it go slowly. 'I guess I'll have to take your word for it, Eiretonne. Let's hope you're right.'

'Aye, Sir, you'll not be disappointed.'

'Still, we only have one wizard for one hundred soldiers... I'd prefer one to ten. Never mind.' Marakon sighed and waved his hand. 'Justenin?'

The tall officer stepped into the light. 'Sir?'

'Protect the wizard at all costs. Take a position beside her and back from the frontline.'

'Yes, Sir.'

Marakon made his way past the waiting soldiers until he stood at the front. He peered into the blackness beyond the torches and dull light of Velistor. Who knew what lay in that darkness…

Eiretonne stepped beside him, the keen edge of his axe reflecting the torchlight. No one said a word as they moved forwards. Thankfully, demons came in large sizes and the tunnel was high and sometimes wide enough to let three soldiers pass side by side.

As he walked, many questions flitted through Marakon's mind but eventually they all boiled down to one: how would he know which way to go when the passage split—and split he knew it would? He placed all his trust in Velistor, but how did it know where he wanted to go? Maybe it only ever sought out demons. He would know, his inner feeling said, just as he had known in that lifetime eons ago.

Eiretonne pointed ahead, snapping him out of his thoughts. 'Look, the tunnel brightens.'

Sure enough, the blackness of the tunnel gave way to an eerie grey light that came from nowhere in particular.

Marakon pursed his lips into a smile, now remembering the mysterious demon light. It grew until everything was bathed in muted soft grey. 'Douse the torches, there's enough light to see and we might need them later.'

They moved forward, the mood of the soldiers changing from pensive to bored as the tunnel continued endlessly. After an hour, the passageway made its inevitable split into two tunnels.

'Halt,' Marakon called and the line shuffled to a stop.

He bent down to inspect the floor and then the sides of each tunnel, looking for a clue. Memory flashed. He held the tip of Velistor against the ground of one tunnel and gently scraped it around the circumference. Velistor hummed and grew brighter. Strange, luminous green symbols flared where the spear passed, making the demon symbols usually hidden to human eyes, visible.

He tried to read them and immediately felt sick.

'Demonic runes. Don't look too long at them,' he warned those closest.

He turned to the next tunnel and did the same thing. Again, runes flared, and he didn't know what they meant. It seemed logical that the tunnel on the left would lead him west—west towards Davono—but the spear pulled ever so subtly to the tunnel on the right.

'Demon tunnels are trickery, like demons themselves,' he murmured. He decided to trust Velistor and took the right-hand split. After several yards the tunnel sloped down and then turned to the left.

'It's turning west,' said Eiretonne.

Marakon nodded and smiled. 'Let's trust the spear from now on.'

They continued and the initial interest in the split tunnel soon faded back to boredom. Being under all this rock and earth felt oppressive. How deep had they gone? Apart from back there, there had been no other decline to suggest they had gone deep, yet somehow he knew they had. Were they nearly all the way to Davono? What if this way led to an ancient demon trap? Were they even in Maioria anymore?

There came another tunnel split, this time into three. Again, Marakon used the spear to scrape each entrance and stared at the meaningless demonic runes. He took the central one when he felt the spear pull and prayed Velistor was responding to his will rather than seeking out demons. Hours passed, and they came to another tunnel divide.

After another hour, Marakon gave the command to rest. 'Half an hour and no more,' he said, setting Velistor against the wall. He realised it was impossible to tell the passing of time down here and then grinned when the wizard pulled out a tiny hourglass.

Marakon sat on the ground and washed down his dried fruit and nuts with some water. When the pink sand in the hour glass was half and half he gave the order to start moving again.

Another hour of marching passed when he came to large blotches of blackened walls. He touched them with his finger. It came away black.

'Demon ash,' he said quietly.

Eiretonne motioned for caution.

They walked on at a slower, muffled pace, passing the blackened marks and piles of ash dotted here and there. Marakon's boot clanged against something in the soot. He bent to inspect it.

Brushing the soot off revealed a small, gleaming blade. 'A throwing dagger,' he said.

He barely touched the edge and it drew blood. 'Still wickedly sharp!' He smarted. 'But it's not demon-made.'

'Here, let me look,' said Eiretonne. Marakon passed him the blade and the dwarf squinted at it turning it over in his hands. His thick eyebrows rose. He passed it back to Marakon. 'It's not dwarven, but Karalanth.'

'Karalanth?' Marakon said, equally surprised. 'What are the deer-folk doing in demon tunnels? They hate the bowels of darkness and anything underground.'

Eiretonne shrugged. 'Could it have been carried here by something else, maybe even in the wound of a demon?'

'Anything's possible.' Marakon shrugged. Tucking the dagger away, he continued walking.

They passed several more piles of soot and blackened walls but no more weapons or clues as to the battle that had taken place here until they came to another tunnel split.

This one was not like the others. One tunnel was much smaller, halfway up the wall and disappeared into pitch black rather than the muted grey of the demon passage. It was roughly hewn, unlike the relatively smooth demon ones.

'Now this,' said Eiretonne, smiling broadly, 'is a tunnel made by dwarfs.' He went close to inspect the entrance. 'See the notch marks here? They were mining. This is a First Tunnel—so called because it is rough. Clearly, they never bothered to smooth and widen it because they tunnelled straight into a demon tunnel!'

'Demon tunnels, dwarven mines and a Karalanth dagger.' Marakon placed his hands on his hips. 'What is going on? Have dwarves tunnelled this far into Frayon? How old is it? Have we reached the Everridge Mountains already or could this even be Venosia?'

Eiretonne shrugged. 'I've no answers to your questions. I'm a warrior not a miner. I was trained from birth for battle and rarely lived inside any rock. Where there are dwarf tunnels, there are mines. Perhaps they were under the commission of an old Frayon King? Such things are common, even today.

'Things don't age underground so I can't tell you how old it is. Here, let me inspect it further.' He took a torch and motioned for another dwarf soldier to follow. With a leg up, Eiretonne pulled himself level with the entrance and peered into the gloom.

'It opens up into a cave. There are skeletons and piles of soot, lots of them,' he said, his voice strained. He pulled himself fully into the tunnel and disappeared before Marakon could stop him.

Marakon walked to the entrance, sword at the ready, followed by several soldiers. He peered over the edge. The tunnel descended steeply, and amongst the piles of rubble and black ash, lay skeletons cast in orange by Eiretonne's torch. The dwarf hastily moved from skeleton to skeleton inspecting each, his eyes wide.

'What is it?' Marakon hissed, not wanting to be loud.

When Eiretonne didn't answer, he heaved himself up. In full armour, it wasn't easy getting through the small entrance built for dwarfs, but he clanged and scraped his way through. Thankfully the tunnel widened into a small cave almost immediately and the ceiling was just high enough for him to stand.

'Dwarfs, all of them,' said Eiretonne staring at a skeleton, his voice cracking with emotion.

'For every one felled by a demon, double it for the ones who disappeared into shadow,' said Marakon with a shiver.

'Bastards!' Eiretonne growled, then bent and picked something up from a pile of demon ash. It glinted in the light. 'Another Karalanth dagger.'

Justenin, Shelley and several soldiers crawled into the cavern. The wizard cast a soft light, illuminating all.

Marakon paused by a pile of bones. The thick short femurs and relatively heavy set skulls of the dwarf were unmistakable. A helmet lay a few feet away, dented and rusted but otherwise whole. Carefully, he pulled at an arrow sticking between two ribs. He barely touched it when the ribs fractured releasing the arrow.

'These skeletons are old. *Very.*' He inspected the arrow, noting the leaf-like head. 'And these are Karalanth arrows.' The ancient arrow shaft crumbled when he tightened his grasp. He frowned, it didn't make sense. What were dwarves, Karalanths and demons doing here?

'Curse the Karalanths!' Eiretonne growled and spat.

'But where are their bodies?' Marakon asked. 'Surely one fell. They aren't *that* good.'

He rubbed his beard, thinking. 'No Karalanth bodies, but Karalanth weapons embedded in demons and dwarfs. To me, it seems, the Karalanths came upon a battle already taking place. Karalanths do not leave their injured or even their dead behind. If they came upon two enemies fighting each other, they would have had easy pickings.'

'Wait,' said Shelley, capturing everyone's attention. 'Look.' She held up a dented dwarven helmet. 'Look at the runes on the rim.'

Eiretonne snatched it from her and stared hard. With a grimace he threw the helmet aside where it bounced loudly against the wall. 'Dark dwarves! Curse their black Tongue!' He kicked a skeleton causing it to crumble.

As soon as he'd said it, the air thickened. Marakon tensed and the wizard fell back, her hands raised and ready to cast. Justenin jumped in front of her.

'Prepare to fight!' Marakon yelled, warning the others back in the demon tunnel. He heard them draw their weapons.

The temperature dropped and Marakon considered his options fast. Should they fight in here or get back into the demon tunnel where there were more soldiers? He turned to the tunnel entrance just as black light shot out of the darkness. It snaked like a living thing on the ceiling and flared around the entrance. Rocks split apart and crumbled in a spray of dust and rubble, sealing the entrance shut.

'Great. We fight in here, then.' Marakon grimaced.

The blackness thickened, and the pressure grew until his temples pounded. The soldiers, ten of them including Justenin and Eiretonne, held their swords ready, eyes wide with fear.

'Bunch together,' Marakon commanded, and they drew close into a circle with the wizard in the middle. 'Shelley, what do you sense?'

'D-dark, old magic and o-others,' she stammered. 'I can't be sure. It's not the Under Flow. The dead are here.'

'Demon magic, once placed, is hard to remove,' Marakon said. 'Demon wraiths cannot be killed, only sent back to the Murk. They will not be on our side.'

'I can *feel* the evil of the dark dwarven runes,' Eiretonne said in a harsh whisper. 'More than one black magic infests this place.'

The pressure suddenly dropped and a deafening noise unlike any sound he had heard assaulted his senses. Marakon released his spear to cover his ears. Adding to the din came a new sound, the thundering of hooves. He focused on it to drive away the other noise and struggled to pick up Velistor. Out of the blackness, a ghostly Karalanth warrior galloped at them. War paint covered his spectral face and his antlers reached high above him.

'Wraiths!' shouted Marakon.

The ghost roared, his face contorting in hatred and his weapons raised as it laid eyes on Eiretonne, its most hated enemy.

Marakon saw a flash. He spun Velistor, only just in time to knock the spectral dagger away before it hit Eiretonne. He hadn't expected the ghost blade to be solid, but it clanged against Velistor like any other dagger. He watched it spin through the air then disappear. *Velistor has power in many dimensions,* he thought.

Eiretonne caught the next dagger with his blade but not the third. It flew so fast and sunk into his shoulder between his armour plates. He roared and dropped to one knee.

A cruel smile spread across the Karalanth's face as it bore down upon them.

Marakon howled and rushed to meet it, spear raised. The Karalanth skidded its charge and reared, hacking at him with a short sword. It clanged loudly off Velistor. Marakon pirouetted, lunged, and sunk the tip into the Karalanth's rump. It bucked and screeched.

Wraith-like howling filled the air. The ghost hesitated and turned around, forgetting Marakon was there, seeing something in the dark the half-elf could not see. With a warrior's cry the Karalanth reared, bounded forwards and disappeared into the rock wall. The howling faded away.

Panting, Marakon bent to help Eiretonne. The dwarf was pale and sweating profusely. Shelley held a glowing blue hand over his wounded shoulder.

'I can stop the pain but I cannot heal a wraith's blade and stop the blood,' she said.

'He'll bleed to death,' said Justenin.

Marakon scowled, he wasn't about to let his friend die here.

'Curse the Karalanths, curse the dark dwarfs, curse them all,' Eiretonne gasped and tried to sit up.

Marakon pushed him back down. 'The wraiths are afraid of the spear. It exists in many dimensions. I think it can destroy the wraith's blade still embedded in your shoulder, but it will hurt.'

Eiretonne gave him a hard stare, brief nod, then closed his eyes. 'Get on with it.'

'Help with the pain,' Marakon said to the wizard and held the spear up. Taking a deep breath, he stabbed Velistor into Eiretonne's wound. The dwarf roared. The spear flared. He withdrew it in a burst of red blood. Eiretonne passed out. Justenin and the wizard quickly pressed cloth against the wound.

'I think the bleeding already slows,' said the wizard after a moment.

'Cauterised by the spear. Something I remembered from long ago,' Marakon gave a weak smile. 'But he won't be fit to fight this day.'

A raging howl, not made by Karalanth ghosts or human throats, echoed around them. Red eyes, dozens of them, flared in the shadows.

'Demons!' the wizard said, her eyes wide.

'Back against the wall!' Marakon shouted. Only the spear could protect them from demons. They fell back, dragging Eiretonne with them.

Shelley made light, halting the thickening darkness. Marakon stepped forwards. A demon wraith lunged for him, red eyes split in two by a narrow pupil, but the rest of its body remained as shadow. Marakon stabbed the spear into it. The demon howled and Marakon's soul shivered. The demon vanished. More came at him and he stabbed and slashed, sweat soon beading his face and stinging his eye.

Light flashed from Shelley, seared past him and flared into a demon. It paused, stunned. The demon drew fully out of the shadows and turned on her. Marakon jumped between them, whirling his spear. Shelley didn't try again. The other soldiers watched helplessly.

Demon wraiths came from every crevice, filling the cavern, forcing Marakon back with his flaring, angry spear. Issa's raven talisman flashed in his mind; had it come from the spear? It wanted the talisman. If only she were here, the spear and the talisman would have ended this fight already.

Demon claws bigger than daggers materialised to his right. They swiped against his armour with a grating sound, its shadow fingers reaching beyond the metal. Icy cold touched Marakon's heart and he fell to the floor. Gasping, he desperately tried to protect the others, plunging Velistor in front of him and striking madly.

Dark red flared to his right. It wasn't Shelley's magic, nor was it coming from the demons. The demon wraiths saw it too and huddled together.

Marakon blinked. Someone spoke in a human voice and the strange words stilled the air.

'…Luf kin damack!'

A thunderbolt exploded past Marakon and smacked into the wraiths. Those not incinerated, fled, howling their demonic noise into the shadows from where they had come. The air became breathable once more and the pressure alleviated.

Marakon stood swaying and panting. He squinted at a young soldier who was in the far corner, on his hands and knees, beside a skeleton. The soldier laughed and held up an ancient scroll he had unravelled.

'Hah! It worked,' he said, pushing himself up. The young soldier was no more than eighteen, tall and gangly with a mop of hair under his helmet. 'I saw it glowing in the dust. Maybe the demons made it glow. All I saw were runes and then I understood them. I don't know—' The scroll suddenly burst into flames, and he yelped and dropped it.

'You fool!' Shelley shouted, making the young soldier jump. He looked at her as she ranted. 'You never read dark runes aloud, not ever!'

'Why?' asked Marakon not understanding.

Shelley turned her glare upon him. 'Dark runes are a deception to the uninitiated! They will make themselves known to even non-magic users if it serves their purpose. But their price is great.'

'So what made the demon wraiths run?' asked Justenin, his frown matching Marakon's.

Shelley sighed as if they were all stupid. 'The demons are enemies of the dark dwarves. The spell was created to kill them. In the presence of the enemy, the spell made its own presence known. When a spell committed to paper is read it will destroy itself and often the speaker unless it is one versed in the magic that made it—in this case, dark dwarven magic.'

Everyone peered at the young soldier and he swallowed. 'I didn't know, I didn't! But I'm still here, right?'

'But we're also enemies of the dark dwarves,' said Marakon slowly.

Shelley nodded, the whites of her eyes vivid. 'A spell may have more than one effect.'

The ground trembled. Everyone fell silent and looked at each other.

'What now?' Marakon sighed, rolling back his aching shoulders.

The tremors came again and everything on the ground began to shake. Fallen weapons and dark dwarven armour rattled against each other and the skeletons they still encased. Dust rose and rocks fell from the ceiling. There was nowhere safe to stand, and soldiers lifted their shields to protect themselves

Something gasped and groaned and then a dark dwarven skeleton sat bolt upright. Shelley squealed. The skeleton turned its creaking head and looked at them through empty eye sockets. Five more sat up, followed by the sound of many more in the darkness beyond the brazier light.

'Not another skeleton army,' Marakon moaned to himself and closed his eyes.

'That cursed spell! It has called the dead to fight,' rasped Shelley.

'At least these ones we *can* fight, right?' said Justenin stepping forwards in front of Marakon with his sword raised. Other soldiers readied their weapons eagerly, determined not to sit out on another fight.

'Yes, but how many are there?' asked Marakon, still sweating from the previous battle.

The skeletons creaked and groaned then grabbed their weapons and stood up. Rusted armour hung off their bones and ancient swords rattled in fleshless knuckles as they advanced towards them. In the darkness he could see skeletons amassing at odds of three to one.

'Fireball,' commanded Shelley and opened her palms.

A ball of white fire flared into the nearest skeleton and it burst into flames. The skeleton's scream raked the air as it crumpled into dust. The skeleton behind it picked up its dropped blade and advanced with two weapons. Another flaming ball flared from the wizard's fingers and took them down. Justenin pushed her back and advanced. Other soldiers jumped to attack, and the room filled with metal clashing against metal.

'There are too many!' Marakon screamed as he shoved a skeleton back and decapitated it. The head disintegrated as it hit the floor, followed by its body.

Another skeleton pressed in to take its place, barely giving him time to parry. Deftly, he switched his sword to his right hand and spear to his left. The spear was mostly useless against the skeletons, spearing them harmlessly between their bones, but he used it to drive them back then swipe with his sword. Two more fell and crumbled but many more pressed forwards.

'Shelley!' he shouted. 'Blast open the tunnel. We can't fight them all!' He hoped she heard him over the din. One of his soldiers gave a death howl. Marakon couldn't even spare the time to look.

There came a boom and flash of light, followed by the sound of rocks falling. Marakon strained to see through the dust but his opponent drove in hard. He sliced his sword, dismembering the skeleton's sword arm and sending it flying into the corner where it twitched. He swung his sword back and decapitated it, only just managing to block the blow from the skeleton behind it.

Another boom came. A flash of light illuminated the cavern and the legion of skeleton soldiers before them. Marakon roared and struck, ignoring their dire predicament. The sound of tumbling rocks was replaced with the yells of soldiers. Behind, and to his left, he glimpsed the rest of his unit pour into the cavern through the crumbled wall. He laughed, the sight of them giving him renewed strength.

With the odds more even, skeletons fell fast beneath his elite army. The battle waged quickly, viciously on his soldiers' part, pent up as they had been in the demon tunnels. Within the hour, not one skeleton remained standing.

Marakon took off his helmet with trembling hands and slapped Bokaard on the back.

'Well met, friend,' Marakon said.

'Why do you always have to fight without me?' the big man sighed. 'Three enemies in one day? We haven't even got to the front line yet!'

Marakon laughed. 'I'm done in before we've even got there. How many dead and wounded?' he asked Justenin, his humour vanishing as he steeled himself against the report.

'Five, Sir, and the same again injured badly,' the tall man's face was flushed with exertion.

Marakon nodded, swallowing his guilt for the dead like so many times before. 'It's unfortunate, but it could have been much worse. We rest here, for a short time, then we get moving again,' he spoke loudly for all to hear.

The soldiers sat or stood upon the ashes of their fallen foe and rested.

CHAPTER 4

Lumenoor

'AND now, we separate them,' said Ayeth, his golden skin gleaming in the pulsing light.

The tall Aralan drew his delicate, six-fingered hands apart, and the white magic filling his palms flared brightly. 'Look at that. Magnificent!'

Freydel held his breath in fear and awe as he watched his Orb of Death throb with power between Ayeth's hands. It began to elongate, its black light sizzling against the Aralan's white magic. Ayeth drew his hands further apart and the orb elongated even more, making Freydel gasp.

Lona leaned closer, her eyes wide and as black and shining as the orb that captivated her. Her pale white face and smooth, hairless head shone brighter in the magic. Every time he came here now he could never find Ayeth alone; Lona was ever at his side, an irritation he let slide in the current magic of the orb.

Ayeth twisted his hands and the orb separated. Everyone gasped. Before them now were two shining onyx orbs resting on the glowing surface of the blue crystal pedestal.

'How is that possible? How can you create this from the very ether?' Freydel understood magic as a force to bend to one's will, to co-create with and command. What Ayeth had done was create substance out of nothing.

'I have a gift,' Ayeth said softly. 'Arzanu has blessed me with the gift of the pre-creative force. As such, all forms of elemental power and substance are open to me.'

Freydel blinked. He only knew one other with the power of the precreative force, and that was Issa. *It seems the Night Goddess gives her gift to only a select few.* But what did it mean for Ayeth to have the gift? Did Baelthrom have the same powers? Falling into the Dark Rift had changed him beyond recognition; he couldn't possibly have the same powers—he couldn't command the Flow—could he?

'And they are exactly the same?' asked Freydel as the magic torrent that Ayeth commanded lessened.

'The same in as much as any two things can be the same,' said Ayeth, the light of the crystal cavern now casting his skin in a blue shimmer. 'The only difference will be that this second orb is created here, so it will hold Aralansia's energy encryption, as well as Maioria's—potentially making it more powerful, although I cannot be sure.'

Freydel licked his lips as he stared at the replica orb. Could it really hold more power than his? A sense of foreboding stole over him, but he didn't know why. He lifted a hand towards the orb, but Lona was faster and touched it first, Ayeth too slow to stop her. Her small hand cupped the side of the orb and she closed her eyes, her smile deepening.

Ayeth swiftly touched it too. 'Be careful of the things you touch after their creation. Like a baby they will attach to the first person they see.'

'A second orb of undoing,' Lona breathed.

'Aralansia's own orb of power,' said Ayeth staring into the black surface.

Freydel picked his orb up. 'If only I could create duplicates of the orbs Baelthrom holds…'

'I must create one for Yurgharon,' said Lona, opening her eyes.

Ayeth frowned, his perfectly smooth brow rising with worry. 'That would not be wise. It could too easily fall into enemy hands.'

Lona dropped her gaze back to the orb and chewed her lip. 'With greater power, we could destroy them once and for all. Then we would be free.'

'Objects of power must not be used for harm. This is where the Yurgharon are going wrong and becoming like their enemies. I would use this orb to do good.' Ayeth, caressed the orb and touched her hand. She dropped her gaze, brooding.

Freydel nodded his agreement at Ayeth's sage words.

'Destruction of another is never the answer,' continued the wise Aralan.

'Help and rehabilitation is, which is why I do not like the name, Orb of Death or Undoing. It speaks of that same destruction and does not befit this new orb's Aralansian nature. I will name it "Lumenoor",' he said, rolling the 'r' in the Aralansian manner, 'for the vast emptiness of space we see in the night sky above us. Lumenoor is also the name of a rare black gem we have on Aralansia, named for the same reason. I think it is far more fitting.

'Lumenoor,' Ayeth repeated, lifting the orb up. Everybody's eyes followed.

Freydel smiled as it reflected them all perfectly in its dark surface. 'You have created something marvellous again, great Ayeth.'

'With it, like you have, I hope to see into the future,' the Aralan said, smiling. 'Only a magical relic made on Aralansia has the ability to accurately reach into Aralansia's future timelines. With it, I might be able to discover what went wrong. Perhaps I might even be able to reach myself there, like you have reached me here so far in the past.' Ayeth looked at Freydel.

'I hope it does not come to that,' said Freydel. 'I worry that Baelthrom would destroy you for your power. But if you can stop what will happen, countless lives—and planets—will be saved.'

'Then I must do it.' The smile dropped from Ayeth's face and he paled. 'I am not a fool, however. There are many timelines stretching forth from a single moment. Nothing is set and sealed. The future is… changeable.'

Lona turned away, her delicate fingers stroking her perfect chin.

'Only you can save our world,' breathed Freydel. 'The hope of millions lies in what you will or will not do.' Relief washed over him. There, he'd said it. He'd been thinking on it for many days now, sometimes waking up in the night to ponder, and now he had come to this conclusion: Issa did not have the power to save Maioria, only Ayeth did.

The prophecies were true once, but now the war had turned, the timeline had changed. Baelthrom was far more powerful than ever the prophecies foretold. No, it would take something far greater than young Issalena Kammy to stop the destruction of Maioria. It would take him assisting the great Ayeth in whatever way he could. The replica orb was the first step.

A sudden, terrible pain in Freydel's chest made him gasp. A hacking cough took a hold of him and he pulled his handkerchief from his pocket, vaguely aware of Ayeth coming to his side as he convulsed.

The pain and lump in his lungs disappeared as quickly as it had come, leaving him gasping and sweating.

'Freydel?'

He looked into Ayeth's concerned face.

'I'm all right,' he whispered but when he took his handkerchief away, it was flecked with bright blood. He scrunched it up and put it back in his pocket, hoping nobody noticed. He didn't want to raise alarm or look weak. 'I must be coming down with a cold. I should go and rest.'

'Of course,' said Ayeth. 'But you must return to us soon. There is more I can teach you and there are things Lona can teach you too.'

Freydel glanced at Lona who was smiling at him. He wondered what she could teach him, and imagined the great technologies of the Yurgha. He suppressed a shiver and, with slumped shoulders, composed himself. The last thing he wanted to do was return to his mundane room in Castle Carvon. All he wanted was to remain here with the greatest wizard he had ever known. But his body was not letting him.

He would return home, rest, feed his body and come back to Ayeth as soon as he could. Within this new orb lay the answer to the future.

CHAPTER 5

Swords and Magic

THE journey across the Venosian Straits was painfully slow despite the weather wizards and wind direction being in their favour.

Issa rested her chin on her folded arms and stared down at the frothing white wash far below. The evening wind whipped her hair about her shoulders and tugged at her shirt. Her feet longed to stand upon solid land or anything that wasn't in perpetual motion. Ehka clutched the bannisters, constantly trying to find balance as the ship swayed. He was bored too. The journey had become tiresome, and now, rather than being nervous about the coming battle, all she wanted to do was get there. Every day that passed provided more opportunities for Baelthrom to discover them.

Now it was officially winter, the days were shorter too. Travel by night was slow as the captains pored over charts fearful of striking unseen rocks or islands. Thankfully, here in the South, winter was mild, warm by her standards, but the weather was unpredictable. Strange winds often blasted in any direction, and the sea was turbulent and uneasy.

Storms were common on these seas, so the captain said, and if the wind blew east like it had the other day, it brought with it the frigid cold of the Everridge Mountains. If the wind blew west, it brought raging storms, and no sane captain dared travel the Straights. *Dangerous storms from Venosia and the sick sky that covers it,* thought Issa. *Unnatural storms.*

The wind currently blew mostly in their favour from the south-east, bringing warm, humid weather from the South.

Issa sighed and stroked Ehka. 'It can't be far now, Ehka. As soon as we see the Devil's Horns, you'll wish we hadn't. Still no Freydel, no Marakon, and no Asaph. But at least the other wizards are with us.'

It was poor consolation. She felt let down on many fronts. Asaph could at least have turned up to keep her company on the journey. Cabin fever had set in far too early. But she would be a fool to let her guard down. Any moment those vicious black spikes could appear, ready to tear into their hulls and rip out their keels.

'All right,' she sighed again. 'How about we do another scout?'

The bird garbled acquiescence and ruffled his feathers.

'Now remember, don't ever lose sight of the ship.' Issa got down into her usual cross-legged position and closed her eyes focussing on the ever-present connection to her feathered guardian. No one paid her any attention now; the crew and passengers were used to her odd behaviour and her strange pet.

Ehka cawed and she felt him jump off the railing and lift into the air, then she was seeing through his eyes. The ship fell away, a floating island in a turbulent, deep blue sea. Around it, more ships ploughed the waves, and behind them followed hundreds more.

Ehka faced east to a darkening horizon. The boredom was swept from her mind and a sense of foreboding grew. She tried not to think about the four horsemen or the Light Eaters or the white raven.

Ehka flew far to the East until their ship was just a speck on the horizon, but he never lost sight of it completely. The sky turned dark tinged with red. She sensed the bird's reluctance to go further.

'There they are!' she said in her mind, knowing he could hear her.

Barely visible dark streaks speared up through the ocean's surface far on the horizon. Ehka flew closer, and sure enough there were the Devil's Horns. Waves frothed around their jagged bases and there seemed hundreds more than she remembered; a monstrous hedgehog sunk beneath the waves, waiting for its prey. She felt sick.

Red lightning flared across the sky and thunder cracked making her jump even from this distance. Did Baelthrom know they were coming? Were they sailing into a trap? She imagined the skies opening, the dark clouds peeling back and the four horsemen charging out of the sky. Ehka cawed and she forced the image away, hoping he hadn't seen her dark imaginings too.

'You'd better come back. Looks like tonight everything changes.'

Issa's heart beat faster as the red horizon approached. This night, no one would be sleeping. She stood at the prow, re-dressed in her Dread Dragon armour with Ehka on her shoulder. Velonorian stood to her right and Naksu to her left, gripping her white staff. Both she and the seer stood in the Flow.

Velonorian was not an accomplished magic wielder, but like all elves, he held a natural ability of his own and his Elven nature magic shimmered ready in his aura. He was dressed in Elven armour of hardened leather that allowed more free movement than the plate armour of the Feylint Halanoi. He wore the new Elven tabard created by Orphinius; dark green with a golden tree upon it. *Sheyengetha,* she thought. *Gateway to the Elven Land of Mists.* With a pang she wished Averen, the Elven High Wizard, were here. They needed all the wizards they could get. *Including Freydel,* she grimaced.

Behind them, on the other ships, she felt the wizards of the Circle standing powerfully in the Flow. Haelgon was surrounded by Atalanph warriors; Drumblodd was much further back with his dwarven ships; Luren was far away, catching them up with his medley of Lans Himay brigands, mercenaries and warriors. The wilting young wizard had become an unlikely advisor to the barbarians of the north. There were many other wizards and magic wielders, but none held the power of those of the Wizards' Circle, or the seer by her side.

A powerful flaming aura entered the Flow making her start. *Domenon?* The Master Wizard was somewhere behind on the Elven ships. *Next to Orphinius, no doubt.* Wherever there was an orb of power, there'd be Domenon. And perhaps that was a good thing. The orb needed the protection of a powerful wizard.

Still, Orphinius was ill-equipped to protect the Orb of Earth that had been thrust into his hands at the death of Daranarta, leader of the Elves. And, in his lack of wisdom, he'd assigned Domenon as its Second Keeper. How this was all going to unfold, she could only worry about.

'Domenon is with us,' said Issa.

Naksu smiled in surprise. 'Indeed he is, somewhere upon the Elven ships. That wizard is a master of appearing and disappearing.'

'So is Freydel, it would seem.' Issa forced a half-smile.

'He will come,' said Naksu, nodding. Issa did not share the seer's positivity. Naksu did not know how often or why he was visiting Ayeth.

Issa glanced up at the sky. The muddy clouds had long since swallowed up the white ones, but under this red sky, night had not fully fallen, and the dull red light gave them something to see by, at least.

The air had become thick and heavy, but not with moisture. She didn't know what it was, only that it was hard to breathe and somehow it tasted stale. Already, she longed to be away from this place.

'Two hours to the Devil's Horns,' the Captain barked, making everyone jump as he stalked the decks.

'Captain, the ships are in formation. Please hold this course.' Commander Septarn walked up the stairs trailed by his officers. The tall commander bowed slightly to Issa. His long white hair was tied back with a black bow and his commander's hat was tucked under one arm.

The captain nodded but said nothing, his face set in a scowl of worry for his vessel.

The ships had been brought into several arrow-shaped formations with one leading the rest of its battalion. Issa's battalion was ahead of the others, and her ship was forefront.

'You and your wizards better have a bloody good plan,' the captain said to her, his grey eyes hard.

'Just thank the goddess Baelthrom appears to be unaware of ours plans,' she said. 'Otherwise this sky would be filled with Dread Dragons— and it wouldn't be two hours to the Devil's Horns, more like one hour to the bottom of the ocean.'

The captain paled, and whatever the commander had been about to say died on his lips for he, too, closed his mouth.

'Thank you, Commander Septarn,' she nodded to him. 'Your expert knowledge on these affairs is well received. Whatever happens—magic or otherwise—prepare for battle as soon as we reach those spikes. Now we have briefed our crews, the way will become known to us when we need it.' She hoped to the goddess she was right.

The commander pursed his lips, seeming to struggle with this. 'My Lady, it's not the way of a battle commander to rely upon the whims of the gods. Battle tactics require clear and absolute planning—'

Issa cut him off. 'I—*we* magic wielders—understand this well, Commander. However, what we have been doing until now has not been working. Please, let us not discuss this again. Now we must trust, and the way will become known to us. We have the most powerful wizards and seers amongst us,' *and there should have been Freydel with his orb! The Wykiry had better be right!* 'along with three orbs of power. This is unheard of in the history of Maioria. It may be hard, but sometimes you have to place your trust in something more than military skill and weapons.'

She tried to remain understanding, for the commander's fears were her own. She wanted assurances and absolutes but there were none. She was actually relying everything upon a dream given to her by the Wykiry—a dream to trust in the orb of power she held. In a way it was a test; the orb was testing her strength.

The Commander nodded politely and turned away, his younger officers in tow.

By the time the black spikes were clearly visible to the naked eye, Issa's heart was pounding, and all her doubts raged in her mind. Trust in the power of the orb, the Wykiry had asked her. That was a hell of a lot of trust. The lives of thousands now depended on her.

'Half an hour to Devil's Horns,' cried the lookout. The captain repeated the call. Issa could feel the captain's eyes boring into her back. She side-glanced Velonorian who smiled at her.

'I trust in you,' he said.

It was a nice thing to say but it didn't help much. The devoted elf would follow her to the ends of the cosmos and die with her willingly. She glanced up at the ugly sky for the hundredth time but there was still no golden dragon in it. At least there were no Dread Dragons either.

'The shield is holding,' Naksu reassured.

Issa looked up again and noted the subtle shimmer of the wizard's cloaking magic.

'And don't forget, the Trinity will be assisting from afar,' the seer added. 'See how my staff glows? They are with us even now.'

'That is comforting,' said Issa, wishing they were physically beside her.

She turned back to the black spikes speeding towards them and pulled out the Orb of Water. It glowed luminous in the dim red light. She stroked its surface. 'The Wykiry had better be right, you'd better know what to do.

I'm just a vessel for your power.' Images and understanding passed between them. Issa frowned, seeing a vague solution in its blue surface. Impossible, it seemed, but there nonetheless. Did she dare to trust?

'Do not slow the ship,' she shouted to the captain, who retained his scowl.

The waves thrashed harder against the bow, pounding the sides and shuddering the hull. The sails snapped taut, filled with a gusting wind. She turned her mind fully into the Flow and the fast approaching spikes of death.

The orb responded readily to her command, drawing on the element of water, speaking to the living thing that was the ocean beneath them. Her breath came too fast and she felt light-headed. She tried to control it by taking long slow breaths, focussing on the Flow that filled her. Her world of magic became filled with blues and greens, from the darkest to the lightest, and above it the dark-light of something that was not of Maioria. In the Flow the sky above boiled and raged, hating her presence. She tried not to look at it, tried not to imagine it forming into the giant shapes of Light Eaters.

'Focus on the Flow. Focus on the orb,' she whispered over and again.

Dimly, she was aware of shouting and the violent rocking of the ship. In the Flow, she could see the blue waves beneath them.

'The sea is angry, but not with us,' she spoke in the Flow, more via thought forms than words. Those in the Flow would have heard her. 'It's angry with the dark magic placed upon it, and it's fighting.'

'Rope us to the rails. We cannot leave this place,' Naksu's voice came from far away. Issa felt something being tied firmly around her waist, giving her stability.

The seer was right, she could not do anything but hold the Orb of Water before her and pool the Flow around her. If she broke her concentration now it would be dangerous to her mind and take hours to regain the control she currently had.

I need more. More magic flowed into her, coming both from the orb in her grip and the ocean below. It filled her being. As in her vision with the Wykiry, she felt herself melding with the element that was water.

The sea found her, a way for it to fight back, a channel for its rage. Its power burst up into her, pounding her head and beating her heart with its own life until she was more in tune with the ocean than her own body. She struggled to maintain control of both her mind and the Flow as she melded with the angry elemental. Wind plastered her hair to her sweaty face.

She let go of the rails, leaned back against the ropes that secured her to the boat, and gripped the orb with both hands. Greater power exploded through her palms and the orb became a blazing blue sun in the Flow. A glimpse into the material world showed the orb flaring bright turquoise, red lightning flashing above and black spikes looming impossibly high only yards away.

'Our cover is gone,' a voice said. Was it her own or Naksu's?

They were exposed. Any magic wielder in the vicinity would feel the power of the orbs. Baelthrom would know where they were for certain.

'Let them know!' Issa growled. 'We have cowered defending for too long.'

The sea surged at her words, hungry for revenge against that which was unholy. Her mind was no longer her own. She had become the element of water.

'Rise up.' Her voice was calm, soothing almost, but it boomed within and without.

The ocean rose.

In her mind she glimpsed purple lights in the swirling blue that was now her body. *Wykiry.*

'Higher,' she commanded.

The ocean swelled and lifted higher. The black spikes that speared her ocean body slid beneath her.

'Higher!'

The black spikes were swallowed by her mass. On her back, hundreds of ships floated. These she had to protect.

Over the top of the Devil's Horns the entire ocean swelled and flowed. Ahead, a dark land loomed. She wanted to thrash against it and lash it in ways the black spikes had prevented her from doing. But to wreak vengeance against it would destroy the precious ships she carried.

'Down.'

Issa filled her giant body with power, feeling herself extend back and forth for miles. She eased herself down, feeling the spikes on her belly.

'Crush.'

The orb pulsed in her hands. Shock waves shuddered through both her human body and that which was melded to the ocean. Beneath her, the spikes snapped and disintegrated as she collapsed upon them. Black rocks shattered and crumbled, sinking into the ocean depths. Joy shuddered through her mighty body.

'Slow.'

The raging ocean calmed dutifully at her command, satisfied that its rage had been somewhat appeased. Issa tried to move her focus to the orb but found herself struggling to extract herself from the elemental. The ocean did not want her to leave.

Wykiry magic moved, faintly purple in its hue, and she felt herself separating from the water. Gentle hands laid her down on hard wood and she saw Naksu, her aura glowing fiercely white in the Flow.

'Release,' said the seer, and Issa knew she meant the power she held.

Slowly, unwillingly, she let go. Calm as she hung between states, then the rocking of the ship, the rushing of waves and the cheering of soldiers filled her ears.

With Velonorian's help, Issa sat up.

His violet eyes shone as he came into focus and she could see Naksu was just behind him, smiling.

'You did it, we made it!' he said. 'I've never seen anything like it! The sea lifted into the sky over the Devil's Horns and smashed down upon them. A great path has been carved through them for the ships that follow.'

Issa smiled. 'Thank the goddess. Thank the Wykiry. I didn't know the sea was so *angry*. I never saw it as a being before. The orb knew what to do.'

The joyful face of Commander Septarn loomed beyond Velonorian and Naksu. He composed himself and took on his serious, commanding role. 'The shore fast approaches. We think we have been spotted. Lights flare in the cove ahead.'

Issa struggled to her feet, wishing she didn't feel so weak.

Naksu handed her a small glass vial. 'Here. The weakness will pass faster if you smell this but come on stronger later.'

Issa pulled out the cork and sniffed. A sharp odour assaulted her and made her eyes smart. Instantly the fog in her brain vanished and her sight regained its sharp focus.

'The essence of a certain rare Elven flower we have been able to cultivate on Myrn,' the seer explained in response to Issa's questioning look. 'Come now, the real battle has begun.'

Issa slipped the now dull orb back into its pouch, gripped the rails and stared at the dark land fast approaching. Lights were indeed flaring into life in the cove, and all along the coast and cliffs on either side. The ship was moving fast as the sea surged beneath them. She felt its rage at the edge of her awareness.

'For once, my Queen, we have mostly retained the element of surprise,' said Velonorian.

Issa looked at the elf and grinned.

The ships became an ordered chaos of activity. Sailors scaled masts and rigging, reefing sails to slow their approach. Tenders were readied, and the shouts of captains and commanders rang over the din. For a blessed few moments there was nothing for Issa to do but watch and rest, but she couldn't relax. Adrenaline coursed through her veins and she frequently searched the skies for Asaph.

'Lady Issa, we must go. Your horse is ready.' Velonorian took her arm and led her to the rope ladder where soldiers clambered down into tenders. Further down the ship, horses in slings were being lowered via a winch over the decks. Thoughts of Duskar filled her mind as she took her seat in the boat rammed between soldiers and Velonorian. Ehka landed next to her.

Oars lifted and splashed into the sea, and the foreboding cove neared. It was similar to the one she had scouted almost a week ago. The strange, low, square buildings of the enemy stretched up the hill. Beneath them, how many dark dwarven tunnels were there?

Issa could see the enemy. The black armour of Maphraxies shining like beetles' backs as they scurried along the coast. She glanced back, wishing the other wizards were beside her. There were hundreds of tenders now in the sea. For a moment it seemed hopeless to spot Haelgon, Drumblodd or Domenon, but then she saw a glowing staff. Her eyes rested on Haelgon some ten boats behind and she sighed with relief.

'We should do as the commander says and stay behind the front line, Lady Issa,' said Velonorian. 'Your magic will be more useful here than your sword. Don't worry, I shall be by your side.' He lifted a hand to brush a strand of her hair back.

She nodded and smiled, suddenly feeling out of her depth. 'I'd hoped Asaph would be here. I can't bring myself to think that something might have gone wrong.'

'There's still time,' Velonorian said, just as the commanders yelled, 'Archers, take aim!'

The archers ahead of them readied their arrows, balancing carefully in their boats.

'Fire!'

A dark cloud of arrows slammed into the Maphraxies. Many fell, but their attack was answered swiftly with a hail of blazing arrows. Late to respond, Issa jumped into the Flow.

'Shield!' She threw up her palms, recognising Domenon's unmistakable magic signature as magic flared moments before hers. The Master Wizard had already created a shield, so she added her power to his. Haelgon did the same and then Drumblodd. The fire arrows bounced harmlessly off it in a shower of sparks.

Her ship ground onto the sand amidst the yells of commanders and officers. Then Velonorian was gripping her arm and guiding her out whilst she maintained her focus on the shield.

The shouting of soldiers was answered by the bellows of the enemy. Frayon and dwarven steel crashed against dark dwarven black iron, and the vicious battle began. Issa breathed fast, sweating, her hand gripping the hilt of her short sword as she ran for a safe spot to cast her magic. Velonorian led her left along the shoreline, dodging past soldiers just touching down. He was aiming for the safety of the rocks ahead where Domenon stood, his unmistakable fiery aura powerful in the Flow.

A Maphraxie broke through the line of soldiers to her right and lunged at her. She ducked his axe but not his boot that sent her sprawling into the sea. Winded, she staggered upright. Velonorian shouted. The Maphraxie dropped to its knees, a surprised expression on its face as black blood oozed from its slit throat and dripped off Velonorian's Elven blade. The elf's eyes were wild.

'I'm all right,' she said, wiping sand from her face. A neigh caught her attention. She whirled to see soldiers falling back from a galloping horse made of midnight.

'Duskar!'

The horse slowed until it pranced in agitation before her.

'You can't ride him until all knights are mounted,' said Velonorian. 'The added height will make you a target. Wait until the knights are in formation.'

Issa nodded even though she wanted nothing more than to ride Duskar straight at the enemy, using swords and magic to slay the undead bastards. 'Once we hold the beach, we'll be able to form ordered units,' she said.

They reached the rocks beside Domenon. The wizard said nothing, but his eyes were vivid turquoise as he looked into, and commanded, the Flow.

To their right, she saw Haelgon running towards them, his staff glowing. A hail of flaming arrows bore down upon him. Had he stepped beyond Domenon's shield? She realised the Master Wizard was focussing his protection on a particular section of soldiers. Elven soldiers. She thought she saw Orphinius' tall stature and pale face. It stood to reason that he would protect a non-wizard Orb Keeper.

Issa held up her hand. Maphraxie arrows flared harmlessly against her shield. The Atalanphian wizard paused, caught her gaze and nodded his thanks to her. He reached them panting, blue eyes sparkling.

'Drumblodd follows. Is Freydel with you? I've not seen him,' he said.

'No. I don't know where he is,' she said.

'One wonders if he has betrayed us in some manner,' said Domenon. He didn't drop his concentration from the Flow. 'We have successfully retained the element of surprise, Raven Queen.' Issa considered that a rare compliment from the wizard. 'And your mastery of that orb you carry is quite impressive. You must tell me how you did that back there.

'I worry, however, that you may have drained yourself for battle. Whilst we have surprised our enemy, there is a whole legion under those barracks. From what I can sense in the Flow there are at least two thousand in this cove alone. But don't worry, I am well rested. I will protect you.'

'Two thousand?' she echoed, ignoring his manner. She'd only reckoned on a thousand at the absolute worst. Whilst they outnumbered their enemy, what of the other bases she had seen? There could be tens of thousands just waiting for them. Dark dwarven tunnels probably connected each and every one of the bases together. They could travel between them fast and undetected.

Despite the bad news, she found herself saying, 'Then we'll have to fight and take them one by one.'

'I hope you have the stamina for a long and bloody battle,' he murmured.

Furious cries captured her attention. Karalanths covered in war paint galloped up the beach to join the fray, weapons held high and their painted faces masks of rage. They even made *her* mouth go dry. The warriors had stepped foot on the lands that had once been theirs and now they were furious to take them back.

Was that Rhul'ynth amongst them? A warrior woman, antlers painted blue, lunged her thick knife at a Maphraxie and then was lost behind a cluster of male warriors. They were all here though, Grast'anth—her trainer, whose sword she held—Diarc'ynth, Cusap'anth their leader, and many others. She longed to fight alongside them like she had before. But her place was here with the wizards, for now.

Feeling it would conserve her energy, she sat cross-legged on the sand and closed her eyes, focussing her attention in the Flow. The black mass of Maphraxies were being pushed back fast, but pouring from the barracks came an ever steady flow of more. If they could destroy the barracks, it would also block any tunnels beneath them.

Emboldened by her success with the element of water, Issa spread her hands and dug them into the sand, willing the element of earth to respond to her commands. Earth magic moved. It was not as responsive as the water elemental, perhaps because she didn't have the orb, but also because the land was sick. She could feel the poison in it, put there by the enemy. Nothing could grow in poison.

Earth, work with me, she put forth her intention. She gathered the energy, losing herself in it and trusting Velonorian to protect her.

Under the ground, her vision moved. There was earth and darkness, and there, cutting through the dirt, was a network of dark caverns and tunnels. She moved her mind through the density and paused under the largest building.

'Pressure,' she commanded.

Everything became heavy. The stone walls of the tunnels groaned and cracks appeared. She clenched her hands in the sand and the caverns bulged inwards. She spread her hands wide and released the Flow. In her mind she saw the main barracks explode. Rocks, dark dwarves and debris flew into the air smashing into other Maphraxies. She opened her eyes. There was no fire or even a whiff of smoke to accompany the destruction.

Domenon glanced down at her and raised one eyebrow, 'Impressive.'

Haelgon guffawed. Issa grinned.

'Nice one, Gal,' said Drumblodd, his eyes sparkling. She smiled at the breathless dwarf leaning on his axe.

'Only another ten to go,' she sighed and dug her hands into the ground again. The fatigue grew. It would be her worst enemy this battle.

Haelgon followed her in the Flow, learning what she did as she did it. Together, they destroyed another barrack and then two more, blocking the tunnels and stemming the flow of Maphraxies.

The enemy frontline was quickly overcome, and their armies now pushed the enemy back beyond their own barracks. The battle turned to skirmishes as soldiers and Karalanths harried an enemy in chaos. They could not let any escape who might warn others. Sensing victory, cheering began amongst the soldiers until the air hummed with it. Issa and the wizards joined them. With relief she released her hold on the Flow and got to her feet.

'Our first success on enemy-held lands, Raven Queen,' said Drumblodd, his voice gruff. 'See how easy it is when surprise is in our favour? But the fighting will be harder from now on. A part of Karalanthia—this cove—may have been retaken, but the Land of the Light Dwarfs will not be freed easily from the hands of the Dark Dwarves.'

'We will take them *all* back, Drumblodd,' said Issa, as she gripped his shoulder.

'Aye, if I do anything, I would rather die doing that,' the dwarf nodded. His eyes suddenly glistened and he turned away.

CHAPTER 6

Barbarian of the North

AS the fighting ceased, the army had no chance for rest.

Hasty camps, hospitals and food tents were erected on the battlefield. A thick perimeter of soldiers guarded the cove in every direction. Tenders left the shores to both assist in docking the newly arriving ships, and to carry the supplies to the shore.

Sailors reported the coves nearby had been successfully taken, though they were smaller than this one, yet despite their victory, everybody was edgy. The enemy had been awakened and was about to come at them hard—they'd need every ounce of strength to keep their foothold on this land.

Issa noted the tough looks shared on dwarven and Karalanth faces as they cleaned their weapons and tended their wounds. The next few weeks were going to be bitter, bloody fighting.

The Karalanths, a tight knot of five hundred or so warriors, kept to themselves at the edge of camp. They eyed the dwarves, sometimes with open hatred, but mostly with suspicion. The dwarves mingled with elves and humans from all factions. They kept their distance from the Karalanths and rarely looked in their direction. When they did, they were wary.

More than once, tall, fair and red-headed men in the mercenary leathers of Lans Himay caught Issa's attention. Twice, she started towards one thinking they might be Asaph, only for them to turn and reveal they were not. *Draxian exiles. At least here they can fight, but I wish Asaph were amongst them.*

Lans Himay was a hot spot for exiles. She even spotted the odd elf amongst them. They all appeared hard, battle-strong and keen for a fight. Some called them barbarians, uncultured, savage even, but all she cared about was that they would fight and fight hard. For that reason, everyone was glad they were here, regardless of what they thought about them away from the battlefield.

She looked towards their leader, a giant brick of a man, towering seven feet high and half as broad with thick muscles knotting his arms. He wore his brown beard short and his bald head shone as if polished. He wore furs over studded leather but was clearly uncomfortable in the heat and sweating heavily. He began slipping them off and dumped them down beside the campfire.

She did not understand what they said to one another in their rolling tongue. Lans Himayan was closer to Munlish, the dialect of Munland, than it was to Frayon, though it was part of the Frayonesse continent. The seas proved easier passage between people than the harsh, mostly impassable Everridge Mountains that divided Frayon from Lans Himay.

As she sat sipping her soup beside Domenon and Luren, she caught the barbarian's glance at her for a second time. The man sauntered over.

'All this is…your doing?' he said in a thick accent, spreading his meaty hands wide. He wore two thick rings, one gold, one silver and both inscribed with letters or runes of a foreign language. Was he accusing her? The man's face and tone were indecipherable, and he watched her without blinking. The question caught her off guard. Domenon looked on with intrigue.

'This invasion was sort of my idea, if that's what you mean,' she said, setting her soup aside.

'They said some girl from some tiny island in the middle of nowhere has managed to unite the armies of the world and start the war that will end it all,' the man said, gesticulating to the milling soldiers and the smoking piles of fallen enemy that were proving difficult to incinerate.

Issa felt herself bristling at the man's tone. Was she being laughed at? Was she being scrutinised and found lacking like she had been when she'd first met the Wizards' Circle? The man continued, and Issa felt her cheeks reddening. 'I did not believe it until today. Now here she sits, a slip of a girl—excuse me, a woman—who calls herself the Raven Queen.'

As if on cue Ehka decided to land on the rock beside her with a caw.

He tilted his head and regarded the man through one eye. The man glanced at him then back at her.

Issa squared her shoulders. 'I did not *start* this war—it was kill or be killed. And I do not call myself the Raven Queen, everyone else does.' She stood up and folded her arms, her eyes hard. She knew they still glowed with luminosity from her use of the Flow and she hoped they had an intimidating affect, although it was unlikely anything could intimidate this man.

'Well, is that so?' The man folded his arms as well.

Issa gave a short, curt nod.

All at once the man's face split into a smile and to her horror he bowed low. 'Then you must have my allegiance, Raven Queen, for you have managed to do what I have tried and failed to do for a decade. We haven't travelled thousands of miles just to help out poor little Davono.'

Domenon snorted. 'Lans Himayans care nothing for others, they don't even care about Maioria. As long as there's the chance to fight someone who's wronged them in the distant past, they'll be there.'

The Lans Himayan leader's grin deepened. He seemed to take the wizard's words as a compliment. 'That and the gold the dark dwarves stole from us. Some say their caverns are filled with it.'

'It wasn't easy, no one wanted to do anything,' said Issa. 'It *was* Queen Thora's agreement that made all this possible, and before that, the attacks on Frayon, our heartland, made people afraid and more willing to do something.'

Another Lans Himayan came to stand beside the leader. He was as tall but not as broad, and a thick scar ran the length of his face from his temple to his chin. From his red hair, she judged him to be Draxian. The leader slapped the man's back with a grin.

'But we didn't come just for gold and violence against those bastards, did we Tarsun?' he laughed. 'The Draxians amongst us have heard the rumours of the last Dragon Lord returning—that he has come to take back Drax, and they are ready to join him.'

The Draxian looked at her in earnest. 'Where is the Dragon Lord, Raven Queen? Is he real?'

Issa nodded. 'Yes, he's real and he should be here. He went north to awaken the dragons.'

The man's eyes brightened.

'Come, Tarsun. Let us eat and make ready for the next battle. Our commander needs a rest,' the gruff leader winked at Issa and she smiled, warming to his manner. They started to leave.

'Wait,' she called out. 'I don't know your name.'

The big man turned, a surprised expression on his face. She hoped she hadn't offended him with her ignorance. He raised an eyebrow. 'You really must be from the middle of nowhere. I am Ghott the Great. Ghott the Dominator. Ghott the Barbarian of the North.' He spread his large hands wide.

'Ghott is the only man to have successfully united the warring tribes and families of Lans Himay,' said Luren, before spluttering on his soup.

'Dominated,' Ghott said firmly, his smile remaining as he pointed a thick finger at the wizard. 'Unified is weak.' He clapped his hands together and, with a deep laugh, left. Tarsun followed him back to their warriors who were eating and drinking around the fire.

'Savages,' said Domenon, smirking. 'Only an iron fist can exert any sense of control over that rabble.'

'As long as they're good fighters,' Issa said.

Tarsun, and the shorter, stockier Draxian he was now talking to, glanced in her direction then looked away, deep in conversation. They wanted Drax back like Asaph did. They just needed Asaph to lead them. For all their strength and barbarity, Lans Himay couldn't win back another continent.

'They need Asaph,' she whispered.

'You think that man can take back Drax, a stronghold of Baelthrom?' Ridicule danced in Domenon's eyes.

'I think your scorn blinds you to the power of others. Underestimating them will be your downfall,' Issa said tartly. She finished her soup without looking at the Master Wizard. Hiding her grin, she hoped he was at a loss for words.

'Dread Dragons!' screamed a Karalanth scout hurtling over the ridge beyond the destroyed barracks.

Issa jumped up and scanned the smouldering skies. Ghott threw his

tankard down with a roar and drew his sword, his warriors following suit.
She glanced at Domenon.

The wizard pursed his lips. 'Now the real battle begins.'

Issa nodded, swallowing. Naksu hurried over with Velonorian. They
had been busy tending the wounded.

'I cannot protect us all from dragon fear, but I'll do what I can,' said
Naksu.

The distant screech of a dragon started Issa's heart racing. She looked
into the Flow. Black specs appeared in the gloom that was frequently the
magical energy of western Venosia.

'I still don't know how best to fight them,' Issa said, half unsheathing
her sword.

'No one does,' said Domenon as he entered the Flow beside her. 'One
thing's for certain, they'll be after the orbs first, and possibly you if they
suspect the Raven Queen is here. My first priority as Second Keeper is to
protect Orphinius. He's not exactly the greatest wizard.' Domenon scowled.

'And I'll protect *you*, my Queen' said Velonorian, standing proud and
unslinging his bow.

The Dread Dragons appeared in the sky and Issa's legs began to
tremble. *Asaph, if you can hear me at all, come fast, come now!*

Soldiers, knights and barbarians swiftly formed themselves into ranks.
Wizards prepared shields that shimmered in the sky, but as the dragons
neared, nothing could stop the dragon fear. Armour rattled and spears
trembled. More than one person sank to their knees and more than one
person vomited.

It hit Issa hard in her magic-weary state. For a moment she lost her grip
on the Flow and felt herself sink to one knee. Duskar stamped and tossed
his head and Ehka made a strangled noise by her leg. She shut her eyes but
behind closed lids she could see the Dread Dragons, the burning eyes and
amulets of the Dromoorai on their backs. Their amulets blazed brighter.
Baelthrom was watching. They were hunting. She could feel their keenness.

'The orbs have been felt,' she said, her voice sounding as though it were
coming from far away.

'It's dangerous to bring them here,' growled Domenon. He stood with
his palms up, holding the shield above them. He was the least affected by
the dragon fear.

She was about to say they didn't have any choice when a Dread Dragon screamed and the noise tore right through her.

Mayhem descended as a wall of dragon fire rolled towards them. Forgetting her sword, she grabbed the Orb of Water. It flared readily in her hands. Water lifted from the sea behind her and sprayed into the fire, turning it to steam and smoke.

Domenon walked forwards, glancing upwards at the Dread Dragons then back to Orphinius ahead whom he was trying to protect. The elf was surrounded by a company of Elven warriors in gleaming armour, all aiming their arrows at the dragons.

He should be using the orb! Domenon was right. The power of the orb was lost on the elf when it could be used to help fight this dire enemy. At this moment she wished the Master Wizard really did have the orb—he'd be devastating with its power.

The dragons landed on the hills surrounding the cove and scores of Maphraxies scuttled off their backs. Freed of their cargo, the dragons lifted into the air and two turned back the way they had come. To get more Maphraxies, Issa assumed. The third came on to attack.

Ignoring a hail of arrows, the dragon swooped and grabbed dozens of soldiers in its mouth and claws. Their screams ended abruptly as the dragon crunched, then swallowed them whole, armour and all. It released the bloody pulp in its claws and the mangled bodies crashed onto the soldiers below.

Issa felt faint. Gritting her teeth, she channelled her anger into the Flow. Fire magic was the most destructive force but it was less effective against dragons. Instead, she focused on the rubble left from her earlier attacks. Rocks, iron railings and debris from the destroyed barracks lifted into the air as she raised her hands. She swept her hands to the left. The debris hurtled into the dragon, knocking it sideways through the air and crashing it into the cliff face. Stunned, it slid to the ground, its Dromoorai rider reeling on its back.

Soldiers cheered.

Not waiting for it to recover, she again lifted debris and flung it. The dragon floundered and fell once more and a pack of Karalanths and soldiers peeled away from the battle to finish it off.

Three more Dromoorai appeared in the sky. They again landed on the hills and dispatched the next horde of Maphraxies, then they launched into the air and flew in her direction.

Issa's heart skipped a beat. Velonorian planted himself in front of her. Luren paled and stepped back. Haelgon jumped into the Flow. Duskar laid back his ears and bared his teeth. Drumblodd raised his hands. The dwarf was to the left of them on a ledge a few feet up the cliff, partially hidden by rocks. A handful of dwarven lesser wizards clustered round him, busily assisting the army of dwarfs pressing against the Maphraxies on the battlefield.

Drumblodd held his Orb of Fire low to hide it, but every now and then it flared fiery red, and her own responded with a flash of turquoise. Had the Dromoorai only spotted her orb or were they after more than that?

A black dragon dropped out of the sky straight towards them only to smash into Haelgon's shield in a spray of orange sparks. Haelgon staggered under the impact as the dazed dragon glanced off it. Its Dromoorai rider yanked on the reins, heaving it back into the sky.

The second dragon smashed straight through it. Luren's fire blasted it first followed by her own. The dragon screamed and wheeled away. The third hesitated and, instead, swooped and torched the soldiers beyond. They scattered, many on fire. Screams of agony filled the air. Too busy fighting the dragons, none of the wizards were able to protect their own army.

Issa closed her eyes and used the orb. Sea water lifted and sprayed over the soldiers, dousing flames and cooling skin. The uninjured dragged the injured away and the fighters pressed forwards once more. The Dread Dragons readied to attack again.

'All the time they attack us, we can't protect the soldiers,' Issa said. She worried they were really only trying to attack her and she jeopardised them all.

They came on, three at once, their red amulets blazing.

With a half-baked plan forming in her head, she grabbed Duskar's reins and swung up into the saddle. The horse pranced, ready to fight.

'Luren, Haelgon, protect the soldiers. Try and get the attention of one of the beasts if you can. Otherwise, I'm going to try and lead them away.'

'What are you doing, Lady Issa? This is madness,' said Velonorian, a look of panic in his eyes. 'I'll get a horse and come with you!' He looked around, but there were no horses nearby, the closest were back by the shore.

'There's no time!' yelled Issa. She held the orb high and it pulsed with latent magic.

It was a brazen move, a taunt to Baelthrom who watched from those amulets. *Let him see, let him come. I'm not afraid. The war has been brought to you now, you bastard, and you'll see that we are mighty!*

'Don't be afraid, Duskar,' she said. 'Trust me.'

With a roar, she let him have the reins. He reared, turned on his hooves, and hurtled towards the coast. She held the orb high, making sure the Dromoorai could see it, and gripped Duskar with her knees, clinging to the reins and saddle with one hand.

The dragons screeched and followed.

'If we want to evade the enemy, we must fly higher,' said Garna. 'We remember this enemy well.'

Asaph side-glanced the red, female dragon, her amber eyes narrowed against the freezing wind, her limbs tucked close and her tail streaming straight behind her. He followed her, climbing higher until the atmosphere turned thin. Pennarc and Rust followed just behind them.

This high, the sun emerged above a blanket of white, and the gentle curve of the planet was just about visible. Pale blue faded into the blue-black of space. If he looked hard enough, he could make out the brightest stars.

He remembered the first time he had flown with another dragon, Faelsun, and the sheer exhilaration. To fly with a whole brood was even more exhilarating. For now they were free, and the whole world was theirs. They could explore all places, beyond even the Kingdom of Fire far to the South, if they so chose. They were mighty and invincible, and the Flow was alive and pure around them.

Ah Issa, I wish you were with me now.

'Your mate is the dark-haired one?' asked Pennarc, coming as close as their wings would allow.

'Yes. We must get to her as soon as we can,' said Asaph, reminded that dragons could read his thoughts easily unless he shielded them. Clearly, they could even see his thoughts as pictures.

They'd tried to show him how to read thoughts, but he found it difficult and wondered if such things were harder for Dragon Lords. As much as he had proven his strength to them in his fight against Morhork, being a Dragon Lord would always set him apart. Loneliness gnawed at him. If only there were other Dragon Lords. *So much has been lost, Father Coronos!*

'Tell me about Morhork. Will he ever join us?' asked Asaph.

'Morhork was the greatest warrior after Arc,' said Rust. A feeling of deep respect bordering on awe came from the big red. 'He's a Grand Architect of War, a master at planning. But his anger at his own brother made us all uncomfortable. It is forbidden to turn on our kin which is why even his closest brood hesitated in their support of him, and how he came to be *pacified* by Faelsun.

'Since that day he has never trusted his own species. He works his own grand plans alone. We do not know what they are, his mind is guarded from us, but we wonder if they are in the interests of dragons or not. We respect him, but our mistrust is mutual.'

'I appreciate your openness,' said Asaph. He hadn't expected dragons to be so open or eloquent. It seemed Morhork was as much alone in this world as he himself was. There was a lot he still had to discover about the mysterious wingless dragon and his grand designs.

'The land you seek looms,' said Garna. 'It will be dark by the time we arrive.'

Sure enough, the sun was already half swallowed by a milky horizon. The dragons began to descend into the thicker atmosphere where it was warmer and wetter, and soon rain splashed onto their scales as they passed through the thick bank of grey. Garna made them remain in the cloud for a long time, obviously choosing to hide themselves for as long as possible.

Asaph found it hard flying, the mix between water and air made conditions unpredictable and he fought against the turbulence. He had to blink the water out of his eyes a lot, too. The other dragons flew with much greater ease so he was thankful when they finally descended out of them, and he was able to shake the rain from his body.

The dark ocean stretched below. He couldn't see any land but he sensed great land masses in each direction. Soon, red-tinged clouds bloodied the dark sky, and the taint of Dromoorai assaulted his senses. Enemy-held lands were ahead.

'I can feel them, my undead cousins,' said Asaph, his voice grim. It was a hard truth; the Dromoorai were the only other beings closer to his kind on all Maioria.

'Whatever inhabits those things is far from living,' said Pennarc with a shudder. 'They're not your cousins.'

'I can feel them too. Some close. Many further away. There will be a fight,' said Garna, her voice showing that she was both excited and pensive.

'You don't have to fight for me or any of the humans,' Asaph reminded them. 'If it starts to turn bad, get away. Don't let them enslave you. We can return to fight another day.'

'We don't just fight for you, we fight for all our kin these bastards have slain. The memory of Drax has returned to all of us.' Rust finished with a roar.

The other dragons joined him, proudly announcing their presence as the dark cliffs of Venosia loomed. Asaph's roar shook the air and he took the lead, constantly checking the Flow for the indigo hue of Issa's power.

Magic flared in an explosion of purple and white far into the distance. *Wizard magic,* he thought, and flew faster. The dark coast sped by on their left, and lights dotted the coves and clifftops.

Enemy lights, he telepathed to the other dragons.

A burst of fire caught his attention out to sea. It could be a ship, he thought, but when it was followed by a flare of indigo, he lunged towards it. The seconds felt like hours as he closed the distance. Not one Dromoorai, but three appeared, and they chased someone glowing indigo blue in the Flow.

Issa!

Issa focused on the Flow, drawing it beneath them. She felt Duskar give the briefest hesitation as his hooves hit the water's edge, then they both felt a slight lift, and he was galloping upon the surface. Duskar raised his head and neighed and she laughed wildly.

She glanced behind her. Three hideous monsters of black wings, teeth and blazing red eyes followed. A horse could not outrun those wings. Issa focused on the orb and the water moved beneath them, carrying them faster.

A terrible howl reached her ears. Glancing back, a Dread Dragon had been ensnared in a blazing net of fire. It thrashed and spun then crashed into the ocean. Issa grinned. *A unique trick, Haelgon.* But the other two were swiftly closing the gap between them.

Issa focused on keeping Duskar galloping on the water's surface, lifting them up and speeding them on with the orb's power. They were soon a mile from the shore and out upon the open ocean, but however far they went, she would have to bring him back. Leading the dragons away had worked perfectly, but what now?

Red lightning flashed, striking the ocean barely yards ahead. Spooked, Duskar reared and she clung to him barely staying mounted. Claws the size of tree trunks swiped past her head. She dodged to the right. Duskar scrambled away, panting heavily, his flanks lathered in sweat.

'Water Wall!' she commanded the orb. Water shot up around them, cocooning them in thick walls of swirling ocean. She screamed as a spiked tail slashed easily through their water barrier and scraped across her chest, tearing her armour and gashing her skin beneath. Water was not going to be enough to keep the dragons out.

'Sink!' she screamed, clutching her wound. Already her armour was knitting itself back together, but the shallow cut still smarted. Her cocoon immediately dropped into the ocean becoming a huge bubble of air with them inside. Duskar turned around, confused.

'Easy,' she soothed. She urged him forward and the bubble moved with them.

Above the sloshing water, dragons howled in frustration. Her head pounded as magical fatigue set in. Commanding the Flow and fleeing Dromoorai was exhausting. Using magic in new ways was always more draining. But if she remained hidden, she risked losing the interest of the Dromoorai. She suddenly felt trapped in her bubble beneath the ocean's surface.

She turned back towards the shore, but moving in this manner was much slower than galloping upon the surface. It was becoming stuffy too. She glanced up and saw the dragon's underbellies and the red flare of eyes and amulets. They screamed and then turned away.

'No!' she said. All she had to do was keep them away from the battle for as long as possible.

'Up,' she commanded the orb, the pounding in her head increasing. The bubble rose, and again they stood upon the ocean. She kicked Duskar into a gallop, now chasing the Dread Dragons.

'Here!' she screamed. Raising her hands she shouted, 'Lightning!'

White light from her fingers tore into a Dread Dragon. It roared and turned back. Not letting Duskar slow, she banked right. The cliffs and the shore loomed close, but between her and them was the other Dromoorai.

One came at her straight on, the other took a wide berth. *It's going to come at me from behind!* She focused on the Flow, preparing to sink again when a strange noise ground and screeched so loudly she flinched. Duskar stumbled and shook his head. The noise expanded in her head like a living entity that was trying to take her over.

She forced her attention to the enemy. Two Dromoorai hung in the air, one in front of her, one behind, and their eyes were no longer glowing red but revolving between red, blue, green and back again. They were taking their time as if waiting for something, but what?

She raised walls of water and just as she tried to sink, the sound came again, louder, piercing, driving all sense from her mind. *The sound of the Dark Rift!* Beyond the awful grinding sound of tortured metal twisting against itself, garbled voices gibbered.

Red clouds bulged above her. They separated to reveal the tear splitting apart the sky, blacker than black. Issa's heart thundered, Duskar's back legs gave way and she slid off his back. The water turned spongy beneath her and she knew she wouldn't be able to hold them on its surface for much longer.

A voice cut through the noise, low and airy.

'Bring the one,' commanded Baelthrom.

Within the black tear, four shapes appeared swathed in darkness. Their mounts breathed soot and their eyes drained the Flow from her hands.

'Duskar, go,' she gasped against her thundering heart. The horse staggered to his feet but he would not move.

'Sink!' she commanded her orb, but something blocked its power. In the Flow she saw the ocean black with the Under Flow. The Dromoorai had imprisoned her with black magic.

What a stupid idea this had been! She cursed herself for her reckless foolishness, her desire to fight everything and anything. Who could help her, out here on the ocean, against the immaterial beasts descending out of the Dark Rift?

Her eyes locked on to the four horsemen. They took on hideous forms as they galloped into the material world. Their long swords and shields reflected the red clouds, and their empty pits for eyes began drawing the life from her, paralysing her in a terror worse than dragon fear. The horses snorted smoke and their manes of spines clacked as they shook their enormous heads.

In her side vision, she saw the Dromoorai descending, could even smell the rotting sulphur of the dragons' breath. Ehka cawed then flew at a Dromoorai only to be swatted away.

'Don't Ehka. Save yourself!'

She held up the raven talisman and commanded it. Lightning flared out, scorching the Dromoorai and forcing them to withdraw. It did not affect the horsemen, for they moved in another dimension. She would have to face them or flee. She had a thought, one last trick to try.

'A'farion, A'farion, A'farion,' she screamed and slammed the talisman to her chest.

CHAPTER 7

Dragon Truth

IN the Realm of the Dead, a blanket of dark grey replaced the red, thunderous clouds of Venosia.

The sky pressed down on Issa, and the sea upon which she stood moved sickly and sluggish. She hunted the skies but the Dromoorai were gone.

A screaming neigh made her whip around. In the fog beyond, shapes formed. Issa ran, her feet slapping the ocean's surface. She gripped the orb in one hand and her raven talisman in the other. The orb's magic was weak here, but it still commanded enough power to keep her on the surface.

Another scream came, this time much closer. She spun around. Four horsemen emerged out of the grey. They reached for their scabbards and unsheathed long black blades. In this open space, they could see her clearly and there was nothing to hinder their steeds. Her flee to safety had become a flee to her death.

Suddenly it became harder to run. The sea beneath her feet began to flow backwards. It felt like she was running up hill, each breath gasping in her throat. She was being drawn back to the horsemen. Clouds raced past and howling winds battered against her, forcing her to stop.

She turned and held up her orb and talisman. Magic flared between them, each strengthening the other. She lifted the sea, forming walls of swirling grey, and smashed them back into the horsemen. Spiked hooves thrashed, and inhumane voices howled as they sprawled, halted but not hurt.

The wind increased, forcing her to a stop. She began to lose her balance. There was nowhere else to turn. Defeated, she slammed the raven talisman against her chest and let the Realm of the Dead go.

Cold water and a vivid world of raging magic and fire engulfed her. Splashing at the surface, she hunted wildly for the horsemen, ignoring the Dromoorai in the sky above. There were none…yet. Perhaps she had got away.

Duskar struggled in the water and Ehka cawed somewhere above. Her arms were so tired she could barely keep herself afloat.

Roaring came from a distance. *Dear goddess, not more Dromoorai!* She struggled with the flagging Flow and glanced to her left. Her heart skipped a beat. There, in the sky, flew dragons. They moved so fast they were streaks of red, green, gold and yellow flames. Ehka plunged towards her with a squawk and Duskar whinnied as a different dragon fear grabbed hold of him.

Spluttering, she stared at the three glorious dragons of Feygriene as they smashed into the Dromoorai in a hail of fire.

'Asaph!' she cried. *Praise the goddess, he did it!*

Issa vanished moments before Asaph slammed into the first Dromoorai.

He had no time to look for her as his teeth closed on a membranous wing and he ripped at it viciously. Its wing torn, the Dread Dragon tumbled in the air and crashed into the sea.

Asaph lunged at the Dromoorai on its back as it flailed underwater. He wrenched it off the dragon and tossed it aside, intending it to sink under the weight of its armour. The Dread Dragon snaked its head back and clamped its jaws on his thigh. Asaph howled bubbles and heaved them both to the surface.

Pennarc was a blaze of green scales and orange fire in his vision as he dropped from the sky onto the Dread Dragon. The green dragon bit down hard on the back of the black dragon's neck, forcing it to release Asaph's thigh.

Shadow stone magic flashed red and the Under Flow moved. Asaph gathered the Flow that swiftly turned sluggish and pulled himself out of the water into the air. The Dromoorai stood upon the ocean surface, red magic glowing beneath its feet, claymore drawn, eyes and amulet flashing. It held one gauntleted hand out and clenched.

Asaph found his throat crushing. He forced the Flow to his bidding, spending it all in one command. He disappeared from his current location, lost the Dromoorai's hold on him, and reappeared just behind it.

Asaph spewed white fire. In the blinding blaze he watched the Dromoorai's armour slowly begin to glow and buckle. As if unaffected by the enormous heat, the Dromoorai inched around to face him, eyes flaring red, fist still out-stretched.

In its amulet, Asaph saw the image of Baelthrom, strikingly similar to the Dromoorai before him, same tripartite helmet, same armour—even his hand was held out in the same manner.

An immense force exploded into Asaph. Hurtling backwards, he spun head over tail, glancing off the ocean's surface before submerging.

He floundered, dazed and stunned. After several long moments, the world stopped spinning and he regained his senses and found the surface.

No Dromoorai or Dread Dragon pursued him. He couldn't feel their presence at all anymore. Blinking salt water out of his eyes, he saw a strange sight.

Standing on the surface was Issa mounted atop Duskar with Ehka circling above them. Rust and Garna hovered just above her and they appeared to be communing. He could sense the dragons' curiosity towards his mate.

There was a huge black lump bobbing between her and him, the body of the Dread Dragon he had just been fighting. Had the blast of magic not come from the Dromoorai? Issa looked pale and shaken as she held up a glimmering Orb of Water.

'Dead?' He asked the dragons meaning the Dromoorai.

'Dead,' Rust replied. 'But more will come.'

Pennarc flew towards them. A bloody gash ran the length of his side but he still flew steadily. Asaph flapped his wings above the surface and pulled on the Flow to help him get airborne.

'You came!' said Issa. 'A little late, perhaps.'

'Dragons can't be late,' Asaph replied. 'I'll carry you,' he said aloud.

Issa smiled at him and reached up. Gently he lifted her from Duskar's back then gripped the horse in his other claws. The horse bucked and whinnied as he usually did before giving in.

'Ahead, there, see those burning braziers? That's where our ships are. There's our war.' Issa pointed.

He nodded, catching her excitement and anxiety, and headed towards the dark cliffs with the other dragons following.

As they neared, more Dread Dragons appeared on the horizon, and between them, legions of scurrying black armoured Maphraxies. The Under Flow gathered heavily here, on enemy lands. Asaph didn't like it one bit.

'Look, we've pushed them out of the cove completely!' Issa shouted over the wind.

The Maphraxies were in retreat as the Feylint Halanoi pushed them back beyond the brow of the hill. Her victorious smile faded as she took in the coast littered with dead. Stretcher-bearers ran left and right, unable to pick up the dead for the number of injured.

She hunted for Velonorian and the wizards, praying none had fallen. The elf she couldn't find, he would be helping his Elven fellows, she hoped. To the left of the cove on a rocky platform a third of the way up the cliff stood Luren, Haelgon and Drumblodd.

She looked for Domenon. Far to the right on the other side of the battlefield came a flare of pale magic. Was that him partially hidden behind a ridge? She saw movement of pale robes beside a darker figure. *Naksu, thank the goddess!*

'You'll be safer on my back,' said Asaph.

'Maybe, but I have to help the wizards,' Issa shouted over the screams and howls and clash of weapons. 'You'll have to drive back the Dromoorai. We must protect the ground army from them. Can your dragons do that if the wizards assist you?'

'There are five.' Asaph clocked the five Dromoorai, three of which were heading towards them. 'We can try,' he growled. 'But I'm not straying far from your side.'

'I was hoping you wouldn't.' She patted the huge claw wrapped around her waist, wondering if he could even feel her small hand. The Dromoorai approached fast and she swallowed. 'Set me down by Domenon, there's no orb that side of the battle other than Orphinius'.'

Asaph turned hard back out to sea and dropped low, trying to create distance between them and the Dromoorai. Dread Dragons followed. He flew faster, then banked back to the coast, moving at such speed that Issa felt the world spin. Pulling his wings in tight he plummeted out of the sky towards the ridge where Naksu and Domenon stood.

Hovering a foot off ground, he set her and Duskar down and leapt into the air to meet the Dromoorai. He dodged the black dragon's snapping jaws and blazed fire over its underside. Swooping low over the battlefield, he scraped his claws into hordes of Maphraxies, lifted them up and threw them at the pursuing Dromoorai.

Naksu came to Issa's side, grabbing her attention from the golden dragon.

'So, the mighty dragons have awakened!' Naksu laughed in wonder.

Domenon smiled but his luminous eyes were hard. He closed them to focus on his magic.

'I only ever dared to believe it would happen,' said Issa, turning her gaze upon the three other dragons further away. 'Now they're here, I can't believe it. Incredible, aren't they? Pray to Feygriene we don't lose any today.'

'Some assistance would be nice,' Domenon's strained voice caught her attention. The Master Wizard had entrapped a Dromoorai in a giant, glowing orange net and the beast was thrashing madly in the air above the battle field.

Issa entered the Flow and Naksu held up her staff. Issa felt the seer's fast command of the Flow. Her staff pulsed once, the air trembled, and the Dromoorai and its dragon vanished.

The seer sagged.

'What the…' said Issa, eyes widening.

Domenon blinked at the seer.

'It's not a spell to do lightly,' Naksu said, her voice weak. 'And neither is it a complete solution. I just put it somewhere else for now, about five hundred miles down the coast. It will return and probably be very angry.'

'I need to learn that,' said Issa.

She focused on the Flow and the battlefield, using it to hunt for Velonorian and his familiar aura. She spied the tall gangly elf amongst a group of Elven archers, closer than she had expected and back from the frontline. His long pastel hair tumbled down from under his helmet.

Velonorian had already spotted her and was trying to make his way through the press of warriors.

'Any news of Freydel?' asked Domenon, hands raised and still commanding the Flow. The wizard pushed his hands forwards as a Dread Dragon hailed fire. A shield of white flared over the elves below, protecting them from the flames.

'No,' said Issa, her voice equally strained as she clenched her hands into claws. The magic she commanded ripped a bunker wall from the earth and smashed it down upon a horde of Maphraxies. Those not crushed, fled.

Domenon lowered his hands, his gaze never leaving the battlefield and the Flow into which he looked. 'Then it seems the Master Wizard has deserted us in our hour of need. The Wizards' Circle will need to consider this most seriously, should we survive this assault.'

Issa pursed her lips. Domenon *was* right. 'I can't help but feel betrayed,' she said under her breath.

'There's no point wasting any emotion on it. If you expect nothing from people, you will never be disappointed. Humans are untrustworthy and weak in the face of power.' Domenon lifted one hand and a knot of fire surged from it, striking a Maphraxie about to behead a stumbling dwarf.

'Not all humans,' said Issa, grimacing. Did he really consider so little of his own race? The Flow shimmered and weakened.

The Dromoorai hovered in the sky, their eyes and amulets flaring in unison. 'What's happening?' Issa blurted, suddenly feeling dizzy.

A wave of black energy swept across the battlefield. The Flow scattered. It bled from Issa's grasp and her orb turned dull. Wind tore across the cove, howling through the cracks and crevices. Clouds rolled like waves and lightning cracked. Everyone on the battlefield fell to the ground. Asaph and his dragons rolled in the air as if they were in the ocean and struggled to stay airborne. Issa dropped to her knees and Domenon growled. She squinted through the tearing wind, holding her hands up and trying to control the Flow.

The only person left standing on the entire battlefield, was Orphinius. Everyone lay prone around him, even the enemy. Nobody was able to get up or move, not even Orphinius. The only things able to move were the two Dromoorai directly above him.

The paralysed Elven Orb Keeper stared up at his impending doom. Issa felt sick.

The colour drained from Domenon's face. 'He has found it,' rasped the Master Wizard.

A strange deep whispering boomed in Issa's head, plucking at her heart and mind.

'Dark Dwarven. Don't listen to it!' screamed Naksu.

Issa clamped her hands over her ears, shutting out the sound of the necromantic spell being woven. She watched helpless as a Dread Dragon reached a claw down to Orphinius. She was aware of Domenon screaming. She sensed him trying to reach the Flow and failing. She couldn't even think to try.

Protect the orbs at all costs. Protect the orbs! Her inner voice screamed helplessly.

Orphinius began to struggle against something. In jerking movements, his hands lifted up the flaring Orb of Earth towards the Dromoorai. The Dread Dragon wrapped its huge claws around him, lifted him into the air and squeezed. Orphinius' terrible scream became a sickening gurgle and blood spurted from his mouth, splashing over his pale skin and golden tree tabard.

Issa watched in horror as the Dread Dragon dropped the elf's limp body. The orb rolled from his flaccid grasp and lay, shining gold, in the growing pool of bright red blood.

Domenon roared. Issa felt the immense strain of the Master Wizard in the Flow. Incredibly, the magic moved to him. Veins bulged on the wizard's neck and forehead, and his face contorted with pain and rage. He held up his hands in a grasping motion.

He's trying to reach the orb! She gripped her orb and talisman, trickling to him what little of the Flow she could draw. It came as a dribble, and then in greater waves. Naksu saw what she was doing and did the same.

The Dromoorai jumped off the dragon's back and landed on the ground with a thud, unafraid of the legions of Feylint Halanoi prone and paralysed around it. It moved in slow motion, its amulet blazing with the gaze of Baelthrom, and reached down to the orb.

The Orb of Earth trembled in the Flow. *More magic!* She needed just a little more magic! The pressure in her head grew and her pulse pounded in her ears as she strained against the Under Flow to bring more of Maioria's living magic to them. The Orb of Earth shuddered, lifted an inch off the ground and trembled in the air. The Dromoorai's gauntleted fist touched its surface and the Under Flow blazed.

Domenon screamed, all his power surged forwards. Gasping for each breath, he drew his hands back as if pulling on something immensely heavy. The orb flared then shot towards him, a blazing ball of light streaking straight to Domenon's out-stretched hand.

The Secondary Keeper of the Orb of Earth caught it and the world stood still. Beatific wonder spread over Domenon's face. The Dromoorai roared, head back, fists clenched. The Under Flow and the Flow shuddered violently, confused at the power change.

The rapture on the Master Wizard's face wavered and then he screamed in utter agony.

'Domenon!' Issa's face contorted, and she ran towards him.

The orb flared, golden magic exploded from it, flinging her back against the rocks. Winded, she rolled to her knees. Domenon whirled left and right, screaming and thrashing as the orb in his grasp flared chaotically. It appeared that he could not release his grip. Her orb responded and flashed sky blue. On the other side of the battlefield, Drumblodd's Orb of Fire flared fiery orange. Immense elemental magic forces, mixed with the Under Flow, ripped across the land.

Domenon thrashed and howled. Impossibly, his body began to grow. His entire form distorted and bent. Issa covered her mouth, reminded of Keteth when he morphed into a hundred beasts.

The wizard's face grew larger and his mouth and nose began to elongate. His arms and legs swelled with muscles and his fingernails became thick claws. A tail sprouted from his lower back and great horns began to protrude from his forehead. The Master Wizard screamed and thrashed in violent agony but still he held the orb as if it would not let go of him.

His body was impossibly huge now, filling the area where they had stood and rubbing up against the cliff face. His smooth skin began to section and turn into scales, and its tone changed from peach to bluish white.

A flare of bright light engulfed him completely, abruptly ending his howls.

Domenon was gone. Instead Issa stared at an enormous ice-blue dragon.

With a sound like a cork being drawn from a bottle, the orb ripped itself from the dragon's grasp and flew straight at her.

Through no will of her own, her right hand dropped the raven talisman and reached to catch the orb. Her hand met its hot surface and immense power coursed through her as she held two orbs.

She could barely breathe as she struggled to hold them both. Her world turned into blazing fields of magic. The Flow raged through her, furiously thrusting back the Under Flow. Time fell away, there was only the Flow and its will as it filled and consumed her.

Through the torrent, she was surprised to feel gentle minds pressing on her own. *Wykiry? They were in the bay,* she realised. The magic burden lessened. Something they were doing.

Another presence joined her in the Flow, equally soft and gentle. *Naksu?* The magic burden lifted a little more, the torrent calmed.

Then she felt Haelgon, Drumblodd and Luren too, all seeking to help her hold the immense magic of the two orbs. She felt herself sinking, floating down like a feather in a world of magic where darkness clawed at the edges.

The Under Flow slammed into Asaph, knocking his dragon magic so forcefully from him it sent his body and mind into spasms. Pennarc's back quivered and Garna tossed her head.

He gathered his senses and followed Garna's rapid descent. They flew low over the anchored ships and landed on a spit of land reaching out from the beach. The Dromoorai he had been fighting had turned back towards the battlefield, no longer interested in him now new commands from Baelthrom had been issued.

Asaph shook himself and tried to decipher what was going on. Where was Issa? Was she in immediate danger? He looked to where he had left her beside Naksu and Domenon, and saw the flash of immense magical power. The golden and emerald Orb of Earth suddenly flew from the battlefield to Domenon's out-stretched hand and flared. The ground trembled.

Asaph watched, stunned, as the Master Wizard struggled against an immense force and then began to morph right before his eyes. The wizard writhed and groaned, his howls audible even from here. His hand and forearm holding the orb began to smoke and turn black, then he grew to impossible proportions.

There came another blinding flare. When it faded, in the place of Domenon stood the enormous form of Morhork. The unmistakable jagged scars along his back where his wings should have been, still angry and red after thousands of years.

Asaph's jaw dropped open as he stared at the ice-blue dragon. A hundred things now fell into place in his mind. All the little things the wizard had said, his hostility towards Asaph, his interest in Issa, his strange disappearance. Asaph inhaled sharply, he needed time to sit down and think, to piece it all together into one big coherent picture.

'The dragon mind I felt but couldn't see,' said Garna, her eyes wide. 'And yet the man is not a Dragon Lord. What magic has occurred here? This is Morhork and yet this is far beyond the design of a dragon.'

Rust landed heavily beside them bleeding freely from his shoulder. Pennarc hovered just above, ready to attack.

'Morhork was always the master planner. While we've been sleeping, he's been busy,' said Rust.

The Elven Orb of Earth tore itself from the dragon's blackened claw and flew straight to Issa. She caught it, the Flow trembled, then rushed towards her. The ice-blue dragon gave an ear-splitting roar filled with absolute rage. His howl turned into one of terrible anguish. He sprang into the air using magic to lift his wingless body, then shot into the sky, moving so fast he was a streak of blue.

His howl was followed by the equally enraged screams of Dread Dragons. More of them had arrived. The two Dromoorai closest, turned to Issa. The other descended upon Drumblodd on the far side of battlefield. The soldiers and Maphraxies who had been flattened on the battlefield now rose to their feet.

'The fight's not nearly done! Protect Issa and the orbs,' Asaph growled and launched himself into the air. The other dragons followed.

With his brood, Asaph attacked the Dromoorai descending on Issa, snapping, clawing, flaming, driving them back into the air. The roars of each dragon gave the others power and fury. Always, in the recollection, Asaph had witnessed the fight for Draxa, flying in the sky and fighting alongside dragon and Dragon Lord, but nothing could have prepared him for the reality of it, the glory of it. Even if he died in pain and agony, it was worth it—he was dragon, this was his glorious might.

He could hear his brood's thoughts and intentions as if they had one shared mind. He saw what they saw, as if the Recollection lay like an open book between them. Their ability to work and fight as one now made them devastating.

The first Dread Dragon, its wings flaming shreds, fell to the ground, crushing the Maphraxies beneath it. Garna harried the other that was fleeing south. Pennarc had split off and was locked into a struggle with the third on the clifftop above the cove. Asaph lifted into the air to help, but the green dragon already had it by the throat in a death grip. The Dread Dragon thrashed in its death throes, spraying watery grey blood.

Lifting higher above the cliffs, he looked east. More Dromoorai came, just specks in the distance. Between them, a thousand Maphraxies marched. The Flow pulsed, capturing his attention. He turned, hunting for the source, and saw scores of Atalanph ships anchoring in the next cove. Already marching from the cove were legions of Atalanph soldiers, their tabards— a yellow sun on white—fresh and shining.

Asaph's heart lifted, there was hope. But the flash of light in the Flow had come from neither of these. There below, on the cliffs between two coves, galloped a lone figure holding a crystal staff aloft. He felt a powerful wizard's mind. *Freydel?*

The man looked up at him and started, his horse whinnying. He whirled his staff in greeting. Finally he had come, Issa would be pleased. Asaph stayed close to protect him but there were no enemies near.

The wizard crested the ridge above Issa and slowed his horse. He held his black orb high and commanded the Flow. Light beamed from him in two directions, towards Drumblodd and towards Issa. When it reached the two orb holders the magic flared again then burst between Issa and Drumblodd, spanning the entire battlefield in a giant triangle.

There came a mighty blaze of light, blinding Asaph. The Dromoorai and Maphraxies above and beneath that triangle of light, shrieked, dropped their weapons and fled.

Asaph laughed bouts of fire as the enemy deserted the battlefield.

Seeing sport, Asaph dove and harried them, burning them with fire and making sure they didn't stop. Out of the cove they ran. Asaph paused, not wanting to follow them further and risk those behind him. With a final look at the fleeing enemy and those in the distance who were approaching, he turned back to Issa.

CHAPTER 8

Precreative Power

THE sound of groaning, twisting metal came again as the Flow left her.

Above, red clouds boiled then began to part. Issa shut her eyes, not wanting to see the gaping black tear of the Dark Rift beyond.

'No,' she shook her head. The horsemen would find her soon, and the Light Eaters.

'Issa,' a familiar voice called from far away.

Asaph? She should go to him.

'There she is! I can reach her now,' said another familiar voice.

Freydel?

The Flow wrapped itself around her, a warm blanket of light that dragged her away from the noise. People's voices became clearer, closer. She blinked. The world of magic disappeared, and two faces came into view. First Asaph appeared, wearing a frown that crinkled the dirt and blood smearing his cheeks and forehead; then Freydel's smiling face followed, deep lines creasing his face and shadows smudging his eyes. He looked like he had aged ten years in the last month.

Issa sighed. *I'm safe, for a time.* But she could still feel the horsemen, out there, hunting.

'Urgh, what happened? I feel like I've been trampled by a herd of horses.' Issa sat up and everything wobbled.

'Magic exhaustion,' said Freydel.

'Here drink this.' Asaph passed her a bowl of something steaming and some corn bread.

She wasn't hungry but she took the bowl and began to eat, hoping it would bring back some strength. Her hands shook as she lifted each spoonful.

The day was lighter than before, night must have ended in the time she had been out. She was in a make-shift tent and the tarp door flapped in the wind. Outside, she caught glimpses of a hive of activity; big men shifting rubble, wounded soldiers carried on stretchers, horses pulling small wagons.

'We have a brief respite and so we're making this place as habitable as possible,' explained Asaph. 'We've gained a foothold on Venosia and we need to make sure we can keep it.

'Haelgon says Atalanph forces have secured several more coves south, though this is the largest. There are tunnels beneath the earth connecting them all, which can serve our needs now the Dark Dwarves have been eliminated from them. You know they're already calling this place Port Issa?' Asaph grinned.

She smiled. 'I didn't know we could do this. I hoped, but… Freydel, you came. You look exhausted.' All her previous anger and disappointment at her former tutor washed away as she looked at the weary, stooped figure.

The Master Wizard settled down on the stool beside her pallet. 'Exhausted, yes, but I'll be all right in time. I returned via the Wizards' Circle, and from there, came here. I had help, of course.' He gave a knowing wink.

Issa couldn't form a smile, but at least he was being honest about being with Ayeth.

'It's lucky you came when you did,' said Asaph, nervously smoothing a hand through his hair. 'With three orb holders down and another legion of Maphraxies on the way, we were in a right mess.'

'It was the Orb of Death,' Issa recalled. 'I felt it reach for me, then it connected my orbs to each other. A great magical force. It was all so surreal. I'm so *tired*.'

'The enemy fled,' Asaph laughed. 'I've never seen Dread Dragons scatter.'

'And Domenon,' Issa whispered.

Asaph looked into the middle distance. 'Yes, there's a lot that needs to be made sense of.'

'That Master Wizard is a Master no longer,' Freydel said, his look turning dark.

Can you unmake a wizard? Issa wondered. *Is he really a dragon?* To her surprise, she found she wasn't angry with Domenon. But how could he be a dragon—be Morhork—and not be a Dragon Lord? The whole confusing thing made no sense. Besides, Freydel kept his own secrets too. She kept her thoughts to herself as Freydel continued in a weak voice.

'With Asaph's help, I've been piecing it together, and it makes so much sense now.'

'It doesn't to me,' Issa snorted.

'This is what appears to have occurred.' Freydel smoothed his robes. 'When Orphinius was killed, the orb was placed in terrible danger. It did what it is naturally inclined to do, sought out its Secondary Keeper, in this instance, Domenon. That wizard's magic is great to be able to override the immense power of the Under Flow. And now we know why. A pure-blood dragon's magic is most potent.

'Well, anyway, the orb went to him. When it touched his hand it tried to meld with him, to understand its Keeper intimately, as orbs are wont to do. But Domenon was not true. The form his mind inhabited was not pure. And orbs cannot tolerate deception. It saw him for what he was, and so forced the man to become the dragon he should be. But herein lies something fascinating! The orb was bound to Domenon, the man, not this dragon—what's his name?'

'Morhork,' said Asaph softly.

'Yes, Morhork...' Freydel shook his head and raised his eyebrows. 'He was lucky to survive the orb's power—only a dragon could! A true testament to his own magical ability.

'Anyway, unable to meld with its deceitful Keeper and sensing peril, it sought out the nearest orb holder—something I didn't know was possible. Yet, we have never been in this position to experience such a thing. So the orb went to Issa. To hold two orbs at once as their primary Keepers...Well, you're lucky to survive it too.' The man's hazel eyes beheld hers.

Issa dropped her gaze. She didn't want the power and responsibility of one orb, let alone *two*. 'I nearly didn't! Luckily I had help. The Wykiry were in the bay, and Naksu was by my side, and Haelgon and Drumblodd in the Flow—wait. You said three orb holders down?'

Freydel paled and Asaph turned away. Naksu entered the tent and paused. The White One smiled at Issa, then her brow knitted together in a worried frown.

'Yes, Drumblodd,' said the seer. 'He's stable but his breathing is shallow. I cannot reach him with such an...infection.'

'What's happened?' asked Issa, suddenly feeling faint. 'How long have I been asleep?'

'Less than a day, but things happened so fast,' Asaph shook his head. 'I didn't see it, but Drumblodd was injured by a Maphraxie arrow soon after Domenon caught the orb. It penetrated his shoulder, a fiendishly lucky shot to miss both armour plates. Well, it was poisoned, we're not sure what with, but we fear it's Sirin Derenax.'

'It *is* the Black Drink,' Naksu confirmed.

When Asaph struggled to speak, Freydel, his face turning paler, continued explaining. 'When the magic of the orbs combined, it stopped him being consumed by the Under Flow. He's become part-trapped in the Flow and part-trapped in the Under Flow.'

Issa looked at the ashen face of the prone dwarf. Even in the orange glow of the lantern, Drumblodd already looked dead, with his blue lips and a chest that barely rose or fell. One shoulder was wrapped in bandages where the arrow had entered. Poisoned with Sirin Derenax for which there was no cure. He gripped the Orb of Fire between two hands, holding it over his chest.

'We cannot get him to release it,' said Naksu softly. 'Perhaps it is the only thing keeping him alive.'

The orb's orange and red surface was flecked through with streaks of black, the colours weaving through and turning over each other, as if locked in some internal battle.

Issa touched his hand and found it cold. She closed her eyes and felt for him in the Flow. He was there but he seemed frozen, untouchable.

'I can't reach his mind. Maybe with more rest...but even then, I can't reach anything in the Under Flow.' Issa shook her head.

Asaph slipped an arm around her shoulders. 'Let him rest, maybe that's all he needs. We all need rest. Just thank the goddess we have not lost any orbs. Come, it's late.'

She let him lead her outside under the red skies that never fully darkened with night nor lightened with day. Their own abode was a temporary tent within which was a pile of hay with blankets over the top. She sorely missed their soft bed and little white house on Myrn. It was a nice home.

Asaph unbuckled his sword and set it down. The candlelight flashed off the red pommel and gleaming crossguard. She remembered when the Guardians of the Portals had given it to her in a vision, a temporary gift to help free Asaph from Keteth's prison. Now it was here physically, with its rightful owner.

'Let me touch it,' she said.

Asaph hesitated. 'It harms those to whom it does not belong.'

Issa nodded. 'I know. I want to see if it remembers me.'

Slowly Asaph held the hilt towards her. She reached, paused, then gripped the hilt. At first it was cold—and then it began to burn. The heat flared up her arm as if setting her on fire. She gasped and gripped harder. Her whole body felt on fire.

And then something changed—it was as if the blade was thinking, remembering; she had saved its master, she had held it before. The burning pain receded to a low ache, reluctantly accepting her.

She let go of the hilt with a smile and looked at Asaph's surprised face. 'It remembered me. But I doubt it would suffer my hand long.'

Asaph set the sword aside and sat down. He yawned, making her yawn too. 'What next, Raven Queen?' He took her hand and kissed it.

'I don't know, King Asaph,' she said, grinning 'A good long sleep and pray they don't attack in the night.'

He pulled her down beside him and they curled up together. Issa sunk fast into an exhausted sleep.

'All that remains of Karalanthia.'

Cusap'anth shook his head, his antlers swaying, his eyes hard as he spoke. Rhul'ynth beside him said nothing, although her face was taut with emotion. Issa could think of nothing to say as she looked from one to the other.

They stood on high ground over-looking the two coves below and the cliffs beyond. Behind them, beyond the wall the Feylint Halanoi had hastily built from rubble, an endless vista of dust and scree stretched out under the boiling red sky. A heavy, cloying wind blew.

'Once this place was filled with forests more ancient than those upon Frayon. There were countless rivers and streams, and now they're all gone. Where have they gone? Karalanths and settlers lived in peace. The dwarves were not a problem then and kept to themselves in the east. Now there is nothing. Look at it, it's all gone. And what for? What is this desolate hell we have won back?

'The forests will grow again,' said Issa, trying to offer some consolation. 'We have won it back. We must praise ourselves and not let what has befallen it mar our strength.'

The hard look on Cusap'anth's face softened. 'You are right, of course. All things will return once the land is cleansed. By the grace of Woetala.'

'How can we cleanse this land?' asked Rhul'ynth.

Issa blinked, the thought hitting her suddenly. 'We use the orbs!'

'What?' Cusap'anth looked at her with raised eyebrows.

'The orbs of Earth and Water—if they can't cleanse the land, I don't know what else can.'

'How?' asked Rhul'ynth.

'I don't know but maybe if we tried…' Issa shrugged.

'I guess there is some hope in what you say. Without fresh water, our victory here will be short lived.' Cusap'anth looked up at the sky. 'I doubt these clouds even know what rain is. Look, the ground is dry and parched. It's more like ash than soil.'

'We have to try,' said Issa. Busy in thought, she started walking the steep slopes back to Port Issa, wishing they hadn't named it that. It may not work, but she had to try, and now was as good a time as any.

The whole camp was alive with activity. Tents filled the entire cove, and more permanent buildings were already being constructed from the rubble of the destroyed barracks. The Dark Dwarf tunnels had been decimated and sealed shut with magic. Issa agreed with the Commanders that they should not be closed permanently for they could be a good way to invade further, faster and unseen into enemy lands.

Another flock of carrier pigeons flapped noisily into the air—the second released today—carrying news of their victory and what supplies were needed, back to Davono, Lans Himay and wherever else troops and supplies might be coming from.

Old stone walls, all that remained of the indigenous community who had once lived here, were being lovingly reconstructed and turned into small dwellings. More supply ships and warships had since arrived from Davono and Atalanph, and the place was fast becoming too small to house everyone.

Now they had their first victory, it was up to the commanders of each unit and company to decide how to progress the war. She really wanted no directional part in it. She was the visionary, the advisor, bringing her powers to battle like a wizard and nothing more. But when it came to facing Baelthrom, she knew everyone would look to her. She prayed Zanufey would come and tell her what to do.

'Issa!' Asaph ran over and swung her into an embrace. He kissed her on the lips and set her down laughing.

She glanced to the sky and saw his dragons flying away. 'Oh, they're leaving already? But we need them.'

'They're leaving for many reasons but they'll return. Their job here is done, and their presence will only draw more Dread Dragons. They need rest. They tire quickly after so long asleep. They wanted me to go with them, but I wouldn't leave you.

'What happened with Dom—Morhork, the other dragons will have seen or felt it in the Recollection but they won't understand. It's possible Morhork may have gone north to Yis anyway.'

'I know but, I'd barely had time to meet them,' she sighed.

Cusap'anth and Rhul'ynth approached. The Karalanth leader gripped Asaph's arm.

'Well met, two-foot,' he grinned.

Asaph laughed. 'Well, I didn't expect you to miss a fight.'

They walked towards the biggest tent set by the cliff side. It was impressive, being of Elven design. Tall poles lifted up thick tarp dyed purple and green. Despite being bright and colourful, no enemy would be able to see past the magic shield that shimmered over it. Most of the command and supply tents had been protected, concealing them from aerial assault, or at least making it that much harder.

Issa tried not to think of any impending attack. The last few days had been quiet on the enemy front, but she knew Baelthrom was amassing his armies.

'King Asaph!' a man called from afar.

Two Draxian men approached, one with a bandage around his head and the other with his arm in a sling. Both were tall, and one had very short red hair whilst the other had his blond hair in the traditional Draxian fashion, long and bound back.

Beyond them, she saw another group of four Draxians following them, their tall statures and tanned complexions betraying their heritage. The men following were either wary or nervous as they eyed Asaph. She turned her attention to the first two whose eyes were wide and searching.

The blond-haired one stood before Asaph. He was older than Asaph by about ten years. 'It's you, I swear it is. You have her eyes and his face.' The man then dropped to his knees, much to Asaph's horror. Asaph opened and closed his mouth.

'Many of us hoped you lived. Some of our Wise Women knew you had,' said the red-haired man, also dropping to his knees. The four men behind quickly followed.

'We are your loyal men. For this mission we serve Northern Lans Himay, but after, we serve you and only you,' said the blond.

'Wait, get up,' said Asaph. 'Yes, all right, I *am* the son of Queen Pheonis and King Ixus. But I am no King for there's no longer a land for us. What am I King of?'

'We can take it back,' said the older man as Asaph helped him up. 'We're a scattered people. There are thousands living in exile, hopefully millions, but all will rush to your side. And you are a Dragon Lord, just as the Wise Women knew. You have awakened the dragons—and no one foresaw that.'

'I'm the last of a dying breed,' Asaph mumbled, his jaw clenching.

'We *will* take it back.' Issa nodded. Looking at the hope and the passion on the men's faces ignited the fire inside. 'Like our victory here today. We will take it all back and wipe these bastards off Maioria.'

The Draxians nodded fervently but Asaph was more sober. 'It will take careful planning and a lot of soldiers. Draxa fell through trickery and is now as impenetrable to us as it was to the enemy. But I have to return…

'Look, let's meet later today and discuss Drax. I need to know everything that happened when Baelthrom invaded the city, anything you can tell me. I shall tell you all that happened to me and Coronos. You shall be the first to hear the truth. Gather all those Draxians who want to know. Go now and tell them.'

The men nodded and hurried off.

'You have yourself a growing, loyal, army.' Issa nodded approvingly.

'I just hope it isn't for nothing. I try not to think about those who will die,' said Asaph as they turned back towards the tent.

Inside, battle commanders of the various legions conversed. Even dwarves and Karalanths were present, appearing to hold an uneasy truce, though keeping their distance and eyeing each other warily.

In one corner, Freydel and Haelgon gesticulated, deep in discussion. Asaph headed to them. Ghott—she couldn't help but think of him as the Barbarian of the North, given his frightening stature and attire—spoke civilly and easily to a well-dressed commander in a pristine uniform.

As she scanned the busy and noisy tent, she realised one person should be amongst them; Marakon. Since he'd entered the demon tunnels—which she assumed he must have—she had been unable to reach him by scrying. She refused to let herself worry he was dead and instead tried to reach him any moment she could.

She sighed and, not wanting to talk battle strategy, quietly stepped back outside to find a quiet place to sit with her orbs.

Carrying one was enough, what with her sword and talisman as well, but carrying two was incredibly burdensome. Aside from Asaph, there was no one she trusted enough to pass the orbs on to. *No, there is one person safe and far away from here. Yisufalni. We must combine them and then she can take them away somewhere safe.*

Issa climbed up onto a jutting rock that offered a good, yet secluded view of the cove, and settled down cross-legged. Ehka landed beside her. He always knew when she was about to do something interesting.

She slipped the Orb of Water out of its pouch, cupped it in her hands and closed her eyes. Slowly, her consciousness sank into the orb.

'Orb of Water, show me the springs, show me the rivers and streams that once ran here,' she commanded.

The orb responded, filling her mind with images of rivers and waterfalls. Her mind was drawn into the earth with it, moving easily through rocks and sand and hidden caverns. Through solid walls she passed, into empty dark dwarf tunnels and deeper.

There came the sound of gushing water. Through a dark dwarf tunnel her vision flowed until she came to a chamber so huge she could not see the ceiling and only the barest light trickled down from above. Water gushed over giant machines of cogs and pulleys, ropes and chains. All of it was made out of Dark Dwarven black iron mined from the bowels of the Maphrax Mountains.

What the machines did, she could not tell. There were also many carts filled with rocks set on tracks that disappeared into the dark. They were mining for something and destroying Maioria in the process. The river gushed through and around the machines, channelled to wash rock or cool mechanisms, she supposed. The land had been bled dry just for them. She scowled.

High up in the ceiling, the river gushed through an enormous pipe. Keeping her eyes closed and inner vision focused, she fumbled for the Orb of Earth and held it in her free hand. Carefully, she entered the Flow. The last time she had used two orbs together they had nearly destroyed her.

Focussing on the Orb of Earth she directed its power—golden in the Flow—to the rock surrounding the pipe. The rock squeezed and trembled. She focused harder. The rock cracked and then collapsed upon and crushed the pipe. The water stopped gushing.

She held the rocks in place, feeling the pressure build swiftly behind it, then she focused on the Orb of Water, adding force and substance to the trapped water.

'Release,' she commanded both orbs.

Rocks and water exploded from the ceiling. A torrent flooded into the chamber, engulfing and crushing the great machines as if they were toys. Within moments, the enormous cavern was filled with water—water that needed somewhere to go.

'Return the river to its original course,' Issa spoke aloud her intention.

Both orbs became hot. The dark dwarven tunnels collapsed, the rocks helping to push the water up, helping it reach the surface as it sought its original course.

Issa flowed with the water through the darkness until it exploded from the earth. She could *feel* the old river bed. A faint, winding indent on the barren earth where once a river might have flowed. The water filled it hungrily, pushing away dirt and rubble as it fought to reach its ordained destination in the sea.

Cries of alarm and then wonder filled the air. Issa opened her eyes and started. Above the cover, exploding through their border wall, came a torrent of water. Quickly she shut her eyes and focussed on the Flow.

'Stick to the course!' she commanded the Orb of Water. 'Do no damage.'

The water calmed, but through the tents it flowed, scattering people from its path. When the water hit the ocean, she heard it give a great sigh. She opened her eyes and stared at the river rushing through the centre of the cove. At first it was muddy, darkening the sea with grey, but soon the water flowed clearer and calmer.

Carefully she released the Flow and looked down at the orbs in her hands, one swirling golden and emerald, the other ocean blue.

'These are just some of the things they can do,' she whispered in wonder. Ehka croaked. What had the Flow been like when Maioria's magic had been whole?

She put the orbs away and made her way to the river. People clustered on both sides, laughing and pointing. Thank the goddess no one had been washed away. Karalanths were the first to jump in and splash in the shallows.

'You did this?' Freydel asked her, eyes wide.

'No, the orbs did. They just showed me how,' said Issa.

'This isn't just orb magic. This is the power to create. Terraforming is a pre-creative power,' said Freydel, laughing and shaking his head.

'Recreate, I guess,' Issa corrected, though she wondered at his words.

CHAPTER 9

Demon Exit

MARAKON glanced at Shelley.

The wizard was crouching over the fallen soldier who had read the runes. The man wasn't breathing. Shelley looked up at him, her face pale. 'He's gone, Sir.'

Marakon nodded, feeling grim. 'Damn dark dwarf runes... Take his sword and use it yourself. We'll pray to Zanufey to carry his soul to the light.'

Shelley shook her head and swallowed. 'His soul will have been taken by the black runes. It's necromantic art the dark dwarves excel at.'

Marakon clenched his fist and sighed. 'Then there's nothing more that can be done. We should not linger here in case anything else decides to attack us.'

Eiretonne groaned. Marakon went to the dwarf who was propped against a wall.

The dwarf opened his eyes. 'Curse it, I feel weak as a newborn. I had the strangest dreams...' He blinked up at Marakon then took in the soldiers wiping their bloody wounds and cleaning their weapons.

'The weapon of a wraith got you and then I stabbed you with my spear,' Marakon said, keeping his face straight.

The dwarf stared daggers at him then broke into deep laughter. 'Argh, my shoulder is on fire! Thank Woetala it's my left.' He rubbed it then tried to move it. Wincing, he gave up.

'Here, have some food and water.' Marakon passed him a pack and the dwarf eagerly took out the provisions. 'So, this is a dark dwarven tunnel and they collided with a demon one. But how does that explain Karalanths?'

Eiretonne mumbled something over a mouthful of bread, shrugged and carried on eating, leaving Marakon to muddle it through.

'The Karalanths used dwarven tunnels when they fled Venosia,' said Shelley, settling down beside the wounded dwarf. 'How else do you think they made it to Davono?'

Eiretonne paused his noisy chewing and nodded, as if remembering something. He swallowed loudly, belched, and spoke. 'Aye, she's right. I may be a Land Dwarf and never lived in King Ashfoot's glorious New World within the Everridge Mountains, goddess bless him, but all dwarves, whether born above or below ground, know the stories of our exile and the wars against the deer-folk. When we tried to drive out the dark dwarves from their hell-holes, the Karalanths attacked us knowing we were weak. Our soldiers perished.'

Marakon frowned. 'But Karalanths will die away from their forests and the light, and these tunnels are surely leagues away from Davono, or Karalanthia.'

Eiretonne shrugged. 'All we have are rumours.'

Marakon rubbed his beard. 'So they discovered these tunnels and told no one of the dark dwarves beavering away beneath Frayon's cities?'

'Karalanths have no love for humans. They care nothing for other races, only themselves.' Eiretonne scowled.

'Why would they, when so many persecuted them?' Marakon sighed, feeling world weary. 'Let's get ready to move on.'

He picked up a torch and inspected the cavern. It narrowed at one end where the tunnel disappeared into pitch black.

'There's no point venturing further,' said Bokaard. 'We'll find nothing holy in this place.'

'I'd hoped for a quick way out, but it seems we must continue in the demon tunnels rather than the dark dwarven ones,' said Marakon.

Stepping into the dim grey of the demon tunnel, Marakon extinguished his brazier. They gathered the skittish horses and advanced once more.

Marakon lost himself in his thoughts. If he were a Karalanth, persecuted on all sides, he would have done the same. Get one enemy to fight another, then hope, one day, that human and dark dwarves would fight each other.

Twice, the tunnel split in two before they rested again. Time had no meaning down here, and after a nervous two hours' rest, expecting wraiths or demons to descend upon them, they continued.

Marakon came to a third split and sighed, bored. He scraped the spear's tip around the circumference. The demon symbols glowed, and one of them captured his attention. He bent close and stared at the fading green lines. The curves and strikes, repulsive and evil to his mind, were familiar.

'What is it?' Justenin came to his side.

Marakon didn't answer immediately as he scoured his mind for the memory. Suddenly it came to him. 'This way leads out. I know it, I'm sure of it.'

'But to where?' asked Justenin.

Marakon looked at the soldier. 'I don't know, I don't think I ever did. But the spear has led us this far…'

'Then let's not dally—out of this hell-hole,' Justenin said. 'Once we're out we can set the souls of those slain free to the four winds.'

Marakon glanced at the shrouded figures strapped to the horses. The commander had refused to leave them behind. Not even the dead deserved to be left here.

With the hope of an exit renewing their vigour, the soldiers hurried forwards and, as some ancient part of him knew it would, Marakon noticed the subtle change in the light from dim grey to dim orange. A memory of glowing amber rock came to him moments before the real thing appeared.

'This is it,' he said, running to the huge, ten-foot high amber boulder filling the tunnel. 'This is the exit.'

The semi-opaque orange rock was polished smooth, and it glowed mysteriously. He held his hand close and felt the tingle of energy.

'What's on the other side?' Shelley asked.

Marakon shrugged. 'Let's find out.'

He heard everyone brace and draw their weapons as he held up Velistor and tapped the spear's tip firmly against the rock. It made an unimpressive, dull noise. There was a moment of still, and then the rock shimmered and dissolved to the sound of gasps and cheers.

Clouds formed beyond the disappearing amber rock and a strong wind blew in.

Marakon closed his eyes in relief and breathed deeply. 'Ah, thank the goddess. This must be Davono where we can rest and drink wine and prepare for war.'

'If that's so, Sir, Davono might have fallen,' said Justenin soberly. 'The skies are red like the cursed sky above Maphrax.'

Marakon's eye flew open and roiling red clouds assaulted his sight.

CHAPTER 10

Hunting Ancients

YISUFALNI watched the Karalanth's and Jarlain fade into the fog, and an unsettling feeling stole over her.

'Something's not right,' she said, focussing her attention on the energy flows. It was faint but growing as they moved deeper into the Sea of Opportunity.

'I know,' said Murlonius, his face grim. 'Look, there, far away. A dark stain. There has never been anything here before.'

Yisufalni squinted into the whiteness. Barely detectable to her eyes was a smudge of dark. 'What is it?'

'I don't know, but it's getting closer.'

Murlonius fell silent for a time as he rowed. He steered a course away from it but the dark patch still grew.

'I don't think it's safe us remaining together,' he said. 'I don't want to leave you but I shan't risk your life either.'

'I'm not leaving you,' Yisufalni said firmly. 'For eons we've been apart. I would rather die by your side than be alone again. Our time here is complete, isn't it? Long have I wished to leave and join our Ancestors.'

Murlonius smiled at her. 'There's the sulky princess I remember.'

Thousands of years ago, Murlonius used to accuse her of being sulky. She smiled, now they were together again, their old personalities were beginning to show themselves.

'I'll take you to Issa or the seers. Alone I can hide,' he said.

The dark patch grew larger, brown on the outsides and red towards the centre.

Yisufalni's pulse quickened. 'Baelthrom,' she forced herself to say his name aloud.

'That or any number of his minions,' Murlonius agreed.

Yisufalni wrung her hands. 'How can it be? Has he discovered us? He never killed us but cursed us from Maioria's planes, though he never knew where.' Yisufalni clutched the collar of her cloak and watched the approaching muddy cloud.

Murlonius stared at it. 'Yes, he didn't know where and gave up hunting us. He knew two of us could do little but perhaps he's realised how much we've been helping the Maiorians. He only kept us alive because of the Orb of Life—the orb keyed to our people. If we are killed, what happens to the orb?'

'Perhaps he no longer cares what happens to the orbs. Our death lies in that cloud,' said Yisufalni, trying to control the rising panic. 'We must hide, and quickly!'

Murlonius tore his gaze away and thrashed the oars into the sea. Yisufalni closed her eyes and whispered to the Flow. The boat streamed through the water. A glance behind told her their efforts were for nothing.

A strange wind blew, hot and heavy, and carrying the smell of sulphur and ash. She found it hard to breath. Something moved in the red cloud, four darker shapes she couldn't quite identify. She closed her eyes and whispered to the Flow in the pure language of her people. Thick fog rolled towards them, blanketing and dampening everything.

'It won't hide us,' said Murlonius, shaking his head. 'They can feel and smell us better than they can see us. We are beacons in the Flow. If we separate, I can lead them away.'

'No,' said Yisufalni. *I cannot let him go alone!*

'If we separate, there's a chance. If we stay together, there is none!' Murlonius Raised his voice.

The sea turned choppy and dark as they entered Maioria's material planes, the boat responding to the boatman's wishes. Yisufalni gritted her teeth. She couldn't fight him and the will of the boat.

The cloud closed on them. She could see them clearly now, four horse-like monsters with spines for manes. Their riders were insubstantial black

smoke, sometimes seeming solid, other times like shadows. The heavy feel
of death exuded from them.

'Where will you go?' Yisufalni clasped his arm.

He gripped her hand, his eyes full of longing. 'Alone I can hide. In the
beginning, I hid from Baelthrom and his Life Seekers in many ways, often
by melding myself with the energies of the Sea of Opportunity. It took a
long time to regather myself, and I cannot protect you that way.'

The boat ground onto sand making her jump. Yisufalni did not even
want to look at where she was. She cupped Murlonius' smooth chin, her
pain reflected in his eyes.

He kissed her palm then pushed it away. 'Go. Hide. I will find you. I
will.'

Unseen hands lifted her from the boat and set her on the ground, her
eyes never leaving his. Behind him the four horsemen galloped out of
bulging black and red clouds.

The boat shifted off the sand and the mist clustered thickly. Then he
was gone, along with the four horsemen. Yisufalni blinked back tears, worry
and loneliness suddenly crushing.

Time to hide, his voice echoed in her head, spurring her into action.
Baelthrom could still find her here.

'Goddess protect you, my love,' Yisufalni prayed.

The mist dissipated to reveal the clear surface of a lake, mirroring
perfectly the blue skies and white clouds above. The trees and forests
surrounding it had turned amber with the onset of Autumn. They stretched
into the distance, blanketing hills and valleys until they reached the rich blue
sea far beyond. A gentle, cold wind blew, rippling the surface of the lake.

She breathed in the clean air and let the beauty of the place sink in. 'My,
it really hasn't aged in millennia.'

She turned from the lake. Behind her soared the great tower of the
Wizard's Circle. The last time she had been here was fairly recent, however,
when she'd saved Freydel from the Ethereal Planes and had been Arla. It
was unaged because of the magical shield she had helped create millennia
ago.

The shield would protect her from the four horsemen, and she'd know
if Baelthrom arrived, yet still she couldn't seem to relax. The narrow,
exposed staircase circled the outside wall all the way to the top where the

twelve stone seats would be. There was power here, power she could use to reach others, maybe even Murlonius. She hurried towards the tower.

Murlonius watched Yisufalni and the wizards' tower fade away, sick with worry. She would be safer there than anywhere. The protective magic on this place would conceal her from anything, even Baelthrom, he prayed.

As the red light surrounded him, he turned his attention upon his own survival. Momentarily disappearing from the realm between planes, the horsemen were there when he returned. They turned towards him, unsheathing their great swords, their black eyes sucking in the light.

Their beasts' hooves galloped above the water's surface. One raised its scaly head and screamed a sound he had never heard a horse make before. It sent his heart pounding. Soot billowed from flared nostrils and the eyes of the horse-beasts and their riders glowed a deeper black, draining his life-force.

Do not look into the eyes of the Knights of Maphrax! His soul screamed. He tore his gaze away and called the Flow. A horseman whispered, the air shivered, and the Under Flow surrounded him.

'Kill the Ancient One,' the horsemen spoke in rasping voices.

Murlonius fought the constricting chains of the Under Flow. They were close now, he could see every glistening scale, every snort of smoke, and the craggy peaks of the Mountains of Maphrax on their black tabards.

He could not fight them, and he could not run from them. To escape he would have to cast himself away. Closing his eyes, he sung in the Ancient's pure tongue of magic. All of his people had once known the spell, few dared used it.

'Efen esah yileth-ahreal!'

The Flow filled him. His physical body began to lighten and expand, turning more into spirit than matter. With a command, he dissolved his physical matter entirely, becoming pure energy and lifting from the realm completely. Murlonius vanished.

The horses screamed and reared. The Knights of Maphrax howled. They turned their prancing mounts, hunting for him.

Disembodied, Murlonius watched. In this state beyond matter he felt no fear, his emotions had detached themselves. Safe, conscious, but unable to effect or be effected by the world of matter. Yet it would cost him his vitality and his power. Magic would be gone from him indefinitely, and on his return he would be utterly vulnerable.

It had been necessary, he thought, watching the raging horsemen, his mind detached and lucid.

The knights turned their mounts and galloped away into their red cloud. The Sea of Opportunity became uninterrupted sparkling light where the sky was indistinguishable from the sea below, and Murlonius drifted.

Yisufalni inhaled sharply as Murlonius vanished. She stared harder into the tiny pool of Sacred Water she had poured from her vial into the centre of the wizards' circle of stone chairs where an orb would have sat. She blinked away the tears. *He got away, I should be joyous!*

'Well-played, my love. Now come back for me, come back now,' she whispered. It would take a long time, but he was safe for now.

She lay down on the hard ground beside the pool and stayed there until the sun had set and the stars twinkled above. Slowly, she sat up and crossed her legs, smoothing the creases of her cloak over her thighs.

Now I return to what I spent millennia doing; watching the world of Maioria and her people from afar. She peered into the pool and whispered, 'Raven Queen.'

The pool rippled and clouded. When it stilled, an image formed. Issa's pale face framed in long, shining black hair. Her eyes were closed. She looked like a sleeping goddess. *A sleeping Zanufey. Thank the light she is safe.*

Issa opened her eyes and looked straight at Yisufalni, making her start.

'Yisufalni?' she said sleepily, her eyes subtly luminous from the Flow.

She can see me? The young woman could feel her presence even when asleep!

'Yes.' Yisufalni smiled. 'There's been trouble but now everything is all right. I was worried. I see Asaph beside you, safe and well, and that is good.'

Issa frowned. 'You came to me like this before. I remember your light, in the storehouses of Little Kammy. It was you wasn't it?'

'It was.'

'Thank you,' whispered Issa. She sat up and lifted two orbs, one golden and emerald, and the other indigo and turquoise. 'I need your help. You must know what has happened for me to now be the Keeper of two orbs.

No one else will agree, but I need your help to combine them. If it can be done, it must be done now. Combined, these orbs will be stronger, Maioria will be stronger.'

Yisufalni looked at the beautiful orbs, amazed that Issa held two in her palms. What the Raven Queen asked felt right in every way. After a long moment, Yisufalni nodded her head. 'The time has finally come to make whole that which was broken.'

Magic exploded off the black walls in an awesome shower of sparks. The pressure expanded, then dropped, then burst outwards in a blinding flash of light, hurling Kilkarn from the iron ring's chamber and smashing him senseless against the thick outer door. Dazed, he lay there on the cold stone floor and stared mesmerised as his One True God raged. Venosia had been invaded successfully by the Feylint Halanoi, and his Lord was venting his displeasure.

The iron ring blazed white and red, its power crescendoing in response to Baelthrom's. His Lord's solid form became ethereal and expanded to fill the chamber. He truly was becoming the god Kilkarn worshipped with each day that passed.

Baelthrom's eyes blazed, not red but dark, furious blue. They changed colour to the darkest smouldering orange and then back to blue as his unfettered power rampaged. His form condensed again, demon wings stretched wide and snapped back, muscular Saurian legs bulged and claws raked the ground. His tail struck the walls, its barbs sending sparks into the darkness. His massive human torso dripped with sweat.

But it was the incredible force of the Under Flow at Baelthrom's command that had Kilkarn so enraptured. His Lord was the first to command the dark flows to such levels. Soon the world would be there to do with as they pleased and no other magic a match for theirs, as their prophecies had foretold.

A long time passed as the magic stormed around the prone dark dwarf. He wondered if he'd passed out for, of a sudden, the chamber calmed, the light no longer flashed, and the pressure released. His body trembled all over as he pushed himself back onto stubby legs.

'My Great Lord.' He sidled into the chamber, eyes darting to the flickering iron ring—the ring that watched all that occurred on this hateful planet, and through which the beautiful power of the Dark Rift flowed.

It was dark for the braziers had all been blown out in the magical maelstrom, but he could see well in this light. His eyes settled on a blacker form beside the ring, and the two even darker patches that were his Lord's eyes.

'West Venosia can be taken again. It's a nothing place,' the dark dwarf placated.

He had watched their defeat through the Dromoorai Shadow Stones. That and the loss of the Orb of Earth so nearly in their grasp. Kilkarn didn't dare mention the loss of the Raven Queen too, and had *never* mentioned losing the Sword of Binding to the last Dragon Lord.

That the last of the Ancient's had also seemingly vanished was a separate issue entirely, one not needed to vex his Lord further. Whilst he had grown in power, the people of this cursed planet still evaded and usurped his rule. Still denied his might.

'I need more power,' Baelthrom whispered, a sound that vibrated the iron ring.

'And you shall have it, Great One,' Kilkarn nodded.

All things his Lord desired would be his and they would help him get it all. It was his Lord's sudden silence that unnerved Kilkarn, for a long time he just stood there in the dark unmoving.

The braziers burst into life. Baelthrom stalked towards the iron ring, his wings spread wide, his tail swinging. A gauntleted hand reached forwards and the ring flared into a swirling mass of grey.

'Hameka,' Baelthrom commanded, his voice booming in the chamber.

After a moment, the pale, gaunt face of a man appeared. His slate grey hair was smoothed back, accentuating deep widow's peaks. His eyes were hard, and though this man was several hundred years old, he only looked to be in his sixties, courtesy of imbibing minute amounts of the Elixir of Immortality. Since Baelthrom's second in command was not willing to succumb to the black drink yet, he still aged, but slowly. A semi-immortal.

'You will know that Venosia has been attacked,' said Baelthrom. Not waiting for a reply, he stormed on. 'Forget the Uncharted Lands, your job is done there. Leave a single garrison and return now. Attack Frayon immediately, in full force. They are spread thinly.'

The man was about to speak but then pursed his lips and inclined his head. 'Right this moment, my Lord,'

His face faded into the swirling grey.

'Cirosa,' Baelthrom commanded.

The striking, cold face of his High Priestess appeared. Her blood red lips and ice-blue eyes were sharply accentuated by her snow-white skin. The immortal woman had once been High Priestess of the Temple to the Great Goddess and second in line to the Oracle. Now she too held the power of a demi-god, power given to her by the One True God.

'My Lord,' she inclined her head and dropped her gaze.

'Take Vornus and attack Lans Himay,' Baelthrom commanded. 'Forget hunting for the heir of Drax, the dragons have awoken.'

Cirosa's face paled, making her seem translucent. Her eyes narrowed. 'I'll kill him,' she rasped.

'Get Vornus. Invade Lans Himay,' Baelthrom repeated. 'Slay the Draxian refugees wherever you find them. They will rally to his call. Go now.'

Baelthrom swiped his hand and her image disappeared.

'Dereever,' he spoke the name of the harpy queen.

In moments, the smooth, tanned face of a black-eyed bird woman appeared. Her dark hair framed her high cheekbones accentuated by the thick, ceremonial scars on her cheeks. A single, shining onyx dangled on her forehead, marking her as Queen. She smiled, revealing a mouth of black fangs. 'Lord Baelthrom.'

'Take your brood and scout the enemy attacking north-west Venosia. Watch the Raven Queen. Report back to me what you find.'

'Yes, my Lord,' Dereever smiled indulgently.

Silence descended upon the chamber as the harpy queen's face faded. Baelthrom's eyes turned from green to orange and back again as he thought. He strode to the pedestal holding three orbs and picked up the brown wooden wizard's staff resting against it.

The staff was filled with the Flow and Kilkarn hated to look at it. It had belonged to the Master Wizard who held the black Orb of Death—the orb that Baelthrom desired more than any other. The staff had been dropped by the wizard when he'd fled from his Lord.

Now, Baelthrom held it in his hands and studied it for a long time. He turned towards the iron ring and, slowly, as if struggling with the name, he breathed, 'Lona.'

The swirling grey became impenetrable black. Time passed. Then, pressing out of the blackness and out of the ring pushed an alien face. Huge, all-black eyes opened and looked at Baelthrom. Even Kilkarn's dark heart beat faster in fear, an emotion he was not used to having.

'Speak to me again of this...*deal* you mentioned,' said Baelthrom, holding before him the wooden staff.

A smile formed upon Lona's face as she looked from the staff to Baelthrom, her eyes gleaming hungrily.

CHAPTER 11

Illendri

ISSA stood with Asaph, Velonorian, Haelgon, Cusap'anth and Rhul'ynth before the lookout tower on top of the cliffs straddling the two coves.

Ehka preened himself on her shoulder. It was night, or at least a darker shade of overcast red. To the East, the firelight of the enemy blazed. There were two spots of light on the horizon, one bigger and closer, the other far away.

'The furthest one is a city. I've seen it,' said Issa.

'Within a week, we'll launch our attack on it, and one by one they'll fall.' Rhul'ynth's eyes gleamed.

'We won't have the element of surprise this time,' said Asaph. 'They know we're coming. They'll have reinforcements. The battles are only going to get tougher.'

'And we shall only get stronger,' said Cusap'anth.

Every day more reinforcements arrived from one country or another. News of their success, and the hope that sprang with it, had spread rapidly amongst the Free Peoples, and now they hungered for their beloved Maioria to be free. Now they had the strength and will to fight.

'Somewhere out there is Marakon and our knights,' said Issa. 'I can't reach him in the demon tunnels, not even the raven talisman can reach Velistor down there, but I know he's somewhere close.'

'He may have emerged behind enemy lines.' Cusap'anth nodded to the enemy in the distance. 'When we fought the dark dwarves, we found their tunnels intersecting demon tunnels at many points. It was through their tunnels so many of us managed to reach Davono.'

'During the war, many of our boats were burnt. It was safer to fight a demon or dark dwarf than it was to sail the Venosian Straights, but few dared venture into the darkness. The goddess only knows how many got lost in that maze beneath our feet.'

'There are dark dwarf tunnels from here all the way to Davono?' Issa had trouble imagining digging that far, and the horror of wandering alone in the darkness until death, or worse, claimed you. 'But no one knows that. I mean, no *human* knows. So, the dark dwarves could attack us at any moment.'

Rhul'ynth shifted her hooves and Cusap'anth gave her a peculiar look, serious, angry and sorrowful all at the same time. 'We did not tell the humans, for why should we? You were mostly our enemies back then, hunting us for sport, never once helping our plight.

'We all hoped that one day the dark dwarves or the demons would arise from their tunnels and attack you, laying waste your lands as you and they had laid waste ours. Besides, we knew of no human friends to tell at the time.' He looked away.

Issa swallowed, ashamed of the past and the suffering that had occurred between even the good people of Maioria. 'I hope, one day when our terrible enemies have gone, that peace between the indigenous people of Maioria will be found.'

'Once, there was peace, between all peoples, between all species, between all things, a long, long time ago,' said Haelgon, his blue eyes sparkling in the dull light. 'Even before the Ancient's ancestors came. We have it written in our sacred books hidden in the desert. But that was before death came, and before the animals and humans ate each other. It was such a long time ago, maybe it was only ever a myth.'

'All myths have their basis in truth,' said Issa.

'One day when this is over, I'll spend time searching the Recollection. Surely the dragons have some memory,' said Asaph. 'Why don't we head back? I can smell dinner even from here.'

'You're always hungry!' Issa laughed. 'Why don't you go ahead and save me a seat? I just want to see if there is any life in the earth with the orb. I think I need to be alone to feel it clearly. Don't worry, I'll be all right. Look, there are five sentries up there watching. I'll be just here.'

This seemed to ease Asaph's worries. 'All right, all right,' he said, and followed the others.

Issa scanned the barren land. There was nothing but the sentries on the lookout above, and the wind and dust. She slipped out the orbs and closed her eyes. Tuning into the orbs, she began to walk slowly. In the Flow, she could see the ground quite clearly. The orbs began speaking to each in their language of energy and her brain subconsciously joined that conversation.

She let the Flow drip from her hands through the orbs onto the earth as she walked. As it hit the ground it sparkled briefly before turning dull. *The soil is dry, but not so much dead as in stasis.*

She walked in a wide circle and stopped. For the briefest moment the breeze blew fresh and pure, and carried the smell of trees and flowers as if she stood in the forests of Myrn. Then it disappeared and was replaced by the stale, heavy wind of fallen Venosia.

Ehka croaked. She opened her eyes and stared at the ground. Where she had walked and dripped the Flow, a sparse ring of tiny indigo flowers bloomed.

'Great Goddess, ehkas! Look Ehka, the flowers after which you're named. Do you remember?' The raven cawed.

Tears filled her eyes and she sank down onto her knees, reaching out a hand to gently stroke the flowers. Only on Little Kammy had she seen the vast blooms of ehkas that came out at night on a full moon. Sometimes the fields were so thick with them, they were like an ocean swaying in the breeze.

There was only a small circle where she had walked and used the Flow, but it was something, it was hope. Ehka nestled against her leg and she wiped the tears away. Carefully, she picked a tiny flower and ran down the hill.

Back at the encampment, she burst into the food hall, and stopped abruptly before her friends' table. 'There are flowers growing here on Venosia, I have seen them! They *can* grow!' she panted.

The Karalanths, wizards and Asaph stared at her, mouths' agape. She held up the tiny indigo ehka and everyone clustered around to look. She passed it to Asaph, and one by one they all inspected it.

'Then it shall be called Ehka Hill,' Rhul'ynth laughed, holding the flower high.

'Life blooms again in our homeland. There is hope,' said Cusap'anth, his eyes glistening.

'You know you cannot come with me to the Wizards' Circle, just as I could not go with Coronos that time,' said Issa.

Asaph wasn't having any of it. 'You're not going alone.'

They stood on the grey sand before the dark ocean. The last thing she wanted to do was go alone without Asaph. It was a dangerous journey, especially with two orbs, across the astral plains. She carried on. 'I wish you could come but you're not keyed to it.'

Asaph's frown deepened with worry. 'I know that but...' he sighed and his shoulders slumped, finally giving in. 'You must go and it must be done, I understand that. I just hope Yisufalni has the power to protect your journey *and* when you are there.'

'The journey part, both there and back, is the most dangerous. Once I'm there, our combined power in one of the most powerful and protected places on Maioria will be no match even for Baelthrom. Besides, she *is* an Ancient.'

Asaph sighed. Nothing she could say would allay his fears.

'I'll wait for you here, don't be gone long. Remember, the flame ring binds us.' He held up her hand, the one she wore his mother's ring upon, and kissed it.

Issa had mentioned her plans to Freydel last night, suggesting he accompany her and combine his orb too. His sudden anger had taken her by surprise. "Preposterous!" He had shouted over and again, igniting her own anger. Both had stormed off and neither had seen the other since.

Never had she seen her former tutor and friend so furious. For the first time she wished Domenon had been there and was here now to offer his thoughts. *Domenon the dragon*, she thought bitterly. *No one is as they seem and few can be trusted.*

Asaph watched the oval white light grow. Issa walked into it with Ehka perched on her shoulder. She turned once to smile at him, and then disappeared along with the light. He let go of his breath slowly, his stomach in knots, then walked the rough path through the destroyed barracks to what had come to be called the Beer Tent.

He stepped inside and the laughing chatter hushed. Soldiers of all factions—from Atalanph to the Feylint Halanoi to Draxians loyal to one of the many warlords of Lans Himay—looked his way, some bowing awkwardly or nodding to him respectfully as he passed. It wasn't just because rumour had spread like wild fire that the heir of Drax was amongst them. He had proved his prowess on the battlefield, both as a dragon in the skies and as a warrior amongst them helping them clear the tunnels of dark dwarves.

He kept his eyes forward, nodding briefly, wishing his cheeks wouldn't burn so, and headed towards a number of Draxians standing to one side, tankards in hand. Beer helped everyone relax, which wasn't easy when they stood on enemy lands. *Our lands now,* he reminded himself.

'Asaph?' Someone called out his name, making him pause. Freydel hurried his way over, his purple robes dusty but his crystal staff shining and freshly polished.

'Freydel, is everything all right?' Asaph asked.

'Yes, as well as things can be in times of war. Let's hope we can keep our foothold here. I've just been scrying with King Navarr, and more reinforcements will be arriving in the next few weeks. This cursed land has no sun, but at least the worst of the winter now descending on Frayon has also been kept at bay.'

'I'd rather face snow and blizzards than exist under this torched sky,' said Asaph. 'But for our purposes, perhaps you are right. Although the weather, or lack of it, isn't hindering our enemy either. They've been too quiet these past couple of days and I don't like it. Anyway, how can I help you?'

'I can't find Issa and thought she might be with you,' Freydel said.

'Oh, she has gone to the Wizard's Circle. Yisufalni is—are you all right?' The wizard had paled dramatically.

'No,' Freydel spluttered. 'I knew Yisufalni was there but...'

'She's gone to see what can be done about the orbs—' Asaph continued then stopped.

Freydel had about-turned and was virtually running out of the tent. Asaph watched him go, confused. Issa had mentioned a disagreement with her former tutor and his reluctance to combine the orbs, but he hadn't given it much thought, not as much thought as it clearly deserved.

Moments later, the light faded and Issa felt herself solidify—it was the only way she could describe it.

She didn't feel Translocation Sickness and she didn't feel dizzy. Yisufalni's magic ensured the translocation spell was completely seamless.

The Ancient's beautiful face appeared. High cheekbones, slanted oval eyes, slightly elongated head and delicate ears longer than an elf's. Despite her simple, grey cloak and attire, her regale grace reminded Issa so much of her Aralan ancestors, although she looked far less alien.

Issa took her out-stretched, six-fingered hands—again reminding her of the Aralans—and looked up into the woman's eyes. A lot passed between them; sorrow for all the pain and hardship suffered, and a shared feeling of uncertainty as to what the future would bring them.

'You stayed by our side all this time as the little girl Arla,' said Issa, humbled. This woman, denied a physical presence on Maioria by Baelthrom's curse, had fought and found a way to return in the frail, tiny body of a child. Banished forever to the Ethereal Planes and torn apart from the one she loved—the only other living Ancient, cursed and banished too.

Tears glistened in Yisufalni's eyes. 'I had no choice. I could not die and leave Murlonius. I did only what one could. I watched over the races of Maioria for millennia, helping where and when I could—but it was such pitiful help…'

Issa held up her raven talisman, an object of power that Yisufalni had recovered for her. 'Without this, I would not be here. I would not have the power to stand against Baelthrom's horde, and I would not be able to enter the Realm of the Dead.'

Yisufalni wrapped an arm around her shoulder, and together they walked between the stone chairs to where a circle of six smooth holes indented the stone floor. The place where the orbs were placed.

Issa paused a moment to take in the stunning view. Evergreen trees mingled amongst deciduous ones whose leaves were now all amber and sprinkling the ground. Clear rivers wound through the valley into the sparkling lake and beyond to the sea. The sky was a rich blue above and the low afternoon sun caressed her face with a little warmth.

She closed her eyes and breathed, feeling the uncorrupted beauty and freedom of the place. 'It's been weeks since I saw blue sky. The torched sky I've been living under lets nothing through and the air is stale. But, Yisufalni,' She opened her eyes, remembering, 'there are flowers growing on Venosia, I have seen them!'

The Ancient's eyes grew wide.

'Look.' Issa pulled out a piece of tissue from her pocket and unfolded it. Although withered and drying, the tiny ehka still held vivid indigo in its petals.

'Oh my goddess,' breathed Yisufalni touching the flower. 'It is true. All things can be healed. Life will return to even the most ravished places.'

They stared at the tiny flower before Issa tucked it back into her pocket. 'This is just the beginning…But let's not waste time. Do you think it wise to try and combine the two orbs I carry?'

'I now think it was unwise to ever separate the magic in the first place,' said Yisufalni. 'I know not what will happen when they are one, but for all that's occurring in this world, we must try. It might not be possible to combine them, but I was involved in the making of them, the only one to still be alive.'

'We can but try.' Issa slipped the orbs out of their pouches and held them up.

Rather than take them, Yisufalni placed her hand gently on top of each, closed her eyes and entered the Flow. Issa did the same. Magic moved powerfully around the two orbs and they began to make a beautiful humming sound.

'Look,' Yisufalni spoke softly, 'feel them already pulling together? The orbs want to be rejoined. Earth and Water are two different elements but always they exist together. Apart, they are nothing, their power is less. Listen, can you hear them talking? They're telling us how to combine them. They're guiding us. Give in to them. Let them lead us.'

Issa surrendered to the power of the orbs. A strange language of notes and symbols filled her ears and vision. The pure language of magic vibrated the deepest parts of her being. The magic grew, filling her with light, power and elation.

Things she didn't know about the Orb of Earth became known to her. The nature of earth magic, the way bark grew and hardened around a tree, the movement of rocks, and the existence of vast crystal caverns deep within Maioria herself.

The Orb of Water also spoke to her of many things—some it had already told her when she had become its Keeper, others were new. She discovered vast ocean-filled crystal caverns deep underground. Thousands of aquifers existed there, and Maioria was not just a solid rock spinning in the vastness of space at all. The rocks and crystals were her bones, the water, magma and other liquids her blood. The planet was alive, but she was hurt and wanted to heal. The elemental powers Issa held in her hands desired to be one so that the planet could heal.

'*We are one,*' the orbs whispered, again and again.

Suddenly Issa knew what she had to do, and she knew Yisufalni did too. She poured the Flow through her hands into the orbs and felt Yisufalni do the same. In the Flow, the orbs flared all colours of the rainbow. They began to lose their solidity until they were no longer physical objects at all but dense balls of golden and turquoise energy. They elongated towards each other like lovers reaching out after millennia apart.

Their energy touched. White light blazed where golden and turquoise combined. The orbs were feeling each other, remembering each other. The light grew brighter, flaring like a fire but without the heat, and the air vibrated and hummed. Pearlescent gold, silver and turquoise glittered in hues Issa had never seen before nor imagined existed.

A different vibration captured her attention, almost breaking it. She couldn't lose her focus now and ignored it, continuing to pour the Flow through her hands. The vibration came again, harder and more like a jolt. It wasn't coming from the orbs. She frowned and pushed it away. The orbs were nearly fully combined now, their energies swirling together in a greater ball of light.

Issa jumped as thunder cracked and black streaks of lightning snaked beyond the light of the orbs. The orbs flared, refusing to pause their destiny. She was unable to take her hands from them even if she tried. She couldn't even see Yisufalni for the brightness, but she could still feel her there, channeling her magic into the orbs. The black streaks vanished and the thunder faded. The orbs gave a final burst of light, and the Flow pouring through her hands dropped to a trickle.

Issa let go of the Flow, finding her hands and Yisufalni's now clasped around a singular orb. The Ancient looked as faint as she felt. Slowly, Issa lowered herself to the ground. Yisufalni followed, both keeping their hands locked onto the orb.

They stared at the beautiful object they held. Gone were the Orbs of Earth and Water. Gone, too, were the swirling energies on the surface. Instead they beheld a different orb entirely. This new crystal flared purple and indigo rays from its centre, like the iris of an eye, or the flaring sun. It was the same size as the previous orbs, and the same weight, but it was twice as powerful, Issa could feel it.

'Something has happened in its making. I feel a part of it now more than I did with the Orb of Water alone,' whispered Issa, not wanting to mar the awe-filled silence but struggling to understand her strange feelings towards the object of power.

'Two become three become one. We have helped birth something new into existence and in its creation we have become part of them,' explained Yisufalni.

Issa nodded her head, understanding her intrinsically. 'Then we are both its Keeper?'

'I guess that must be the truth.' Yisufalni did not lift her gaze from the orb. 'But what is it called? It has a new name…Listen, can you hear it? It's a vibration. It is Illendri. In our ancient language a similar word means 'The One'.

'Illendri,' Issa breathed, feeling the wholeness of the word. The orb flared as she spoke its name. 'For the one it has become. The symbol of all things being rejoined. Take it, Yisufalni, take it to the astral planes or to Murlonius. Take it far away from here and hide it.' Issa tried to push it to the other women but Yisufalni shook her head.

'No, we are hunted too. The Knights of Maphrax—ahh, your look of horror tells me you've seen them. I knew you would have. Baelthrom's hunters.'

Issa didn't want to think of them in this moment. 'They came for me a few times; in the bath in Teramides and again on the battlefield—they can reach me anywhere and I must run. Even in the Realm of the Dead they follow me and I cannot fight them.' Issa's throat constricted at the memory, her mind seeing horsemen made of shadow and scales.

'No one can fight them, Issa. They came for us too, that's why I'm here. I told you we fled. Baelthrom's Knights of Maphrax whose souls live in the Dark Rift and are lost forever.'

Issa imagined a horse screaming in the distance, black eyes leaking smoke, shadows becoming swords and armour. A hand reached towards her and she shivered. A hand with a ring, and on the ring, a horse...

The Flow jolted suddenly, breaking her out of her terrible memories. The air shimmered where they sat, the telltale sign of another wizard arriving. They jumped up and Yisufalni stuffed the orb into Issa's pouch. Before Issa could protest, Freydel appeared. The wizard's ashen face was a mix of fear and anger.

CHAPTER 12

Falling Circles

'WHAT have you two done!' Freydel roared.

His eyes were bloodshot and he clearly hadn't combed his hair or beard in days. He looked thin and utterly bedraggled.

Issa stepped back. Yisufalni laid a hand on her arm. The Ancient stood tall, her back straight, her melodic voice calm yet commanding.

'My dear Freydel, we have done what the orbs commanded us to do.'

'You have endangered everyone!' Freydel virtually screamed, almost mad. Had the wizard lost his sanity as well as his cool?

The air shimmered and that strange magical jolt came again. Issa frowned and looked around. *Where was it coming from?*

A light beamed down from the sky striking the Wizards' Tower where they had just been sitting. Issa stared at it. It didn't feel dangerous, just had a peculiar magical signature. In the pillar of light, a tall, slender being swiftly formed.

Issa stared up into the serene, alien, golden face of Ayeth. He was at least seven feet tall. Her legs gave way and she sank to the ground, all the magic dissipating from her grasp. Yisufalni was frozen to the spot, all colour draining from her face. Freydel, in the presence of his beloved teacher, regained his sanity and composure and rolled his shoulders back.

Ayeth did not take his deep blue gaze from Issa. Slowly, an enigmatic smile formed on his flawless features. 'You are the one who is trying to stop it,' he said.

Issa realised he spoke an entirely different language and only recognised one of the Aralansian words, but he somehow had the power to make her understand him.

'You cannot be here,' Issa whispered, her voice an ugly rasp compared to his. He was regal and calm, poised and elegant.

Her mind and emotions churned in turmoil. Here was the one who had started it all. Here was the cause of the death of her family, her friends, and the destruction of her homeland. Here stood the being who had destroyed her life in this and lifetimes past, and yet all she could see was wisdom, benevolence, beauty.

With a sinking feeling, she realised she could never, ever kill Ayeth. In that moment, hope for the end of it all died a little—for she must stop him so that Maioria might live.

'He helped me arrive here safely,' Freydel said, smiling proudly, his character calm and vastly different to when he had arrived. 'Now we must undo what you have done. This war must end and only Ayeth can stop it.'

'The orbs stay combined,' Issa said through clenched teeth.

Ayeth walked towards her. With an honest, benevolent smile he held out a hand.

Issa's heart thumped in her chest as a thousand thoughts and emotions battled within her.

'I was chosen as are you,' Ayeth said.

For a moment it seemed only she and him existed. Images, memories, feelings flooded into her, both of her life and his. His words unlocked a watershed of emotion, tears and pain. She wiped at the tears, struggling for composure.

Zanufey had chosen him and he had fallen. Now he stood here with her, the great being before it all changed. Was she going to fall too? Could Zanufey even be trusted? Slowly, she reached to take his hand. As their palms touched memory jolted through her.

She witnessed again the destruction of Aralansia, the screaming people, the vast and terrible energies ripping apart the planet. Then she saw Zanufey on the blue desert beneath a star filled sky, the hopes and fears of an entire race within her, and within Issa and within Ayeth.

Was there any hope for Ayeth? Was there any way to save him? If she killed him now, all this would end and Maioria would be free.

But as she stared into his fathomless eyes, she only saw herself reflected. A being given a grand yet terrible task. A being filled with devotion and power, and bringing into him all the pain and suffering of a world so that he might help it.

They had both been chosen; he to save another race, and she to save her own from what he had become.

Compassion swept over her. Could she help this man? An incredible need to assist him and stop him from falling filled her, just as it had when she fought Keteth and Zanufey stepped into her being. Could she bring this man home like she had Keteth?

Thunder peeled and black lightning flared, splitting the sky apart and tearing her out of her thoughts and memories.

Issa glanced up at a sky no longer blue but filled with racing, muddy clouds. Wind tore around them, not fresh but stale and heavy.

'The shield is breaking!' Yisufalni screamed.

A great crack appeared in the shield, as if they were under a huge dome of glass about to shatter.

'Ayeth, you must leave this place,' said Freydel running to his side. 'It's Baelthrom, and you must not meet!'

Ayeth stared up at the sky frowning but he still held Issa's hand. He turned his gaze upon her. Beyond him, Freydel lifted his black orb and crystal staff, and incanted. The erratically moving Flow surged to do the Master Wizard's bidding, and then Ayeth began to fade. The Aralan looked confused. In this place, the Master Wizard of the Wizards' Circle held the most power. Right now, Issa doubted even she could match Freydel's strength.

The shield above shattered. They fell to their knees, except Ayeth, his partially material body remained unaffected by the explosion. He stared up, mesmerised, they all did.

Black energy poured through the shattered shield towards the Wizards' Tower as if being channelled through a giant funnel. It struck the tower, and cracks snaked beneath them. In the swirling black, another being began to form.

Fear iced the air. Issa's heart beat heavy and slow as time slowed down. Demon wings spread wide and a tripartite helmet appeared as the enormous shape of Baelthrom materialised.

Issa gasped. Ayeth became fainter as Baelthrom solidified. Ayeth looked from his abominable future self back to her. Fear narrowed his eyes, and his gaze was searching. Was he asking her to do something? He disappeared, and she became aware of Yisufalni screaming something and dragging her to her feet. But Issa moved in a detached, sluggish haze.

Dark blue eyes, like the colours of Ayeth's, blazed to life within that helmet. If Freydel had had any power before, the Flow was gone now.

In a daze that placed her beyond terror, Issa let Yisufalni pull her back but she could not tear her eyes from her enemy. Ehka squawked madly from somewhere, she had forgotten all about the bird. Her raven talisman burned at her side, and Illendri pulsed. The Under Flow surrounded all, there was nothing to protect them from Baelthrom.

Issa lifted her hands. It seemed foolish to try, but the magic of the orb and the talisman willed her to. A wall of fire rolled towards Baelthrom. He stepped forwards, a clawed lizard foot stepping out of the black cloud. The Under Flow responded and shattered her wall, sucked the magic into itself, and doubled in strength as it slammed back into her. She fought it, spreading her arms wide to push it back but the Flow was an uncontrollable mess.

The hurricane of magic shunted her backwards. Her power was not nearly enough. She realised she was screaming. The blackness pouring from the sky filled Baelthrom with magic she could never hope to match.

He stepped forwards again and lifted his other hand. Black magic ripped into her, throwing her backwards, a doll spinning head over heel into the air.

Time speeded up.

Helpless, she tumbled over the edge of the Wizards' Tower. Lightning flared and she tried to reach for her raven form but it was impossible to call.

The ground sped towards her.

Something large and blue streaked in her vision, something huge clasped around her waist. Dazed, she looked up at huge ice-blue scales. Her eyes travelled over the enormous body to stare into the huge golden eyes of Morhork. The claw that gripped her was blackened, hurt from when he tried to take the orb. They were airborne but he had no wings, instead, great magical forces flared around them. Powerful dragon magic. But even Morhork floundered under the assault of the Under Flow.

Dragon magic surged, a gale blew, and everything became a blur. New forces overwhelmed her.

Yisufalni stared at the fading form of Ayeth. He was a Great One, the Ancient's ancestors of old whose power far surpassed their own. Beside him the ugly form of Baelthrom took shape—the terrible being that the Aralan would become.

She tried to catch Issa as the incredible force of the Under Flow knocked the Raven Queen backwards, but her body failed to obey her mind, and the Flow was ripped away in the maelstrom onslaught.

Ayeth disappeared and her eyes locked onto Baelthrom's. He held a wooden staff, a wizards' staff. *Freydel's old staff, is that how he'd found them?* The staff would always be linked to its wizard.

Yisufalni understood that she could not run, and the cold terror paralysing her abated in that realisation. An odd calm stole over her and her heart pounded less; she faced her death and there was no running from it. She would face the inevitable with calm dignity.

In these moments of calm acceptance, the roaring of wind and magic melted away and time slowed down. Her capable mind worked fast, seeing the unfolding of events that had led up to this point, and now to her inevitable death.

In a final act of defiance, she used the last of her magic to shove Issa away from Baelthrom, lifting her high into the air. Death would be better than enslavement if the Raven Queen could not break her fall.

Yisufalni had known the wingless dragon lay hidden, she'd felt him arrive while she looked into her sacred pool, and had even sensed his murderous plans, not unto herself, but to others. *Wizards and orbs. His mind was consumed with wizards and orbs!* But she had not expected him to help.

Her eyes widened as he streaked behind and below Baelthrom, out of view of the Immortal Lord's gaze, and captured Issa in his talons. Yisufalni marvelled at events, at redemption—perhaps Morhork could be forgiven. The universe had an enormous amount of leeway when it came to doing wrong. Too much, she felt.

Her eyes travelled back to the gnarled old wooden staff in Baelthrom's hands. With it, he had followed Freydel. All objects formed a link to their owners, especially magical ones. Baelthrom would know this as well as any magic user. That was why he carried the staff with him now. But he would not have been able to enter the Wizards' Circle, or even find it, had Ayeth not come there first. For Baelthrom and Ayeth were the same being separated only by time. The shield would not have known to stop one and not the other.

Freydel had, unwittingly, led Baelthrom here, and Baelthrom was exceedingly clever. But she could not hate Freydel for that, the wizard's intentions were pure, he thought he was doing good, and intention was everything. She found she could not even hate Baelthrom, not even now.

With some surprise, she watched the wizard not turn and run from Baelthrom, but stand his ground, his body trembling as he tried to speak with the Lord of Immortals. An admiral act, Yisufalni thought, but from the raging black magic surging through Baelthrom, this was not a being to be reasoned with.

The black magic consumed Yisufalni, and within it four horsemen stood.

The Under Flow smashed into the Wizards' Circle, cutting off Freydel's incantation. The ground split apart and the stone seats that had stood there for millennia exploded into rocks and dust, hurling Freydel over the edge. Barely hanging on to his staff and his mind, Freydel managed to cushion his deathly fall. He rolled on the grass at the edge of the forest beneath the tower, and lay there.

In horrified awe he watched the Under Flow pouring from the sky into Baelthrom rampaging at the top of the tower. A great fissure snaked through the ancient structure all the way to the ground, rending in two the tower that had stood strong for thousands of years. It shuddered and crumbled brick by brick, the masonry tumbling faster and faster in a deafening roar.

Baelthrom lifted into the air and hovered on demon wings. Holding his old staff in one hand, the Immortal Lord pointed at Freydel. Cold black liquid-like fog seeped up from the earth and smothered him.

In the blackness of the Under Flow, the Knights of Maphrax approached. All power had gone from Yisufalni, leaving her to her inevitable demise. In a way, she'd always known her end would be in darkness. Millennia spent alone, trapped within the Ethereal Planes and cursed to watch the fall of millions from afar, had taught her to accept torment and death, and helplessness.

She could not run—where would she run too?

Yisufalni breathed deeply, trying to control the terror in her heart as each knight surrounded her. There was no violence, just acceptance. Black smoke billowed from the beasts, eight pairs of smoking eye sockets trapping her in their gaze and feeding off her living light.

In unison, the knights lifted a hand and shimmering chains fell about her, biting like broken glass into her skin. Cold seeped through her body and into her heart and bones.

They lifted her from the ground and between them dragged her away. Their mounts galloped on darkness as they descended into lower dimensions unknown to her. She dangled and jolted in their chains, each jerk a searing pain as the chains bit deep into her flesh.

'Maphrax,' the horsemen whispered.

She closed her eyes and focused on the one thing she loved most of all. *Murlonius. Goodbye, my love.*

CHAPTER 13

Orb of Fire

HAELGON staggered to his knees, one hand clutching his staff, the other the collar of his robes.

Luren swayed and grabbed the table for balance. Asaph looked from one wizard to the other then rushed to help Haelgon up. All the officers ceased their discussions abruptly. The wizard's blue eyes turned luminous as he looked into the Flow. Velonorian hurried over, abandoning his conversation with the new Elven commander Asaph had yet to meet.

'Haelgon, what is it?' asked Asaph.

Without looking at him, the High Wizard reached a hand out and gripped his shoulder, eyes wide in horror as he stared at something the Dragon Lord could not see. 'The Wizards' Circle, it has fallen. I feel…weak. Baelthrom…'

Asaph's mind raced, his thoughts ending with Issa.

'It's fallen, Prince Asaph. Our power is…diminished.'

'How? How has it fallen?'

'He came. We were tricked. He has Freydel's staff. I glimpsed three others. Yisufalni, Issa, and…one not of this world!'

Asaph stepped back. 'I must get to her!'

Haelgon grabbed his arm. 'Do not! Baelthrom is there.' He paused and looked to the floor his eyes seeing far away. 'She's escaped—where, how, I don't know. The orbs are gone—safe? I pray. The light is dimming. Our connection to the Circle fades.'

Haelgon blinked and sagged against his staff. 'It is lost.'

Luren, assisted by a Feylint Halanoi soldier, came to stand beside him, his face drawn and suddenly aged. Words escaped the young wizard.

'How can I reach her? How can I be sure?' Asaph pressed.

'I can scry for her.' A quiet voice cut through Asaph's panic. Naksu came to his side. She held her thin white staff lightly, her face serious. Seeing Asaph's desperation, she said, 'Follow me.'

Asaph, the wizards, and Velonorian followed the seer out of the tent. Naksu halted abruptly and Asaph nearly ran into her. The seer frowned, her forehead creasing in concentration.

'What is it?' asked Asaph.

Naksu didn't immediately speak, and instead closed her eyes. 'Something's not right. Something is…'

Asaph couldn't feel anything, but the wizards and seer jumped. Their eyes darted in the direction of the hospital tents. Asaph followed their gaze and did a double take. A swirling black cloud hung above a tent.

'Drumblodd!' Haelgon gasped and ran towards it.

Asaph followed and quickly overtook the wizard. He had no idea what the wizards had sensed but he was ready to fight it. Pulling his sword free he lunged fearlessly into the healing tent. The air shivered and turned thick and dark. He didn't know if the others followed, all sound had ceased. He squinted into the darkness then pushed forwards, it was like trying to walk through a wall of cotton wool.

Further in, the blackness cleared, and there lay Drumblodd. His face was greyer than before but his eyes were open wide, all black and shining like onyx's. Asaph's heart leapt.

Beyond Drumblodd moved another figure, petit and slender. Her strange clothing and cloak were black, and at times it seemed she melded with the blackness seeping around the room. Her face was alien, beautiful but not of this world—pale white skin and a smooth hairless head. Her eyes matched Drumblodd's, all-black onyx's.

She smiled victoriously at Asaph and slowly held up her hands. In one was a black orb just like Freydel's, and in the other…

'The Orb of Fire!' Asaph gasped. He lifted his sword, not sure what to do and wishing he could call the Sun Fire to him. Shouting came from the others behind in the blackness. He was just about to shift into his dragon form when a force smashed into him hurling him from the tent. He hit the ground and rolled, winded.

Spitting out dirt, he looked up. The black cloud had become a swirling vortex. Howling wind gushed around him as the vortex extended into a twisting tornado that reached into the sky, then vanished.

Asaph pushed himself up, picked up his sword and ran back into the tent. The strange black air had gone, and instead a sorry sight greeted him. Naksu was bent over Drumblodd, her hands over his eyes and deep sorrow etched in her face. Haelgon and Luren had hung heads, and Velonorian was inspecting the smoking hole where the vortex had come through. No one spoke.

Naksu closed the dwarf's eyes and straightened. Asaph sheathed his sword and gave a heavy sigh.

'He's gone.' Naksu's voice was barely a whisper. 'Not gone to his rest but to his torment in the Dark Rift.'

'Did you see it? Did you see her, the one who came?' Asaph asked, struggling to keep his voice level.

Naksu looked at him then shook her head.

'I did,' said Asaph. 'It's the one who attacked Issa, the one in league with Baelthrom through this Ayeth I mentioned before. She had an orb, one like Freydel's, exactly the same.'

'Impossible,' said Haelgon, but his eyes lacked conviction.

'It's what I saw,' said Asaph. 'If she has an orb of power, we're up against far more than previously thought. Who knows what other powers are coming out of the Dark Rift?'

Everyone was too grieved to say anything, to do anything, and nothing could be done for Drumblodd. Anger seethed through Asaph and he wondered what he could do now. 'We must scry for Issa and see if she's all right.'

'Yes, of course,' said Naksu weakly.

'I see her,' said the seer, passing her hand over the bowl of still water collected from Issa's Spring, as the river flowing merrily through Port Issa had been named.

Naksu raised her eyebrows. 'She is...*flying!* I see a pale blue dragon.'

'Morhork!' said Asaph, shocked, then pleased, then worried. Would he hurt her? He chewed his lip. 'Where are they?'

'I can't tell. They're moving too fast, I can't keep up with them.' Naksu rubbed her eyes and sat back. She looked exhausted. 'Why don't we try again first thing tomorrow? They won't be flying then.'

Asaph wanted to press for more, but seeing how drained the seer looked, he relented. 'At least she's safe.'

Issa regained her senses. They must have slowed for she was able to make out the rocky features of the ground far below. She still felt woozy and nauseous from the tremendous speed at which Morhork had flown. The sky was pale, indicating the sun had set, and cold wind rushed by making her thankful for the dragon's warm grip.

She looked down at a rocky flat land dotted here and there with copses of short stubby trees. It soon gave way to wetlands, and large swathes of water and reeds stretched all the way to the horizon. The air was hot and humid, and thick swarms of flies rose and fell in the dusk. White and blue plumed birds with long orange legs and beaks hunted the still waters of the swamp.

'Where are we?' Issa raised her voice over the wind and angled her head, trying to get a better look at the dragon.

Morhork took his time answering, his voice quiet. 'We just passed into Western Ostasia.'

Western Ostasia? Why had they come here? She'd never been to the endless swamplands of the South East, and never wanted to go. She didn't know if they were enemy-held lands or not but the sky above, though blanketed in clouds, was not red and raging like Venosia or Maphrax. She wanted to ask him why he had come here but sensed the dragon didn't want to talk.

Instead, she inspected his right paw which he held curled up tight towards his chest as if it hurt him. It certainly looked painful. His scales were blackened and blistered all the way from his scorched claws up to his elbow, and the many red-raw cracks still seeped blood. She wanted to help him, it was the least she could do when he had just saved her life.

They descended towards an unusual round jut of smooth red boulders rising a hundred feet out of the swamp. A strange magenta oasis in an otherwise flat and watery landscape. Morhork circled it and landed before a wide hole where two giant boulders had fallen against each other creating a cave of sorts.

He waddled inside, still holding her in his paw and limping on his blackened one. His chest rumbled as he breathed in and then roared fire into the cave. Issa covered her ears. A bird fled out, squawking in fright, and angry at losing its perfect nesting spot.

Without a word, Morhork set her down towards the entrance, crawled to the back and collapsed. In moments, the dragon was asleep and breathing heavily.

'Magical exhaustion,' Issa nodded. Using magic to fly at such speeds was impressive, but it was clearly costly. The exhausted dragon was now terribly vulnerable. Perhaps it wasn't worth flying without wings, she decided.

She looked around. The cave was empty, and she couldn't sense anything dangerous. At least the dragon had taken her somewhere safe. She sat down on crossed legs and studied the dragon before her. The jagged red scars where his wings had been made her wince. *A dragon who hates humans and yet became one.* She felt sorry for him. The world just wouldn't work the way this dragon wanted it to.

Her eyes travelled back to his burnt paw and she got up. Her own magical reserves were also spent, but she could use a little of it to help him. Carefully she touched his cindered flesh, looking back at his face for any sign of pain or awakening. The dragon slept deeply. Closing her eyes, she let the Flow move through her into his wounds. The seeping blood thickened, and the bloody welts drew together a little. In time, they would heal completely, but she wondered if he would always have a blackened paw.

Realising she ached all over, she settled herself down beside him. Nothing could prevent her from sleeping.

Issa awoke with the dawn as it slowly crept into the cave. Her throat was parched, and her stomach growled almost painfully. She looked up at the enormous ice-blue dragon she lay against. He hadn't moved an inch, not even a claw, and he still breathed heavily. The welts on his blackened talons weren't as angry as yesterday.

Beside her, to her relief, nestled Ehka. He blinked open his eyes and ruffled his feathers.

'There you are, thank the goddess.' Issa stroked his back.

She got up and went to the entrance. The swamp was vast, the endless pools completely still and mirrored the reeds and scattering of trees perfectly. Dragonflies darted above the water, hungrily devouring the clouds of flies that rose and fell. Toads made a continual croaking cacophony and a kingfisher dove into the water, darting back out with its beak filled with frantic fish.

Harpies also inhabited the swamps of Ostasia, Issa remembered, and Saurians too, if there were any lizard-folk left in the world. Her stomach rumbled loudly, and she swallowed against her dry throat. The water of the swamp began to look enticing.

'Well, if there's one thing the Orb of Water can do, it can purify water,' said Issa. *Not the Orb of Water anymore, Illendri—something much more.*

She scrambled awkwardly down the boulders, having to dangle her legs over the edge and lower herself down in places. At the bottom she paused and checked her surroundings, hand resting lightly on her sword. She could hear only the buzz of flies, the croak of toads, and the squawking birds. A bright green dragonfly the size of her hand landed on a reed in front of her, bending it down under its weight. It flew off as she neared causing the reed to whip back up.

She selected a small pool and peered into the muddy water. Dubious, she lifted Illendri and dipped it into the water. 'Purify,' she commanded.

The orb sparkled, turning more blue than purple, and the mud disappeared. Issa laughed and scooped a hand into the crystal-clear water. Tentatively she sipped from her hand.

'It's pure, like spring water,' she said to Ehka. She scooped up some more and slurped it down, and the raven dipped his beak in.

Finally satiated, Issa sat back on her haunches. The water would keep her hunger at bay only for a short time. Unless she wanted to eat frogs or insects, there didn't seem to be too much to eat here. Maybe there were eels, but the thought made her stomach churn.

She pushed herself up and the Flow suddenly jolted. She turned in time to see an enormous ice-blue streak shoot out of the cave and disappear into the clouds.

'He woke up,' she said to Ehka. 'But where's he going? Has he left us here to rot?' Ehka croaked and flew up on to her shoulder.

'We could follow him as ravens, but he flies too fast. I don't know how to use magic like that.' She felt too magically exhausted to even become a raven anyway.

Just as she was pondering what to do, the giant blue streak returned, flying straight into the cave without a pause. Fire burst from the cave, then billowing smoke. What on Maioria was the dragon up to?

Issa ran to the boulders and began the exhausting climb back up. Every now and then heat and fire burst out of the cave. Panting, she staggered into the cave.

The smell of cooking made her stomach rumble, but the sight made her want to vomit. Morhork was busy devouring the charred remains of an enormous crocodile. He took the whole head in his mouth, bit down and twisted it off with a snap. He chewed once and swallowed it whole.

Issa turned away, gagging. *Never have dinner with a dragon…*

'I saved you some over there,' the dragon rumbled over a mouth-full. 'Weakling humans can only eat cooked, tender meat. It just doesn't taste as good as when it's fresh and dripping.'

Issa swallowed, not sure what to say. 'Uh, I'm not sure lizards are my thing… Is there anything else here in the swamps? Maybe some fruit, or something,' she barely whispered the last.

'Ha-ha!' bellowed Morhork. 'Dragons aren't equipped to pick fruit. Eat it or starve. It means nothing to me.'

Issa turned around and forced herself to be grateful. 'Thank you.'

On hesitant feet, she went to the ledge where Ehka pecked at a mound of charred crocodile meat. It was chewy and not to her liking, but her starving body needed it and she forced it down. She ate to the sound of snapping bones, gulping and gnashing, reminding herself over and over to never share dinner with a dragon. When the crocodile's tail finally disappeared down Morhork's throat, she found her own meal a little easier to eat. At least her stomach no longer rumbled, and she felt stronger.

Morhork settled himself down and closed his eyes. Fearful he would go back to sleep, Issa sat down in front of his snout.

'Wait, you've been sleeping for hours. Why are we here?'

Morhork opened one eye and she sensed irritation. 'The trouble with humans is they never shut up. After flying at that speed for so long, I need at least a week of uninterrupted sleep to recover.'

'Thank you,' said Issa, dropping her gaze and toying with the lace of her boot. 'For saving me, that is. It must be hard when your…it must be hard without wings.'

'No. Wings get in the way of the forces I am able to generate and the speed with which I fly.'

Issa considered this and changed the subject. 'But how did you know we had arrived at the tower? Why were you there?'

Morhork eyed her with a golden eye larger than her head. His pupil narrowed to a slit and his voice became a growl. 'When the orb betrayed me, my power bled away. I left before it was gone completely, rather than stay and fight a *human* battle. I went to the Wizards' Circle and there I waited.' He hissed the last, opened both eyes and lifted his head close.

Issa refused to let the dragon intimidate her. 'What were you waiting for?'

He gave a low chuckle. 'To kill the first wizard who arrived, and take their orb, if they had one.' His eyes glittered dangerously.

'So why didn't you?' Issa whispered, fear tickling the hair on her neck.

The dragon looked out of the cave. 'I had no idea an Ancient was there. When I saw her, I felt…differently. The Ancients have helped dragons before. And then you arrived. I planned to stop you but the Flow was gone from me while you combined the orbs. I could not fly, and so I watched. Then *he* came, bringing the Under Flow.'

Issa jumped to her feet. 'We must return to the Wizards' Circle at once. We must find Yisufalni and help them!'

She hadn't finished speaking when Morhork snapped his head closer, his long neck snaking. 'Idiot! The Wizards' Circle is gone, destroyed. Yisufalni is dead. You cannot stand against Baelthrom, you fool. No matter what that goddess has said to you.'

Issa clenched the pommel of her sword, her mind in a panic. 'It cannot be, Yisufalni's not dead. I would…I would know.' Was she really? No, it didn't feel right.

'Dead or captured. It amounts to the same thing,' Morhork sighed and shifted his girth. 'Now the circle's been destroyed, all wizards will be weaker. Even I can feel it in my…other self.

'So what happened to Domenon? Did you kill him?' Issa planted her hands on her hips.

'I cannot kill him, he *is* me. He resides within me, in a way.' The dragon turned thoughtful. 'It's as if I have absorbed him into my true form, and yet, I can still become him.'

Issa began to laugh. 'So, you have become that which you despise, a Dragon Lord.'

'I'm no half-breed!' the dragon roared.

Issa covered her ears.

Slowly the echo faded away and she dropped her hands. Morhork fell into a brooding silence, his talons raking back and forth on the ground, creating deep grooves. 'But I can still become the man,' he rumbled to himself.

'So are you going to kill me and take Illendri?' Issa goaded.

The wingless dragon considered her for a long moment then looked away. He seemed almost *sorrowful*. 'When the orb forced me back into my pure form, memory returned to me.'

'Memory of what?' asked Issa.

Morhork gazed at her without blinking. 'I have tainted myself with human thoughts, human feelings. I have become impure, compromised.'

'You have empathy, you mean.' Issa nodded and folded her arms.

The dragon spoke slowly, thoughtfully. 'Perhaps. But that's not the memory I meant. I remembered I was there when your parents cast their powerful Web of Forgetting.' Issa caught her breath. 'Sheyengetha knew all along, for trees are immune to such spells, trees can never forget. So are dragons…but my pet human was not. Now we are one, their spell has fallen away, and that memory has returned to me.'

Issa stepped closer to the dragon. 'You know where they went, where they are?' She paused and stared into those huge golden eyes. 'They're here aren't they? That's why you brought me here.'

'No, I don't know for sure. But there were rumours a long time ago, and in the Recollection there are memories held by dragons now dead— killed by Baelthrom when he invaded Drax—of a bard and seer living amongst the Saurians. Now all those things add up, and we are here.'

Issa turned towards the cave entrance and slowly walked towards it. 'My parents might be somewhere out there, even now.'

'Perhaps. I did not say they were still here, maybe they are both dead, but the Saurians will know. I brought you here, it's up to you to find them. You'd do well to remember that Saurians despise humans.'

'Thank you, Morhork,' Issa whispered, her heart thumping as she stared out over the swamp wondering where her parents might be. 'You are a being of conflicts. I don't know why you choose to help me now but thank you.'

The Flow rushed towards Morhork. She turned and saw Domenon standing in the place of the dragon. He looked at his blackened hand and winced as he tried to move his fingers.

'It hurts, the change to a man,' said the wizard. 'And this form feels so weak and cumbersome. The limb also hurts more in this form, though it pains me less today.'

'I tried to heal it with magic. It helped, but it's going to take a long time,' said Issa.

Domenon nodded, perhaps his way of saying thank you. 'It may always be like this.' He took a cloth from his pocket and wrapped it around his hand. Holding it by his side, he walked towards her.

The tall man was impressive with his sweep of black hair, dark eyes, black leather clothing and purple wizard's cape flowing out behind him. She laid a protective hand on the orb at her side.

'You have no need to worry, I'll not try to take it,' said Domenon coming to her side. 'The thought of touching any of them again is abhorrent. At least my power has not diminished as much as it will have for the other wizards, my magic is not tied to the Circle.'

'You forget that Freydel has power taught to him by Ayeth,' said Issa.

'And that is another thing,' said Domenon. 'You should not have withheld such information from me. That Freydel is now in league with Bael—'

'Ayeth,' Issa corrected him.

'Whatever. He will soon be one and the same. Maioria is in grave peril,' said Domenon.

'Is that why you chose to help me—us—now your own plans of domination have failed?' she asked caustically.

Dark eyes regarded her, but he said nothing. She knew she had spoken the truth, but what did it matter now?

'So, are you coming to help me find my parents?' She changed the subject, not wanting to talk about Freydel until she had thought about it some more.

'No, that's for you and you alone. I go north to my own kin.'

'And what of the battle?' asked Issa.

'That, too, is for you humans,' Domenon snorted, forgetting for a moment that he was a human.

'I thought as much.' Issa sighed and turned back to surveying the swamp. She massaged her sore shoulder with one hand.

'Are you hurt?' Domenon asked.

'I ache all over! But no, not really. Forget about me, what about the others? What about Yisufalni? Will you look for her? I *know* she's still alive. Perhaps I'll call the boatman.'

Domenon took a deep breath and let it out slowly. When he spoke, he sounded weary. 'I'll try.'

Issa closed her eyes, gathered the Flow and mentally called the raven form to her. Unlike Domenon's change, it did not hurt. She looked up at the man staring down at her. With a squawk, she jumped into the air and circled above him.

He pointed south. 'Hallanstaryx is that way.'

She cawed and turned in that direction with Ehka. The Flow moved, a blue streak shot beneath her, turned and disappeared to the north.

CHAPTER 14

Hallanstaryx

ISSA scanned the endless swamps, the warm wind humid and heavy beneath her wings.

She couldn't imagine being here in summer, the cloying heat would be unbearable. The day wore on and her wings began to ache, they'd seen nothing but swamp. With her avian senses she could feel the ocean hundreds of miles ahead. Knowing these things instinctively made her wonder if birds were ever truly lost.

She followed Ehka's lead and descended to land and rest on a stumpy tree. The thick bough looked strong enough to take her human weight, so she shifted form.

'There's nothing here, Ehka.' She slumped back against the trunk. 'We've been flying all day and still nothing.'

The bird appeared unconcerned and busied himself preening. She slipped down the tree to the water's edge and took out the orb to purify a pool of water. They then continued their search with Ehka leading the way.

Morhork had said there'd been rumours of a bard and seer amongst Saurians, but it didn't mean they were still here, or that they were even her parents. Perhaps they'd left a long time ago, after all, who'd want to inhabit a swamp? *There's a whole world they could hide in, why would they stay here?* Worse, they might be dead. The sun began to sink into the horizon and her hope with it.

A high-pitched screech snapped her out of her musings. Looking up, she saw something flying high in the sky. *Harpy!* She'd know that creeping feeling anywhere. Issa dropped low amongst the reeds and landed on the grass clumping around a small tree. Ehka landed beside her and they both watched the sky.

More screeching came and four harpies circled high above. Harpies ate anything meaty, humans, birds, deer… *But they don't normally hunt at dusk,* Issa thought, her heart thumping.

The tree they hid under was small and withered, it offered poor protection. She waited several long minutes as the sky turned a deep orange, yet still the harpies remained.

They came closer, Issa could make out their black eyes and smooth breasts. How long did she wait for them to attack? There were only four of them, she could take out two with magic before they even knew what had hit them. Ehka could harry one while she fought with her sword against the other. It was either fight or sit here all night. Harpies could see well in the dark, too. Perhaps that's when they would attack, and she didn't fancy fighting in the swamp in the dark with crocodiles about. Besides, was she the Raven Queen or not?

Flattening herself against the tree, she looked at Ehka and the bird looked at her. She moved fast. Jumping into the Flow, she grabbed at the magic. In the same instance she released her raven form, struck the talisman up and shouted, 'Fire!'

Indigo fire exploded into the two closest together. They didn't even have time to screech. White and brown feathers floated down like snow and two blackened, smoking bodies plunged into the swamp.

Their companions screamed and attacked. Harpy magic moved, and dark fire rolled towards Issa in a wave. She held her shield firm as it rolled over it, then unsheathed her sword.

The first harpy swiped her talons at her. Issa ducked then jumped up as it passed, grabbing a handful of slick, auburn feathers in her free hand. For a moment, she clung onto the back of the harpy. Unable to carry her weight, the harpy rolled in the air and fell towards the swamp. Issa raised her sword and slammed it deep into the harpy's back.

Cold, muddy water blasted Issa's face. She floundered, found the swamp bed and shoved herself up, her feet sinking into the soft mud. She gasped, stood, and looked at the bloody water and the bobbing body of the harpy.

Ehka squawked, barely dodging the other harpy as she zoomed past. Issa raised her hand, felt the Flow rush through her, and a hail of mud battered the bird-woman. The harpy tumbled senseless into the swamp and sank.

Issa waited but the harpy did not emerge. The orange sky was fading fast. Far away she heard another screech. 'Let's go!'

She clambered onto the bank, shifted form and launched into the air. She looked behind and wished she hadn't. Between her and the horizon, a small dark cloud moved. Harpies, lots of them, maybe even a whole brood! She swallowed. She was in their land now. *We'd better find Hallanstaryx, and fast.*

She used the Flow to push the wind under their wings, but another glance back told her the harpies were still gaining. Magic was stronger in one's true form, and as a raven she couldn't best her magically adept harpy pursuers.

Suddenly the wind vanished from her wings, she didn't even know what had hit her as she spun in the air and fell alongside Ehka. A shimmering green net revealed itself and engulfed her, its enchantment forcing the raven form from her.

She hit the water hard. Winded, she thrashed in a wild panic to find the surface to fill her burning lungs, but the net dragged her under. A strong hand suddenly gripped her arm and leg in a crushing vice and pulled her up. She burst into the air, gasping and spluttering. In the blur, it looked like a crocodile's claw gripping her arm, all green and scales. She fought against it, but this only made the net tighten, crushing her arms against her body.

Harpies screeched and the thing that held her hissed and screamed back. Ehka struggled beside her also caught in a net.

'Don't fight it, it will tighten,' she said to the bird with her mind since she could barely move her chin to talk. At least she could breathe and see, and so she helplessly stared at the scene unfolding in the dusk.

Torches lit up an area of swamp, about five lights flickering at the end of tall sticks thrust into the mud. Between them ran huge upright lizards on two, heavily muscled legs. They had long, rounded snouts and gleaming gold, brown or green eyes with black slitted pupils. Red forked tongues darted in an out and when they spoke in their croaking hissing language, she glimpsed mouths lined with dozens of fangs.

Thick tails swayed behind them as they ran, helping them to keep their balance. Their arms and hands, though covered in scales, were much like a human's with four fingers and a thumb, but their fingers ended in sharp talons. In the firelight they seemed to range in colour from green to brown and all shades in between. Some were slender and smaller than others, maybe they were young or female.

They wore not so much clothes but adornments. They wore leather belts within which were tucked thin knives, and brightly woven blue and red bands on their arms and legs. They held spears or bows decorated with red, blue and yellow feathers. The spears they hurled into the cloud of descending harpies. It did not escape Issa that not one of those spears missed. Bird women thudded and splashed into the swamp, spears embedded through chests and wings.

Issa struggled to reach the Flow but the enchanted net she was in prevented her. Maybe if she rolled, she could get away, *and risk sinking into the swamp!*

The shadows around her moved and gathered oddly. Two yellow demon eyes blinked at her.

'Maggot!' she gasped. 'You shouldn't be here, it's dangerous right now.'

A Saurian jumped from the swamp to land on all fours before her. Issa froze in terror. His green eyes stared at her, pupils narrowing to mere slits, red tongue slithering out to almost touch her face before sliding back into its mouth. Then the lizard man bounded away to rejoin the battle.

Maggot's eyes materialised again. Although worried for him, she was very glad he was here.

'Maggot, stay safe. I don't know what will happen, but they haven't killed us yet when they could have. Stay in the shadows but don't let them see you.'

A group of Saurians ran towards her, spears held high, expressionless faces more frightening than if they had been howling. She closed her eyes expecting them to trample or spear her but instead they bounded over her and all she felt was the wind as they passed.

From the whoosh of spears and arrows, the strange hissing howls of Saurians and the screeching of harpies, Issa couldn't be sure who was winning the fight. As the battle moved, all she could see in the growing dark was the tall grasses in front of her face and the flickering of the torchlight beyond.

Maggot chewed, clawed and pulled on the net that wrapped around her like a vice. 'It won't break, Issy,' he groaned.

'Leave it, Maggot, and go hide.'

The sound of screeching and growls of Saurians became fainter and suddenly stopped. Issa's eyes darted around. Had they left her here to die?

A Saurian leapt from the tall reeds and splashed into the shallows beside her. It was dark green with a lighter scaled underbelly. She was too frightened to make a sound. The Saurian pushed its thick round snout into her face, its golden eyes narrowing to slits, its tongue flicking out to touch her cheek. It raised its spear and she clenched her eyes shut. She had never met a lizard-man before, their powerful physique was frightening enough.

The blow never came. She opened an eye.

Another Saurian jumped beside the first. This one was sand coloured with pale yellow eyes. It bent to inspect Ehka.

'Don't hurt him,' Issa gasped. She found the net tightening with every tiny move she made, every breath. She prayed Maggot had disappeared into the shadows.

The Saurians spoke to each other, croaking and hissing, then looked at her. The green one gripped her arm and inspected her wrist. *Ely's bracelet,* Issa thought. Were they thieves? Dragons liked gold, did Saurians like silver? They were both reptiles after all.

The paler one leaned close, eyes widening and narrowing, tongue flicking in and out. She began to feel dizzy, mesmerised. Then the snout of the green one darted from behind. It opened its jaw, and two long, almost translucent fangs flipped down from the roof of his mouth.

She screamed as it bit deep into her shoulder. Agony seeped through her shoulder and then it went numb. The world wavered and disappeared.

Under a red sky Marakon and his soldiers walked—not quite marching but seeking to move quietly, always looking upwards, always afraid Baelthrom was watching from above. Even their conversations were hushed.

It had taken them days to navigate down from the cave where the demon tunnel exited. They had to make a path through rubble, heaving rock and sweating in the clammy atmosphere, daring to use magic when necessary. Now and then icy winds froze the sweat on their faces and made their joints ache even more. They slept under only blankets listening to the howling wind.

It was slow and dangerous. A particularly narrow section of path had already crumbled under the weight of a horse. Both horse and soldier had fallen with the rubble screaming to their deaths a hundred feet below. Another path had had to be cut.

It took a day for them to reach the fallen soldier, no one wanted to leave him. They buried him under piles of stone and, against Marakon's conscience, butchered and ate the horse to save the last of their meagre rations. It also hid the evidence that they had passed this way. *What a cursed place to die,* Marakon had thought, *leaving your body in this barren, forsaken place.*

Now they'd almost reached lower ground, the wind was less frigid, but their supplies were pitiful and waterskins empty. The landscape north, west and south was the same, endless hills of what could only be described as scree. There was no water to be found and no food, neither animal nor plant.

'Where in the Abyss are we?' Marakon sighed and leant against his horse, ignoring his growling stomach.

'I've been hunting for ley lines,' said Shelley, coming up to him. She'd found a gnarly old stick and used it for support. Her face was pale and drawn. They'd all lost weight. This was the opposite of how he'd wanted to arrive for battle. Weak, exhausted and spent before he'd even used his sword. Not that there was any battle to be had, even the enemy wasn't here.

'They're hard to read and almost non-existent—it's unnatural,' she muttered, and he struggled to hear her over the howling wind. 'But if what I've read is correct, we're south of Diredrull in what was once called the Low Hills. Once fertile green lands where grapes grew.'

Marakon squinted over the wasteland, struggling to imagine it was ever fertile. 'It's all gone.'

Issa floated in and out of a surreal dream.

She knew she had been poisoned but the details were hazy. In parts of the dream she was being carried by strange lizard men. Thick, short trees spread their canopies above, and among the leaves shone beautiful lights in all shades of purples, yellows and oranges. She wondered if they were fairies but as she peered at a glowing pink one, it didn't dance or disappear and instead remained still, like a light in a bottle.

A lizard-man came into view and looked down at her. He was all hazy, then he looked away and the dream moved on.

The trees were gone now and instead she saw buildings made of grey stones. Some were small, no larger than a cottage, and others large. All were covered in angular writing or images of animals and plants carved expertly into the stone.

The houses faded away and a huge structure came into view, pushing up through the trees. A pyramid, but not like the ones on Aralansia. This one was a giant stepped pyramid, and whilst it was shorter, it was certainly wider. Steps led all the way up its steep sides, and there was a dark doorway at the top. There were statues up there too, but they were too far away to make out clearly with her hazy vision. She saw many Saurians walking at the pyramid's base. They looked at her, paused for a moment, then carried on.

The pyramid faded. It was dark now. She peered into the blackness waiting for her eyes to adjust, but they didn't. She fell asleep.

A terrible pain in her shoulder broke into her dream and then she was rushing back to consciousness. Whatever gripped her shoulder, released and with it went the pain, the fog, and the poison.

She stared into the face of a green-scaled Saurian. It may be the one she had seen earlier, but they all looked alike. Beside him stood the sandy one, and beyond them, a large grey ceiling rose in steps to a distant central point. Every layer of stone had text or scenes. Orange light flickered, cast by a hearth or braziers she couldn't see. She had to be inside the pyramid, or *a* pyramid.

'Where am I?' she asked, her voice weak.

The two Saurians said nothing, looked at each other and then moved away. Ehka landed beside her, his presence comforting. So, they'd set him free unharmed, that was a relief. His soft feathers against her thigh told her her armour had been taken.

She tried to move and found she couldn't. Was the poison still in effect? She tried again and slowly strength tingled through her body. She looked around and found she was lying on a stone bed. With shaking arms, she pushed herself up.

Two fires burned in sconces a short distance away offering some warmth. Beyond the fires, a large stone staircase led up to a wide central doorway which was pitch black beyond. Braziers on the walls also lit up the giant stone chamber.

Apart from her underwear, she was naked—her armour, her weapons, her orb…gone. She looked around for the Saurians, but they had disappeared. Gingerly, she touched the two bloody bite marks on her shoulder.

'They will heal fast and with no marksss, especially with that bracelet you wear.' The female voice was too low and soothing to make her jump, but Issa looked around, heart-pounding, wondering where it had come from.

'But you will be weak for a while. It was necessary, to ensure you cannot harm usss.' The voice continued, ending every 's' in a long hiss, then added ponderously, 'We have been waiting for one such as you.'

'Where are you? Where are my clothes?' demanded Issa. How dare they take the orb.

'Illendri is safe. And you needn't worry, we are not in league with Baelthrom.'

Issa rubbed her wrist around Ely's bracelet, surprised she still had it when everything else had been taken. 'Then why has it been taken along with my stuff?'

'To protect us from you,' hissed the voice.

'Then why not the bracelet?' asked Issa. She pinpointed the voice to be coming from the pitch-black doorway at the top of the stone staircase.

'We knew the one who forged it,' the soothing voice echoed softly in the chamber. 'And that might be why we let you live.'

Issa was taken aback. They knew Ely's mother, Harianna?

As if reading her thoughts, the voice said. 'The Tree of Life is sacred to us. The one who made it came to us in the same manner as the priestesses of old; seeking wisdom and healing powers. Priestess Harianna was the last to make the journey here to acquire such knowledge. We have seen no priestesses since.

'The Order of the Goddess is corrupted. They have given in to greed for power, with many now turning to Baelthrom and the powers he can offer.'

Eyes flashed in the darkness of the doorway, large and pale blue. 'We have seen it and watched many things come to pass. I am what you humans call the Oracle.'

'You know many things yet remain hidden. Why don't you show yourself?' Issa challenged.

Her breath caught in her throat as a massive white snake appeared in the doorway, then its huge coiling body unfolded rapidly out from the entrance. Ehka squawked and flew up to a safe ledge as the great white snake flowed down the steps like liquid. It slowed as it approached Issa, its red forked tongue darted out of its muzzle and a hood flared out from its neck. Blue eye slits narrowed, it opened its mouth and hissed, two huge fangs protruding.

Issa pressed herself back against the wall, her heart pounding and cold sweat running down her back. The snake closed its mouth, blessedly hiding its fangs, but pushed its smooth head barely a foot from Issa. She swallowed as the snake glared at the raven mark on her chest then back up at her face.

The snake turned away abruptly then lifted itself impossibly high into the air to inspect the strange inscriptions halfway up the wall.

'Who are you?' Issa asked, her voice trembling.

'I am Hallanstaryx, Queen and Oracle. All Oracles of the Saurians are called this, the name itself means 'Oracle'. And you are she, the Raven Queen, there can be no doubt. But will you remain as she?' The snake whispered the last as if to herself.

'What do you mean?' Issa frowned. 'If you're the Oracle, have you seen an end to this war? Have you seen us win?' She suddenly found a hundred questions.

The snake's tongue flicked in and out. 'The future is dark concerning the survival of Maioria, this you know from your wizards and witches. You have come here to find something lost to you, and you will find it. But you will also discover things you do not want to know but must.'

Everything the Snake Queen said felt loaded with mystery. Issa shook her head for all the questions she wanted to ask.

'If I fail, then there is no more Maioria,' Issa spoke quietly her greatest fear, her greatest, crushing burden.

'If you fail, and that time is close, there can be another,' the Snake Queen lowered herself and looked at Issa, her whole body motionless apart from her flickering tongue.

Issa frowned. 'I don't understand. There is only one Raven Queen, and she cannot fail.'

'There are three *potential* Raven Queens. The one that came through the human Oracle died, and the other is far away and unaware, just as you were unaware.'

Issa felt sick. She knew there *could* be three but had always thought they had all failed or died. In truth, she didn't want to know about the other Raven Queens or the prophecies and all they meant. A part of her still wished to be free of the whole thing. *But now another still lives?*

Breathing heavily, she placed her hands upon the altar. She knew and accepted she was the Raven Queen, but what if she failed? She could finish it all right now. Find the other Raven Queen and divulge herself of the responsibility and this awful war. She would be free.

'I know you've seen the White Raven in your dreams,' the Snake Queen's voice cut through her thoughts. When Issa didn't say anything, the Oracle continued. 'It signals death and danger. The end is unfolding quickly now, as surely it must. There is always chaos at the end. The time of your failing is near, but this other Raven Queen can pick up the mantle. However, she will not be as strong, she will not have experienced all the things that has made you hard as iron—for now.'

Issa stared at the enormous snake, her heart in her throat. Deep within she knew the Oracle was not lying.

The Snake Queen continued. 'There are others who have come to know of the Prophecies of Zanufey, beings who have no place on this planet. Beings who reach out to us through time and space through the Dark Rift.'

'Lona... The Yurgha,' Issa breathed.

The Snake Queen blinked, her second eyelids sliding swiftly back after the first. 'They are hunting for this third Raven Queen even as they try to destroy you. They will rise her to power—power that comes from within the Dark Rift, I have seen it, I am the Oracle.'

'What can I do? What can be done?' Issa stepped around the altar towards the snake. The snake remained motionless for a long moment, silently regarding her.

'I only tell you what I have seen. Only one Raven Queen can rise, the others will fall. When the darkness comes into you—and come it must—

then will begin your greatest trial. Fail, yes, you might.'

'How do you know so much? Why hasn't Zanufey said anything?' Issa demanded. She needed answers, not more questions!

The snake retreated towards the stone steps, her voice sounding ponderous. 'We are not polluted by corruption like humans are. Our race is pure, kept apart from all the others. We hear our Great God Staryx as a clear voice in our minds, but it is not in the nature of our gods to tell us what to do. They only guide us.'

Issa let out a long sigh.

'You are not alone in this,' said Hallanstaryx. 'For many years we have awaited the coming of the Raven Queen, for she signals our end, too.'

'It's not my choosing.' Issa shook her head, feeling very weary.

'You bring war to us,' the Snake Queen said simply. 'Though we do not wish for it, we must comply. The war will come to us whether we fight alongside the Raven Queen or not. It cannot be undone. But by her side there is a chance. Without her, there is none. And after? Ancient prophecies tell us a vastly different world will come into being. The Raven Queen signals the end of endings.'

The Snake Queen spoke in riddles. Issa rolled her words over and again in her mind. *The end of endings. There is something important in this. Something I can't quite grasp!*

'I don't understand. How does the darkness come into me? There must be a way I can fight it. Why is everything unfolding quickly now?' The questions weren't good enough. She paced the cold stone floor as the Snake Queen spoke.

'We do not know how. But you will enter the darkness so all else has a chance to reach the light. Things unfold rapidly now because our Great Goddess Woetala is dying. The life energy, the female magnetic energy of our world is draining into the Dark Rift. The Orb of Life that Baelthrom took ensured the enslavement of this planet to his will, and now the last female Ancient and true Keeper of the Orb of Life is in his chains.' The Oracle spoke with sorrow, her head moving back and forth as she looked into the distance.

Issa had for so long thought only of Zanufey, the guardian of Aralansia. Rarely had she considered the guardians of Maioria; Doon and Woetala. There was too much to consider, too many huge problems that she alone could not solve. She struggled to gain perspective on what had to be done. Unable to grasp a solution, she turned her attention on the reason why she had come here. 'You, or the one before you, met my parents. You know where they are, don't you?'

The Snake Queen looked at her. 'The seer and the bard came to us a long time ago, fore-warned were we by a raven. The musicman is not amongst us anymore, though he is near. But he is not the man he used to be, he was drained by our enemies and now grief has taken part of him.'

Issa's heart and hope rose and fell with the Oracle's words, they had to be her parents. 'He has to be my father, what's happened to him? Where's my mother, the seer?'

The huge snake regarded her for a long time without moving apart from her tongue flicking in and out. Then she turned away with a hissing sigh. 'After the musicman and his seer came to us, we were attacked by the entire brood of harpies, both from the East and the West. Then came Baelthrom's Dread Dragons. It was too coordinated to be chance. Hallanstaryx nearly fell.' The snake rolled a portion of her long body over to reveal an angry red scar slicing several feet along her side. Issa winced.

'The musicman believed they were betrayed.'

'What do you mean, betrayed? By whom?' asked Issa, her mind whirring.

'By the demon who helped them in the demon tunnels.' The Oracle did not elaborate.

Issa swallowed audibly. *Never trust a demon!* And yet, her friends were demons. Did Gedrock know about any of this? Surely he must!

'When the enemy came, many Saurians were injured, including your mother and father, and many were killed,' said Hallanstaryx. 'Your father felt guilt and sought revenge. Much changed. The music left him and, unable to play for us as was the agreement for him to live amongst us, he left for fear of another attack, and went into the swamps. We saw little of him after that. But it is better you find out for yourself.'

CHAPTER 15

Musicman

ISSA decided not to protest as the blindfold was pulled over her eyes.

It was either that or be bitten and poisoned again, and her shoulder was still sore from the previous bite. Helpless and at their mercy, they lifted and tied her on to the back of a Saurian.

'I can walk,' she said indignantly, but they ignored her, and so began a long jolting journey through the swamps.

The Saurians didn't speak much, not even amongst themselves, but with careful questioning, she learned a little about them and their history. Baelthrom hadn't bothered invading the swamps, who would? He didn't need to for his allies the harpies had grown more powerful and numerous. The Saurians now fought a war of resources, and their vitality dwindled in response to Maioria's.

It was with a certain amount of horror that she realised this race of lizard-people had resigned themselves to their fate, that one day there would be no Saurian on Maioria. *We shall leave this realm and go to our Pure Place. There is no going back, we look only forwards at what must be,'* they had said.

She was about to ask how much further when they stopped and lifted her from the back of the Saurian she'd been riding. The blindfold was pulled from her eyes and she stood swaying and disorientated. Ehka cawed, letting her know he was there.

The dark green Saurian she had first seen when captured, pointed a long, clawed finger into the distance. 'That way,' he said.

Issa squinted over the flat swamp but could see nothing other than swarms of flies and flocks of long-necked birds. There weren't even many trees in the area, just long swathes of water broken up by clumps of reeds and tall grasses.

The Saurian passed her a bag. 'Food and water. Enough to survive for a few days should you get lost.' They turned to leave.

'Wait!' she said, afraid to be alone out here. 'Er, what are your names?'

'Ekem,' said the dark green one.

'And I, Ata,' said the tan-coloured lizard-man, his voice was deeper. 'Watch the skies for harpies.'

'How will I return?' Issa asked.

'The musicman will know,' said Ekem, and then they bounded away through the reeds leaving her at the mercy of the swamps.

Skin-creeping magic moved, and something pressed on her leg.

'Maggot!' Issa watched the demon materialise from the gathering shadows, his yellow eyes wide and shining. 'You've been watching all this time?'

'Only when you left the pyramid, Saurian magic stopped me following. I waited to see if you were alive or dead.'

'Thanks,' said Issa sourly.

She thought about what the Snake Queen had said. Should she go to the Murk this very moment and ask Gedrock what the hell was going on? What *had* happened to her parents at the hands of demons? But as she looked out over the swamp her heart called to her. Out there was her father.

She started stomping through the water. As each step sunk into the mud and clung to her foot, her energy waned. It wasn't long before she was soaked through and muddy.

The journey was slow going but she pushed on. As she walked, she considered turning into a raven and flying over this muck. *But I want to find my father with my own eyes, in my true form.* Perhaps it was a silly thing, but it felt important that she be Issa, his long-lost daughter, and not the Raven Queen. She wished she didn't even have her Dread Dragon armour on. And so she slogged onwards, hands hovering near sword and talisman in case any crocodile or harpy should suddenly appear.

Heavy rain clouds clustered and the day turned overcast. Without any wind, it became close and muggy, and sweat stuck her clothes to her body in a most uncomfortable manner. Annoying flies slapped into her face and clung there with increasing frequency.

Maggot, however, was having a great time, jumping into the air and gulping them down. Every now and then he'd release a huge belch that echoed across the swamp—shocking for his tiny size. But no matter how many he ate, there always seemed to be a hundred more. The sky began to darken as dusk fell and she hugged her arms. She certainly didn't fancy wandering the swamps at night.

'Over there, Issy.' Maggot pointed a clawed finger to the horizon and rose into the air on flapping wings.

Issa squinted and spied a thin plume of smoke rising in the still air. She took a deep breath, suddenly feeling overwhelmed, and quickened her pace.

The house poking out of the swamp was tiny, little more than a small barn, and made entirely of wood that was old and warped in places. A wide roof made of planks hung over a porch, protecting it from the frequent rain. A chair stood on the porch beside the front door. The door itself was a rickety thing that clung on to its hinges at an odd angle. There was one small window and possibly light beyond, but a curtain was drawn across it.

Ehka landed on the bannister as Issa took the first creaking step up to the front door. Maggot hid behind her knees. She paused and swallowed. What if her father wasn't there? What if it wasn't him? What if he was dead? It was all too much. She suddenly wondered if she could bring herself to knock on the door at all.

The decision was made for her. The door flew open and magic in the form of luminous yellow-green energy exploded out. Issa barely had time to duck as it whizzed past her crackling. Maggot vanished into the shadows and Ehka squawked into the air.

'Wait! I mean no harm,' said Issa, flattening herself on the stairs. 'Are you Thanon Bard?'

'Who's there? What do you want?' a male voice rasped.

Issa lifted her head and dared to peer over the top step. Stood in the doorway was a thin, stooped old man whose grey, tattered shirt hung off his bony shoulders. His grey and white beard was poorly cut, and his grey hair hung limply to his shoulders. Around his eyes a rag of cloth was tied. He couldn't actually see her, she realised. Was this frail old man her father? He was surely far too old. She struggled to find the words.

'I'm your... I'm a friend,' Issa forced the words out.

'You don't sound or smell Saurian and there are no *friends* round here,' the man said. He reached behind the door and pulled out a sword.

'I came from the Saurians,' Issa said, daring to stand up. 'Please, put away your sword. I—'

Ehka cawed loudly then flew to the man's feet where he continued to caw.

'A raven?' whispered the man. He bent down and reached a searching hand towards the bird. When he touched Ehka, he paused and inhaled sharply as something passed between them. His mouth opened, and his face contorted, then he sunk to the floor, his shoulders shaking.

Issa ran to him. 'What is it? What's wrong? I can help you. I have some healing ability.'

The man reached up to her with gnarled, calloused hands, feeling her arms then her shoulders, chin and up to her cheeks where he rested them gently.

'Can it really be so? Is it really you? Our little Issalena?'

Issa began to cry.

All the past terrible months and years came crashing down upon her as they embraced. Issa lost herself in a sea of emotions. Nothing was said, not even when the tears had dried and the shaking had subsided.

When they finally drew apart, Issa looked at the old man who was her father, old before his time. The faded green swirls of the bardic tattoos on his tanned skin reached up beneath the worn collars and cuffs of his clothes.

'What happened to your eyes?' Issa asked gently, holding his arms, not wanting to let him go.

After a long moment he said, 'You'd better come inside.'

Warmth from a small log fire engulfed her as she stepped inside the house that was little more than a hovel. The heat drove back the damp of the swamp, and behind the glass of the log burner she could see clumps of peat burning.

There was one tiny stove and oven, a single bed pallet, one chair with an old cushion, and a table made out of a thick tree stump. Using his hands to feel everything he did, Thanon hooked back the curtain covering one of the two windows and the fading light of day filtered in. He poked a stick into the fire until it was alight and then lit a couple of candles. Soon the place was glowing and almost homely. He clearly didn't need candles to see, so perhaps he did it for her benefit and perhaps for the extra warmth they provided.

Without saying anything he passed to her a misshapen, firm peach-coloured fruit and set about pouring some small round vegetables and water into a pan. Issa was bursting with questions, but she sensed he needed to take his time. A thick cloak of sadness draped around his shoulders, and her presence had helped lift it, if only momentarily.

'What is it?' Issa asked, sitting down on the only chair. 'The fruit, that is.' She added hastily, remembering he couldn't see what she held up.

'It's a swamp apple. I've come to prefer them to the others, thankfully. It *is* possible to survive in the swamps, but the food is the same every day. There is little variety, and I can no longer catch fish or the unfortunate croc.'

Issa's stomach rumbled, and she bit into the hard fruit. A burst of tart and sweet hit her tongue and she devoured it, setting the core aside. Ehka jumped onto the table and pecked at it.

Issa shook her head. 'I've so many questions, so many years have passed... When the Dread Dragons came... When Fraya told me she wasn't my real mother... The raven came too. Uh, I don't know where to begin.' She stopped suddenly as overwhelming memories threatened to make her cry again.

Silently, Thanon reached over, found her hand, and squeezed it. Tears slipped down Issa's face, so much time had been lost.

'I'm all right,' he said. 'Alive, but nothing more. Now you're here I...I can believe again, I can love, again. But anyway, the most important thing you want to know is where is Eritara. Where is your mother?'

'Yes,' Issa said in barely a whisper. 'Why isn't she here? Why are you living out here in this bleak and defenceless place so far from people who can help you?'

Leaving the pan to slow boil, her father let out a long sigh and sat down on the edge of the bed. He was about to speak then instead reached under the bed and pulled out a long covered object with a bulbous end. He rested it lengthways on his knees and pushed back the old cloth. Underneath was a beautiful lap harp, its smooth polished wood gleaming happily in the firelight. Issa was reminded that before her sat a Master Musician, and she longed to hear his music.

Lost in thought, Thanon stroked the wood, his hands seeing what his eyes could not. 'There's too much to tell, too much to explain. I've not played or sung since the day it happened, Eritara. Since the day you were lost to me.'

Issa leaned forwards, butterflies in her stomach. 'Tell me,' she breathed. 'I must know, no matter how bad.'

Thanon gripped the harp, his mind made up, and began to play with a sudden firm hand. Rich notes flooded into the cabin, immediately capturing Issa's attention and soothing the butterflies in her stomach.

The music was neither happy nor sad but carried within its notes a story. She leaned back and let the music flow into her and carry her with it. Ehka settled down and ruffled his feathers, dozing.

Issa felt herself drifting too, but not to sleep. Her father's playing was seamless, beautiful, a part of his being expressed. Mesmerised by his strumming fingers, she didn't even notice he had begun to sing until his voice rose a little higher. As he sung his words created pictures in her mind so that she didn't so much as hear his words as see the pictures in her mind his music was making.

Entranced, she saw her mother, Eritara, just as Sheyengetha had shown her with her sea-green eyes and long, dark-brown hair. She was smiling, and her father took her hand. Around them clustered Saurians, and before them Hallanstaryx the white snake. There was joy in the air.

The images changed, her mother's belly swelled.

'Another child?' Issa's eyes widened. *I have a brother or sister?*

'It was a miracle, after all that had happened,' said Thanon without pausing the notes. 'But one day, years later, we were expecting another child. However, it seems a happy life was never meant for us.' His voice trailed off into a whisper and his music turned dark and turbulent.

In her mind, harpies filled the skies, thousands of them, and peaceful Hallanstaryx descended into chaos. The music moved faster, and the images of a bloody, violent battle whizzed past as if Thanon didn't want to linger on the details. Bloodied grass…Weapons and bodies—both Saurian and harpy…Screams, howls, screeches, and the clash of weapons and magic assaulted her senses. She captured glimpses, nothing more.

Thanon, then a younger, fitter man, fought harpies, his sword swinging, bardic tattoos glowing. Behind him stood her mother, her hands raised commanding the Flow. For the speed at which the images moved, the battle lasted a long time.

The music calmed, becoming low and sorrowful. The images turned blurry and dull and then empty. Thanon ceased singing, letting the harp carry them gently in the aftermath.

'The demon who helped us through the demon tunnels betrayed us to the harpies who hunted us the other side of the yew. Together, they made a bargain.' Images formed in her mind again as Thanon narrated.

'The harpies only wanted us, they had no interest in the Saurians. Many died because of us being amongst them. So we ran, hoping to draw them away and then hide. But there were so many harpies, and their magic so strong. They caught us.'

Issa watched in horror as the bird-women plucked her parents from the ground, binding them with magic so they could not fight. Thanon they lifted into the air, but Eritara they took in a different direction. The sound of her parents screaming for each other as they were carried apart would haunt her forever.

'Me, they took to their nests. For days they tortured me trying to get my seed. I wouldn't give it to them. Bards have powers that can nullify harpy magic, but they were relentless. I think they wanted to make something more than just more harpies.'

Issa saw a high place atop rounded crags. Huge nests made out of sticks covered the tops, and scores of harpies brooded there. Thanon's bloodied face and cries of anguish faded into a grey mist. She saw his shoulders tremble.

'I resisted ferociously but they broke me, and, in the end, I was unable to resist their magic. Through my mind they discovered what we had done. That we had given you to Fraya and that you were far away. They became enraged, especially when I did not give them my seed, they drained my soul and took my life-force. They took, and they took and made me an old man, weak and feeble. And then they took my eyes. I can still feel the agony...' Thanon's voice broke. Issa went to him and sat beside him on the bed, wrapping her arm around his shoulders.

'I survived long enough for the Saurians to come. I can't believe they came for me, but they did, and they wanted revenge. Unawares, the harpies were easily outnumbered and, thankfully, slaughtered. The Saurians, when prepared, are devastating warriors.

Thanon focussed on his music once more, finding solace. His voice became strong, filled with anger as he beat the notes out. In her mind she saw Saurian spears fall as rain onto the harpies with devastating accuracy. Thanon, bloodied and blinded crawled out of their nests and was carried away by the lizard-folk. The images faded.

'When I was well enough, I hunted for Eritara with a Saurian friend to be my eyes. For days and days we wandered the swamps, and then I found her broken body.'

Issa gasped as she saw her mother, lifeless, discarded in the swamps. Quickly, the image faded as if Thanon didn't want her to see. He seemed about to say more but instead stayed silent and turned his focus on the music. Issa hardly breathed for fear of what she would see next. The harp made long, mournful notes.

'She wasn't dead,' he whispered. 'But her baby, our daughter—Eritara was certain it was a girl—was gone. It had been beastily cut out of her—there were vicious, bloody scars. I carried her back. The Saurians tried to heal her with their powerful arts but even they failed. Black magic held onto her, all the Saurians could do was form a mind-link and discover her last conscious moments. These are her memories.'

Hazy images formed in Issa's mind. A wall of rock and then a grey, gloomy place as Eritara fell forwards. Harpy cackles faded away, and a hundred pairs of demon eyes appeared in the shadows, yellow eyes gleaming. Eritara cast light and the hairless, dark grey and brown skin of the demons was revealed, some huge, others small, some with wings, others heavily muscled. *Grazen and Shadow, yet I recognise none of them,* Issa thought.

'Eritara they gave to the demons, as they had bargained for within the yew tree,' Thanon explained. 'The demons got Eritara and the harpies got me. The harpies knew she no longer carried Zanufey's Chosen, and so she was of no use to them, unlike me.'

The demons surged towards Eritara, gripping and grabbing, dragging her deeper into the tunnels, their excited demonic howls echoing loudly off the walls.

'When the demons took her, the black vortex came.'

A cold chill ran down Issa's back. The music clanged and scraped out of tune.

'To this day, I don't know if the demons were in league with this…*alien*. Perhaps I'll never know, but she came out of that dark and evil energy, and she took our child. For what purpose, I do not know.'

Issa felt the Under Flow grow from just the image she saw in her mind. A black hole appeared, no bigger than an egg, spinning suspended in the air. It grew rapidly into a rushing vortex and the demons scuttled away from it. The tip surged backwards and up, unconstrained by the tunnel walls as it moved into another dimension, forging a connection to the Dark Rift. Painful pressure built in Issa's mind and she felt sick.

Eritara struggled but the demons held her. Her laboured breathing came in gasps. Issa clasped her hands over her eyes, but the images were inside her head. In the centre of the vortex, a figure walked forwards.

Thanon paused and the single note he played slowly faded. For a moment there was silence.

'Lona,' Issa whispered.

Issa saw Lona's face clearly, her pitch black eyes gleaming with predatory malice, her paper-white skin glowing in the gloom. Black magic swamped Issa's mind and the images became broken and garbled.

'Over and again I have relived these images, but they never get any clearer,' Thanon's voice shook.

Demonic growls intermingled with Lona's voice. Screams cut through both, perhaps the screaming of her mother. Issa didn't want to listen. A pain filled howl, then the sound of a baby crying. Issa's heart thundered in her chest. She realised her cheeks were wet and her hands shook as she wiped them.

'The demons drank her blood, the alien took our child. Then they discarded Eritara into the swamps like garbage.'

The music faded to nothing and Thanon sat hunched over his instrument, shoulders quivering, his tattoos no longer glowing.

At the edge of her sorrow, red-hot rage grew. She felt betrayed by the demons, even by Gedrock and Maggot, and yet the little demon had done nothing but help her. Gedrock had to know something of this, was he tricking her? Confusion befuddled her mind. She sat up.

'You said she wasn't dead, so where is she?' Issa dared to ask.

'There is little left of Eritara, save for her broken body barely housing a soul that lingers in some cursed place,' said Thanon.

Issa jumped to her feet. 'We must go to her at once. Maybe I can reach her. I have a gift…it's too much to explain now. I must see her!'

Thanon nodded. 'Indeed, you must, though I wish it didn't have to be this way. I'll take you to her, though it won't be easy, I stopped going to that place long ago. I'm so sorry, Eri, I could not bear to see you in that state. I didn't have the strength to help you pass on.'

'We must go now!' Issa swept towards the door and flung it open. Before she could stride out, a small green light hurtled inside, sucked in by the sudden vacuum of the opening door. The light squealed and circled in the air.

'Thiashar?' Issa blinked in surprise. This is a swamp, thought Issa, so it wasn't unusual for a swamp fairy to be here. *But Thiashar?*

'Seer Iyena knew you would find your father,' said the swamp fairy in her quiet yet high-pitched voice.

Issa smiled. 'Seer Iyena knows many things.'

'You make interesting friends,' said Thanon thoughtfully.

'Yes,' agreed Issa, then eyes went wide as she looked beyond Thiashar. Outside, Saurians gathered. The lizard-folk sat on the porch, or stood in the swamp, their eyes gleaming in the light spilling out of the cabin.

Thanon came to stand beside her, his hands feeling for the doorframe and she wrapped an arm around him. He was still tall despite his stooped form.

'They are here?' he asked.

'Yes, but I don't know why,' she said.

Ata and Ekem, stepped forwards. 'We waited to see if she would find you, to be sure that she is yours. Then your music called to us and we came, like the old days.'

Thanon nodded and leant heavily against the door. 'It has been a long, long time. My daughter brings me strength, and a little of my music returns.' He squeezed her arm and she took his hand and held it against her cheek.

'So, you've told her all, as we knew you would,' said Ata. 'And we are ready to take you to your mate once more.'

Issa looked at Thanon in surprise then back at Ata.

'The swamps are dangerous at night for humans,' explained Thanon. 'Normally I'd wait until daylight before making this journey. The place we go to is a Saurian graveyard, hidden and barred to any non-Saurian.'

Issa would have been intrigued had it not involved her mother. She waited anxiously as Thanon grabbed his walking stick then stepped out into the swamp. Ehka flew to her shoulder and Thiashar stayed close as she held Thanon's arm and followed the group of Saurians into the dark swamp. Two held torches to light the way but still the night pressed in close as they waded rather than walked.

Saurians surrounded them on all sides, not too near, but not too far either. Always they looked around them and held their spears ready, but her eyes and ears, though better than most in the dark, picked up nothing of note apart from reeds, giant frogs bigger than her hand, and tiny geckos jumping between the grasses.

For a long time they walked until Issa longed for her bed. Thoughts of her mother helped pushed back the tiredness and never did her hand leave her father's. Often her eyes strayed to him and she wished he were more talkative, but she was content to just be with him.

Frequently he would squeeze her hand, father and daughter finally united after decades of pain, too much had happened for it all to be shared and understood. Issa looked forward to the future times they would have together. She dared even imagine a future without war, and walking with her father in the beautiful, peaceful countryside. *Beloved Zanufey, I long for such a time.*

The Saurians slowed.

'We are here,' said Ata.

The party paused, and Issa looked around. The swamp seemed the same as it had the whole journey. A Saurian dressed in a short white robe with a hood walked ahead of the others. Issa realised he held a short staff, not a spear, topped with a shard of white crystal.

A smaller Saurian dressed similarly came to stand beside him, perhaps female. The smaller one spoke to the other in Saurian, her voice low and hissing, then they both held up their hands and were still.

'Priests of Staryx, their Snake God of whom Hallanstaryx is emissary,' whispered Thanon. 'They are both priests and wizards to us.'

Earth Magic moved, and the white crystal flashed. The whole swamp rippled as if an invisible wall of water just in front of them had been touched. It reminded her of the liquid black entrance to the Star Portal.

The ripples deepened and the swamp beyond it changed. The trees were larger, and lights of all lights sparkled amongst the leaves—lights like those she had seen in her strange dreams after being poisoned. Though it was dark she was certain there was green grass and no swamp. The two robed Saurians stepped forwards and vanished into the rippling wall. Issa blinked. She must have made a noise for Thanon chuckled.

'They've entered, then. I can see this wondrous place in the Flow,' he said softly.

'Where is here?' asked Issa. She looked into the Flow but all she could see was swirling golden-white light.

'It's where all Saurians come to bury their dead. No matter how far away they are, they all bring their dead here. It's more deeply sacred than we can fathom, for the Saurians know they are a dying race.'

Issa inhaled sharply. 'Surely something can be done.'

'Their lands border Baelthrom's and the sickness spreads to them as their life-force is drained. Few now are able to conceive, which is why they treated Eritara with so much respect bordering on awe. They almost worshipped her when she was pregnant. It's also why they allowed her to be brought here. You will see.' Thanon led her forwards and she realised he must be looking into the Flow to see where they were going.

She closed her eyes as they moved into the shimmering wall. Passing through the watery veil was just like passing into the Star Portal, a period of intense cold moved through and between every particle of her body, and then a warm rush of pure air greeted her the other side.

Thiashar followed closely and Ehka ruffled his feathers whilst still perching on her shoulder.

Issa stood blinking, taking everything in. The place was silent save for a gentle breeze rustling the leaves and carrying the scent of sweet flowers. The ground beneath her feet was firm not sodden, and the grass rich green and thick. Ancient hazel, oak and chestnut towered above them and the night sky was filled with stars but no moons. The Blaze of Eight was just dipping into the trees beyond.

The area was deceptively large and there were indeed lights within the trees, but they were not fairies as she had first suspected. They filled the place with beautiful diffuse light. To say it was serene was not quite right. *Holy,* Issa thought. She stepped closer to a silvery yellow light and saw it was contained within an exquisite, thin glass vial very much like the baubles they hung on trees for the Mid-Winter Celebrations.

'They are souls,' whispered Thiashar, inspecting it with her.

'Saurian souls?' asked Issa, the notion shocking.

'Yes. They know their souls are trapped on Maioria when they die, so they bring them here,' said Thanon.

'Because Zanufey cannot reach them.' Issa pursed her lips.

'Trapped, but safe from Oblivion.' Thanon squeezed her hand.

'Only for now,' said Issa. 'When the Dark Rift is gone, we'll all be free.'

She peered at a silvery light. A Saurian face formed within and looked right back at her making her jump. Unnerved, she stepped away and glanced at the other trees, every one was covered in soul lights, thousands of them gleaming like the stars above. Tears blurred her vision and she wiped them away.

The Saurians had moved on ahead. Humbled, she led Thanon after them.

Not one of the lizard-folk had uttered a word since they'd entered, all walked bowed in reverence. Was her mother here, somewhere? Just as she was about to ask her father, the Saurians paused and formed a circle around a simple stone statue. Being taller than she, she had to peer around them to see.

The statue was of a coiled snake, head lifted high but bowed and its hood flared though its eyes were closed. The Saurians bowed their heads and closed their eyes, mirroring the statue. Issa wondered if she should be doing the same but was too intrigued not to look. The priest-wizards spoke, lifted their hands, and Saurian magic sparkled. Issa's eyes widened as the stone snake came to life. It opened its eyes and looked at them through sparkling white orbs.

The male priest spoke. 'Come forwards, Raven Queen, Daughter of Seer and Bard, Chosen by Zanufey.'

Issa straightened.

'Don't be afraid, it's the only way in,' her father reassured, making her even more nervous.

Hesitantly, she walked towards the priest and stone snake, and stopped a few feet before it. Everyone stood silent and still and she wondered if something were expected of her. The priest motioned to the living statue and she looked into those shining white eyes. She instantly felt herself relaxing and settling into a meditative state.

Faster than lightning, the stone snake whipped its head forwards. In a blur she saw stone fangs then a sharp pain in the place where the Saurians had bitten her before. The pain took her breath away. She fell back and felt her body stiffening. Time slowed down as she fell, making it so she floated down to the ground, then she sunk right through the earth.

The last thing she saw was Ehka following her, behind him a green light, and behind that a slinking black shadow.

CHAPTER 16

Staryx

IT was impossible to say how long the nothingness lasted.

Issa opened her eyes moments or maybe hours later, her mind alert and senses sharp. She knelt on the ground with Ehka on her shoulder and Thiashar a flash of green beside him. The shadows by her feet moved oddly, letting her know Maggot had also come along. *All here then,* she smiled inwardly at her menagerie of companions.

She was in a round stone chamber, some thirty feet or so in diameter, and several arched doorways led out of the room into darkness beyond. The ceiling was low but high enough to stand. Three braziers lit the room and gave it warmth, but they did not flicker. The flames were oddly still— either magical or made of a substance she did not recognise. Everything was starkly real and sharp, and in many respects akin to the Star Portal. Perhaps it was the same, but a sacred place for the Saurians alone.

A soft pale light grew beyond a doorway to the right and she went towards it. She entered into a small round room and in the centre lay a prone figure draped in white and pastel blue fabric atop a thin, fluted stone altar. The light clustered densely around the figure. Issa's breath caught in her throat as she looked at the serene, pale face of her mother.

Her heart in her throat, she inched forwards and looked down at the woman. Her mother hadn't aged like her father, she still looked young, beautiful, frozen in time. Her long, dark brown hair was freshly combed and lustrous, and her dark lashes brushed flawless cheeks. There were the faintest lines around her eyes and the shadowing of circles beneath them.

Her skin was so white and bloodless, she looked dead. Arla had looked the same when her soul had been trapped in the Ethereal Planes. *No, Arla had looked more alive than this!*

Issa lifted her hand to touch her mother's cheek, but couldn't bring herself to do it. It seemed wrong, sacrilege even. Perhaps she would disturb her and break her slumber.

'What has happened to you?' Issa spoke softly but her voice echoed loudly.

'Like Woetala, she's in stasis, trapped by the failing life-force of Maioria.' The low masculine voice made her jump. Her hand went to her sword as she stared around but there was nothing there.

'Who are you? How can I free her?' Issa asked, peering into the glowing air.

'The only reason she's alive is because she was brought here. Otherwise her soul would have fallen into Oblivion when the one-from-beyond took her child.'

The light shadowed in places and clustered into a cloud. A smooth round head and a blunt nose formed within the cloud, becoming clearer until a snake-like head appeared. White eyes with long black slits for pupils looked down at her and a dark forked tongue flickered out.

An awesome feeling tinged with fear flooded through her and she felt her legs trembling under the weight of ancient wisdom. She dropped her gaze and took a deep breath. *Staryx.* Nothing other than a god could make her feel like this. When she next looked up, the snake made of light and shadow hung in the air over the body of her mother.

Issa found her voice. 'Great Staryx, can I reach her in the Realm of the Dead?'

'To reach this one you would have to go so far you could not return. Your mother is dead to Maioria, we only keep her soul alive in stasis until a time when Zanufey can reach her or we all fall into Oblivion. All our souls are waiting, as you know.'

A sob shook Issa, it wasn't what she wanted to hear. She bent over the body of her mother and hugged her cold, lifeless form.

'Your father tried everything to reach her,' the snake god spoke softly in a long, hissing whisper. 'He drained his own life force just trying to reach her. But the one-from-beyond who took her child, also took the life of Eritara.'

'Lona,' Issa growled. Everything began to fall into place, possibly aided by Staryx's presence. Lona hoped to raise and control another Raven Queen. 'Where did she take my sister?'

'Into the Dark Rift.' Staryx hissed and swayed his head. 'Do not think you can save her. Save yourself and end this war, Raven Queen. When you do, your mother's soul will be free to find the light.'

Issa wiped the tears from her face. Grief mixing with furious rage made her whole body tremble. She looked back down at her mother. The snake god was right, Eritara wasn't here, this was just her shell. She gently stroked her pale cheek with the back of her hand. Cold. Empty.

'I'll find your daughter,' Issa whispered.

'Do not,' warned the snake god. 'Your sister is her no longer. Changed. Run from her or do that which few siblings can do—destroy her.'

'Kill my sister?' The thought was heart-stopping. She'd only just learned she had a sister and now she was told she had to destroy her. 'She can be helped in some way. It's not over for her—'

'It is,' the shimmering snake cut her off with quiet words. 'All the while she lives, she's a threat to you and so to all Maioria. This is what those-from-beyond understand deeply. Should she survive and become more powerful than you through the powers of the Dark Rift, then the third Raven Queen has arisen, and you have fallen.'

Issa's mind was a whir. She remembered the prophecies, the talk of a terrible warrior bringing death, and the emotionless woman in her dreams who scared even herself. There always seemed to be two Raven Queens spoken about, one the saviour and one bringing death and war. Was this what her sister would be if she failed?

Oh, how clever Lona is! To learn the prophecies and find my sister, travelling through time and dimensions to bring her to power. Her parents and Fraya had done such a good job of hiding her, Issa, that Lona and the Yurgha could not even find her. *They had hunted, though. Had it not been for you, my beautiful Ehka...* She reached up and stroked the bird on her shoulder.

She brought her attention back to the chamber and focused on her mother's lifeless face.

'Mother,' she whispered, imagining the life they might have shared together—a family together, complete. 'I may not be able to bring you back, but I can set you free.'

Anger and resolve straightened her back. The battles against Baelthrom's hordes were merely skirmishes, they were not battles against Baelthrom himself or the Dark Rift. *I have to go to him, I have to face him, and I have to pitch my power against his. This I've always known, always dreaded.*

The commanders and officers of all the armies on Venosia's soil were far more adept at war than she ever could be. She could advise them, she could relay to them all she had witnessed on her scouting mission, but she could not lead the war. She had to let them do that. *And I must do what must be done!*

She looked up at the ethereal snake, he watched her without blinking. His eyes began to glow golden as she felt him read her thoughts.

'Coming here has given you what you needed; strength, resolve, direction. Go now, Raven Queen, and do what you have to do.'

The sky above the swamp blushed pink with the dawn.

Toads had stilled their incessant night warbling, and in the brief moments between night and day, everything fell silent.

Issa took hold of her father's hands as they stood beside his house. They were cold, and she tried to warm them as she spoke. 'The final battles have begun against Baelthrom and all his horde. If you see them come, you run. You go to Hallanstaryx.'

Ekem stepped forwards. 'There will always be a place in Hallanstaryx for a musicman, even one whose arts are sleeping.' He held his brightly feathered spear like a staff. Ata emerged from the reeds, lizard eyes darting left and right, knife lowered but always ready.

'I wish with all the world that I could come with you,' sighed Thanon. 'My long-lost daughter who has come to me now, only to leave again so soon.'

There was so much Issa wanted to say, the few days they'd spent together were not nearly enough. All she could do was pull him into an embrace. He returned the hug, and there was strength in his arms he'd not had a couple of days ago.

'I'll come back to you, I promise. And when I do this will all be over, and Mother will be free,' said Issa.

Her father nodded. 'Find your sister. Bring her back to us.'

Issa bit her lip. She had only told him in part what had happened in Eritara's chamber. She couldn't bring herself to tell him that her sister had been taken and corrupted by a fallen race from another world. Maybe she would when this was all over. And if she failed? Well, then it wouldn't matter anyway.

'Promise me you'll play your music, the life-magic of Maioria needs your voice, your power,' said Issa. She smiled when he nodded, though he couldn't see it.

'Too long have I been silent, lost in sorrow. Since you returned to me, the light has come back into my life. Zanufey is with us through you, I can feel her.' He fumbled inside his worn jacket and pulled out something shining. 'I kept this next to my heart wanting to keep her close, but now it is for you. I think it will help you.'

Issa stared at the ring he pressed into her hand, silver leaves wrapped around a green stone. The ring had an earthy power that she recognised instantly. *Witch magic... and something else.* She lifted the ring and stared hard at it. The green gem felt so familiar, *but it cannot be!*

'Green crystal from the Murk...' she said in shock.

Thanon shrugged. 'I know little about it, only that it belonged to Belledyn, Eritara's mother, your grandmother. Now, it's yours.'

She knew so little about her grandparents, if anything at all, and now there wasn't time to ask the questions that filled her mind. Blinking back tears, she slipped her mother's ring onto a finger on the opposite hand to Asaph's flame ring. 'There's so little I know about my family, we have years upon years of catching up to do.'

'There will be time, when you return. I'm not going *anywhere.*' Thanon squeezed her hands.

Issa looked up at him with a question she longed to ask. 'Was my grandfather a wizard? Someone wondered once, and I didn't know.'

Thanon broke into a grin, the widest she'd seen. 'He was. My father was a man of great ability, but he chose solitude rather than rising in the arts to become a Master Wizard. Much like I choose solitude now, I guess. His gift passed on to me in the form of music. Perhaps you too can learn a bard's arts.

Issa blushed. 'The last time I tried to sing, next door's dog joined in.'

Her father laughed. 'Like anything, it takes time and practise. When we're together again, I'll teach you.'

Overwhelmed, Issa pulled him into another embrace. 'When we're together again,' she echoed. 'I'll come for you, I promise.'

'I'll be here, waiting,' Thanon reassured her. 'Go now and do what you need to do.'

It took an enormous amount of will to let go of her father's arm. She left him standing next to his hovel in the growing light of dawn and followed Ata and Ekem through the muddy water. Her father stood straighter and stronger than when she'd first met him, but soon he was lost in the swaying reeds.

Thiashar had disappeared sometime in the night after they had returned to Thanon's house. Ehka flew high in the sky checking for danger, and the odd movement of shadows at the base of the reeds suggested Maggot was still with her.

When they had lost sight of Thanon, Ekem held out a blindfold. 'It is either this or poison,' he said.

There was no swaying a Saurian, and the thought of being bitten again made her bow her head and let him put it on. She *had* agreed to it earlier. No human could be allowed to see where Hallanstaryx was for the safety of the Saurians. Despite feeling indignant, she let them lift and tie her onto the back of a Saurian and awkwardly she clung on as they bounded through the swamp.

Hours passed as she bounced uncomfortably on the Saurian's back. Eventually, they slowed and stopped and set her down. She found her legs could not support her and she sunk onto the damp grass. Pulling her blindfold off she looked around, seeing the same swamp stretching out in all directions for miles around.

Silently they passed her a waterskin and a swamp apple. She drank the water and tucked the apple into her pocket.

'West is Diredrull and the enemy,' said Ekem pointing. 'Here we rest.'

Issa nodded and lay down on the grass.

When she awoke, it was night and the swamp beyond their dwindling torch pitch black.

She looked at Ekem. The Saurian sat on his muscular haunches completely still as a statue, not even his huge, dilated eyes blinked. The night was filled with the sound of frogs warbling and the splash of fish jumping. Ata slept curled up on his side, hugging his tail that reached to his nose. She couldn't feel Maggot's presence and even Ehka was absent, probably out terrorising frogs, she thought.

Issa tried closing her eyes again but all she could see was her mother's lifeless face and still form. Giving up on sleep, she quietly walked down the hill to the water's edge where a large toad jumped out of her way with a disgruntled croak.

She squatted down, cupped her hands into the cool water and splashed it on her face. *If only there was a bath…* She'd build a house with her father and make sure it had a wetroom. She already missed him. *At least he'll be safe in the swamp,* she hoped.

She sat down cross-legged and drew out her raven talisman. Light shimmered across its surface as she stilled her mind and thought of Asaph.

The swamp quietened with her mind, the waters becoming so perfectly still there was not even a ripple as they reflected the reeds above. *A beautiful, perfect, serene world.*

Issa took a deep breath and a warm breeze blew, lifting her hair from her shoulders, but it did not touch the surface of the water. *How strange,* Issa thought. She heard a voice, soft and low, coming from somewhere. Her ears pricked, and her hand went to her sword, but she felt that was silly, rude even. The voice spoke again, a man's voice carried on the wind. She didn't understand the words, but the voice was filled with the wisdom and power of the natural world. In her mind she saw giant trees, a world of moss and ivy and earth so real she could smell the moist, dark soil. *I am the wisdom of the Wild Wood,* the voice seemed to say. She longed to hear the voice speak again.

A hazy golden light gathered before her, hanging above the surface of the still water. Her hand slipped off her sword hilt and she put away her talisman. The light expanded into a six-foot-wide circle and opened into another realm, a realm of ancient, giant trees and moss and ivy. The deep voice came from within it, calling to her with sound more ancient than language, more sophisticated than words, and wholly male, making her think of her father, her grandfather, and all her male ancestors. The voice spoke of nothing but love, wisdom, and protection.

Issa got up and walked towards the opening. In the hazy forest within, something moved in the trees, as large as a tree. Emerging from the oak trees, great antlers spread high into the air. Letting go of her breath, Issa stepped into the other realm.

Warmth and diffuse golden and emerald light replaced the cool damp of the night swamp. Song birds fluttered between ancient boughs and deer moved unhurried and graceful through the glade. Tiny white flowers swayed between tall grasses and the tinkling of a river could be heard.

A huge figure loomed in the trees, less solid than the world around it. The bright light coming from behind it, cast it in shadow. Issa blinked and marvelled at the enormous antlers as the figure stepped towards her and took solid form.

Muscles rippled across his arms and chest and soft brown hair grew from his waist downwards, reminding her of the Karalanths—but this was no deer-man. Heat rose in her cheeks as she saw he was naked but then she felt more embarrassed herself for being clothed. They weren't born with clothes, clothes were unnatural if worn to conceal, so her thoughts flowed in this place. The being did not have legs as such, his rippling thighs became solid wood, like tree trunks, and his feet were flowing roots that twisted and turned with each step.

Powerful energy flowed from this being, like that which flowed from Zanufey, only different. This being's power was one of raw physical strength, of confidence and bravery, of protection and assertiveness, of loyalty and fortitude. *Male energy,* she thought. The hairs on her arms rose and fell, and she understood a little of what the seers had said. Masculine energy is light and electrical in nature, like the lightning in storms. It pushes out from the One Light, seeking, exploring, creating. Female energy is sound and magnetics, like the thunder in storms and it returns to the One Light, creating the pathway back to the Source of All.

Issa stared in awe up at the being and understood that she gazed upon the Guardian of Maioria. She thought about kneeling and bowing her head, but unspoken words told her this would be inappropriate. Instead she stared up with her mouth hanging open. Now she could see his face, she saw it kept changing. Sometimes it was a man with incredible eyes whose colours kept shifting. Other times, it was a bear's or an eagle's or a deer's or any type of forest animal.

'Doon,' she breathed.

Maioria's male guardian held out an enormous hand towards her. When she touched it he either began to shrink, or she grew. Images, thoughts and words flooded into her mind, too fast to process and understand. The forest around them faded into golden light.

She looked up at Doon. He was still large but not impossibly so. His face no longer changed, and he was indescribably handsome in a way in which Zanufey was beautiful, though the guardian deities were beyond these qualities.

'Raven Queen,' he said. There was music in his voice and it made her think of her father. She looked at him again and saw Thanon. There were even green tattoos upon Doon's body though the tattoos moved. She blinked and now she saw Coronos' familiar features, the only man she'd thought of as her grandfather. Doon was all things. Doon was father, brother, lover, all. Things were different in the calm of spirit.

He spoke in words deep and rich and nourishing, she could listen to him speak forever. 'You have the power to see and understand.'

Issa shook her head. 'To see and understand what?'

But he didn't reply and instead took her hand in a warm, strong grasp and led her into the golden light. They descended, and the light became thicker, darker and colder. She shivered. Death and mortality hung in the air, sharply contrasted to the world of light and life they had just left. Even Doon by her side was greyer, his face ashen and aged. She looked at her hands and gasped. They were mottled with age spots and wrinkles.

'Do not fear what you will see,' said Doon. His beautiful voice still strong and reassuring yet filled with sadness—sadness that no guardian should have. If a guardian was sad it spoke of hopelessness. If a guardian was hopeless, what was she?

The scenery became all shades of grey and black, like the Shadowlands only there were no trees or ghosts or objects of any kind. There were only grey and black *somethings*.

Her breath was a cold cloud in front of her face and in the distance, a white shape appeared. Doon gripped her hand a little tighter. As they neared she saw the shape was a giant statue, a female figure prone, her body swathed in white cloth. Entwining around her marble body were thick, black vines. Issa stared at the woman's face and the whole scene reminded her of her mother lying there dead, trapped in a world she could not leave.

Fear clasped cold hands around her heart and Issa drew back, not wanting to see or go further. Doon looked down at her, his eyes green emeralds, all faceted and shining, the only colour in this place.

'Yes,' he breathed to her unspoken questions. 'They are bound by the same thing.'

Issa dropped her eyes trying to understand. She let him draw her onwards and knelt before the statue as he did. A guardian kneeling…it made her heart race. The thick ugly vines had thorns that cut into the figure. They wound around her neck and over her head, barely leaving her face revealed.

Issa swallowed and trembled as she stared at the statue's face. The woman looked uncannily like her mother. 'It cannot be,' she breathed.

The woman gripped an arrow in one hand, and the other, hanging over the side of her stone bed, held a bow. The bow was broken.

Issa touched an ugly vine wrapped around her wrist and jumped. It moved and hissed, tightening around the woman like a snake.

'Who is it? Who is the statue of? Those things are alive! What are they?'

Doon did not look at her but instead reached a giant hand to stroke the statue's face. The motion was so tender and loving, Issa swallowed, then her eyes widened for where his hand touched, the cold marble became peach, her lips turned pink and her eyelashes long and black.

Issa could barely breathe as the woman's face came to life. 'Why does she look like my mother? Where are we?'

Doon looked at her, his eye's gleaming amber. He spoke to her like Zanufey, with direct cognition.

'*She is that which is female in all things,*' Doon said without speaking. '*All are bound to her.*'

'The Orb of Life is bound to her,' Issa spoke aloud the understanding flooding into her.

Doon spoke again. *When the darkness came from the Dark Rift, so did death and the fall of the female power, that which sustains and nourishes. That which gives life. When the Ancients split the magic and the Orb of Life was taken, Woetala fell into darkness.*'

'If we take the orb back, she will be free? Will my mother be free also? But where is this place?' Issa asked breathlessly.

Doon spoke aloud. 'The life force of all things draws into the Dark Rift. This is a place between Maioria and the rift. Soon, all will pass through it.'

Unfathomable sadness descended upon Issa and she wanted to run from this place. In the distance something drummed.

'I'll get the orb. We'll get them all back.' Issa wrung her hands.

'Time is short,' said Doon, rising to his full height. 'The last of the Ancients are falling. That which was done can only be undone by those who did it.'

'Only they can combine the orbs?' Issa asked.

'If they do not do this soon, Maioria's magic will be forever broken,' said Doon.

Something screamed in the darkness far away. Issa's heart began to pound, and Doon looked into the black.

'What is that?' asked Issa.

'That which you fear most,' said Doon, turning his gaze upon her.

The drumming grew louder. *Not drums, but hooves!*

'The horsemen? The Light Eaters? I cannot fight them, any of them!' she drew her sword uselessly, horror clenching her stomach.

'One day you must,' Doon said.

'How? How can I possibly fight them!' Issa shouted over the growing thunder. A blood-red light grew in the blackness.

'You must enter the darkness and make your stand,' Doon said. 'Until that time, you must run.'

A giant raven landed on Doon's shoulder. It stared at her, cawed noisily, then spread its wings and flew over her head.

'Until then, run Raven Queen. Follow the raven.'

A horse screamed and something not human howled. Issa turned and ran after the giant raven. What about Doon? She couldn't stop to think about the guardian, all she knew was to run. Black wings fluttered ahead and beyond them an orb of light, within the light, a torchlit swamp. Increasing her pace, she threw herself into it.

CHAPTER 17

Fear of the Dark

ASAPH scanned the endless swamps.

His excellent dragon eyesight searching the layers of water between clumps of swamp trees, tall reeds, swarms of flies and flocks of long-necked birds. Cloaked in dragon magic and invisible to all, he was still wary of the enemy. Harpies lived here, and they could also hide their presence with magic. Every time he saw a crocodile he grimaced for Issa's safety, it wasn't just the undead and those in league with Baelthrom who were a threat.

In the Flow, he hunted for the flame ring on Issa's finger. There, to the west, came the faintest pull, just enough for him to angle his wings towards the setting sun.

He spotted movement amongst the reeds. A bird squawked and Ehka darted in front of him, his black feathers glinting gold in the sunset. Though Asaph was cloaked, the clever bird had detected his presence.

He followed the bird and slowed before a strange sight. Talking to two giant, upright lizards on a patch of grass, was Issa dressed in her Dread Dragon armour. He blinked at his distant lizard cousins who clearly meant her no harm.

She's made friends with Saurians? Relief washed over him.

The Saurians paused to sniff the air and Issa scanned the skies. With a deep chuckle Asaph hovered, dropped his magic cloak and revealed himself, the waving reeds and billowing wind already announcing his presence. The Saurians hissed and howled and bounded away. Issa turned pale and sunk to her knees. Asaph abruptly stopped laughing and dropped himself into the swamp with a splash.

He let go of his dragon form and strode towards Issa. This seemed to dissipate the dragon fear and she stood up. A nervous smile spread across her face and then she was running into his arms. He swept her up.

'Asaph, thank the goddess. I found him, I've found my father!'

'How? Where? What happened? Where have you been? How did you get here? I've been worried sick about you.' He hugged her tight.

Issa stared up at the handsome, fair-haired man with gleaming blue eyes.

'And I you! So much has happened,' Issa rushed on. 'I went to the Wizards' Circle, and Yisufalni and I combined the orbs. Asaph, it was amazing. But then Freydel came and he was…he was *furious*.' Issa rushed on. She remembered Ayeth and the memory sent her heart racing.

'I saw him, Asaph. I saw Ayeth—beautiful, powerful, regal—everything Freydel said he was. But I realised I could never kill him, or any innocent being.'

She drew away from Asaph and stared at the ground, emotions conflicting. 'Freydel's translocation alerted Baelthrom. He came, Asaph, Baelthrom physically arrived. I've never seen anything so terrifying, so… He was huge, grotesque and the power he wielded… He destroyed the Wizards' Circle and I couldn't do anything! My power was nothing.

'But then something incredible happened. For a moment, for one brief moment, Ayeth and Baelthrom stood there before me, both in the same time and place. How is that possible if they are the same being? I don't understand it. Then Baelthrom attacked and I tried to fight back but I couldn't. Light and dark magic struck me and then I was falling.'

Asaph listened, his eyes wide as Issa explained all. When she spoke about Morhork, he frowned. 'Gone there to kill a wizard and take an orb' Asaph echoed.

Issa nodded. 'But in the end, he saved my life and brought me here. You see, when he tried to take the Orb of Earth, his human form was forced into his dragon form and he said all forgotten memories returned to him. It's a long story but he remembered old gossip from long ago about a musicman and a seer living with Saurians. He brought me here, safe from Baelthrom, and to where my father might be. And he *is* here, Asaph.'

Her eyes misted over, and she paused to catch her breath. She hadn't even mentioned her mother yet, but even thinking about her brought a lump to her throat. In the corner of her eye she saw Ekem and Ata peering through the reeds.

'I'm so pleased you found your father, Issa, after all the years you've spent without one,' said Asaph. 'I cannot imagine having lived without Coronos, even though he wasn't my blood father.

'Other things have happened too, back at the camp.' His voice softened, and he looked pained. 'Drumblodd is gone, and the Orb of Fire lost.'

Issa inhaled sharply and steadied herself on his arm. 'No.' She shook her head. Another orb lost? It couldn't be. 'Baelthrom was with us, not you.'

Asaph smoothed back his hair and looked into the middle distance as he recalled events. 'The Dark Rift and the Under Flow came into our midst. We ran to Drumblodd's tent, Haelgon, Luren, Naksu, me—all of us—but we were too late. There was a black vortex, an evil bloody hole, opening right into his tent! A whole passage to another dimension ripped into our reality. The one you told me about was there, the alien woman with the black eyes.'

'Lona,' Issa gasped, and looked up into his eyes. 'Lona the Yurgha.'

Asaph nodded sombrely.

The Saurians emerged fully out of the reeds. They kept their distance and stood silent several paces behind Asaph, silently watching and listening.

Issa tried to make sense of what Asaph had said. 'It all happened at the same time; Baelthrom, Ayeth, Freydel, the Wizards' Circle, Lona and the orb. And, oh Great Goddess, Yisufalni!' Surely she got away, surely Murlonius had come for her. She could easily evade anything in the Ethereal Planes. *But nothing can escape the four horsemen, they go where they will!*

'Listen,' said Asaph, taking her fingers out of her mouth when she began chewing them. 'We can do nothing about what has happened, there's *so* much happening, we must protect ourselves and return to the others. There's also unconfirmed news of a massive invasion into Lans Himay with Draxians being targeted.'

Issa inhaled sharply. 'By Baelthrom?'

'Yes. We must formulate new plans. Whilst you've been gone, the armies of the Free Peoples have pushed towards Diredrull. As we speak, border strongholds are being attacked. If we're lucky the city will fall to us.

'I never knew dwarves had such strength and ferocity within them. They fight for their ancient homeland with little rest and great drive. Only the Karalanths match their bravery and stamina. There's even a new respect growing between the two. After everything, who'd have thought Karalanth's and dwarves would ever fight on the same side again?'

The thought brought a little warmth to the cold that chilled her bones.

Asaph looked into the distance. 'But something calls me away from these battles. My place is in the North, fighting for Drax—and it absolutely cannot wait. If Baelthrom really is killing Draxians, he's doing it to quell the uprising. He knows I'll rally them and invade Drax—and I must do it now.'

Issa thought about what he said. Was their place really on the battlefield beside the Feylint Halanoi? It didn't feel like it. The leaders could always use their magic, but who was going to take the fight directly to Baelthrom? 'You're right, I don't think my place is here either. I was the catalyst to get things moving, the inspiration behind it. Now our destinies call us elsewhere, where we are needed most. Besides, by striking other places, we can distract Baelthrom's attention from our take-over of Venosia.'

'Exactly,' said Asaph, his eyes shining. He noticed the emerging Saurians and eyed them curiously.

'Asaph, meet Ekem and Ata,' said Issa, nodding to the Saurians. Without elaborating, she added, 'They fought off the harpies and looked after me before taking me to my father.'

Asaph and the lizard-men regarded each other and then the Saurians lowered their gaze as if in respect. Asaph bowed stiffly, clearly unsure of the protocol or the history between them.

'Greetings, Dragon Lord, cousin to Saurians,' said Ekem.

'I'm honoured to meet you,' said Asaph awkwardly. 'Thank you for protecting her.'

'It is our duty, to the Queen of Ravens,' said Ata.

'Ata, how far is it to where you saw the soldiers?' Issa asked.

'Directly north to the border, maybe a day on foot,' he said, pointing a claw. 'The swamp dries up and the ground turns into rocky hills. It's very dangerous, harpies inhabit the borderlands.'

Issa looked at the horizon. 'We can make it from here. Thank you for bringing me this far. If you would like, Asaph can carry you closer to home?'

Ata and Ekem's eyes widened and their long, red tongues flicked rapidly in and out. They spoke to each other briefly, then Ekem said, 'We never fly.'

It was with some reluctance that Issa said goodbye to the Saurians. She wished she could be back with her father, building a house together far away from the troubles of the world. *Until Baelthrom finds us.*

Asaph gently picked her up and she watched them, and the swamp disappear beneath the clouds. A keen wind grew up and she was thankful to nestle into Asaph's huge claws.

Ekem and Ata watched the giant golden dragon lift into the sky, circle once and then speed away.

The Saurians looked at one another, then Ata spoke. 'It's as the Oracle foresaw, the last Dragon Lord has returned and now our dragon cousins awaken.'

Ekem nodded. 'We are being called to war, the last. Whether we win or lose, live or die, our world will never be the same again. We must gather our warriors and march to the Black Mountains to meet our enemy, the last battle will be there. It's as the Oracle foresaw.'

Ata looked back up at the sky. 'It's as the Oracle foresaw,' he repeated with a nod.

'Diredrull,' rumbled Asaph, slowing and lifting higher into the clouds.

Issa stared at the dark mountain looming monstrous on the horizon like some terrible beast. Cormak had told her of the once splendorous city that had stood here hugging the lone mountain—itself a source of awe and mystery in a land that was otherwise low country. Tarvalastone, the wonder of Dwarven architecture, gleaming with gold, and more impressive inside than out. She imagined glistening marble walls, great turrets reaching into blue skies, surrounded by the Low Hills of green grass and fertile valleys cut through with gushing rivers.

Diredrull was none of that. Whatever gold there was, was long gone. Even from this distance she could see the grand turrets were no more.

Instead great blocks of black rock formed enormous walls ensnaring the mountain in a deadly embrace. The parched, cracked earth had seen no river or rain for hundreds of years. No sun rose here, there was only the angry red sky and the endless rumble of thunder, the sickly feel of the Under Flow moving just beneath the earth.

Issa shivered.

'There are Dread Dragons,' said Asaph in a low voice. 'I can feel them.'

Issa strained to see through a break in the clouds and thought she saw black shapes flying. 'What about the others, Freydel, Haelgon, even Marakon? Can you feel them?'

'I can only feel dragon minds. What's left of them.'

'Don't get too close. I feel strong magic, and not the good kind.'

Asaph took a wide birth of the ugly Dark Dwarven stronghold and came up on the far west side. Much further west, the sky brightened.

'Look,' Issa said, butterflies in her stomach. 'The lands we've taken back, the sky is changing!'

'It's recovering,' said Asaph. 'So Maioria can heal herself, there *is* hope.'

'I hear drums,' said Issa, picking up the faint sound of a monotonous dull beat. She recalled standing with the Guardians of the Portals beside the giant oak tree as the Sword of Binding was passed to her. 'They are the drums of war,' she whispered.

'The Feylint Halanoi is marching, look beyond that ravine,' said Asaph, flying lower.

Issa inhaled. Sure enough, several miles ahead, marched thousands upon thousands of soldiers in neat, ordered lines and units, their armour and weapons gleaming in the dull light.

They came closer and she saw the tabards and pennants of every country and faction, Davono, Frayon, Atalanph, Feylint Halanoi, and hundreds of mercenary flags she did not recognise. There were dwarves, elves and Karalanths—Issa had never seen so many people moving, there were at least ten thousand soldiers marching and the thump of their drums beat victory into the land.

Asaph chuckled long and low. 'Look what you managed to do. We'll take back Tarvalastone and Venosia will be ours.'

Issa swallowed. ' "We." I didn't do this alone. Thousands will die. I saw not one but many Dromoorai back there.'

'They are willing and ready to fight for their freedom. This is the only way,' said Asaph.

'I don't want it in my name,' Issa shook her head, the horror of battle bringing unwanted images into her mind. Visions of bloodied fields, a dying man reaching out to her before falling face down into the mud, and through it all a cold-faced warrior woman dressed as she was now.

A horse neighed, and she spied Duskar prancing to the rear with the pack horses. The nimble horse looked to the skies as if sensing her. He was tied on a long rope to another horse ridden by a man in Elven armour. *Velonorian*, she guessed. The poor elf would be worried sick about her.

'Let's join them,' said Asaph, excitement in his voice.

The talisman grew warm in her belt and she looked at it. A white spear flashed on its surface.

'Wait, where's Marakon? Can you see him?' she scanned the lines of soldiers but there was no sign of the half-elf commander.

'He's not here,' said Asaph.

'He should be by now, it's been days, even weeks.' She bit her lip. What if he'd been killed in the demon tunnels? What about Velistor, Staff of the Gate? Even if they were allies, it was an uneasy truce that held between demons and humans. There were still enough unhappy Grazen who might attack, who might steal the spear. A Star Portal magical tool falling into demon hands would be a terrible thing.

The talisman was hot now and she felt it pulling to the South. She pictured Marakon, focused on the talisman and entered the Flow. Fields of moving energy appeared before her, far into the distance came a flash of white and then of black. Good magic *and* evil? Was Marakon in trouble?

'No, we must go south. We can be with the others soon,' said Issa, squinting into the distance where a jagged spine of rocks reached into the sky. 'I think I can feel Velistor, and Marakon.'

Yisufalni swam through a sea of darkness.

It filled her body, entering her with every breath, finding every orifice, chilling every particle. She called for Murlonius, but her mouth only let the darkness in. He was far away; this blackness was her end.

'The Immortal Elixir,' an airy voice whispered, shuddering through her like thunder. The voice *was* the darkness, the sound of Oblivion. 'I let none of your kind have it. You are privileged.'

That voice, I know that voice from long, long ago! She gasped and choked, trying to get whatever was in her, out. Pain bolted through her body, she convulsed and screamed, and then the pain faded. It returned stronger than before. Parts of her were dying, she could no longer feel her extremities.

'At first, there's pain. Then there is only power and beauty.' The voice turned quiet, pondering. 'I no longer despise you and your kind, it could be said I have almost *forgiven* you. All things that occurred in the past are petty, are nothing compared to what lies before us. As a gift to you, I have allowed you to join me.'

Pain came in the form of burning within then a bolt of lightning brought a different agony. Her body contorted, and she made a horrible gargling sound. She couldn't breathe. She opened her mouth and sucked but no life came from the air.

The pain passed. Her vision became a little clearer. A huge dark shape moved towards her. She tried to move back. Deathly cold chains wrapped her arms behind her back, tightened. The black magic upon them could not be undone.

Pale orange eyes flared, illuminating the massive tripartite helmet. Baelthrom reached a hand down and clamped under her chin jerking her up off the ground. Pain exploded down her spine as she flopped in his grasp.

'An hour left, my Great One,' said the yellow-eyed dark dwarf at his side. His repulsive gaze travelled over her naked body.

'Find the other one, find the male. I want them both. He'll be hunting for her,' said Baelthrom, dropping her.

Yisufalni fell to the floor, twisting an ankle and crying out. Waves of pain rolled over her. She drifted, sinking deeper into the dark soup where there was no pain, but there was no life either.

Bright light exploded in her mind, calling to her, drawing her on.

'Murlonius?' she whispered, shielding her eyes against the brightness. It came closer. Warmth pushed back the cold. The light began to flicker and flash silver and gold and pink.

'No, I know you,' she smiled and reached for the power of the Orb of

Life. 'You survived here, alone in the darkness, waiting.'

The orb spoke to her with feelings, joy at her presence, the desire for freedom, fear of the dark, and the calling for union.

'Yes, this is the only way. We must become one for you and I to survive. It is the end, but at least it is not Oblivion,' she whispered, giving her agreement.

Yisufalni touched the light and it filled body and soul. Enraptured, she became one with the light, and the darkness, the pain and the cold fled.

The Orb of Life burst into blinding light, filling the chamber with the Flow. The iron ring shuddered angrily, red lightning flickered across its surface as the Flow assaulted it.

'What's happening?' Baelthrom roared.

'I don't know, my Lord!' cried Kilkarn. 'Urgh, the light, the pain, make it stop!'

But the light increased. It spewed from the Orb of Life, snaked up into the air, then poured down upon the Ancient at Baelthrom's feet. The woman groaned as the light touched her. Baelthrom grabbed at her but the light flared, burning his hands and forcing him back.

He drew upon the Under Flow. It came in powerful waves, but before he could direct it, the Ancient's body became consumed by the light. The light and the Ancient flared brightly, then both she and the light blasted back into the orb.

Unspent red energy hummed around Baelthrom's hands waiting for his command. The Ancient was gone and the Orb of Life now dull and empty, like it had been since he'd taken it thousands of years ago.

He stalked over to the pedestal where the remaining orbs were, Kilkarn hobbling after him.

'She's in the orb?' Kilkarn chanced an intelligent conclusion for once.

Baelthrom lifted his arms and roared.

CHAPTER 18

Battle for Tarvalastone

'THERE!' Issa spotted a gleam of metal in the distance.

A hundred soldiers with a score of horses moved just below a rocky ridge, armour and weapons polished and gleaming. *They've not seen war yet*, Issa thought.

'Look, there's Marakon!' She laughed and pointed at the tall, bearded half-elf with the eyepatch leading the unit. He carried the white spear, Velistor, and her raven talisman glowed in response to it. 'And there's Bokaard.' The heavily muscled Atalanphian captain followed him.

Asaph slowed his approach and she felt the tingle of his strong cloaking magic. It was wise to be cautious, she thought. Now they were close, she could see most wore the Feylint Halanoi tabard but then her eyes widened. A handful of others wore a different tabard. 'Look at their tabards! A black raven on an indigo moon.' The raven was stylised into the same shape as her raven talisman, cleverly formed into a circle with wings flared, talons out-stretched and head turned to one side.

'The Knights of the Raven,' said Asaph, approvingly. 'You should be wearing one as well.'

Indeed, Issa thought, *and a thousand others, too.*

Ehka cawed and she sensed something wrong. The soldiers were moving hurriedly but their progress was hampered by the rocky terrain. A female dwarf paused and looked behind—she seemed out of place amongst the soldiers, even her armour looked awkward. Wizard magic moved, and Issa glimpsed the edges of a shimmering shield above them. The dwarf hurried on. Marakon leapt over a rock and shouted something. Horses stumbled, and soldiers scrambled, weapons drawn at the ready, further slowing their progress.

'But what are they running from?' She squinted below but couldn't see anything. Peculiar magic moved, it wasn't the Under Flow, but it wasn't good either.

'Harpies!' growled Asaph just as she spotted a dark cloud cresting the ridge behind the soldiers.

Issa lifted her raven talisman and caused it to glow a bright indigo blue. The spear in Marakon's hands burst into white light, startling the half-elf. He stopped and stared up. He could probably see the indigo light but nothing else through Asaph's cloaking magic, she realised.

'There are thousands of them,' Asaph's voice was filled with horror.

Issa looked ahead and saw the mass of screeching harpies, a wave of harpy magic rippling the air around them.

'Far too many,' Issa whispered.

Asaph must have heard for he grinned and said, 'It's foolish to bunch so close together before a dragon.'

They were suddenly hurtling through the air towards the bird women. Issa gripped his talon tight, squinting against the rushing wind. She entered the Flow. A hundred beautiful faces with cruel black eyes loomed into her vision, and then were engulfed in a sea of scorching flames. Screaming and the stench of burning feathers filled the air.

Asaph arced upwards so fast her stomach somersaulted. She didn't even get a chance to use the Flow before he was coming at the harpies with another bout of fire. Most moved out of his way but a score weren't quick enough and exploded into flames.

Harpy magic flashed, but Issa was ready, and it bounced harmlessly off her impenetrable wall. Asaph turned, and she glimpsed Marakon and his soldiers besieged by harpies far below. She watched as more harpies fled from Asaph and descend upon the soldiers.

'We have to help them,' she screamed over the rushing wind.

'I can't use fire, it will kill them too,' growled Asaph.

'The clever bitches know that!' shouted Issa. 'We have to fight them on the ground.'

'Yes, but I cannot,' said Asaph, his voice unusually quiet and strained.

Then she spotted what he had already seen, and her heart skipped a beat. 'Dread Dragons!' Between them and the far distant dark walls of Diredrull, flew at least five of Baelthrom's most prized abominations. 'They'll kill us all.'

'No, I'll lead them away. They're after me, I can hear them in my mind,' Asaph said. 'With magic, I can fly fast, much faster than they can. That's one thing I can thank Morhork for.'

'I'm not leaving your side,' growled Issa. She looked down. A bloody gash streaked across Marakon's cheek, and more than one soldier lay unmoving on the ground in a pool of blood.

'Let me get you somewhere safe from all of them,' said Asaph, his voice weak. He knew she'd refuse, she thought. 'If I don't do something fast, we're all going to die. I'll take my own life before I become one of *them!*'

'All right,' Issa slumped her shoulders. 'Set me down over there by those rocks. With the power of two orbs, I can help Marakon. You lead away the Dread Dragons.'

Asaph banked and descended, setting her down in a smooth motion without landing. With her heart in her throat, she watched him rise and turn towards the Dromoorai, golden scales bright and gleaming. Dragon magic shimmered, and he shot away.

The Dromoorai spread out, ready to intercept him.

He's right, they're only after him, thought Issa. 'Blessed Zanufey and Feygriene, please protect him.'

A harpy screamed, and a harrowing cry grabbed Issa's attention. A man struggled with a harpy, her talons embedded deep into his shoulders making his arms useless. Issa pulled her sword free and ran at her. She leapt the last few feet and swiped her sword with such force the harpy's head flew from her shoulders. Blood and feathers sprayed over her.

Issa didn't pause and ran to the next soldier fighting two. One gripped his spear and the other clawed his face so that blood ran into his eyes.

Issa roared. Her sword sliced through the harpy's leg, releasing the man's spear. The harpy screeched and struggled into the air gushing blood from her stump. The other harpy turned on Issa. She raised her sword, but the man's spear burst through the bird woman's chest.

Issa ran on to the next, too busy with her sword to think about using magic. Talons scraped across her back, hard enough to penetrate Dread

Dragon armour, and she sprawled on the ground. There came a scream and a thud, then a strong hand gripped her arm and pulled her up. She blinked up into Marakon's bloodied face.

'There are too many. At least six to one,' he shouted over the din. 'We're good, but not *that* good. Our wizard is tiring.'

She glimpsed the slender dwarf wizard surrounded by soldiers trying to protect her. Her face was pale and drained, and she swayed from left to right.

Harpies attacked Marakon from behind. Issa leapt forward, and they were locked in battle again. She forced her mind to magic whilst she swung her sword and slipped into the Flow. Her free hand found Illendri.

'White Fire,' she commanded.

Magic moved.

The harpies nearest burst into white fire. They fled screaming into the air, beating their wings and tumbling trying to put out the flames. Again, Issa commanded the fire, forcing more bird-women into the air.

'Shield us!' she shouted. A shield rose immediately above her and Marakon, giving them time to breath. She closed her eyes and focused on strengthening and lengthening the shield. Soldiers bunched together under it.

'I can't hold this and fight them at the same time. They'll find a way through eventually,' said Issa.

Harpy magic struck and vibrated off her shield, weakening it.

'We have to run,' said Marakon.

Issa scanned the scorched terrain. There was nowhere to hide, not even a rock to sit on. 'I'll bet there are dark dwarf tunnels right under our feet but hidden by magic.'

'Aye, the Missy is right.' A dwarf with fierce eyes and a thick black beard knotted with silver rune beads pushed towards them. 'There'll be those bastards' tunnels aplenty.'

'How can we find them?' asked Marakon.

The dwarf set down his axe, reached into his pocket and took out a palm-sized, oblong wooden box. He flipped open the lid and inside were two small compasses. One dial was red with black runic lettering and a black hand. Issa's skin crawled just looking at it. The other dial gleamed copper and had dwarven runes etched into it.

'The black hand points always to the Mountains of Maphrax,' said the dwarf. 'Don't look too closely at its runes. The other points true north. It is the black hand that will lead us to a dark dwarf tunnel. When we pass their filthy magic it will glow red like the fires of Maphrax.'

A harpy breached the shield with a screech. Magic flared. Soldiers leapt and struck her down.

Issa turned her attention back to the Flow. She tried to strengthen her shield, but it had weakened in too many places. 'I can't hold it,' she gasped.

Marakon grabbed her arm and ran. She stumbled along after Eiretonne who held his strange compass before him.

'There, maybe five hundred yards ahead,' shouted the dwarf, pointing.

Issa squinted into the distance but could see nothing of interest. The harpies began dive-bombing the soldiers.

'We're not going to make it,' Marakon panted, echoing her very same thoughts.

'White Fire. Wave,' Issa commanded. A sheet of fire blasted over their heads. Harpies screamed but she didn't pause to look. Harpies in their hundreds swept overhead, moving in a huge cloud.

Staring up, Issa slowed. Her sweaty palms made gripping her sword difficult. The bird-women screeched as one, a sound so deafening, all sense was driven from her mind. She was aware of dropping to her knees, her sword clattering on the ground and her hands clasping over her ears. The noise drove deeper into her skull. She couldn't even think to cast a spell.

The harpies closed in. Issa tried to take her hand from her ears to pick up her sword, but her whole body was frozen by harpy magic.

Something whizzed over her head and speared a harpy knocking her from the sky. Another spear followed the first, moving too fast to see clearly but it looked colourful. *A spear with green feathers on the end,* Issa realised.

Scores of spears exploded into the air, casting a shadow beneath them. Harpies screeched and fell as each spear found its target with deadly precision. The flock panicked and scattered.

The magic that had bound Issa vanished. She grabbed her sword and stood, only to flinch as hundreds of Saurians bounded past her. They pulled their spears from the downed and writhing bird women and aimed them once more.

A light-skinned Saurian paused to regard her, she thought it was Ata, then he bounded along with the others.

The flock of harpies drew back, lifting out of range of the spears, and many fled. One harpy screamed orders, circling high above them and out of reach, but she was unable to form any control over the panicked flock.

Issa stared at her. Was that a blood stone amulet on her chest? Was she the Queen, Dereever?

Perhaps the harpy could hear her thoughts and stopped her screeching. For a moment Issa was certain she locked eyes onto her. In her mind she pictured herself from above and saw herself staring up, pale-faced and dressed in shining black armour. A spear hurtled upwards, but it bounced off the harpy's shield. With a howling cry, the harpy lifted higher and left.

'They'll be back,' said Marakon, wiping the blood off his sword with earth. 'The vengeful witches will probably return with their entire race.'

'The Queen must be killed to stop them. She follows Baelthrom's orders,' said Issa, wiping the sweat from her brow. She turned her gaze from the sky to the approaching Saurians. At least fifty warriors trotted towards her, all armed with spears and knives decorated with red and green battle feathers.

Marakon raised his sword, and his soldiers readied their weapons.

Issa grabbed his arm. 'It's all right.'

The commander scrutinised her then lowered his sword. 'Stand down!' he shouted to his soldiers.

Issa stepped towards the Saurians. 'Ekem? Ata?' she asked the two closest as they slowed.

They nodded once, their long red tongues flicking in and out.

'We're indebted to you.' She bowed. She wanted to reach out and shake their hands but was unsure of Saurian manners.

'Yes, we're indebted to you,' Marakon echoed her, uncertainty in his voice. Nobody here had ever dealt with the lizard-folk, or probably even seen a Saurian, she was the only one with some experience. The Saurian warriors were bunched together, and though their weapons were lowered and their faces completely unreadable, she sensed extreme wariness. Humans and Saurians weren't friends, so she would have to take on the responsibility of being the intermediator.

'How did you find us and get here so quickly? Asaph and I, we flew for hundreds of miles.' She tried to fathom how many leagues they might have flown and gave up.

'We do not give up our secrets easily,' said Ata. 'Let us say only that the veils between realms are thin in our lands, and Saurians may pass where the fae tread.'

Issa was intrigued. They had passed through the veil to their sacred graveyard, perhaps it was like that? She wanted to know more but felt it would be rude to press them.

'War is coming,' said Ekem.

'And we're ready,' said Ata. 'When we saw the harpies fly in great numbers, we knew the end times had begun. Our most hated enemy will leave their nests in the final days.'

'It is as our prophecy has foretold,' said Ekem. He bowed his head reverently. 'Our Great Oracle sent us to follow them. We are the First Warriors and we're proud of this honour. If we don't return to Hallanstaryx, more warriors will come. The Second Warriors, then a Third and a Fourth until none of us remain. It is a great honour.'

'You will fight and die until none remain?' Issa raised her brow.

'It is as the prophecy has foretold. If we do not, there will be nothing left to live for,' said Ata simply.

'Well, we're not all going to die right here and now,' huffed Eiretonne. The dwarf had been fidgeting throughout the whole exchange. He winked at Issa. 'Right there by that pile of rocks is a tunnel. I say we get in there before those winged witches—or worse—deliver our end times before the battle's even begun.'

Asaph sped towards the Dromoorai.

There were three flying side by side, he could see their raised claymores and gleaming red Shadow Stones. Was Issa safe? He glanced behind and a strange sight greeted him. Streaming out of an invisible vertical wall were dozens of Saurians armed with knives and spears. The wall rippled like water as they leapt through it and hurled their spear with shocking power and accuracy at the harpies.

A Dread Dragon roared, the noise sweeping a chill through his body. He forgot about the others and turned left sharply. The Dromoorai followed, all three of them, they weren't interested in Issa below. Perhaps Baelthrom hadn't spotted her through their Shadow Stones yet. Instead, he had their deadly, undivided attention. He had to lead them away.

The Under Flow moved, he saw it as a shimmering black net in the Flow. He banked right and blasted the net with magic and fire, disintegrating it. Already the Dromoorai were creating another.

'The last will soon be one of us.' A Dromoorai spoke in a voice low and howling like the wind. Its eyes shone blood red, its face forever hidden behind black metal.

Asaph tried to imagine what they might look like without armour and shivered. He turned due west away and flew fast. The Dromoorai pursued.

Now then, my brethren, how would you like to go for a long, fast flight? Asaph grinned, bared his fangs, and roared long. He filled himself with the Flow, beat his wings hard, and watched the ground and sky become a blur of browns and reds.

The dark dwarf tunnel turned even darker when Shelley closed the entrance.

The initial feeling of safety from aerial attack was soon replaced with fear of the all-enveloping darkness. Issa gripped her talisman and Ehka huddled closer to her neck.

'Light,' she commanded. Soft indigo light lit up the tunnel ahead.

Shelley created a ball of golden light above her. The tunnel was rough-hewn but high enough to stand up in. *And wide enough for Maphraxies to walk two abreast,* thought Issa, grimacing. Now she was inside all she wanted to do was get out. The place, the energy, crawled across her skin, and breathed damp and foul upon her neck.

The soldiers and knights stood there for a long time, all expecting hordes of dark dwarves, Maphraxies and death hounds to attack. Nothing emerged from the darkness except the darkness itself.

'With our armies approaching, the enemy will be preparing above ground,' said Marakon, inching forwards, sword raised. 'One can hope, at least. Let's rest a short time. There are some rations and a little water left, but not much.'

Issa looked at his bloodied face and nodded. At least the blood had dried.

The Saurians, fresh to battle and keen for more, lit their strange thin braziers and scouted the tunnel whilst the soldiers took rations from their packs and sat down on the hard ground. Those not eating tended each other's wounds. Issa dampened a cloth with a water flagon and set about cleaning Marakon's wounds.

'It's not deep, but harpy talons leave infections and all sorts of awful magic,' said Issa inspecting the bloody gash on his head. Using the Flow, she cleansed the wound.

He touched her arm when she was done. 'Thank you, and by the goddess, am I glad to see you.'

Issa grinned. 'What took you so long? We thought you'd died in the demon tunnels.'

'The demon tunnels…' Marakon sighed. 'Don't even ask.' He removed Velistor from its sheathe on his back and slumped against the wall. Bokaard, sitting to his left, passed the commander a small flask. Marakon took a swig. From the grimace on his face Issa decided it wasn't water.

'Dwarven spirits,' said Marakon approvingly and passed it to her.

She hesitantly took a drink. Burning sweet and sour liquid filled her mouth and warmed her throat as Marakon spoke.

'The spear led us as close as it could. Perhaps there are other tunnels, but we couldn't find them. We ran into trouble when we crossed a dark dwarven tunnel and what appeared to be a Karalanth passage.' She listened as he told her everything that had happened since he'd first entered the demon tunnels.

'There must be other tunnels, one that exits on West Venosia,' said Issa, thinking. She wished she had a better understanding of how Velistor worked.

Marakon shrugged. 'Perhaps they are closed or no longer working. I followed the spear with clear intention. If I were a Karalanth fleeing, I'd close every damn tunnel behind me, so nothing could follow. Anyway, how long has it been? What has happened?'

Issa's eyes shone. 'We've taken West Venosia.'

She told him about their successful invasion and watched his face light up. The other soldiers came closer as she spoke, pain and anger dancing across their faces when she told them about the lost orb and destroyed Wizards' Circle.

'The army is marching to Diredrull this very moment. It's massive, Marakon. Feylint Halanoi, Karalanths, Elves—hundreds of companies, warriors and mercenaries from all over the Known World. It has begun. Diredrull will fall and become again Tarvalastone.'

Marakon smoothed back his hair and took a breath, letting it all sink in. 'Lans Himay invaded, Domenon a dragon, Drumblodd and an orb gone, all nations drawing together to take back what is ours. I want to be there this moment, not in another underground hellhole. I'll be thankful if I never go in another tunnel again.'

Issa nodded, feeling the same.

'Wait a moment, Commander,' said Eiretonne. 'There's something on our side few will realise. These tunnels go right into the belly of Diredrull. It's too dangerous to join them overland, harpies and Dromoorai will attack us. But we can attack from within whilst our armies attack from without. Weakening it from the centre, perhaps?' The dwarf chuckled.

Marakon's eye gleamed. 'By the goddess, you're right. Let's hope we can reach the heart before our rations run out, we must move quickly. But what about Yisufalni, what about Murlonius?'

Issa dropped her gaze, worry for her friend knotting her stomach. She opened her mouth to speak, but an inhuman roar and clash of metal tore through the air. Soldiers grabbed their weapons, and a group of Saurians bounded towards them, their powerful thighs rippling and claws scraping on the stone.

'We've found battle,' hissed one, struggling with the human language. 'Dark dwarves, necromancers—scores of them.'

Issa couldn't be sure, but it looked like glee in his bright yellow eyes. She glanced at Marakon, but the high commander was already pushing forwards, a keen, deadly look in his eye.

Issa ran after him and the Saurians, with Eiretonne and Bokaard hot on her heels. The sound of metal clanging against metal and the screams of battle grew louder.

Asaph lost the Dromoorai quickly.

Arcing high, he shot into the thin layers of the atmosphere, then curved downward. He did not intend to avoid fighting the Dromoorai for long. Everything was a blur of red clouds, even this high up. It wasn't natural, even the wind felt muggy and clung to his scales.

He slowed. The land came into focus. Ahead, the lone mountain stood, with Diredrull clinging to it like a predator trying to down a proud and mighty beast. Before it marched tiny specks in perfectly ordered columns, the armies of the Free Peoples.

He panned around, hunting for his pursuers but they weren't there, which was more worrying. They must still be hunting him in the clouds, so he circled back and scouted the area where Issa had been. There was no sign of her, Marakon's knights or the Saurians or harpies. There were no bodies, so they must have escaped. She would be safe with Marakon and the Saurians, he convinced himself.

He turned, almost lazily, and headed back towards the armies. Circling above them, he kept up his cloaking magic to avoid spreading dragon fear unduly. He could smell their anxiety and excitement, it was infectious. Not long now before they reached the city.

The dark walls of Diredrull stood impossibly tall and impenetrable. Along its ramparts and ugly tower blocks, Asaph's keen sight made out thousands of Maphraxies and dark dwarves jostling. Their black armour gleamed in the dull red light, iron blades raised and shaking defiantly above them.

He swallowed a lump. Never had he seen so many of the bastards in one place. He realised how little he knew of armies and of warfare, of sieges and scaling great walls, of fighting in close quarters as the screams of a thousand friends and enemies assaulted the senses.

There would be necromancers, hidden. He would seek out and destroy them first, like he had at Avernayis. There would be death hounds too, and the Dromoorai would soon catch up with him.

He swallowed again. With a glance at the people below, he looked for hope. *Look at them, their shining armour. These are seasoned soldiers, warriors and fighters—Maioria's strongest and finest. They know what they're doing.*

He wondered for the third time if he should fly north and rally the dragons. But it was far too late, and once again a strong feeling told him this was not their fight. *This is our fight, for dwarves, Elves, Karalanths and humans. The dragons are waiting for Drax. They need their strength.*

He spied a tight pack of Karalanths on the southernmost flank of the marching companies. There were at least a thousand warriors. He dipped lower and spotted Cusap'anth in the lead with Rhul'ynth and Grast'anth.

'*Greetings, friend,*' he spoke with his mind to the Karalanth leader.

Cusap'anth paused and looked up. *'Asaph?'*

'Yes. There are Dread Dragons coming. I'll focus on them and the necromancers.'

'Where is the Raven Queen?'

'She's safe with Marakon and the Saurians. As safe as can be.'

'Saurians? Is that possible? Incredible.'

A mighty horn rang out. The armies slowed and halted before the black walls of Diredrull. All turned still and silent. The bright pennants of each company billowed proudly in the wind. Horses, nervous with excitement, flicked their heads and stamped their hooves. The Free Peoples stood before their foe, eyeing up the enemy. Even the enemy stopped their guttural hollering.

Asaph scanned the walls, looking for weakness and finding none. He glimpsed the flash of a pale white hand and a face half concealed by a hood in one of the foremost turrets, then it was gone. He looked into the Flow. There, concealed by magic, stood five necromancers. They pushed back their hoods and lifted their hands. Powerful black magic washed into the Flow.

Asaph dropped out of the sky towards them, fire rumbling in his belly. He clenched his gut and added magic to it. Quickly now, they were about to cast their spell. With a roar that rocked the walls, he spewed blue fire into the turret. The flames revealed the five necromancers for a brief moment. Their faces captured with mouths open, eyes wide, their spell hanging on the end of lips and fingertips. Then each one exploded into blue fire. The fire raged for a second then went out. There were no bodies, not even a scrap of cloth remained. They had been utterly incinerated.

Asaph glanced back at the armies, realising his cloak had dropped and dragon fear spread. At the head of the army stood a commander in shining armour on an enormous black steed. The horn he held to his lips but did not blow. It was as if he had been frozen in time.

Had he inadvertently started the battle before it had even begun? Even the enemy looked frozen. Feeling oddly guilty, he did what he could only think to do. With a face-saving roar, he swooped aggressively. But the horn never sounded, and instead a hundred thousand human voices screamed, yelled and whistled. In one great wave, the armies of the Free Peoples poured towards the walls of Diredrull.

The battle for Tarvalastone had begun.

CHAPTER 19

Beneath Diredrull

THE Under Flow flared, weapons clashed, and the press of soldiers in the narrow tunnel quickly became suffocating.

Pushed back by bigger men, Issa was grateful to finally sheathe her sword and focus instead on using magic. Shelley stumbled beside her. The dwarf gave a weary half-smile then entered the Flow. From within the Flow, Issa watched streaks of energy order themselves into interweaving lines, creating a geometric shape. Shelley spoke a dwarven word and the shape bolted forwards.

Issa added her own magic to it and the shape moved faster and grew until it filled the entire tunnel. It passed harmlessly through the glowing shapes that were the soldiers' auras but further along, it exploded, and the screams of necromancers and dark dwarves echoed loudly.

Shelley formed another shape and Issa added to it again, combining their magic to create more potent spells than any could formulate alone. Slowly, they and the soldiers moved forwards.

Issa held her own circular, geometric shape, the magic flaring in lines of energy. Ehka began squawking, but to lose her concentration risked dropping the shape and harming herself. Ehka would not squawk without a reason, she told herself.

She forced her attention out of the Flow and Shelley took over. With a sharp inhalation, she unsheathed her sword. Coming up a smaller tunnel behind her hurtled a baying pack of death hounds.

'Enemy at the rear!' Issa screamed.

The first death hound virtually flew at her. She threw herself aside, slashing her sword, slicing it from tail to shoulder. The hound smashed into a wall, yelping and oozing pools of dark blood.

Two more came on. She hurled magic at one and a ball of fire smashed into its muzzle, the other was already in mid-air and descending upon her. Too late to dodge, she dropped to one knee, sword upraised. It crushed down upon her, hard, and howled. Dark blood gushed over her hand from her embedded sword. Gagging, she heaved the twitching body off her.

She barely had the blade free before the next hound sent her back to the floor. It was lifted by unseen hands and crushed into the wall, bones snapping. It fell as a bag of limp flesh.

Issa jumped to her feet, nodded her thanks to Shelley, and engaged the next hound. From the sounds of howls echoing in the tunnel, many more were coming. Shelley couldn't protect her and all the other soldiers.

'Help!' she screamed.

Tiny hands gripped her calf. 'Maggot?' She stared down into the demon's huge eyes. 'You can't stay here, you'll get killed!'

A soldier ran to her side, sword and shield raised. The man's face paled. Ahead, dozens of gleaming eyes filled the tunnel, the howls of the death hounds deafening.

'Too many,' Issa said breathlessly, laying a hand on his arm and pulling him back. Maggot clung to her leg.

Sheathing her sword, she grabbed hold of Illendri. She had no idea what to do. 'Help!' she cried.

The Flow poured through her into the orb. It flared dark purple, held the magic for a moment, then released it in an explosion. Issa stared into the Flow, barely able to breathe for the forces pouring through her body, out of her hands and into the orb. The tunnel began to shake and tremble, rocks cracked as the walls heaved first out and then in. Rubble exploded onto the death hounds. Issa and the soldier fell back, shielding their eyes from the light and debris as the walls caved in. Howls of pain fell silent under crashing rocks.

Issa coughed, took a deep breath and straightened up, brushing the dirt from her jerkin. The soldier sneezed. He blinked at the rubble for a long moment, his eyes the only clear things in a face that was black from dirt. Without saying a word, they turned and followed Shelley to catch up with the others, stepping over bodies of dark dwarves and the empty robes of dead necromancers that littered the passage. Holding up her glowing raven talisman, Issa finally spotted brazier lights ahead.

The tunnel wound on and eventually opened into an enormous chamber, so large she could barely see the ceiling. Huge chains dangled from above, free falling or holding enormous metal containers. There were giant cogs, easily the size of her house, and mechanisms, devices and constructions built of stone and metal. Despite eyeing them from all angles, Issa had no idea what they were for. It was the strangest place she had ever seen.

Narrow stone steps led to an even narrower bridge over a chasm whose depths could not be seen. Swallowing loudly and without looking down, she inched over the bridge to where the soldiers and Saurians gathered on the other side on a wide stone platform. Many stood guard, ready for imminent attack; others tended the freshly wounded. At least five soldiers lay unmoving, their tabards covering their faces as was the custom for a fallen soldier when there were no physicians with their white sheets.

Two Saurians lay unmoving, one covered in horrific wounds, the other seemingly sleeping without a mark on its body, lay still and silent. The lizard warriors clustered around them, murmuring.

Issa's heart grew heavy as she came to stand beside Marakon and Eiretonne. Marakon's face held its usual grim-but-determined expression but Eiretonne's was filled with wonder as he looked above him.

'What is it? Where are we?' Issa asked the dwarf.

His eyes glistened, and he looked away. 'Ah, it's been a long, long time.' Eiretonne took a few paces, rapping his fist against his chest plate. 'These are the mines of Tarvalastone. Many ores are rich in Venosia, as any dwarf will know. Look, the chains are not even rusted, it's been left exactly as it was. The dark dwarves have no use for the things we so cherish—they just want their black magic and blood rites. Bah, the sick bastards!' His voice raised to a roar, echoing off the high walls as he walked deeper into the chamber where huge wheels and cogs, once forever moving, had been still for hundreds of years.

'Don't go too far,' Marakon called after him. 'We don't know what other horrors await us.'

But if he heard, the dwarf didn't stop.

'I'll go with him,' said Issa. The high commander nodded.

She hurried after him, keen to explore the dwarven mine. Ehka flew between the chains, making the smaller ones jangle, and Issa glimpsed the shadow of Maggot seeping across the floor like a moving black puddle.

She caught up with Eiretonne in a small domed chamber. It was so expertly hewn out of solid rock, its dark walls were smoothed to a high sheen. The dwarf stood before an anvil and huge hearth that had been cold for eons. Tools still hung from the walls and lay on benches, discarded and forgotten.

The dwarf didn't hear her come in. There was a faraway look in his eyes as he absently smoothed the surface of the anvil with his thick hands. She came closer and realised he was staring at the skeleton of a dwarf beyond the anvil, a Maphraxie arrow embedded in its chest.

A lump rose in her throat. She laid a hand upon Eiretonne's shoulder.

'It's all been left exactly as it was. Those bastards know nothing about creating, they only lust to destroy.' His eyes glistened.

The brazier he'd placed in the wall gave the place a warm glow, as if the hearth might still be lit. She imagined she could hear the clang of the weaponsmith as he worked, the heat of the furnace, the gleam of metal.

Issa turned towards the hearth, her boot accidentally thumping into a metal bucket, causing it to spill its contents. She looked down at the curiously long pieces of pale metal and picked one up. It wasn't as heavy as it looked, and the metal had an almost creamy sheen to it.

'Tarvalastone metal,' said Eiretonne, peering at her from the other side of the anvil, 'for forging weapons.'

A sharp pain came into her head along with the flash of a vision.

'Are you all right, Missy?'

Eiretonne's voice came from far away. The sword shimmered in her hands and the light of Illendri blazed in its pommel. The image went, and she blinked back into Eiretonne's frowning face, the pain subsiding.

'A vision…I'm all right. I saw a sword, made with this same metal.' She held up the metal, wondering. 'But it had my orb as its pommel. Who can make such a sword? I don't know what it means, it's just what I saw.' She shrugged.

'Well, this smithy is as it was left—for all else that was destroyed. If we can take and hold this damned city, this place will come alive like nothing you have seen, Missy.' Eiretonne's eyes shone with glee.

Issa smiled. 'I truly hope so, Eiretonne.'

Marakon, Issa, and all the soldiers walked the enormous mining chamber.

The narrow path was held up from the unfathomable depths by giant stone arches. Issa dared to look over the edge and peer into the abyss only once.

The path led on and on until Issa's feet began to ache, forever pounding on the cold hard stone. Eventually their braziers lit up a crossroads. In the middle stood a giant pedestal carved out of solid rock. Eiretonne hurried ahead and climbed the steps. At the top, he peered into the huge carved bowl and chuckled.

'Someone hand me a torch,' he said.

He took the flaming torch and swept it into the bowl. Fire burst into life, illuminating the entire chamber.

'He-he, praise the goddess' he laughed. 'Who'd-a thought the oil would still be in it after all this time?'

A sight caught Issa's eye, making her gasp. She pointed at the walls of the chamber. They shone gold and silver in the sudden light. 'It's beautiful!'

'Aye, Missy,' marvelled Eiretonne. 'That be real gold and silver and not the fake rubbish. This is what made Tarvalastone such a city to behold. Now I've made it back to the heartland of my ancestors, I vow to devote my life to making this mine function again.'

The road ahead narrowed and became an even thinner bridge over the abyss. It reached the far wall where hundreds of steps led up to a door which looked tiny from this distance.

'We'll rest here by the sconce,' said Marakon. 'Warmth and light will put off the dark dwarves, and at least we'll be able to see what we're fighting if attacked. Shelley, Issa, do what you can with a shield.'

Issa nodded, thankful to stop and rest. She helped Shelley set the shield boundary over the soldiers, then settled down next to the pedestal, leaning her back against it. Many Saurians simply laid down on the floor and curled up, their spears beside them, hugging their thick tails up to their noses. Others stood watch. They did not speak often to the humans, but Issa watched intrigued when Marakon finally approached Ata and engaged in conversation. She was too far away to hear what was said.

'Hey girl,' said Bokaard grinning. He passed her something wrapped in paper. 'Eat.'

'Thank you, I'm famished.' She took the hard bread and cheese and devoured them, tearing off bits for Ehka, though he was nowhere to be seen. Neither of them spoke as they ate, both were too hungry. Instead, they watched Marakon and the Saurian conversing.

Marakon finally came over and sat down to eat. After, swigging a little dwarven spirits, he said, 'Ata confirmed what I suspected. We're being followed and watched—whether by magic or not, he can't tell either.'

'Perhaps it's Issa's demon friend,' chuckled Eiretonne.

'Maggot comes and goes at will. I wish I could,' said Issa.

'No, he doesn't think it's him,' said Marakon.

Issa chewed her nail. The news was worrying, especially when she hadn't felt anything in particular—everything felt weird down here. Perhaps she should talk to Ata. She got up and went to the Saurian. 'You didn't have to come, you don't have to die here,' she said.

'What affects Maioria, affects us all,' he hissed. 'Our Oracle and Great Staryx has spoken. We will not perish without fighting to the end.'

Issa considered that, then nodded. *It is their choice, a noble one at that.* 'Tell me more about what follows us.'

Ata's tongue flicked in and out as he studied the great walls. 'Eyes. Something watches. I feel it stronger in the astral planes.'

'Baelthrom?' Issa's pulse quickened.

'I do not think so, I would know it.'

'I'll keep alert,' said Issa, for there was little else she could do.

Leaving Ata to watch, she went back to the others. There was a deep frown on Marakon's face as he stared at the ground.

He looked up as she unbuckled her short sword, laid it gently down and then sat beside him, waiting for him to speak.

'Tell me what happened to Yisufalni,' he said, his voice low and filled with concern.

'He took her,' said Issa, feeling the darkness creeping closer. 'To Maphrax. It hurts to even think about it…She's alive, I'm sure of it, but if she is killed, all may be lost—only the Ancients can recombine the orbs, that much has been made clear to me.'

Marakon let out a long low sigh. 'Murlonius will follow her. He needs *our* help now. Despite our victories, that immortal bastard still holds all the cards.'

Eiretonne leaned in. 'I know nothing about these Ancients, they are as distant to me as the stars. All I know is how to use my axe, and all I've been trained to do is kill Maphraxies.'

Bokaard grinned and slapped him on the back.

Issa hugged her arms feeling none of their humour. 'I thought about going there, to Maphrax to find her. But what could I do? Where would I look? I pray Murlonius has a trick or two up his sleeve.' She didn't dare think about Freydel. If he hadn't arrived when he did, none of this would ever have happened. The wizard had now deserted them in their greatest hour of need—worse, he had betrayed them.

Ehka flew down from the rafters and landed beside her, quickly gobbling up the bits of food she had left him. He looked up at her and croaked, and the Mountains of Maphrax came into her mind.

Understanding, she shook her head. 'No, my little one, you cannot go to Maphrax and find her, it's too dangerous, even for you.'

'He said all of that?' asked Bokaard, his blue eyes glowing in the gloom.

Issa nodded. 'He speaks in pictures, it's faster.'

'We can summon Murlonius, perhaps he can take us,' said Marakon.

'Let's finish one battle first before we get ourselves into another,' said Justenin, overhearing as he stepped away from the watch. 'No one's prepared to go to Maphrax right now, and besides, I'd need more gold in my wages.'

Issa slipped out her talisman and turned it over and over in her palm, half-listening to the others. The talisman that Arla had found for her, risking her own life. *Yisufalni, how can we help you?* She'd have to scry for her in Maphrax—which would be terribly dangerous, even if it were possible. The sound of the others talking faded into the background as she was drawn into the talisman's shimmering, star-filled surface.

She reached out with her mind, far out into the darkness where it was cold. *Yisufalni,* she called. *Yisufalni.*

Illendri grew warm at her side. The orb was with her, calling and searching. A faint, multicoloured light answered in the distance. *Yisufalni?* Her heart leapt for joy.

'She's not dead,' Issa said in wonder, her eyes seeing not the mining chamber and the men talking but the light in the darkness shining brighter. The men ceased their debate. 'But she's not what she was, I feel only her pure essence. I don't understand.'

The orb at her side became uncomfortably hot. In the Flow, it flared purple, its magic shooting through the darkness towards the rainbow light. Angry red lightning streaked around them and something roared. A wave of dark magic rolled towards her.

Issa pulled back, snapping the connection so fast she reeled. Strong hands steadied her as the roar faded. She blinked and looked up at Marakon. 'She's not dead,' she repeated.

'And Murlonius? What about Murlonius?' asked Marakon, gripping her arm, his expression intense.

'I saw nothing of Murlonius,' Issa shook her head.

Marakon slowly released her and looked away.

'When Baelthrom came he... he appeared so fast, I tried to help but... Freydel will have got away with Ayeth, I'm certain of it.' Issa wanted to say more but found herself repeating what she had said earlier. 'To lose Yisufalni is to lose Maioria. As Doon said. The orbs must be recombined by those who split them.'

'I made a vow to the boatman,' said Marakon, staring into the middle distance, the indigo light of her still-glowing talisman casting his face in soft blue. 'I vowed to help Murlonius with his curse, just as he helped me with mine. We must try to find Yisufalni and bring her back to him. Alone, he will die, just as I almost died.'

Issa nodded and hugged her legs, resting her chin on her knees. 'It's all so impossible.'

'No,' said Marakon. He stood and lifted Velistor from where it rested against the wall. The spear glowed at his touch and he shook it. 'We retrieved this against the impossible. You raised a hundred armies and invaded Venosia, against the impossible. Now those armies press forward to Diredrull, and one day soon this place will be called Tarvalastone once more.'

Issa managed a faint smile—half of her proud of what had been achieved, and the other half sick with worry for Yisufalni. She watched the commander lay the spear down. Before her stood a High Commander of the Feylint Halanoi and a leader of the Knights of the Raven. Once an ancient, powerful King, now a soldier who remembered all his past lives, their triumphs and transgressions.

'What is it like? To remember them all,' Issa asked. She must have caught him at the right moment for he understood what she meant.

'I shut them out. They get in the way of this life, mostly. But all of them have led me up to where I am now. Lately I find a sense of peace I've not known before, yet there's so much still to do.

'In the North, before we took an excursion into enemy lands and I lost everyone except Bokaard,' he winked at the big man. 'I met a young elf-girl in Port Nordastin. She had the Sight and knew who I was—or *had* been— long before I had any idea. She told me "one lifetime is not enough". Just one life is not enough to do all the things we came here to do.'

Issa considered his words. That was why she had come here, to complete a task, a quest she'd started eons ago. 'I think I know what you mean. Sometimes I get glimpses of my life on Aralansia, before the...' she swallowed the pain and the visions of a planet being destroyed. 'It gets in the way of this life. I can only deal with the pain of one life, let alone hundreds.'

Marakon didn't say anything immediately, perhaps he was remembering something from long ago, like she was. When he came back to her, he changed the conversation. 'Those things in the Dark Rift you spoke about, the Light Eaters, do they come from Aralansia?' He took another swig of dwarven spirits, winced and stoppered up the metal flask.

Issa shuddered, remembering the giant formless beings and the tortured noise they made, the deep hatred and loss they exuded. 'No. They're ancient, even older than Aralansia. Maybe from when the Dark Rift was first formed.'

'And the four horsemen, you said they were Knights of Maphrax?' Marakon asked and continued when she nodded. 'Sent by Baelthrom to hunt the other planes, they'll hunt Murlonius down too. Where do they come from? Who are they?'

Issa didn't want to think about them. They were waiting for her to reveal herself. Not even the Realm of the Dead could hide her. 'I don't know what they are but suddenly they were there, hunting down all that Baelthrom desires.' She swallowed and closed her eyes, but they were there behind her closed lids, dark and immaterial. They walked towards her, the spines that were the horses' manes clacking, their breath as soot in the grey fog, their eyes leaking darkness and swallowing the light. One reared, scaly, oil-slick skin glistening, its reins clenched in the gauntleted fist of its rider. On that fist a ring flashed.

Issa forced her eyes open. 'I remember something odd. I remember seeing it at the time and thinking how strange it was, how out of place for something undead to be wearing an adornment. One of them has a ring, a gold ring. On it is a prancing horse.'

Marakon dropped the flask. It clanged on the stone floor and Issa looked at his stricken face.

'No,' he breathed, his eye wide. 'It cannot be.'

'What is it?' asked Issa, a cold chill shivering down her back, Marakon's face was a picture of horror.

'Meyer.' Marakon whispered the name of his knight but it went through Issa like a knife. 'Meyer was taken by them.'

He jumped up, screaming, 'You bastard!' He punched the air then spun away and leant upon the pedestal, panting heavily. Anyone who had been asleep was now on their feet, weapon in hand, looking wildly from left to right.

Bokaard and Eiretonne held up their hands for calm. The Atalanphian laid a tentative hand on Marakon's shoulder. Issa got to her feet not knowing what to do. Could the horseman really be one of his knights of old? Had Baelthrom taken them and damned their souls eternally to Oblivion like so many others?

Slowly Marakon stood upright and composed himself. He turned around, rage still vivid behind his composure.

'I'm so sorry,' said Issa, aware of how weak it sounded.

'I have to kill them, I have to kill them to set them free, kill my knights, my own friends,' Marakon whispered. A tremble shook his shoulders.

'They're not your friends anymore,' Eiretonne said. 'There's nothing in them but darkness. They're gone—'

'Into Oblivion, into that bastard *thing* in the sky. I know.' Marakon hissed, staring up at the ceiling as if seeing the Dark Rift there and daring to challenge it. 'They must be killed before they take Murlonius too.'

Issa nodded, wishing for all the world she knew how to be rid of them.

She sighed. 'I feel like we're going around in hopeless circles, saving people and losing others, taking back lands and losing more.'

Eiretonne laid his axe against the pedestal and sat down beside it. 'Lans Himay may not have fallen—yet. But until the Dark Rift is gone, until *he* is gone, we can never be free.'

The ground rocked and the air sizzled, tearing Issa from her sleep.

She awoke looking into the Flow. A spray of dark magic hit the shield which shuddered and flickered wildly, threatening to collapse. She bolstered the shield, then squinted into the darkness trying to locate the source of the attack.

There, on a ledge back the way they had come, stood necromancers. Hurtling towards them ran a horde of Maphraxies clinging to the chains of rabid death hounds. Along each crossroad except one, Maphraxies streamed.

'They came out of nowhere,' gasped a soldier who had been on watch, his sword tip quivering.

'Necromancer magic,' hissed Ekem, his spear at the ready.

Issa gripped her sword, trying to fathom how many there were.

'At least two hundred,' said Marakon, reading her mind. 'Run!' he screamed. 'We'll fight them on the bridge and in the tunnel where they cannot attack us from all sides.'

Issa lifted her hands. 'Fire,' she commanded. A wall of blue flames spread before her and smashed into the Maphraxies. Without waiting to watch, she turned and fled after the others.

She made it onto the long narrow bridge and slammed into the back of a soldier who had suddenly halted. Streaming out of the doorway ahead came more Maphraxies, roaring their commands in guttural speak. Beyond the din of baying death hounds, she felt the necromancers' magic building.

A death hound lunged for her. She stepped away and stabbed her sword into its side. It staggered and tumbled over the bridge, its desperate howls taking a long time to fade away.

Another came on, followed by its Maphraxie handler. She barely missed its snapping jaws as she sank her sword into its neck. It fell, dragging her down. The soldier behind her grabbed her and she yanked her sword free.

A green feathered spear slammed into the Maphraxies throat before she could reach it. It tumbled over the bridge, silent.

She didn't have time to counteract the necromancers' magic. It snaked above and below. The bridge between her and the Maphraxies exploded, rock and stone spraying into the air, leaving a gaping chasm. There was no way forward. A second explosion sounded. She glanced behind. There was no way back.

The whole bridge trembled. Issa staggered for balance on the narrow walkway. 'It's falling!' she gasped.

'With us on it!' said the soldier.

Issa grabbed hold of Illendri as the bridge swayed sickeningly. She drew upon Earth Magic, feeling it fill the orb. 'Balance!' she cried. Their swaying section of bridge gently righted itself. Shelley entered the Flow. Issa prayed the dwarf would keep the necromancers at bay whilst she focused on the bridge.

Earth Magic, assist me, Issa prayed.

There was a ledge, far down on the opposite wall, and what looked like a doorway with no bridge or steps to reach it. The din of cracking rocks filled her ears and soldiers screamed. Sweat trickled down her face. Illendri flared, straining to hold the bridge upright, its magic pulsing through her in powerful waves. But it was not enough.

The bridge emitted a sighing groan as it fell. She tried to control it, to turn the bridge in some manner. In the Flow, time slowed, the bridge moved in inches. A great crack told her it had lifted from its arches completely and she now held the entire bridge with all the soldiers upon it. She could barely breathe. Her pulse pounded in her ears and her teeth ached from being clenched so hard.

The ledge loomed ahead and then they were hurtling towards it. The bridge slammed lengthways onto it and everyone sprawled. One soldier was thrown over the edge, his horrified screams cut short as he slammed into the cliff face. Issa rolled and crashed into a rock, the breath knocked from her lungs.

Black magic surged, bringing her back to her senses. She clawed onto her feet. Ehka squawked madly and flew to the doorway. Illendri turned cold in her hand, spent. Shaking all over, she gripped her talisman and formed another shield. It was weak; she couldn't keep this up for long.

'Into the tunnel, follow the raven!' Marakon screamed.

Issa followed the others inside, each step staggering. She heard a magical explosion followed by the agonised screams of the soldiers behind them, but she couldn't stop.

Rocks tumbled from the ceiling as the tunnel began to crumble. A boulder fell, knocking down the soldier beside her. She glanced back and wished she hadn't. The man was crushed and lifeless, blood trickling over the ground. The whole tunnel shook, and she leapt onward. She tried to pull on Illendri to calm the rocks, but it would not respond.

The ground groaned and splintered, an enormous crack yawned before her. It grew wider as she leapt over it, barely making it to the other side.

She turned, ready to help the next person, but all she could see was billowing dust and rubble. She staggered onward. The soldier in front of her stumbled, forcing her to leap over him. The ground opened up again and then she was rolling into the chasm.

Marakon!' she screamed, scrabbling wildly to grab hold of something, anything, but her hands were scraped raw on rocks as she helplessly rolled into the darkness. Somehow, she managed to stop tumbling and instead slid forwards with the rubble into the blackness. Unable to stop her descent, the floor vanished and she found she was suddenly falling.

A moment later she hit the ground hard. The darkness completed itself.

CHAPTER 20

Hall of Memories

ISSA awoke to the cold hands of Maggot on her cheek.

The rotting smell of the demon so close assaulted her senses. She stared blearily up into his face, one grimy tooth protruding over his lip, the only light coming from his yellow eyes which really did glow in the dark.

'Issy?'

'Oh, my head,' Issa groaned. There was a sore lump on the back of her skull but thankfully the skin hadn't broken. She trembled all over but was otherwise whole. Gingerly, she sat up. There was no sound, no light, no anything. There wasn't even black magic. The nothingness made her shiver.

'Thank the goddess you're here Maggot.' She couldn't imagine being down here alone, dying slowly in the dark.

'Where is here, Issy?' he asked.

'I don't know.' Taking long slow breaths to calm herself, she created a little indigo light with the talisman.

She was in a perfectly square room only a few paces wide. At head height, there were several small square holes and a slight breeze of fresh air came from them. Could this be some kind of airshaft? In one corner of the room was a carved doorway, about dwarf height.

She got up, drew her sword and went to it. Maggot followed. Peering around the corner of the stone wall, she saw nothing but a straight tunnel of smooth rock. She considered sending Maggot to find the others but, again, the thought of being down here alone chilled her to the bone.

She let out a long, dejected sigh. 'Well, come on then, let's get moving.

There's no point crying down here.' Hunched over, sword in hand, she made her way forwards.

Further on, the tunnel heightened and she found she could just about stand up straight. There were no bends or turns or branches—it just went on in one direction. She trailed a hand along the smooth walls. 'At least this was made by the light dwarves,' she said, finding solace in the thought.

A green light flashed in the tunnel far ahead. She stopped and raised her sword. A noise echoed—it sounded like a squawk.

'Ehka?' she dared to call out.

Maggot flew ahead.

'Wait, Maggot. It could be a trick.' Not wanting to be alone, she rushed after him, coming to an abrupt stop when the tunnel ended and branched left and right. Another squawk sounded, closer, then the green light appeared and rushed towards her. In moments, it was buzzing in her face and squealing.

'Stupid swamp fairy!' growled Maggot.

Issa wafted at the fairy irritably. 'Thiashar? Stop that. What are you doing here? *How* did you get here? Ehka?' The raven landed at her feet. The swamp fairy squealed and buzzed around Maggot.

'You found me, praise the light,' said Issa. 'Did you find the others? Are they coming?'

'What others?' Thiashar giggled and bounced on Maggot's head, jumping to avoid his swatting hand. 'I came alone and found your raven lost in the tunnels looking for you. Anyway, I've found it, after so long hidden, it was me who discovered it again. You have to come.'

'Found what?' Issa frowned.

Thiashar giggled again. 'There's a place—an ancient, forgotten place deep in the ground beneath Tarvalastone. The Seers know of it but few others. It was lost long ago, even before the Dwarves of Light made this their home. When you and the necromancers destroyed the tunnels, the magic revealed older ones. But it's not exactly in Maioria, more sort of between here and the world of fae.'

'Thiashar, what are you talking about? This is all meaningless to me. Did Iyena send you? Ah, I thought she did. Now all we need to do is get out of here and back to the others.' The thought of adventuring right now was abhorrent.

Thiashar hummed excitedly and bounced in the air. 'Yes, but you must see what has been found.'

'Why?' Issa shrugged, trying not to be irritated. 'We're trying to take back a city and all you can do is go on about some forgotten place. I don't see why…' The swamp fairy zoomed away into the darkness. Issa slumped and Ehka croaked.

'She's so annoying,' Maggot harrumphed.

Issa closed her eyes and tilted back her head. *I can't just ignore something ancient found!* Her own insatiable curiosity getting the better of her, she hurried after the swamp fairy.

At the end of the tunnel before an exit—or entrance—Thiashar waited. A strange haze filled the doorway. Issa sheathed her sword and held a hand to it. It felt fuzzy, like static.

'It's a gateway,' said Thiashar knowingly.

'I can see that,' Issa murmured. She swallowed audibly, watching Maggot peer into the strange white mist. He sniffed it, wrinkling up his nose.

'Is it safe?' she asked.

Thiashar buzzed up and down excitedly. 'How do you think I got here? There's nothing evil, silly, it's only an ancient place of *mystery*… and a touch of fairy.

'Iyena had a vision. She said that when the Free People's invade the lands of the dark dwarves, a forgotten place will be revealed. In that place, answers will be found. She knew it would be discovered soon and told me to lead you to it. She wants to know what you will see.'

'Maggot, no—' but before Issa could stop him, the little demon disappeared into the mist. Moments later, he stuck his head out again.

Issa let go her breath. Ehka jumped after the demon.

'Come on, scaredy-cat!' Thiashar giggled and disappeared after the bird.

Issa wondered about Marakon and the soldiers and all that might be occurring on land that she should be involved in. *It's not like we have a city to take back or anything.* But without Thiashar, she was stuck down here. Besides, she hadn't noticed another exit, anyway.

Holding her sword high, Issa stepped into the doorway.

Dar watched Iyena's eyes turn first blue and then completely white as she stared into their Holy of Holies.

Suli sat beside her. The water in the pool of the small crystal cavern shimmered with effervescence. The white crystals shone even whiter in the glow of the three staves resting on the floor beside the pool.

Iyena spoke, her voice strong and filled with wonder, 'Thiashar has found the Hall of Memories. As it is written, "When the forces of light entered the dark city, then will the Halls reopen again." And now they have. She has led the Raven Queen there, just as we have foreseen. What Issa will see now, will shape the things to come.'

Iyena sat back on her calves, her shining eyes never blinking, never leaving what she saw in the still water. When she spoke again, her voice was a whisper. 'Is this the end? No, it's just the beginning of the end. The shield protecting Myrn is failing, as we have also foreseen.'

An image formed in the pool. In it, the shield above Myrn flickered purple then became transparent. It began to crack, like glass. Dar took a silent breath and wiped away a tear. The cracks had appeared a few days ago, and each day the shield weakened under Baelthrom's assaults. He hunted relentlessly for them now. But it wasn't just his power causing this— the close proximity of the Dark Rift and the flood of the Under Flow into Maioria was now overpowering their own magic.

'We cannot withstand Baelthrom's attacks for much longer.' Iyena shook her head. 'He knows the end times have begun and will fight ever harder. We must prepare to protect only that which is most sacred: Sheyengetha; the Star Portal; our crystals; our people, and our knowledge.

'On the Endless Planes the last battle for Maioria will occur. We may be able to save a fraction of Myrn, but we cannot hope to protect the other islands. We must leave here, soon. Do not cry, beloved Dar, it is as we have foreseen. We must be strong; all things change in time.'

Dar smiled through the tears at Iyena. Despite the weariness in the older woman's face, the love and compassion therein moved her. Iyena stood and the three seers embraced, hands clutching and trembling.

Issa felt a strange dizziness as if she were shifting form, and then the feeling was gone.

She stepped into a very large stone chamber with a high ceiling. Thick square pillars decorated with strange lettering held up the ceiling and the whole place was smoothed, polished and unaged—with not a speck of dust in sight. Indeed, every letter on the pillars looked fresh and sharp as if freshly chiselled. It was as if time had decided to leave this place.

'A place between time,' Issa breathed.

Soft mist hung above the floor and the place was silent as the grave. She stepped further into the hall and the mist swirled up to her waist.

'This place is strange,' she said, trying to determine whether it was magic or enchantments she felt hanging thick here, though there appeared to be no obvious danger.

She inspected a pillar. The script was angular, not like Dwarven, or even Elven. 'I've not seen any writing like this.'

'Look, the mist's changing,' said Maggot. He was hazy beneath the fog. Sure enough the mist was turning blue and her talisman began to glow in response.

'You say this place is ancient, before even the Ancients?' asked Issa.

'Yes,' said Thiashar, swirling around a pillar. 'Iyena says the Ancients discovered it and hid it from the Dark Dwarves. But no one knows for sure. Come, look at these.' She darted to a corner of the room. Issa cautiously followed, there was something about this place she couldn't quite put her finger on—magical, ancient, important. Or perhaps it contained artefacts or visions or truths she wasn't ready to see.

The fairy hovered before a giant picture frame ornately carved out of stone. It was at least seven feet high. On either side of it, many more stretched along the wall in both directions.

Issa stared at the empty picture and touched the smooth stone. It was cold. Suddenly the surface rippled out from where she had touched it, the stone moving like water. She gasped and stepped back. Maggot clung to her leg. An image appeared.

'The raven talisman,' whispered Issa, her eyes wide as she noted the familiar raven with wings outstretched and forming a perfect circle. Beneath the raven was a long shard. 'Velistor. The likeness is perfect, but what does it mean?'

Thiashar didn't speak and instead hummed and bounced in the air before the next one. Issa went to it and touched the surface again. It rippled, and another picture formed.

This time, people appeared carved out of stone. Men on one side and women on the other. They all held staves and wore robes—so expertly carved they appeared to ripple in the wind. Wizards and seers, she thought. Some even looked familiar, though she couldn't, and didn't want, to be sure. She swallowed.

They all stood before a woman who was robed and hooded so that only her chin was visible. She held no staff, but a raven perched on her shoulder. They were all smiling, as if something wonderful was occurring.

Issa frowned and went to the next stone frame. She touched the surface and marvelled as an incredibly detailed scene depicting a battle unfolded.

On the left, identified by their tabards, Knights of the Raven sat proudly upon prancing mounts. Beyond them, as far as the eye could see, clustered legions of soldiers sporting Feylint Halanoi, Davonian and many other tabards. *All the Free Peoples are here.* There were proud elves, Karalanths and even armoured bears carrying people.

On the right, the hordes of Baelthrom roared. Maphraxies, their huge, deformed bodies, repulsive even in picture form, hefted giant weapons. Death hounds and Foltoy, even Dromoorai flew in the skies ready to meet the dragons of the North.

In the centre of the picture, the armies clashed. So life-like was the image, Issa fancied she could hear the screams of man, horse and beast, the ring of metal, and the thud of drums.

Her eyes were drawn to a lone figure on a cliff looking over the battlefield. She sat atop a large horse, her face grim and unyielding. Mirroring her, on the other side of the battle atop a hill, stood Baelthrom. His wings spread wide, great sword drawn and magic flickering around him. Above them all, the Dark Rift ripped apart the sky.

Issa's pulse quickened. She turned away from the two figures facing each other and forced herself to the next picture frame.

As the ripples smoothed, a far simpler scene was revealed. A tree formed in the stone, so detailed she could tell from the leaves it was an oak, and a body swung from its bough. Another figure huddled on the ground, her back to her, head in hands. Cold swept through Issa.

'Ely,' Issa's breath caught in her throat. She reached to touch the serene face but couldn't bear the thought of feeling cold stone instead of warm flesh. 'It will not be for nothing, my beautiful Ely.' Her eyes misting over, she let her hand drop.

'What is this place?' her voice was a harsh whisper.

Thiashar no longer buzzed so gayly but was thoughtful, almost withdrawn. 'Sad things, these,' she mused. 'It's known only as the Hall of Memories. It reflects back what is so, the things that have come to pass, and sometimes the things that might be.'

But that battle she had not lived, was that what was going to be? *But the future is not decided!*

She moved on and the surface of the next picture rippled under her touch. Asaph's handsome face looked back at her. All the love and warmth he had in real life exuded in the image, pushing back the sorrow and making her smile. He hugged a woman with long hair, her back also to her. Issa closed her eyes, she could no longer deny it was herself in these murals.

She glanced around the hall. Soft indigo mist glowed everywhere and there were many more stone frames to look at. 'There must be hundreds in here, I must see them all. Who made them? Why?' Issa knew before she spoke that no one in particular, no one here knew, not even Thiashar or the seers.

She touched the next one and another scene from her life appeared. Freydel's study in Castle Elune, and the man himself smiling beyond a pile of books and scrolls. She sat in an armchair, cradling a steaming mug. The serenity and innocence of the scene filled her with yearning for a time before now. *Celene, my home, now gone.* She turned away.

The next was of a raven perched on a fence, a horse looking on from afar with a mane that stuck out at all angles. 'Haybear.' She laughed, then sighed, feeling overwhelmed. 'There are too many to look at them all. Maybe I don't want to see everything again.'

Her heart heavy, she walked to the opposite side of the hall. Perhaps something different would be depicted there, something from the future? But as she touched each frame, again only scenes from her life were reflected back; Keteth, the man and the beast, Rhul'ynth and the Karalanths, Asaph the dragon, and dear Coronos. Even her beloved father was depicted, but where were the ones of the future she hoped to see?

On she looked, her heart beating harder as each scene brought back memories relived anew. It was all here; the record of her life. Faster and faster she moved through each picture until she felt faint.

Her head pounding, she finally paused and leant back against a frame to steady herself. *It's all too much, reliving every painful and joyful scene from my life.* She focussed on breathing deeply and slowly until a sense of calm returned. Why was she here? What had Iyena expected her to see?

She stood and stared at the picture she had been leaning on. Reflected back was herself, just as she stood now, even the flick of her hair tickling her cheek that she was about to brush away was carved into the stone.

Maggot appeared beside her feet and the shape of a star beside him. *Thiashar.* Barely breathing, she walked to the next empty picture and touched the surface. For a long time it rippled, longer than all the others— but this one did not turn into a picture. Instead, the ripples began to swirl like a whirlpool around a central point.

'What's happening, Thiashar?' Issa rested her hand on her sword pommel.

'I don't know, Raven Queen, it reflects only what is so.'

The centre of the vortex began to open. Issa stared, mesmerised as a face formed. It became clearer, a female face, smooth-skinned and young. It looked like her own, only younger – more girl than woman. There was pain in that subtle frown, and deep sadness reflected in the downturn of her perfect lips. Her eyes saw things Issa didn't want to see. Issa stepped back.

'I don't like it, Issy,' said Maggot.

'Courage, Maggot, like Carmedrak taught you.' But her voice was a whisper, and she felt no courage at all. Sweat beaded her face.

Issa turned back to the previous mural that had mirrored the current moment. It was changing. The picture melted away and the stone began to swirl in a vortex just like the other. With a sound that made her jump, the stone suddenly cracked and turned black and liquid-like.

'The vortex has become real!' Issa gasped, staring at the whirlpool of black paint.

Thiashar shrieked and shot away, disappearing out of the chamber. Maggot squealed and vanished, leaving nothing but the glowing green symbol of the Murk on the floor.

'Maggot, you coward!' said Issa, even though her legs trembled.

Ehka squawked and landed by her feet. He jumped and crowed, urging her to leave.

'I know it's the Under Flow!' Issa replied, but something made her stay.

She grabbed her sword and entered the Flow. Darkness was all about. The Under Flow seeped everywhere above and below the Flow, seeking to smother it. She gripped her raven talisman. The vortex grew and the face she had seen in the other picture formed, only this one was not made of stone. This was *real*—pale flesh and pink lips. She wanted to run, but something about that face…it seemed familiar.

She glanced back at the last mural. It now depicted another person behind the first, a bald female scowling, but at least it remained in stone, not like the one before her.

The pale faced-girl opened her eyes and Issa gasped. They were so pale they were almost white. The girl blinked and squinted as if she couldn't see properly. Then she scowled and cried out in pain before becoming still and frowning in confusion. She did not act normally at all—she acted as if possessed and struggling against some awful darkness within her.

Shoved from behind, the girl jerked forwards, almost falling out of the vortex. Issa stepped back in alarm. The girl's dark brown hair was scraped back into a tight band, and a thick choker hung around her neck and it seemed to be controlling her. *Not a choker, a leash!* Issa realised.

The collar jerked back, savagely pulling the girl upright and making her groan in pain. She was draped in a simple white dress that hung loose to her pale calves. Her arms and feet were bare, and every visible patch of flesh was bruised or welted.

Beyond her, the face of the other woman became clearer; gleaming white skin and shining all-black eyes. The Under Flow came from her and in her hands she held an orb as dark as the black drink, an orb that mirrored another. *Freydel's orb!*

Issa lost her grip on the Flow as the Under Flow smothered it completely.

'Lona,' Issa rasped, feeling weak.

The Yurgha smiled at her, her predatory eyes gleaming, and Issa glimpsed the end of the girl's leash in her hand.

'Go on, go to your sister,' said Lona, her accent unlike any Issa had heard before.

Issa's world rocked. She stepped backwards shaking her head, her sword trembling, her eyes darting from Lona to the girl and back again.

'This is a lie,' Issa growled. 'You always lie. I've seen everything! You lied to Ayeth and now you lie to me. *You* killed my mother.'

The rage grew in Issa so fast she had trouble seeing straight. This strange puppet on Lona's string was not her sister but some hideous trick. Lona would pay for all that she had done. Pulling on both the talisman and Illendri, their combined magic surged into her.

Issa's eyes blazed with power. 'Let the girl go, she needn't die.'

Lona laughed, a beautiful musical sound devoid of any warmth. 'I'm the only one keeping her alive. All she needs is your life-force, the life-force of her sister to sustain her, and the two Raven Queens will be destroyed. All that exists within the Dark Rift will make it so.'

Issa could barely breathe through the rage. All that halted her was the thought of sparing the innocent girl's life.

'Impossible! She's too old to be my sister, fool. Let her go and come fight me, coward, whether by blade or magic, it matters not to me,' Issa's voice trembled as the magic surged within waiting for release.

'How archaic, how barbaric! We Yurgha do not fight with *pathetic* blades. Your *sister* is a child, but her body is full-grown. Your backward race has so much to learn, it's incredible how far you have to go. Now touch her!' Lona shouted.

The girl lunged forwards, driven by her handler's command. A bruised pale hand with torn nails shot forward and grabbed Issa's arm in an icy vice. Heat and something more, something vital, flooded out of Issa's body, making her stagger. Her heart slowed, and the air became thick in her lungs.

The girl groaned, her eyes fluttering, and the bruises on her body began to lighten. Issa tried to twist her arm away, but the girl grabbed with her other hand. Something happened in that touch, a communication, a knowing she could not deny.

This is my sister!

The shock sent Issa to her knees. All the rage, all the fight, left her. Beyond the pounding in her ears she heard Ehka squawking. He tried to attack the girl but blackness flared smashing him to the floor where he lay still.

'Ehka,' Issa screamed. She swung her left arm, punching her sister in the face. The girl fell, the shock enough for Issa to wrench her arm free.

Issa staggered back, her heart labouring, her weakened soul struggling to form a hold on the Flow. Her sister recovered faster and there was colour in her cheeks where before there had been none. Issa sobbed, seeing her mother and father reflected in the features of the face before her.

'What have you done to my sister?' Issa held her sword up then lowered it. She couldn't kill her sister.

'Take her essence, it's yours to have,' hissed Lona, letting out a yard of chain. The Yurgha took care to not step away from the vortex and the power of the Dark Rift.

Her sister stepped forwards, white eyes wide and hungry.

'Yes,' said Lona, 'that is what life tastes like. That is the soul. Take it!'

Her sister moved with frightening speed. Issa ducked her grasping hands, the merest brush searing cold as they glanced off her cheek, stealing more of her life-force.

'Sister, it's me,' Issa sobbed, her back hitting a pillar. 'Can't you see? Can't you feel? Remember Mother, remember Father.'

Her sister came on, not listening. The hunger in her eyes reminded Issa of a Dread Dragon, the way it lusted after death, lusted after the life blood of others, and devoid of all else. All it did was feed.

This *was* her sister and yet it was not. Was anything left within her? What had been done to her? Her sister suddenly weakened and fell forwards with a gasp. Uncaring of the peril, Issa caught her, felt her frigid cold hands grab her shoulders. Terrible pain exploded there, and Issa screamed. The cold both paralysed her body and convulsed it at the same time. Beyond the pain, she glimpsed the gleeful eyes of Lona. The cold spread, eating into her mind and making everything go numb.

The Flow waited within Illendri and her talisman, making its presence known. It took all Issa's strength to lift her dead arms and place her shaking hands on the collar around her sister's neck. Magic flared from her palms shattering the glimmering collar. It snaked up the chain held by Lona and exploded, flinging the Yurgha backwards.

Her sister shuddered and blinked as if coming back into herself.

'Sister,' Issa gasped, finally feeling the air in her lungs, 'you cannot take what's mine. Come with me, let's go together.'

Lona jumped to her feet, her face a mask of unfettered rage. Briefly, Issa wondered if Ayeth had ever seen that face—if he'd ever seen who Lona really was, but there wasn't much time to save her sister or herself.

'A'farion, A'farion, A'farion!' Issa screamed.

The Realm of the Dead engulfed them.

CHAPTER 21

Sorrow and Fury

HER sister shuddered, and the outflow of Issa's life force halted as the ghost world took shape.

The place felt stronger and more real than it ever had. The pillars of the hall, the stone beneath her feet—it was all more solid. *My soul is weakened, my body closer to death, closer to this place.* Ehka twitched, got off his side and huddled against the ground. Not well but at least he was alive. *As alive as one can be here!*

Far away, horses screamed and her sister's hands, which were still gripping Issa's shoulders, clenched. Issa tore them from her but as their palms connected, images flooded into her mind. She gasped and dropped to her knees. Her sister fell limply beside her, their palms still connected.

She entered a world of darkness that lasted hours and terrible pain such as she had never felt. Her skin stung all over and the very marrow of her bones burned, as if on fire. She screamed and howled until her voice broke. When the pain subsided, a desolate loneliness descended.

The Yurgha, with their pale faces and black eyes, surrounded her but they did not alleviate the loneliness, they did not push back the darkness. The pain came and went as they did things to her with strange devices, small and large, with liquids and gasses—medicines and technologies she didn't understand.

I'm a child, she realised, *I'm a child and these are my sister's memories.* Fear, loneliness, pain…and then one face in the darkness. *Lona.*

'Mother,' said her sister in her mind.

'*No it isn't. This is mother,*' Issa replied, and in her mind gathered together all the memories of her mother she possessed. A smiling woman with long dark hair and blue-green eyes dressed in pale blue seer's robes.

Horses screamed, closer. Issa ignored them and the growing terror, instead focusing on images of her parents.

'*And this is father.*' She shared her memory of her parents smiling down at her when she herself was a babe.

Her sister cried out in agony, breaking the memories. She clawed at her own face, scratching welts into her bruised flesh. 'I know only darkness,' she howled.

'No, sister stop, please!' Issa grabbed her hands and struggled against her surprising strength. 'Sister, don't! Feel the life-force you took from me; the memories are within! They are yours too. Reach for them.'

She held her sister close, trying to avoid her clawing, punching hands. In her arms, Issa noticed her sister's hair was long, straight and brown, more umber and lighter than her own.

'Your hair's like our mother's,' she said. 'Look, mine is dark, more like father's.'

It seemed the most frivolous thing to say but her sister slowly ceased her flailing. She looked at Issa's hair with wide, child-like eyes. She touched it and lifted a few strands closer to her face. Was there a flicker of her sister in there?

'Yes, sister, reach.' Issa smiled through the tears.

Her sister convulsed, her back arching painfully. Her watery-pale eyes suddenly rolled back in their sockets and then turned completely black. She scowled, just like Lona scowled, and a tormented howl tore from her lips. She moved in a stagger, as if possessed, and her hand whipped towards Issa so fast, she barely glimpsed the dagger as it plunged towards her throat. It was strange, made of beautiful crystal, and she did not have time to stop it.

She became aware of the hooves pounding behind her and the clacking of horns, so loud she wondered why she hadn't heard them before. A black sword flew past her nose and slammed into her sister, piercing the left side of her chest. She jerked violently in Issa's grasp and the dagger missed her throat as she fell. The black sword ploughed on, embedding itself all the way to its hilt. Red blood spilled down white cloth.

A woman howled, it sounded like Lona but came from far away. Her sister's black eyes turned milky white and shock spread over her childish face. Issa pulled her close, felt her labouring heart shudder against her own. Silence fell. Hot wetness spilled over her hands. Issa held her tighter, willing her life force into her, but it could not be done.

Pounding hooves halted. A beast snorted smoke that billowed over her, the blackness stark in the grey of the shadow world, the stench of something long dead.

In the glaze covering her sister's eyes, Issa saw the four horsemen reflected back. Black knights on beasts, three with swords aloft pointing at her.

'Sister,' gasped the girl in her arms. 'I still feel the light. I still feel it.'

Tears streamed down Issa's cheeks. Her sister's heart stopped, and she became limp. Issa grabbed her close and screamed, feeling the light of her sister pass right through her and upwards.

A huge metal hand reached down and gripped around her throat, shutting off her scream and lifting her up by her neck. Her sister flopped from her grasp and lay still, so pale and lifeless she was already a ghost in the Realm of the Dead.

Issa had no fight left within her. She surrendered.

Ehka cawed loudly.

I've got nothing left within me, Ehka.

A flash of magic blinded her. The hand around her neck jerked and she was falling, but the hand still gripped her neck. The ghost realm vanished, and she hit the ground of the Hall of Memories hard. The metal hand dropped from her neck, dismembered at the elbow. Beside her lay Velistor, bloodied and thronging and flashing bright. Beneath her, a giant symbol of the Murk slowly dimmed.

The hum of the translocation faded into chaos.

Four demons, their backs and wings filling the space in front of her from floor to ceiling, slashed demonic weapons against a sea of black flooding out of the vortex.

Through the swirling mass, Issa glimpsed Lona and other Yurgha, their pale hands raised, black magic surging from their palms. To her right, on the far side of the room, Marakon, Eiretonne and Bokaard, along with Cusap'anth and Rhul'ynth, battled against the Knights of Maphrax. Maggot stood back from them all hurling Jabber, his beloved tiny spear-like weapon, whilst Thiashar whizzed wildly left and right, desperately dodging magic and blades.

Clanging metal, demon howls and the screams of beast-horses deafened her ears, and the crush of black magic stole the air from her lungs. She pushed herself to her feet and readied to enter the Flow, but her eyes fell upon the still, pale form of her sister on the ground, beside whom Ehka huddled.

The noise and mayhem faded away into silence.

Gone, and I could not save her. The sorrow cut deep, tears instantly springing into her eyes—but there was rage too. Not knowing what else to do, she picked up Velistor and felt it rumble with a desperate need. She aimed it at a Knight of Maphrax, struggled to find her mark on the moving target, then hurled it, screaming her rage.

The spear plunged through its chest, ignoring the armour the knight wore. Its terrible mount reared and pawed the air as if it, too, had been struck.

Seeing his chance, Marakon lunged in, raised his sword, and smote the knight's head from its shoulders. Without pause, he swung his sword back and slashed at the horse. Horse and rider jerked backwards, becoming immaterial as they faded from the world. The beast's hind quarters turned into smoke and then the whole horse and knight exploded, smoke and soot filling the air in the place they had been. Velistor fell and clanged upon the floor.

Issa looked at Marakon. He caught her glance as he looked up from the smoking knight, her own pain and fury mirrored in his face. With deadly calm, he snatched up Velistor and turned upon the next Knight of Maphrax, once his knight, once his friend. Now only the spear in his hands had the power to kill them.

Issa entered the Flow too late. Black magic slammed her against a pillar, knocking the breath from her lungs. She gathered herself, drew upon the Flow fast and hurled it at the vortex.

Sonic booms shook the chamber and they plunged into darkness. Demon howls filled the air.

'Lightning,' Issa commanded.

White forks streaked from her hands into the vortex. The air shuddered, pressure grew, crushing down upon her until her head pounded and bones creaked.

Someone entered the Flow and magic added to her own. *Naksu*, she recognised the signature. The Under Flow groaned as the Flow surged. The pressure shattered, cutting off the screams of beasts and demons. Immediate silence and a void in magic descended. The darkness receded.

Issa slid down the wall, panting. Was it over?

Demons, half shadow and half materialised, looked around, their scowling faces softening. Marakon and the others, paused in mid-battle, now slowly straightened and lowered their weapons.

Naksu sighed, a relieved smile growing on her exhausted face as she smoothed her robes.

'We shut the vortex, somehow,' Issa panted.

'They couldn't cope with the purity of Maioria's magic,' said Naksu.

Ehka hopped unsteadily over. She pulled him onto her lap and lay her head back against the pillar. 'Thank the goddess you all came when you did. How did you find me? I fell down a long airshaft. Never mind. How many horsemen did we take?'

'Two down,' said Marakon, a pained look on his face. 'Two got away.'

Rhul'ynth came over and Issa looked up into the face of her friend, dried blood marring the swirls of blue warrior paint. Issa forced a smile. 'I'm all right, but how in hell did you get here?'

'We breached the south-western wall through the hidden gate, and ran right into Marakon,' said Rhul'ynth. She took a cloth and bent to gently wipe the blood and dirt from Issa's forehead.

Marakon stood beside her. 'The swamp fairy was leading us to you after we lost you in the collapsing tunnel.' He nodded to Thiashar who hung close to the ceiling, her light unusually dim.

Cold hands pressed on her leg and Maggot dared to materialise his face. She smiled at him. 'So, you didn't run away but went to get help.' She glanced at the demons to her left. They clustered together and eyed Marakon warily, knowing him better as Demon Slayer.

'King promised warriors. Now was a good time,' said Maggot.

Issa watched the demons shuffling awkwardly, clearly not used to humans, and certainly not fighting alongside them. 'Will you fight for us?' she asked.

'We fight in the shadows until we can bear this world no longer,' one growled. 'Then we return to our king.'

'Thank you,' said Issa, moved, but her emotions were conflicted. The demons had betrayed her mother and caused so much pain, and yet here they were helping her. She couldn't hate them, but Gedrock had better have some answers for her. Apart from Maggot, she wondered if she could ever trust them fully.

With Rhul'ynth's help, Issa got onto her bruised feet, and in halting steps, she went to her sister. Marakon followed, then the others.

'Who is she?' Cusap'anth asked.

Issa knelt down, trying not to see the ugly black sword impaling her body. 'My sister,' she croaked over the lump in her throat. *She doesn't even have a name! All those years we could have spent together, gone. I could have loved you, I do love you. You could have met father. We could have healed you and made you strong, but not now. What can I tell father?* Issa smarted in bitterness.

Marakon knelt beside her. As gently as he could, he pulled free the hateful sword and threw it on the floor. It hissed and turned into smoke.

'Only a few days ago I had a sister,' Issa whispered. 'Already she has been taken from me. That *thing* that came out of the vortex, out of the Dark Rift, took her as a slave and killed my mother. My sister might be gone but at least she's free of this bitter world of pain and torment.'

Before the sobs could come, Issa entered the Flow and pulled indigo magic to her, cool and gentle. Tears blurring her vision, she worked indigo light from her hands into her sister's body, the blue flames engulfing her swiftly. The magic fire flared brightly for several moments and then disappeared, her sister's body along with it. *Turned to light. Zanufey carry you, beloved!*

A strong hand gripped her shoulder. She looked up at Marakon, and he pulled her up and into an embrace.

'Find solace in battle,' he whispered in her ear.

'And there's a big one occurring right now above our heads,' said Cusap'anth, his sensitive ears overhearing.

Issa nodded, and a steely resolve came over her. 'I can fight.' *I'll lose myself in battle, so the sorrow cannot touch me!*

Marakon hung back as the others left the strange chamber of stone mirrors.

Alone, he knelt beside the pile of dark ash on the floor, all that remained of one of his knights. *My knight killed by my own hand, like so many had been in those dark times.* He had deliberately targeted the knight with the ring on his finger.

'Meyer,' he whispered, casting his mind back to memories of conversations shared thousands of years ago.

'I'll train your horse. You'll never want to ride another again.' Meyer's hair caught the sunlight, his white teeth shining as he grinned.

Meyer had trained horses for the Knights of the Shining Star. He had a way with them, a special relationship, like a Daluni but only with horses. This pile of ash was not Meyer but the remains of something twisted and evil.

Where are you now, Meyer? Does anything remain of you in the tormented darkness? Forgive me, for everything. Cold wrapped around his heart for all the wrong doings of a life lived long ago. *I'm sorry I could not save you.*

He forced back the tears, he would not grieve, not here, not when there was a battle to be fought. He would find solace in the sword and spear in his hand.

Gently he stroked the pile of ash, his fingers touching something hard and round. He picked it up and stared at the gold ring with a prancing horse engraved on it.

Giving a long sigh he stood, slipped the ring into his pocket, and hefted Velistor. Feeling the spear's need draw him on, he followed after the others.

Naksu took Ehka from Issa's arms as they walked out of the hall. 'You save your magic. Let me help him.' The seer began her inspection of the bird, who sat quite calmly in her arms. 'So, you found the Hall of Memories?' Naksu smiled knowingly.

'Yes, and I don't care to ever come here again,' said Issa.

'It's not an evil place, but it's always a trying place,' Naksu nodded. 'What happened to you in there was not normal.'

'Nothing that's happened to me in this life can be considered normal,' said Issa. She stopped suddenly and looked around. 'Wait, this isn't the place I entered from.' She noted the wide cellar filled with ancient barrels lining the brick walls as far as the braziers would stretch. Many were smashed and empty.

'And how *did* you find me? I fell all the way to the end of an air shaft, maybe a mile deep.'

Naksu smiled enigmatically and continued walking. 'The Hall of Memories does not stay in the same place. It moves at will. That's why it's so difficult to find. This must be the ancient dwarven section before the dark dwarves took it. Look at that old barrel of wine. Dark dwarves don't drink such fine beverages.'

Issa looked at the old barrel laying on its side. 'A place that's not quite in the real world…more in the land of fae,' she murmured.

'That's it,' said Naksu.

Issa rolled back her shoulders. 'I hope I don't end up in any more of those places.'

Stone steps led up into a long corridor. Something must have been heard for Marakon paused and raised his hand for quiet. Bokaard padded silently ahead to scout. Issa followed Marakon's lead and pressed herself against the wall beside him.

'Where are the others? Your soldiers and the Saurians?' she whispered.

'Ahead, fighting. They might have reached the courtyard by now. When that swamp fairy found us, we split off to come and find you. We thought you were gone.'

'Thank you, Thiashar,' Issa nodded to the green light high above.

Bokaard came back. 'Can't see anything obvious.'

Quietly they made their way through several wide, empty stone corridors. Issa imagined them in their heyday, adorned with rugs, chairs, tapestries and paintings—much like Castle Carvon or Castle Rebben. Now there was only dark emptiness. At least they were in the light dwarves' old home rather than the dark dwarves' evil tunnels.

There came the distant sound of clashing and Issa thought of Asaph. Was he out there somewhere battling Dread Dragons? She gripped her sword and pushed on, keen to get outside into the light.

Voices shouted ahead, and everyone paused.

'Let me go,' whispered Eiretonne to Marakon.

The dwarf inched forwards up the stairs and peered around the corner.

He didn't return immediately so Cusap'anth silently stepped beside him and both scouted. The moment captured Issa, two bitter enemies now standing side by side, giving hope that an old rift could be healed.

The seconds passed like hours and Issa's skin prickled. She longed to fight or move or do something.

Finally, Eiretonne turned back to them. 'Dark dwarves,' he mouthed.

The dwarf glanced up at the Karalanth and the deer-man down at the dwarf, a fiery look shared in their eyes. Eiretonne lifted his axe and gave a low chuckle. Cusap'anth drew his bow and broke into a smile.

As one, the dwarf and the Karalanth leapt around the corner. Issa looked at Marakon who shook his head then grinned. Together, they ran after them.

CHAPTER 22

Battle of Queens

FROM wall to wall, the hallway ahead teemed with dark dwarves, their black axes raised, yellow eyes gleaming as they stomped forwards.

Behind them came a horde of Maphraxies, their eyes narrowed, mouths opened to roar as the enemy ran to meet them.

Issa, barely a pace behind Marakon, took the Maphraxie on the farthest left swinging its black iron flail. Her sword whistled, shuddered into its shoulder then stopped, forcing her to pull it free. The Maphraxie howled a gust of putrid, rotting breath, from a mouth filled with grey, broken teeth; its eyes alight, not with life but with Sirin Derenax.

Issa smarted, rolled under its flail and slashed its exposed calf. Dark blood oozed but the Maphraxie remained standing. She rolled desperately to avoid its return swing, black spikes swishing past her nose.

With the barest intention, Issa threw her hands forwards and the Flow responded without her even entering it. Shards of paving tore from the floor, hurtled forwards and impaled the Maphraxie. It gave a surprised look, then fell straight as a plank. The ferocity of their attack was already pushing the enemy back.

Naksu helped her up, her staff glowing. 'How did you do that?'

'I don't know,' Issa said, looking at her hands and feeling the pulse of Illendri in its pouch. 'Illendri responded to my whim and the Flow was there. I didn't *choose* to enter it – it was just … already there.'

Naksu nodded, considering her thoughtfully. 'The magic users of old never had to enter the Flow. It was once as you describe, always there, an integral part of us, like breathing.'

The baying of death hounds broke off anything else she might have said. The undead dogs bounded towards them, long tongues dripping drool, fangs bared. Naksu held her staff up and magic moved with a flash. The dogs catapulted back over the heads of the oncoming Maphraxies.

In the light, Issa glimpsed the swarm of the enemy filling the halls. She swallowed. They were outnumbered.

A Maphraxie filled her view. The shadows moved between them and then a demon stood there, the muscles of its back bulging. The Maphraxie paused, the demon screeched and leapt. Both Maphraxie and demon became shadow and then were gone whilst Issa stood blinking.

Rhul'ynth screeched. The Karalanth warrior struck swords with a Maphraxie whilst kicking a death hound attacking her rump. Issa ran and leapt on the death hound's back, sinking her blade into its neck.

Magic exploded nearby, it wasn't coming from their group, and the entire wall to their left shuddered. Everyone jumped back as stones cracked and splintered. A thunderous noise erupted as the wall and ceiling ahead collapsed onto the enemy. Issa dodged the falling debris, pulling Naksu with her.

The thunder stopped. Daylight spilled through the cracks into the darkness. Well, it wasn't quite daylight but the sickly red-brown light of this cursed land, Issa thought.

A dragon roared, followed by the ear-breaking scream of a Dread Dragon. Giant, ice-blue claws smashed through the wall and ceiling and clawed the rubble out. More of the hallway collapsed. Through the tumbling stone, Issa glimpsed a Dromoorai raise its sword only to be catapulted into the air by an unseen force. She stared at the flailing Dromoorai disappearing into the sky. The enormous head of an ice-blue dragon appeared and then was gone.

Morhork? She paused in shock. A howl from behind captured her attention. She whirled then dropped to the ground to avoid a Maphraxie's swinging blade as another horde descended upon them from the other hallway. She screamed for help as two death hounds also ran at her.

Bounding over the rubble rushed a clan of green and tan coloured Saurians. A spear slammed into the shoulder of her opponent, green feathers swinging. She nodded her thanks to Ekem as he wrenched his spear free.

'The harpies have returned,' he said and rushed on towards a Maphraxie.

Now he'd said it, Issa could hear their cackles and feel their strange magic. She thought of her father and the venomous taste of revenge filled her mouth. She had to get out of these dark halls and fight them! Clambering over fallen masonry she went out the way the Saurians had come in.

Outside was chaos. Bodies littered the ground—mangled death hounds, Maphraxies, Saurians, Karalanths, Feylint Halanoi, dwarves—both dark and light—and elves. The enormous body of a slain Dread Dragon lay on top of most of them, the massive wound on its neck still spilling watery blood. Its whole throat had been ripped out, *by another dragon,* thought Issa.

Black and red blood slicked the paving stones of the large courtyard. Many walls had been torn down but still the outer walls remained, giving the place an enclosed feel. Destroyed stairwells stopped half way down or half way up, making getting to the higher ramparts difficult at best.

Beyond the slain dragon and by the outer gate, the battle raged hottest. She thought she saw Ata, then beyond him, Grast'anth, then they were lost in a surge of Maphraxies. She started towards them.

Necromancers—protected by shielding magic that most others could not see—clustered in high turrets and rained down shards of ice and fire. Dark dwarves battled alongside lumbering Maphraxies. Dread Dragons wheeled in the sky and harpies chanted, the screeching swoon of their words making her woozy. The howls and roars of rage and pain filled the air alongside the whoosh of arrows and clang of metal. The stench of death, of blood, of the undead and Sirin Derenax made her stomach churn, and upon it all the sickening feel of black magic moved.

She scanned for Asaph, but her field of vision was dictated by the towering outer walls. He would be out there, somewhere, she prayed.

'I'll try to stop the necromancers,' shouted Naksu over the din. Issa immediately worried for the slight woman who was wearing robes that were hardly fit for battle. *Seer magic is not to be underestimated,* she reminded herself.

A harpy screamed, and Issa looked up. High in the sky circled one who did not attack, one who watched the battle from above, ordering her sisters to attack.

The queen. Issa licked her lips and hunted for a high place she could get to. Ehka cawed. He was perched on the sconce on the outer wall. Beneath him were the remains of a staircase leading up to an apparently empty turret. She ran to it.

The first few stairs were missing. She'd have to jump onto the edge of one and pull herself up. A black arrow thudded into the ground barely a foot in front of her. She dropped to her knees. A Maphraxie on the wall was already aiming another arrow and a dark dwarf had turned in her direction.

The arrow never came. A golden shaft suddenly protruded from the Maphraxie's neck. It convulsed, took a step forwards, then fell from the balustrade.

Another golden arrow thudded into the dark dwarf running towards her. It pierced his leather armour with such force, the bloody tip burst through its chest. The dwarf dropped his axe and fell into a dirty pool of blood.

'Issa, here!'

'Velonorian?' She scanned the chaos for the elf.

There, on the ramparts with two other elves dressed in bloodied and shining armour, was the young elf-man waving his bow.

A band of dark dwarves appeared above them on the higher wall, knives and axes raised.

'Look out,' Issa screamed.

In a blur, Velonorian leapt like a gazelle, spun in the air and sliced his Elven dagger down. A dwarf fell without a sound, followed by the other two with arrows embedded in them. Maphraxies appeared along the wall and Velonorian was running with his elves.

'I'll cover you,' he shouted, dodging the mace of a Maphraxie.

Issa couldn't see how he'd be able to fight *and* help her at the same time, but she nodded anyway. She ran and leapt. Her hands caught the edge of the lowest step. Grunting, she swung a leg up and heaved herself onto the ledge. She flinched as arrows whizzed past, chipping out chunks of mortar in front of her face. Glancing across, Velonorian and his elves were now engulfed in a battle against harpies as well.

A Maphraxie jumped in front of her and roared before she was even on her feet. Her hand found her talisman before her sword and she wrenched it up, smashing it like a weapon into the enemy's blade. Indigo light exploded, knocking her back against the wall and shunting the Maphraxie over the ramparts to the ground where its body lay crumpled and smoking.

Two harpies fell beside it, golden arrows embedded in both. The elves were covered in blood, possibly theirs, possibly from the harpies, but probably from both. Issa hunted the ramparts for a way to get to them, but the wall had fallen between them and the gap was too big to jump.

Her knees trembled before the Dread Dragon even screeched. It came low, the wind gusting as she fell to the ground. The amulet on the Dromoorai's chest flared and whispering began in her skull.

Issa roared against the dragon fear. With shaking fists she held her sword and talisman high. *Now of all times, let that bastard see me!* Her stomach somersaulted as she locked eyes with the Dromoorai.

Fire spewed across the sky, blinding her. A golden dragon slammed into the Dread Dragon, hurtling them both out of view beyond the wall. Issa yelped with joy. *Thank the goddess you're alive!* But her joy faded as a flock of harpies appeared.

'Shield,' Issa commanded.

In the Flow, an indigo shield of energy flared around her. Ehka hopped to stand by her feet, not even trying to attack. Issa closed her eyes, stilled her mind and tried to ignore the hellish sounds of the battle around her. Harpy magic flared off her shield again and again, hard and relentless. Sweat soon trickled down her brow. Defending was not fighting, and she couldn't keep them off for long.

She gripped the talisman and the Voice came to her, echoing loudly in the stillness of her mind. She let it fill both her and the talisman, reached far away for the ravens, and spoke aloud, 'Ravens, come to me.'

Alongside her, Ehka also cawed, calling them. Through the dimensions they would come in all their wondrous numbers.

Five black birds appeared immediately and circled around her. They must have been close to arrive so quickly. More arrived soon after, appearing in the air as they moved from all corners of Maioria through the dimensions, like the Saurians appearing through the veils of fae.

A hundred ravens now filled the sky, wheeling and cawing around her.

'Go,' she commanded softly, but the Voice reverberated through her and echoed loudly.

The ravens lifted up to meet the harpies and a vicious fight unfolded. Upon her shield, blood and black and brown feathers pattered. Issa filled herself with the Flow and with it, hunted for only one: somewhere up there was the queen. She clambered onto the wall beside the rampart and ran towards the turret. Heaving and scrambling she pulled herself onto the roof of the turret. The scene before her caught her breath.

Diredrull stretched out around the central peak of a relatively low, yet wide mountain—a mountain crawling with Maphraxies and vast swathes of the armies of the Free Peoples. Beyond the outer wall, Morhork was locked in a savage battle against a grounded Dread Dragon and Dromoorai. The wingless dragon was covered in wounds and blood, yet he fought as one unmaimed, tail whipping and jaws snapping.

In the sky above, Asaph struggled against another Dromoorai, whilst another hurtled towards him. The sky flared with their fire.

Harpy magic slammed against her shield, destroying it and flinging her backwards. She staggered for balance, seeing the ground sway far below, and touched Illendri. The Flow moved, stabilising her, and she rebuilt a hasty shield. Black arrows pinged off it. Were Naksu and Velonorian still able to protect her? She couldn't see them in the press of battle below.

She focused on the Flow, letting the magic fill her until lightning flickered from her finger tips. Holding her arms up she screamed, 'Dereever!' The name of the harpy queen boomed into the sky.

Ignoring the flock of ravens, a harpy split off from the rest. With a blood-curdling scream, she descended until the red amulet was visible on her chest.

'Come to me, Dereever. Do you remember Thanon Bard? I have a message for you from him,' Issa hurled the Daluni mind-speak at the bird-woman.

Only a long, glee-filled cackle returned. Powerful harpy magic, filled and strengthened by the Under Flow, fell upon Issa. The battlefield disappeared as a strange, dark, magical world engulfed her. She could only feel rather than see that Dereever was there, up and to the left of her.

In Issa's hands, the Flow became a glowing indigo shaft. She hurled it high. A harpy screamed, then something smacked into her head. The dark, magical world shook, and she fell to her knees. Dereever cackled. Red magic flickered and Issa swayed, dizzy. She formed another shield.

A strange groaning filled the air, as of words spoken by one in torture.

The air turned thick and terror seeped into her heart. The Dark Rift was near—the power of it overwhelming. She shook her head, trying to think clearly, hunting for Dereever, readying for the next defence or attack.

Black magic pulsed, shattering her shield. The harpy queen hurtled out of the dark, talons outstretched and gleaming, onyx stone shining on her forehead, matching her black eyes and fangs. She slammed into Issa sinking her claws into her shoulders and wrenching her from the ground. Issa screamed and felt hot blood trickle beneath her armour. The talons clenched viciously, Issa screamed again. Dereever laughed.

The black magic fell away, along with the battlefield as Dereever lifted her high in the air. She couldn't reach her sword through the pain in her shoulders. If she changed into a raven now, Issa doubted she'd be able to fly at all. She pulled on the Flow, but the harpy queen opened her talons.

The jagged rocks of the mountainside rushed up to greet her. Illendri flared and the ground shimmered. Issa slammed not into rock but soft earth that caved gently inwards under her weight, as if the rock itself had turned soft and springy. Ignoring the pain in her shoulders, Issa rolled and unsheathed her sword. In her other hand she gripped Illendri. Dereever's talons scraped the rock where she had been moments before. Issa jumped and hurled her sword, daring to let her weapon fly from her hands despite Grast'anth's teachings of never letting go your weapon. She had a chance and she took it.

Dereever moved fast but not fast enough. The sword missed her breast but sheared off the end of her wing before clanging against a rock. The harpy screamed with rage and flicked blood from her bleeding wing at Issa. Without her lead feather, the harpy queen could not easily get off the ground.

'Your wings needed clipping, you bitch,' Issa growled.

Harpy magic slammed into Issa, taking her by surprise and rolling her into a boulder. Gasping, she grabbed her raven talisman with her free hand and heaved herself onto her feet. *So, this is how it will end,* she thought, *raven queen against harpy queen, magic to magic.* Had the fight not been on enemy-held lands, the power of her magic would be stronger, purer, and had the blue moon been closer, the fight would have already been finished. But here, she was at a disadvantage, the Flow was already weak, and the power of the Under Flow strong. Exhaustion gnawed at her, pain throbbed in her shoulders, and beyond the harpy queen lay her sword.

Harpy magic flared. She fought it back, stepping first right, and then left, attacking just enough so she could inch her way towards her weapon. White fire flared from the harpy and she ducked, pretended to fall, and rolled to her sword. Whirling, she lunged at the bird-woman.

Dereever hastily counteracted her blows with magic and talons. Issa was fast but her wounded shoulders ached terribly. She roared, slicing left and right in a fury, but talons knocked her blade away again and again.

Tiring, the harpy finally moved too slowly, and Issa's sword bit flesh. A talon flew off in a spray of blood. Dereever howled, and renewed her attacks, the pain maddening her into a rage.

Claws raked Issa's leg and wings beat against her. Issa stabbed and sliced, finding only air, then she tripped and fell onto the harpy. Neither were able to break their fall and they tumbled over a ledge. Together they rolled, slamming against rocks, sliding through crevices. Issa struck her sword whenever she could, still trying to kill her enemy even through their perilous descent. The harpy clawed back at her and hurled magic. Issa's rage at what the harpies had done to her parents, to her father, burned strong and she didn't care if she lived or died, so long as she took the harpy queen with her.

They bounced and rolled off another ledge. Issa hurled herself into the air and stabbed at the ball of feathers. Her blade found home, she didn't know where but the frantic struggles of Dereever told her it was a good spot. She twisted the blade, the harpy screamed, then they hit the ground. Her vision filled with blood and sky and rocks, then blackness.

Noise returned first; a kind of rushing sound, followed by an immense pain that radiated from her shoulders downwards throughout her whole body.

Her wrist grew hot – Ely's bracelet and healing powers making itself known. Slowly, Issa lifted an arm and winced. Her shoulders ached deeply but there was no break in the smooth material of her Dread Dragon armour; it had already mended itself. Her shoulders would take longer.

She prised open her eyes and stared up at the muddy sky. She lay at the base of Tarvalastone Mountain, and the ongoing battle was now at least half a mile away. To her left lay an unmoving mound of feathers. *Dereever!*

Ehka landed beside her and cawed. Issa rolled onto her side and almost vomited as pain radiated through her body. Slowly, her head pounding, she got onto her hands and knees and crawled to the bloody mound of feathers.

Dereever's once pretty face was now, sickeningly, smashed in on one side, and Issa's sword was embedded in her stomach. The red talisman flared between her blood-smeared breasts. Grimacing, Issa grabbed it, and burning heat exploded in her hand. She wrenched it from the harpy queen's neck and held it up, ignoring the heat as she glared into its blood red surface.

'This and more,' she growled and filled herself with the Flow. Holding her head back she screamed, 'Aralansia!' and poured the Flow into the amulet. Blue magic exploded, and the amulet shattered. She watched the shards scatter upon the ground then turned away to look towards the city. She didn't have the strength to even walk half a mile, let alone fight when she got there.

A dark cloud passed overhead. Issa moved and wrenched her sword free of Dereever. Looking up, she almost fainted when she saw Asaph gliding down towards her. She tried to control the tremble in her legs and failed, sinking gracefully onto her haunches.

Asaph listed to the left. His wing was crooked, and blood smeared his golden sides red and black. Without landing, he deftly scooped her into his front paw. The gentleness with which he held her despite his size was still a source of wonder.

'Are you injured?' he asked, beating his wings and turning towards Diredrull.

'Bruised and battered, mostly. I don't think I can lift my sword again today, though I want to.' Issa touched her aching shoulders. She wanted to fight alongside the others, perhaps she could still use magic.

As they passed over Diredrull the sheer scale of the battle was revealed to her. It still raged in the enormous courtyard where several more walls had collapsed, and fires ravaged many parts. Ravens still fought harpies but now in scattered pockets. Occasionally, Elven arrows assisted them.

'The goddess only knows what's going on underground,' Issa breathed.

'The Dwarves of Light are fighting their dark brethren beneath their great city,' said Asaph.

'Look, there's Morhork,' said Issa, pointing.

The blue dragon was on the ground atop a collapsed wall and turret, surrounded by Maphraxies, their shining black armour making them seem as ants beside the enormous dragon. He swiped his tail at a horde sending scores of them into the sky. They crashed onto their comrades and many did not get up again.

She scanned the skies for Dread Dragons but couldn't see any. A shimmer of magic came from the gatehouse at the East Gate. She entered the Flow but could see nothing. *Cloaking magic,* she thought.

'Go there, by the gatehouse.'

Asaph nodded and turned towards it.

Issa held up her talisman. 'Fire,' she commanded.

A ball of blue flames smashed into the gatehouse, revealing the invisible dome. The dome flickered, then collapsed, revealing four necromancers huddling beneath it. Pale faces looked up in shock. They raised their hands, but before they could use magic, Issa blocked them. Asaph roared and swooped showering them with fire. Their howls of pain died in the roar of flames. Asaph lifted up.

'There, the elves!' shouted Issa, pointing to a group of elves helplessly surrounded by Maphraxies.

'Protection!' Issa commanded as the Maphraxies surged forwards. A shimmering barrier surrounded the elves. Maphraxie swords smacked uselessly against it. Unwilling to use fire and risk the elves' lives, Asaph swiped and grabbed Maphraxies into his talons. With a clench, their armour crumpled, and black blood oozed over his claws. He threw away the bloody mess to the sound of cheering elves.

An explosion to the left caught her attention.

Asaph turned. An enormous black hole yawned open in the courtyard. Feylint Halanoi and Maphraxie alike fell howling into the blackness. Issa stared. What horror was this now emerging? Heavy drum beats came, echoing dully. The battle paused as opponents watched.

A Dread Dragon screamed within the earth, then out of the cavern spewed hundreds of dark dwarves, Maphraxies and death hounds. The fresh enemy ran into the Feylint Halanoi lines, cutting them down like blades of grass. Over their heads soared a Dromoorai, and it came straight for Asaph.

Heavy magic hit him, shunting him upwards. The wind disappeared, his wings became flaccid, and he fell out of the sky.

Issa gasped as they spun. Asaph desperately flapped his wings, but it was as if he were in a vacuum. She grabbed Illendri and closed her eyes. Air magic did not come naturally to the orb of earth and water, but she remembered Haelgon's lessons in weather magic. Air came, but barely. She filled Asaph's wings only enough to slow his plummet so that he floated down.

'I cannot fight grounded and protect you,' Asaph growled, staring up at the fast descending Dromoorai.

Issa bit her lip, watching the ground loom towards them. 'That hole they opened, they must have created massive tunnels, maybe even portals. More could come, perhaps the entire legion of Maphrax straight from Maphrax. We *must* block it!'

Asaph hit the mountainside. With his wings spread, he slid down it before coming to a controlled stop on a ledge. He ran along it on three legs, still holding her in his fourth, his limping gait jolting every bone in her body.

He reared up to meet the Dread Dragon. It slashed at him with giant talons, tearing the scales on his back. He sprayed it with fire and raked his teeth along its belly, unable to get a good grip as it passed. The Dread Dragon arced around and returned. Issa pulled on the Flow, shielding them from the fiery torrent.

Asaph managed to get airborne again, but the wind moved strangely, and he struggled and panted. Shielding him swiftly became exhausting and the Flow sputtered in her grasp. She glanced back at Diredrull. Maphraxies continued to stream out of the black hole. How long before more Dromoorai came? They were all tired and exhausted, and this new enemy fresh. If they became outnumbered, they would lose this city and thousands would die.

'Set me down, Asaph. I must—' her sentence was cut off as the Dread Dragon dropped into Asaph. They weren't high in the air and slammed back onto the mountainside. Issa was thrown from his grasp. She rolled over and over, dirt filling her mouth, nose and eyes. Coughing and choking she got onto her knees, her hand grabbing her sword. Asaph was already neck to neck with the Dread Dragon.

Issa held Illendri up and focused on the earth. Rocks tore themselves from the mountain, lifted into the air and smashed into the Dromoorai, nearly dismounting it. It turned towards her.

'No!' Asaph roared, snapping at the Dromoorai to get its attention back. 'Issa get away!'

Issa nodded and stepped back, looking left and right and wondering how to help. Ehka squawked, wanting her to get airborne. Something caught her eye. In the distance far to the West, a giant dust cloud grew. Had another army come to their aid, or was this a new enemy?

'Ehka, can you go look?'

He flew away. Issa closed her eyes and connected with the bird. The dust cloud neared, and within it she saw people—soldiers marching. It took her a long moment to believe what she was seeing through Ehka's eyes. Hundreds of soldiers, most dressed as knights in plate armour and riding horses, whilst others were dressed in leathers, armed with spears and riding enormous brown bears. She stared at the bears as they loped towards Diredrull following a woman seated atop a massive beast. The scar on its muzzle was familiar. Issa stared harder, but the woman had a helmet on and she couldn't see more than that.

Ehka had keener senses and a picture of a woman came into her mind from him along with the word, *Navadin*.

'Jarlain,' Issa breathed. 'Oh my goodness.' There just might be enough knights and Navadin to hold off the enemy.

Issa reluctantly tore her gaze from the bear riders and focused upon the hole through which Maphraxies poured. Suddenly she knew what to do, she just didn't know if she had the strength or energy left to do it. *I have to try, even if I lose myself in the Flow, otherwise we are doomed.*

CHAPTER 23

Two Become One

TRYING to ignore the roars and clap of jaws, Issa held Illendri before her, absorbing her mind deeper into the orb which reached into the earth, reading the energy lines, hunting for water. Deeper it searched, through dark, ancient rocks never touched by the light of the sun, until it found a gush of water feeding an underground pool.

With Illendri leading, she followed the water. The river spoke to her of times long past. Once, it wound all the way to Tarvalastone, but since the city had fallen it had been blocked. The Fallen City, the water element called it, and the river here yearned to find the surface and reach the light once more. With Illendri, she could see a way, and all she had to do was coax that elemental yearning.

'This way,' she whispered to it, '*this way to the light.*'

When Illendri reached a rock blocking their path, a word came into her mind and she whispered it. The rock cracked and moved apart, allowing the water passage.

Onwards they flowed, the river, Illendri and she, until they reached another barrier of impenetrable stone. Another word, more a tonal vibration, came to her lips and the stone sunk into the earth, creating a new course through the firmament towards the Fallen City.

As she worked, Illendri found new water pools and sunken springs, lost since the fall of Tarvalastone. '*Rise,*' said the orb to the water, '*rise up.*'

They hit a wall of stone, the outer walls of Diredrull. The water frothed and churned, Issa felt the pressure of it build against the city's foundations, and still more water came. Illendri called it from every nook and cranny, urging the liquid element to it from all directions, and it filled Issa with anxious excitement.

A great crack developed deep in the earth. She felt it reverberate through the soil reaching her body even here, far away on the mountainside. Eyes still closed, she saw a tsunami explode through walls and thunder into the darkness beneath Diredrull, filling that gaping black hole. Dark things moved, fleeing from the torrent. Howls, distorted and strange to her remote senses, echoed over the roar of water that tore at everything. It ripped rocks off the walls and ceilings and carried them like toys.

'Rage,' whispered Issa, sending forth her command, and the water raged. The ground trembled, distant thunder sounded, coming not from the air but from the ground. The great hole in the earth collapsed upon itself.

Issa opened her eyes and stared. In the distance, the entire courtyard and centre of the city crumbled and sank into the hole. Great turrets tumbled, entire walls vanished. Earth and debris billowed thickly into the air as light dwarf towers and Maphraxie bunkers sunk into the ground together. A torrent of water spurted upwards and out, the river of old gleefully reaching the light. It flowed where it willed, seeking to create a new course, seeking to wash away the creatures that had enslaved it.

Asaph staggered towards her, his clothes and leather armour in shreds, black and red blood smeared over his face. He limped, and exhaustion etched deep into the frown on his brow, but there was a smile on his face. He took her hand and sank down beside her without a word. Together they watched what she and Illendri had done.

The Feylint Halanoi retreated back from the river now raging through the city. The enemy were in complete disarray, and those not caught in the flood fled in all directions. Wherever they went, they met the Feylint Halanoi, Karalanths or the Navadin and soldiers just reaching the city. The soldiers, fresh and unsullied, cut the enemy down in their hundreds.

Issa watched the Navadin in awe as beast and human worked as one powerful unit, spearing and clawing together, the roars of bears echoing over the mountain.

'It's over,' said Asaph nodding. 'The city is ours. Tarvalastone lives again! What's left of it…'

Issa blinked back tears and hugged him, then gasped. 'Look Asaph, the sky!'

Above them, the muddy red clouds paled to grey. In the patches between them, faint blue could be seen. From the West, a shard of brilliant golden-orange light burst through the clouds over the mountain and onto the city.

'So the sun is still there, and it's glorious,' she breathed, marvelling at the final rays of a sunset that had not been seen on this land for so long.

'So it's true,' Asaph said after a time as he got to his feet and pulled her up. 'When we take back our lands, the land itself heals.'

Issa laughed and buried her face into his chest, tears of joy filling her eyes.

Asaph landed in the rubble of the city, and an ecstatic crowd of cheering soldiers surrounded them.

He set Issa down and resumed his human form. Ehka landed on a broken section of wall next to her and surveyed the celebrating throng. Cusap'anth and Rhul'ynth pushed forwards.

'Well met, Dragon Lord and Raven Queen,' said the deer-man.

There was no time to reply for Marakon and Bokaard came to them, then Eiretonne and Naksu, followed by a nervous Ekem and Ata.

'Thank the goddess you're all alive,' said Issa, looking at each of them. 'And the demons?' She raised an eyebrow at Marakon.

He grinned. 'They've returned to report back to their King. They said they had a good time and hope to return.'

Issa laughed.

'Issa! Issa!' someone yelled.

She turned to see Velonorian pushing through the crowd. The elf's face was flushed, and he was breathless as if he'd just finished fighting and run all the way here.

'Velonorian!' She embraced him.

Pulling away, she realised she'd made his face flush even redder. He smiled indulgently. 'My Queen, I did all I could to protect you.'

'You saved my life several times, Velonorian,' she said, her voice serious.

His eyes sparkled. 'What do you need of me now? Tell me and I shall joyfully get it.'

'Just water… and to check on Duskar.'

'Of course, my Lady, it is done.' He took her hand, bent low to kiss it, then whirled away to do as she commanded. She watched him go, flattered and bemused by his unfaltering devotion.

'I hope you don't expect that kind of behaviour from me,' said Asaph, winking when she looked at him.

'Well, he's just so darn helpful!' Issa grinned wickedly.

Haelgon and Luren emerged from the crowd. Though they were smiling, they hung off their staves and looked exhausted. Their capes were covered in dirt and more brown than purple, and their eyes glowed turquoise, just as hers probably did. Freydel was not with them. She felt a stab of pain, the severity of it taking her by surprise. Forcing a smile, she refused to think about the traitor wizard who had once been her beloved tutor.

'That was some trick you pulled back there,' said Haelgon, smiling enigmatically.

Issa shrugged. 'Not so much me, Illendri has its own powers. Just think of the power all the orbs combined could command.'

He was about to reply when the crowd murmured and parted. A bear rider made her way towards them. Soldiers eyed the bear nervously, on its face, a scar pulled up its lip enough to reveal huge fangs. But the bear was placid, and his eyes lazily focused on the ground.

Marakon ran to them and swept the woman from the bear's back. She lifted off her helmet and a shock of curly black hair sprung out. Soldiers cheered as Jarlain and Marakon kissed unabashedly.

Asaph stepped hesitantly towards a young man seated on an enormous brown bear.

Without his dragon form, he could not communicate to the beast with his mind, but it seemed contented enough to let him approach. The mounted man wore leathers instead of a full suit of armour, though he did have a Feylint Halanoi helmet on that mostly concealed his features. But it was the way he moved, and his unruly dark brown hair…so familiar as he dismounted.

'Jommen?' Asaph called, his heart pounding.

The man turned.

'Asaph?' His golden eyes widened.

The two men ran to each other, laughing. Jommen tore off his helmet to show a large scar which slashed from cheek to cheek across his nose. The redness was fading but the flesh would always be puckered.

Asaph stared at his old friend, homesickness flowing over him in powerful waves. 'It's so good to see you, I never thought I would again! Where are the others, Kahly and Tillin, and what about Gurapoha?' He scanned the dismounting Navadin looking for people he recognised but it was hard to tell when they all wore helmets. There were people from all of the other tribes—even the far southern tribes he'd rarely met.

'No, Asaph,' said Jommen quietly, drawing Asaph's gaze back to him. The man shook his head slowly, his eyes dropping to the ground.

Asaph swallowed against a painful lump and they embraced silently. In his mind he saw Kahly's smiling face, athletic shoulders drawing back her bow strong. *Gone...*

When they pulled apart, Jommen spoke.

'Barely two hundred of our people remain. Other tribes were luckier, but not by much – some are less than a hundred. The evil ones came on black ships in their thousands...we could not fight them. We fled.' Shadows passed across Jommen's face and he swallowed. 'She fought like a tiger before the end, so they said. Her family, too...all gone. We think they took most of the children away, and that's the worst bit—' Jommen's voice broke and he turned away, his fists trembling.

'Don't, Jommen.' Asaph gripped the man's shoulder. 'I know how it is. Don't relive it.'

'So we fight, me and Ooster, and all of us.' He looked from his bear to Asaph, eyes red rimmed and glassy. He swept his hand over the Navadin. 'We'll not stop until they—or we—are all dead.'

Asaph forced a smile at his fiery friend. 'You sound like a Karalanth. I'd never even heard about the Navadin until now. Together we are formidable indeed.'

Jommen nodded, the pain fading from his face a little as he tried to smile. He looked at his people tending their bears. 'Despite everything we have suffered, all of us are together again as one people, like once we were.

Great Doonis came to us through our leader, Jarlain. The old power within us has awakened and every one of us remembers an ancient land lost long ago.'

Jommen turned and patted his bear who looked at his rider adoringly. 'But you, Asaph…You just disappeared one day. Only Gurapoha knew where you had gone. Said you had returned home and would say no more about it. Now look at you! We always knew you were weird, but a *Dragon Lord?* There's so much we have to talk about, my friend.'

Asaph grinned. 'Of course, and soon, but not now. Let's feast and celebrate. We'll share a meal and drink dwarven spirits and you can tell me all about home.'

Asaph and Issa approached the enormous ice blue dragon.

He rested, paw over paw, head raised but dozing, at the base of the mountain where the remains of the city wall lay in rubble. He was covered in a thousand wounds, more numerous than they were deep. Most had closed but some oozed puss. Asaph was reluctant to disturb him, but Issa kept on walking.

'You wouldn't let them tend your wounds,' said Issa to Morhork.

Many Draxians had come to help the wingless dragon, curious to see their ancient allies of old, but Morhork had sent them away, some running for their lives. The temperamental dragon maybe helping them, but he was still difficult.

Morhork opened a golden eye a crack and looked down at them. 'I don't need men to help me, they need me to help them.' He lifted a claw to inspect it, then set it down.

'You came to fight,' said Asaph, it was a statement rather than a question.

Morhork took in a deep breath and looked to the North. 'If I had not, no one would still be alive here now. None could have survived that many Dromoorai.'

Reluctantly, Asaph nodded. 'We couldn't have fought so many at once. But more will come, I have no doubt. Maybe they're already on their way.'

'No,' Morhork let out a smoky breath. He sounded weary. 'No, they will not. They're heading north, north to the dragons to destroy them, and

I'm too weak and exhausted to get to them.'

A chill went down Asaph's spine. It couldn't be true. What care did Baelthrom have about the North when he'd just lost Diredrull, his ancient city?

'How do you know?' Asaph asked, folding his arms over his chest.

'A dragon knows another's mind, even a Dread Dragon's mind. You'll learn this, in time. I can feel them now, thinking about the North.'

'Those dumb beasts actually think?' Issa snorted.

'Not really,' said Morhork. 'They have thoughts, orders, directions placed in their minds by the Dromoorai—who in turn take orders from Baelthrom. They are not truly autonomous.'

'Then we'll go north,' said Issa. Asaph stared at her, clearly shocked she would suggest such a thing and be willing to go.

Morhork regarded her for a long time. 'There's a reason Baelthrom isn't sending all his efforts here to Venosia. It's plagued me for a long time but now I think I know why. He simply doesn't care.'

'What?' Issa laughed and looked incredulously at Asaph.

He shared her shock. 'You're saying that Baelthrom does not care about Diredrull?'

'Yes, that's exactly what I'm saying. All of this was too easy.'

Issa laughed and tossed her head. 'Easy? You're saying Baelthrom was prepared to let this fall? That all this meant nothing to him? That it was also a waste of our time? Hundreds died here this day—and the days before, thousands! They still haven't finished burying them.' Issa's face turned red. Asaph laid a gentle hand on her arm, but she pulled away. 'One thing hasn't changed, Morhork, you're still able to irritate everyone.'

Morhork growled. 'He doesn't care because he thinks the game is won. You cannot see it yet under this cursed sky, but that Dark Rift is enormous. Nothing, save a miracle, can now stop us being pulled into it, it's simply a matter of physics. Everything you see here today is nothing but collateral damage. What he *does* want is the dragon race to become his own monstrosity. Like pets for him to play with, he wants to enslave *all* dragons for use in the Dark Rift.'

Asaph felt sick. Like Issa, he wanted to deny what the dragon said, but an awful feeling told him it was true. He put his hands on his hips and hung his head, thinking it through. 'I cannot let that happen.'

'Why?' Morhork snorted this time. 'You awoke them. It would all be fine if they had not been awoken.'

'What, and have them sleep their way into the Dark Rift?' Issa laughed incredulously.

'Better that than become a deformed slave for all eternity,' growled Morhork, bristling. He scraped the ground with his claws, leaving deep grooves in the dirt. 'When I've recovered my magic reserves, I'll go to them. I'll fight and die with them. The end is close.'

'I'll go with you, but not to Yis,' said Asaph. 'I'll raise an army and go to Drax. The dragons will come. There we'll fight alongside each other.'

Morhork looked at him and his lips lifted into an ugly grimace.

Within a sky turning dark blue, twinkling stars emerged.

Beneath it, giant sconces and bonfires were lit for the gathering people. Soldiers washed in the cool river running through the city, and endless crates of food were stacked in a cleared section. Those in charge of the meals set about preparing a feast, and soon the air was filled with the delicious smells of cooking.

People worked tirelessly, erecting tents and securing walls, but darkness fell swiftly, and most would have to camp out under the stars, though no one complained.

Issa patted Duskar and looked up at them. *So beautiful compared to that awful dark sky.* The horse chomped noisily into his bag of oats. She ran her fingers through her damp hair, almost dry from being washed in river water. Now the dark spell on the place had been broken, cool fresh air blew, bringing the promise of a new dawn. But it was a chill wind, reminding her that they should be in the depths of winter. There would be snow even on parts of Little Kammy by now.

She pulled up the collar of her seer's robe, given to her by Naksu who always came prepared with plenty of supplies. Her armour, now washed, was drying by the fire, and Eiretonne had taken her sword to fix the notches in it. The dwarf had been itching to get back to the forge as soon as the battle had ended.

'There you are,' said Asaph grinning and striding towards her. He was washed and clean-shaven and the firelight caught his hair in a blaze of red.

He scooped her up in his arms and kissed her long and hard before setting her down again. She had to steady herself against him.

'Food's ready,' he said, taking her by the hand and leading her towards the delicious smells.

Giant cauldrons and pots hung over fires. They filled their bowls full of steaming stew and grabbed as many hard rolls as they could carry. The bread was old but once soaked in the stew, it softened up and everything tasted divine. They settled down on blocks of rubble next to Marakon, Jarlain, and the wizards. At the next fire along, crouched the Saurians. She raised her eyebrows when she spotted Naksu amongst them. The seer was speaking easily in their own language, further surprising Issa.

'She can even speak Saurian,' said Issa, blowing on a spoonful of stew.

'She's a Wayfarer, a traveller. It's her job,' said Haelgon, wolfing down his.

Issa chuckled, marvelling at the seer's talents. She turned her focus onto her food and managed another half bowl of stew in the same time that Asaph finished three. 'It's lucky they aren't rationing tonight,' she said.

Asaph laughed and set down his bowl. 'I could eat enough for a dragon.' He put his hands behind his head and leant back, a satisfied look on his face.

She sighed and leant against him. 'Ah, if only Drumblodd could be here with us now. To see our victory and everything he fought for. Goddess bless him.'

'Goddess bless him,' echoed Luren. Haelgon nodded but said nothing, his eyes seeing into the middle distance.

'And Hally and Drenden and all the others,' said Marakon, staring at the fire. Jarlain squeezed his arm and he smiled sadly at her.

Asaph laid an arm around Issa's shoulder, lost in his own emotions.

'Hey, lads and lasses.' Eiretonne came stomping over, cradling half a dozen or so dusty brown bottles, eyes gleaming with joy. 'You won't believe what we've just discovered!' He handed out the bottles, and Issa noticed his face was rosy. 'The finest Tarvalastone dwarven spirits. Get yer lips around that and you'll find your aches and wounds gone by tomorrow.'

He winked at Issa as she took a bottle. She pulled out the cork and brought it tentatively to her lips. Cool liquid filled her mouth, sweet, strong and suddenly warming. Her cheeks flushed, and she felt herself relaxing.

Asaph took the bottle from her and drank deeply, smacking his lips appreciatively.

Eiretonne chuckled. 'Yes, me lad, that'll put hairs on yer chest, *and* yer feet. Get it next to the fire, the warmer it is the better.' The dwarf placed his bottle near the hearth then seated himself next to Bokaard.

Whilst everyone ate, drank, and talked about their battles that day, Issa considered telling Asaph more about her sister, but emotions threatened to overwhelm her when she wanted only to be peaceful and joyful this moment.

'Whilst you were tending Duskar, I went exploring,' said Asaph. 'I found a room in a turret with all its windows still intact. There's a fireplace too which I'm sure we can light if we take some kindling. It's draughty though, tricky to get to and unimpressive when you do, but given that it's pretty full down here, I thought it would be a nice place to be alone, to sleep and watch the stars.'

'Sounds perfect,' said Issa, yawning and stretching. 'Show me now before I drink too much of this.'

Asaph helped her up and led the way through the fires and groups of soldiers eating, drinking and laughing. He grabbed a wrap of kindling from the pile and she took two wool blankets from the stack.

They climbed the stone stairwell and had to jump the gaps between the missing steps. They clambered under fallen beams and masonry until they reached a short hallway. Asaph turned left and emerged out onto a rampart. At the end stood the tiny turret, nothing more than a guard house but at least it had an intact, heavy wooden door. He shunted it aside and led her in.

Narrow windows lined the hexagonal room from ceiling to chest height and the stars above trickled their light through. They set about filling the tiny fireplace with kindling and lit the tinder with flint. Soon, a fire blazed and warmth filled the room.

Asaph stood behind her and held her close as they looked at the stars. He took a dram of liquor and passed it to her. She took the bottle, raised it to her lips and drank, shuddering as the contents warmed her thoroughly. He ever so gently kissed the exposed part of her neck, his lips brushing against her skin, making her whole body tingle with anticipation. The raven mark on her chest began to throb.

Feeling butterflies in her stomach, she turned and kissed him fully on the lips, loving his warmth. He smoothed back her hair, then ran his hands down her back, caressing her bottom, and when she leant her head back, he kissed her throat and lowered his face to her collarbone. His hands loosened her robe. She let it fall from her shoulders and gasped when he kissed her breasts, feeling the whole world melt and waver.

With fumbling fingers, she undid first his shirt and then his trousers, desperate to feel his naked skin next to hers. His eyes were alight with desire and his expression was serious, eager and tender all at the same time. This time, she wasn't afraid. This time, she was free.

She helped him push the robes from her hips and sank down to the floor beside him, noting how hot he was, how flushed his skin and how hard he had become. A flash of overwhelming fear passed through her and was gone. Asaph stroked his hands over her skin, everywhere he wanted, and she allowed him free passage - tonight he was in control, and she would trust him. When he kissed her she returned it with equal passion and followed where he led.

The Flow opened up before her as he moved on top, stroking, whispering, feeling. When their marks touched, magic flared consuming them both; he became golden fire in the Flow and she a sea of indigo. Together they lifted, their beings blending and becoming something new, something more than the sum of their parts, something beautiful.

She gasped as his power filled her, orange flames warm within and without, and she found herself moving with him in wanton abandon. The magic intensified, the world became pure energy and she was vaguely aware that it wasn't always like this; that this was otherworldly, special, divine.

She heard herself groan, felt something building to a crescendo inside her as Asaph's whole body trembled upon her; and the noise he made, the burst of his breath on her face—she didn't want him to stop.

A wave of ecstasy exploded through her and she felt him shudder and pause, his whole body straining as she lost herself completely.

A new world opened before her. One of light and the most beautiful sound she had ever heard. She moved along an endless hallway of light, and when she wondered if she walked, she found her legs appeared, as if thought alone had created them. She was serenity and ecstasy combined, and she knew where she was, where she was going. Ahead beamed the light of the One, the Source of all, and it bathed her in peace, beauty, and absolute trust.

'I am One,' she said, her voice a melody vibrating harmoniously with the exquisite tinkling sound.

'I am spirit,' she said, and the light resounded.

'I am eternal,' she breathed, and the light became a chorus.

Then she was drifting back down, a feather floating through clouds of light. Hot lips kissed hers tenderly and she kissed them back, wound her hands in his hair. She looked up into Asaph's blue eyes and saw, echoed within his, the wonder she felt.

'I saw the Halls of Creation,' she whispered, stunned.

He nodded, and his brow furrowed. 'We were one and it was...' he struggled helplessly, '...it was beautiful. So beautiful, words cannot describe it. Issa, I saw the Source of all Creation!'

He lay down beside her and pulled her close, the fire crackling and warming their entwined feet.

CHAPTER 24

Baelthrom's Grace

'WHY do you come to me,' Baelthrom's voice rolled around the dark chamber.

It was cold too, even to his ethereal form. Freydel shivered again and thanked Ayeth for teaching him this particularly potent projection spell. Through Ayeth's tutelage and the power of his staff forged from Aralansian crystal, his form was just a projection. Baelthrom would see him only as a ghost, shimmering and opaque, and be unable to harm him in any way—or so he prayed.

"A ghost in colour," Ayeth had said. Only Freydel wasn't dead. His physical body stood in the remains of the crumbled Wizard's Tower under a sky that raged with red clouds that never rained and a storm that never broke. Thunder rolled around and around, and the air tasted heavy and stale. The shield was gone, along with the power that had once been here.

Freydel glimpsed his hand in the projection, it was pale, indistinct, and trembling. This was indeed the most powerful mental projection he had ever been able to create. Had his staff been made from Maiorian crystal, he doubted it would have the power to hold such magic.

His teeth chattered slightly, as if he could feel the coldness of the room, but more likely because of Baelthrom's looming presence chilling his very soul. Larger than a demon, he hulked in the shadows, the barest light from a distant brazier catching on the tips of his helmet making them look like horns. In the darkness, the Immortal Lord's eyes blazed first red, then blue, and his wings stretched wide. Enormous! Surely he had grown, thought Freydel.

Black magic coiled like snakes on the floor around them. A warning. He was here by Baelthrom's grace alone, even as a projection—perhaps he could enslave a projection too! Freydel forced his mind to calm.

'Should you not be battling with your friends? Thousands are being slaughtered in Diredrull, and thousands more will fall before the end.' Baelthrom paced, his claws scouring the stone floor.

'There are greater things to be dealt with,' said Freydel, hating the stammer in his voice. He gripped his staff so tightly his fingers turned numb. 'Do you remember yourself before you came here, before you became Baelthrom? I implore you to remember.'

'You implore nothing of me!' Baelthrom roared. Braziers around the room burst into flames, lighting up the chamber. The Immortal Lord lifted his wings and his form grew, becoming ethereal and made of a smoky substance.

'I'm sorry, my Great Lord,' Freydel stuttered and stepped back, dropping his gaze dutifully.

Baelthrom considered him. 'All that has gone before means nothing in the face of what is to come. You fools still think you can stop your inexorable fall into the wondrous Dark Rift.' He laughed, great bellows reverberating around the room, vibrating the giant iron ring that hung in the centre. 'Not even I could change the movement of this planet.'

Freydel paused, the thought chilling him utterly. *Ayeth and the crystal pyramids—could they do such a thing? Surely they have the power to alter a planet's course, he always spoke of their incredible powers.* But right now he didn't feel so sure—in fact, he suddenly felt stupid. Coming here was an act of terrible bravery—*or foolishness.* Did he really hope to sway Baelthrom's mind? To make him simply stop his plans and…and what? Go home? He hadn't thought this through nearly enough. *But there had been no time to plan anything!* He tried again.

'You were a wise and powerful being, possibly holding more power than you do today,' Freydel stepped forwards, beseeching.

Baelthrom chuckled, a strange sound that almost held glee. He lifted and flexed a gauntleted hand. Black magic shimmered around it and his whole form solidified and then grew indistinct, surrounded by shadows. 'It is not so. This power fills me like nothing before. It *becomes* me. The Rift has never been this powerful. Every moment, a new world falls into it, feeds it, and it grows. I grow too. That puny being I saw beside you in the Wizard's Circle…that's barely a fragment of me. I've become so much more even I cannot fathom where I will end. I see an endless universe of dark power—and it is beautiful.'

He is becoming one with the Dark Rift! Freydel realised, his stomach twisting painfully. *He's filled with the power of it.* He felt the Under Flow growing, pulling on him, urging him, seducing him. The power was strong and pure, here in Baelthrom's chamber. *Pure darkness!* Did Ayeth know more about this power? Perhaps if he understood just a little, he could disseminate it, learn how to break it.

Freydel swallowed, if he learned such black arts he would never want to break it, which is why all wizards were forbidden to use black magic. After all, this was not the first time he had looked evil in the face—but it was the first time he had felt it so strong and so pure. He shook his head, trying to rid himself of the desire.

'The Dark Rift will destroy you and consume you as it has all others,' he said.

'No, it will become me,' Baelthrom breathed, his rumbling voice filling the chamber.

He's mad, it's clear to see, but is he wrong? Freydel pursed his lips, did he dare say it? *I must say it.*

'The one you used to lo— The one who stood at your side. She is…It's not…Curse it!' Freydel took a deep breath trying to find the right words. 'The Yurgha, they are *not* your friends. She will betray you. She *has* betrayed you. That is why you fall into the Dark Rift. It's *her* fault!'

Sweat beaded on Freydel's forehead, rolled down his face and dampened his collar uncomfortably. Could Lona see what was happening now? Ayeth said she had the ability to see into the past and future, and now with the replica orb…

'I have seen this one you mention.' Baelthrom moved closer, Freydel stepped back. 'But she does not have the power she thinks she has. Those given to the powers of emotion have strength but lack stability. Nothing can overcome or withstand a process both accurate in its design and perfect in its execution.'

'No, but she and her entire race believe as you do, that they can rule the Dark Rift,' said Freydel. He understood the wisdom in Baelthrom's words. Lona and the Yurgha were unstable in a way Baelthrom was not. Was such wisdom a part of Ayeth coming through? Could he reach anything of Ayeth in Baelthrom if he tried harder? Just the thought gave him hope, but also filled him with terror.

'This Ayeth, who was once you, he's trying to reach you to stop what you *will* do.' Freydel's voice was barely a whisper. 'There are those willing to help, you have only to reach for the light.'

Baelthrom paused his pacing and stood for a long time beside the orbs. He stared at them inlaid in their stone pedestal. They were dull and lifeless, the pale Orb of Life, the muddy Orb of Fire and the grey Orb of Air, so unlike how they had been when brought together at the Wizard's Circle— all flashing colours and harmonious sounds. Freydel was deeply saddened. He was looking at the waning life of Maioria.

His gaze rested on the sickly Orb of Fire. Fighting back sorrow for Drumblodd, his colleague and his friend, Freydel's thoughts turned to Lona. Why had she given Baelthrom the orb rather than use it to progress her own dark ambitions? What vile pact had occurred between them, and who would suffer and die as a result of it? Perhaps Maioria's orbs were useless to her, perhaps they did not work beyond the realm of Maioria herself. All these things he could only guess at as a shiver slithered down his back.

After a long moment, Baelthrom said, 'Then it's *I* who must stop *him*.' He picked up a long, wooden, misshapen object leant against the pedestal and held it towards Freydel.

The Master Wizard inhaled sharply. 'My staff!'

Baelthrom smacked its tip on the ground and the staff burst into erratic, magical light. Lightning flashed around it and reached towards the iron ring. Freydel's mouth hung open, he had never seen his staff hold such power or act in this manner. The Under Flow flooded from the iron ring into the staff where it began to build up. Lightning cracked in the darkness that clustered around it hungrily.

Freydel felt the raw power pulling on his projected hologram, overpowering his own magic. His old wooden staff knew it belonged to him and was trying to return to its master, but Baelthrom held the staff and his power was greater. It was Freydel who was being drawn to it.

Fascination turned to horror. Freydel resisted, and the staff pulled stronger. Dark magic spilled closer. He felt the pull even on his physical body located thousands of miles away in the rubble of the Wizard's Tower. Freydel gripped his crystal staff, entering the Flow fully, and began to fight.

The Under Flow poured out of the iron ring into his wooden staff making it vibrate with a loud, distorted hum. His crystal staff, an exact replica of his wooden one, responded and began to pull towards it. Freydel tried to pull back but the magic of the two staves was unstoppable. Sweat poured down his brow as incredible forces fought against each other. The Flow weakened in his grasp as he struggled against the will of his own two staves.

Great goddess, help me! He gave himself fully to the Flow, feeling the magic course through him and become him. With his will he clung to his crystal staff, filling it with all the power he possessed, feeling the solid crystal become almost ethereal as the raw power turned its dense structure to pure energy.

With his staff and through Ayeth's tutoring, Freydel could barely breathe for the amount of power he was able to command in this moment. He was vaguely aware of howling, he could no longer feel his physical body anymore. All he saw were the enormous energy structures of the raging Flow, and the black and white lightning flaring from his wooden staff. He would have to lose himself to the Flow rather than be enslaved by Baelthrom. He probably already *had* lost himself to the Flow. He reached higher and more power flooded through him as he fought with every fibre of his being.

It was not enough.

The Under Flow surged between the two staves, finally finding a connection. Black tendrils shot through the Flow, paused, then smothered him. The magic trembled and exploded into darkness. Freydel was thrown forwards into nothing.

Then, in the darkness, two staves connected. Blinding magic flared. Thunder peeled and cracked. Consciousness faded.

A disembodied, haunting howl tore through the destroyed and deserted Wizard's Circle. It echoed through the empty valleys, over dwindling rivers and across forests withering beneath an angry red sky.

CHAPTER 25

Sword of Illendri

ISSA stood beside Asaph watching the people working hard to rebuild a broken city.

They surveyed from a high rampart that had mostly survived unscathed. Anything that had been built by the dark dwarves was being torn down and even the rocks destroyed. Anything that had been built by the light dwarves was preserved or being rebuilt.

Legions of soldiers marched day and night around the perimeter, and scouts and rangers could sometimes be seen in the distant foothills. Already, greenery was pushing through the soil now fed by the Tarvalastone River. It would be a while before food could be grown, but every day new supplies came, and along with them, settlers—mostly eager dwarves—as news of their victory spread back to Davono, Frayon and the Free Lands.

The Karalanths had returned west a week ago to start rebuilding their own home. Karalanthia would indeed live again. Marakon and Jarlain and her Navadin remained to help rebuild Tarvalastone, though news of war in the North made them keen to get moving.

Having heard of unrest on the Isles of Tirry, Naksu had left in a worried hurry. Issa was torn, she wanted to go with her, but she did not want to leave Asaph's side again.

'As much as it gives me joy to reclaim new lands, my place is not here,' said Asaph. 'King Navarr's correspondence is taking too long. I need soldiers on the border at Port Nordastin—and any Draxians now fleeing Lans Himay must go there. I just wish we knew what was going on.' He shook his head and leant against the wall.

Issa felt frustrated too. Reports of attacks on Lans Himay had turned out to be true, confirmed by carrier pigeons from Atalanph and Frayon. Refugees now flooded the northern border and the entire region was in chaos.

'We must continue to attack where they least expect us,' said Issa. 'My heart says Draxa, but I fear we will not have the legions we had here at Diredrull, and Draxa is far more formidable. Marakon will come, and all his soldiers, along with our Knights of the Raven. But still, though I'd happily fly with you, it will take us weeks to get everybody there.'

'What about the spear, Velistor? What about demon tunnels?' asked Asaph.

Issa shrugged and held up her hands. 'You saw what happened to Marakon? They're unstable and unpredictable. He ended up many miles away from where he'd anticipated.'

'It worked out in the end though. What about Maioria's portals? You said it opened the interplanetary gates. Why don't we just use those?' Asaph face was alight.

Issa let out a sigh. It was all very well having powerful magical relics, but only if one knew how to use them properly. Such knowledge had been lost a long time ago, along with a great many things. 'I would, of course, if I knew how. It requires one to know where the gates are, and we do not. Apart from the Storm Holt, which is very different anyway, I don't even know what a gate looks like, and since no one has seen one, they're probably hidden by magic – if they are even there anymore. There was an ancient book that recorded it, The Book of Maps, but that hasn't been seen for a thousand years.'

Asaph's shoulders slumped, and he returned to staring at the people working below. 'Then perhaps we must try calling Murlonius. Now they've banked the river, we've at least got a body of water through which he can travel.'

Issa said nothing. Just the mention of the Ancient's name brought up images of Yisufalni and a terrible sense of helplessness to add to her frustration.

'Come on, let's get some lunch, I'm starving already.' Asaph took her hand and they made their way down through broken stairwells to what had come to be called The Kitchen—a huge room with an ancient oven. However, it was exposed to the elements now one of the walls had collapsed in the battle.

'King Asaph! King Asaph!' someone shouted as they crossed the courtyard.

Asaph grimaced at the name. Four tall Draxian men hurried towards them, the ones they had met before, and they struggled under the weight of something they carried between them. They were followed by Velonorian, another elf, Eiretonne and several dwarves she remembered seeing working in the forge.

They hefted and heaved the thing, then set it down before Asaph and pulled off the covers. Issa stared at it. It was made of metal that shone gold, although it couldn't have been, it was too big for that. The metal curved and joined in odd places. There looked to be a seat in the centre along with chains welded here and there. Issa looked at Asaph and saw his eyes widen.

'And here's the rope,' said Eiretonne, heaving thick rope with the other dwarves and dumping it beside the strange metal thing.

'Every Dragon Lord and Dragon Rider should have a dragon harness, my King,' said the Draxian with long fair hair tied back at the nape. His face was completely serious.

Issa stared at the seat, trying to imagine it on the back of a dragon and failing. She noticed the exquisite leaves and whorls worked into the metal.

'It's stunning,' she said, peering closely.

'Made out of Elven metal,' said Velonorian proudly. 'This metal will not heat up if touched by flame, nor will it burn its rider.'

'Built by dwarven hands,' said Eiretonne proudly. 'Right here in Tarvalastone.'

'…To a Draxian design,' said another Draxian with red hair and a thick beard. The scars of battles and lines on his face showed he was the oldest there. He smiled. 'I remembered how my father made them.'

'You two can't go into battle with him holding you like that,' said the fair-haired Draxian. 'You need a proper Dragon Harness like the Dragon Riders of old.'

'I'm a Dragon Rider?' asked Issa. She hadn't considered the idea.

'Of course,' said the fair-haired man.

'And I'm supposed to sit in this?' She chewed a finger.

'Yes.'

'On his back?'

'Of course.'

Issa swallowed.

'Even the rope has been enchanted to resist fire,' said the elf. He was tall and slender with pale silver hair set free about his shoulders. Issa sensed magic about him; possibly he was the one who'd cast the enchantments.

'You're the last Dragon Lord,' said the Draxian to Asaph, emotion shaking his voice. He turned to Issa. 'And you're now a Dragon Rider. You make us a proud people once more.'

He started to kneel, but Asaph quickly grabbed the man's shoulders and slapped him on the back before turning back to the harness.

'I'm indebted to you. What a gift!' Asaph stroked the metal. 'I see it now in the Recollection. So, the design has not been lost to us. With Feygriene's blessing, the Dragon Lords will not be lost either.'

'With Feygriene's blessing,' echoed the Draxians and bowed their heads.

Issa walked the dark hallways towards the underground forge that glowed red and warm in the distance.

A few sconces burned low but gave off enough light for her to find her way. It was late, and most people slept, but not all. The sound of Eiretonne's hammer striking metal rang out soothingly, reminding her of all the times she'd worked at a blacksmith's.

A spray of sparks lit up the dark, followed by the sizzle and smoke of hot metal hitting cold water. Why he had sent for her was an intriguing source of mystery.

'Ah, there ye are, Miss,' said the dwarf, standing straight but still only coming up to her chest. He arched his back and wiped his face, smearing even more soot over it. His eyes gleamed in the red light of the furnace and he said, 'It's ready.'

'What's ready? Why did you send for me? Surely you should be sleeping and not working.' Issa stifled a yawn as the dwarf went the other side of the anvil and picked up a long object wrapped in cloth. He set about polishing it with the cloth and she watched, curious.

'This couldn't wait, Missy. I know in the next few days you'll be leavin' and you need a decent weapon.'

'I have a good weapon already. Grast'anth gave it to me.'

'Indeed, it *was* a good, strong weapon—notched and bent though it was, but you need something more than that now. Something enchanted, something far finer, something much more than just a sword.'

He let the wrappings drop to reveal the most beautiful sword she had ever seen. It was like a jewel—the metal so pale it was almost white. The blade was thin at the base and tip and wider in the middle, like a willow leaf. It was longer than her short sword but shorter than a longsword. The pommel was a strange basket that made the whole sword look rather odd. It gleamed in the firelight.

'This is no ordinary sword, Missy.' Eiretonne proudly turned over the stunningly skilfully made blade. 'It was designed by an Elven weaponsmith and forged by my good self, Eiretonne Coldhammer, in pure Tarvalastone metal. Then it was set in the fire of a dragon and enchanted by a Master Wizard.' He deftly spun the hilt towards her. 'Have a feel of it.'

She took the hilt. The cold metal, though unleathered, sat perfectly comfortably in her hand. She could feel an enchantment on it, testing her hand, wondering if she were its master.

'It's so light,' she breathed, gently swishing it too and fro. It dipped left and right awkwardly. 'Hmm, as beautiful as it is, it doesn't feel right, I don't think it's balanced quite correctly. And who is this dragon? I've been with Asaph the whole time, and Master Wizard Freydel is nowhere to be seen.'

A cool, quiet voice spoke, 'There are other dragons and wizards besides them.' Domenon stood in the doorway, shoulder leaning on the frame, his arms folded. The firelight lit up his face and shone off his hair, but the rest of him, dressed as he usually was in black leathers, was lost in the darkness.

His dark eyes sparkled and held her gaze without blinking. She noticed his burnt hand now wore a glove to hide his injury. Despite his usual cool and superior demeanour, he actually looked exhausted, paler than usual, with dark circles under his eyes and bruises on his face, and he was thinner too. *But he still looks handsome, still powerful,* thought Issa.

'The metal was set in the white fire of a pure blood dragon, not a half-breed,' Domenon said though there was no venom in his words. 'But the enchantment…my magic is not what it used to be since…However, it's as strong as I—or anyone—can make it, and will bind to the owner on first touch, once the sword is whole.'

'It's not finished?' Issa frowned at the sword, her eyes resting on the strange basket.

'Your orb, Missy,' said Eiretonne, urging her with a nod.

Knowing that Domenon was watching, Issa was reluctant to take out Illendri, but she did so anyway.

'Push it in, the magic and the sword will know what to do,' said Eiretonne.

Not seeing how it could possibly fit into the basket, Issa pushed the orb against the metal. She gasped as the metal grew warm, twisted upon itself, then opened to allow the orb in before wrapping itself protectively around it. Illendri hummed gently.

Issa held the sword up and laughed in amazement. 'It's perfectly balanced now, and somehow even lighter with the orb,' she said in wonder.

'The sword will never break, notch, or allow the orb to damage. Such are the effects of my enchantments,' said Domenon. 'It will remain in the sword until the orb finds and rejoins its sisters, as I now know it surely must.'

Eiretonne nodded and winked at the wizard. Issa stared from one to the other. 'This is such a gift—I don't know why you made it for me or how I can repay you.'

She bent down and hugged the dwarf. He chuckled and blushed. Then she turned and hugged Domenon, catching him by surprise. He hesitated then a strong arm embraced her. His chin was smoothly shaven, and he smelled slightly of soap, fresh and clean. She released him, blushing despite herself.

'Luterian does not design swords for just anyone,' said a familiar voice. Domenon stepped aside to allow Velonorian through. 'There you are, my Lady. I've been worried sick and hunting these eerie dark hallways for an hour. I know the elf who designed your sword, it's made to ancient specifications.'

'I must meet him, Velonorian, but, hmm, perhaps another time. It's late and we need sleep.'

'Of course my lady. I'll accompany you to your room,' said the young elf.

'Let's all go. I am indeed tired,' said Domenon.

'You kids go,' said Eiretonne wafting his hands and relaxing down onto a stool. 'I need a bit more time alone here, within the forge of my ancestors.' He looked around, instantly losing himself to the past and the once-magnificent city of the Dwarves of Light.

'Murlonius.'

The final call of the boatman's name echoed into the darkness. Issa stood on the banks of Tarvalastone River outside the city walls and watched the water calm and flow silent as a thick mist rolled over it towards them.

Too stunned to speak, she boarded the boat without a word, followed by Asaph, Marakon, Bokaard and several hundred soldiers; Knights of the Raven, Navadin, Elves and Dwarves. No one spoke, the bears didn't even grunt, and she watched mesmerised as the boat grew without a creak to accommodate them all.

Ehka seated himself on her lap and Asaph sat down beside her, his eyes locked onto the still, cloaked form of Murlonius. There was no Yisufalni. Issa burned with questions but feared to ask them and break the stillness.

Murlonius pushed them from the riverbank and the river carried them into the mist. Apart from the softly lapping water against the boat, a deeper silence descended. An ethereal light shimmered off the surface and in the air, beautiful yet peculiar. Issa imagined spending an eternity in this place and shivered.

The pull of sleep grew, and already Asaph's eyes drooped as they entered the realm above and between the physical plane of Maioria. The higher the frequency of other realms, the harder it was for the physical body to process them and it tired quickly.

Issa fought sleep.

She glanced behind her. The Knights of the Raven—trained under Marakon with her assistance—slumbered. Beyond them, sleeping against their bears, were Jarlain and the Navadin—at least another one hundred bear riders. Eiretonne, though reluctant to leave his beloved forge, had hand-chosen the scores of dwarven fighters now around him, some Feylint Halanoi, some Knights of the Raven.

Velonorian would not leave her side and brought with him some of the finest Elven archers. There was even a company of Draxians, and though currently led by slumbering Gott, the Barbarian of the North had conceded leadership to a reluctant Asaph as soon as they reached Drax.

Cusap'anth, Rhul'ynth and Grast'anth had wanted to come, but were needed to rebuild Karalanthia far away on the western-most edge of Venosia. She'd been sad to say goodbye and couldn't help but wonder now if she'd ever see her friends again. If she didn't, it would be because all of Maioria had fallen.

This tiny boat now accommodated over five hundred soldiers and their horses and mounts, including Duskar. Issa thanked the goddess the Sea of Opportunity was always calm in this open-topped vessel.

Forcing her eyes open, she bent forward to Murlonius.

'My heart bleeds, for they took Yisufalni.' Her voice was barely a whisper.

He nodded ever so slightly, his face lost in the folds of the hood that he hadn't even bothered to push back, even though age no longer touched him.

'I could not save her,' she explained. 'Domenon saved me—'

He cut her off. 'I know, Raven Queen,' he rasped, raw anguish in his voice. 'I tried to follow, to lure them to me, but they got away. I chased them to the edges of Maphrax where I lost her.

'When they eventually came back for me, I did not run, I stayed. I wanted them to take me, I wanted them to kill me. Either I will be with her or I shall die.

'I turned myself into ether and it took me near half a year as time passes in the Ethereal Planes to pull myself back together again. So many months have passed and still this body is frail and spent! I almost expected them to follow me into the ethers, but something happened, and they turned away. They left. I don't know why nor where they went but they have not returned. When they do, I'll be ready.'

'The Hall of Memories,' Issa whispered. 'They left you and came for me, and there was Lona and my sister…it doesn't matter. Please, Murlonius, do not surrender yourself to them. Come with us, fight with us. If we lose you both, the orbs can never be recombined. She's not dead, I have felt her, she's within the orb. You *must* stay alive and together we'll try to save her.'

Murlonius gave a long low chuckle as he rowed, an odd, hopeless sound. 'Valiant Raven Queen, I have nothing left to give and no fight remains within me. It's all gone now. Do you really think we can just walk into Maphrax and take the orbs for ourselves?'

Issa shook her head, his hopelessness infectious. How could they get the orbs? How could they ever defeat Baelthrom? Lona would kill her before she ever set foot on Maphrax. 'I don't know how,' she whispered.

In her mind an image of a great battle formed. Soldiers and Maphraxies fighting on a ravaged plane under a thunderous sky. Baelthrom standing omnipotent on one side, and she, seated atop Duskar, upon the other. *The Hall of Memories...I see a great battle that will destroy us all before the end.*

'Yes, there will be great destruction before the end.' Murlonius nodded and she realised then that she had spoken aloud. 'Rest, Raven Queen. Our lives are still our own, and you have a long journey before you. Heed the White Raven, Raven Queen.'

His voice faded as sleep overcame her. She drifted uneasy over an endless plane of shimmering light.

CHAPTER 26

Foreboding Dreams

IT was the deathly cold that awoke Issa, followed by the rough rocking of the boat as soldiers disembarked.

As frost bit deep into her fingers, she shivered, and Ehka buried himself into her lap when she tried to lift him up. So long had she been in the South and the strange wastelands of Venosia, she had forgotten what real winter was, but having never travelled further north than Frayon, she was utterly frozen. She hugged Ehka in her arms, grateful for his warmth.

Asaph pulled her to her feet. 'Come on, we're here, and you need a hat and gloves.' He took her free hand into his surprisingly warm one.

'I can't imagine how cold Drax must be,' she stammered, blinking. Even her eyes felt frozen. 'Where *is* here?'

They disembarked onto a beach, to the right of which rose the hulk of a great harbour where huge sconces burned bright along the harbour walls. Stars twinkled icily in the frigid sky and there were no moons to offer more light.

Her feet plunged into the frozen water and she was glad for the water resistance of her boots, although by the time she had taken the few steps to shore, she could no longer feel her feet. She turned back to Murlonius who stood silent and shrouded at the helm of his boat. She stepped back into the water towards him and gripped the side of the vessel as the last soldier disembarked.

'Please, for all our sakes, don't give in. We *can* find Yisufalni, I'm sure of it—she's not dead. We can be free, all of us.' But Murlonius did not reply, nor did he even nod. Instead, he drifted away from the shore and the mist engulfed him.

'Come, Issa, you'll freeze to death,' said Asaph dragging her back to the shore. 'He knows what he has to do better than any of us.' She reluctantly turned away from the fading mist.

Marakon led them along the outer walls of the harbour and port, through the endless rows of well-ordered, semi-permanent tents and shacks to the Feylint Halanoi barracks. It took some time to find anything empty; the place had swelled with refugees from Lans Himay, but a section of tents had been vacated by a unit of soldiers who were on expedition.

Eventually, Issa and Asaph found a tent for themselves and they huddled against each other for warmth in the few hours that were left before dawn.

Sleep evaded her as she worried about Yisufalni and Murlonius, his words tumbling over and over in her mind. *Heed the White Raven, Raven Queen.'* When sleep finally came, it brought with it disturbing dreams.

It was very dark.

In the distance, a drumbeat—a single, slow beat, like the rhythm of a heart, like the drums of war. The cold seared her nose and fingers—so icy it burned. A frigid wind blew, and she shivered, hugging her arms, arms that were bare. She looked down and saw she was naked, but where had she left her clothes?

The cold now came from within, starting in her stomach and radiating out through every cell in painful waves.

'Light,' she commanded, but her orb and talisman were gone, and the Flow wasn't there. She stumbled along stony ground, peering into the night.

Something moved, a white wing flapped, feathers starkly bright in the blackness. *The white owl?* Thinking of Cirosa, Issa paused, her heart pounding.

Dawn spread a grey light and the bird turned and cawed at her – not a nice sound but an angry grating one. Issa stared at the white raven, its white beak, even its white legs. It watched her with pale, unblinking eyes. The pain in her stomach grew worse, an intense, icy, stabbing pain, that made her double over. She struggled to breathe as something smothered her, dark and powerful like the Under Flow. She choked and clawed for air.

'Issa, what is it? Wake up!' A voice commanded from afar.

Issa forced opened her eyes mid-choke and stared up at Asaph. The pain in her stomach eased and she found she could breathe again. She lay gulping in the cold air. It was light in the tent, and his tanned skin radiated warmth.

'It was just a dream,' he said, smoothing back her hair. She shivered. Her frozen fingers hadn't managed to warm themselves since they'd arrived. 'Look, you're freezing. You need a thick cloak and gloves. We'll get them today. It's past dawn and I can smell breakfast already.' He rubbed his taut belly. Sure enough the smell of toast and coffee wafted agreeably in from somewhere.

'Just a dream,' Issa echoed, still seeing the white raven in the darkness, still feeling faint stabs of pain in her stomach. She tried to push the foreboding dream aside, but the ominous feelings remained.

Asaph kissed her on the cheek and pushed himself onto his feet. He pulled her unwilling and groaning body up beside him and together they dressed, pulling on every item of clothing that they possessed.

Asaph stepped outside, eagerly following his nose, then sheered back, startled.

Twenty or so unarmed Draxians stood before his tent, dressed warmly in furs and armour. Some were sitting on the frozen grass but seeing him, all stood and eyed him eagerly, the ones at the back straining to get a better look.

Velonorian emerged from the tent next to theirs, his sensitive hearing must have heard him getting up.

'Are they still here?' sighed the elf. 'Sir Asaph Dragon Lord, I tried to get them to leave at dawn, but they would not. Now even more have come.'

A Draxian with long red hair walked forwards, his helmet tucked under an arm. He spoke nervously. 'Sir, uh, is it true what those from Venosia have said?'

Issa stepped out beside Asaph. 'Oh,' she said and looked at him. He shrugged and spread his palms.

'He called him Dragon Lord,' said a fair-haired Draxian woman, pointing at Velonorian. She removed her helmet and a thick braid of flaxen hair swung over her shoulder. More Draxians emerged from between the tents to stare at him. Asaph's cheeks grew hot.

'He looks Draxian,' said another man coming closer, his heavy furs making him look even more enormous than he was already. 'So, the fighter from Frayon did not lie. This is he, the one he fought and to whom he has pledged his life. Behold the last Dragon Lord, behold our King!'

Asaph's mind raced as all the Draxians dropped to one knee. He thought of Leaper and his loyal men, was that who the man was talking about?

Issa grabbed his arm when he went to stop them. 'Don't,' she said, shaking her head. 'Let them do this. They need this. They need you, their King, they need something to believe in.'

Asaph held her gaze before nodding. She looked so regal and wise just then, so different from the broken girl he'd found on the shores of the Shadowlands. They had both changed a lot in a short time, he thought, they had grown strong.

Awkwardly, Asaph reached down and gripped the first man's arm, raising him to his feet. At his motion the others stood. Two, who he recognised from Venosia, came forwards.

'All who are Draxian, in whole or in part, now know *you* have returned to us,' said the one with red hair, his face solemn. 'More come every day fleeing the war ravaging Lans Himay. That land is gone. Now we'll fight to take another, the one we should never have lost.' Tears filled the man's eyes and he clenched his fist and held it high—just like Coronos had once done after a victory against the goblins in Kuapoh lands. The others followed the gesture and Asaph slowly followed.

'We will fight,' said Asaph, the passion for his homeland rising. 'We will fight for Drax once more, until it is ours or we are all dead and free to join our ancestors.'

The Draxians cheered, startling him with their ferocity. Other non-Draxians came close to see the spectacle.

'Asaph?' said a familiar voice.

A wiry man with a scar and tied-back fair hair pushed through the crowd.

'Leaper?' The two men laughed and slapped each other's shoulders.

Asaph pushed the man back to look at him. 'I can see you're well. How are you here? You got my message?'

He nodded. 'Yes. King Navarr got your message and he discharged us immediately to go north. He said we are your men now. We're loyal to you, King Asaph. We're all here, ready and waiting for your word.'

Other non-Draxians came forward, smiles forming on their faces. Green-eyed Danny, Renno the giant, dark-haired Jekk and quick-eyed Blaise. They were all fully armoured and armed, and wearing the Feylint Halanoi tabard.

'And this is your beautiful maiden?' asked Leaper. He took Issa's hand and bent low to kiss it, making her blush crimson.

'Issa, yes,' Asaph grinned at her. 'Issalena Kammy.'

'Your Dragon Rider,' said the closest Draxian, nodding approvingly. 'Everything is complete, we're all gathered together, now is the time.'

'When do we leave for our homeland, my King?' asked the Draxian from Venosia.

Asaph opened and closed his mouth. 'At least let's wait until after breakfast,' he said. Everyone laughed, and he felt foolish—certainly he didn't feel like the King he was supposed to be.

'We already have Frayonesse ships waiting for us in the harbour, courtesy of King Navarr. We just need to know how many will be boarding,' said Leaper.

Issa giggled when Asaph rubbed his beard, struggling to come up with a plan. He side-glanced her, eyebrow raised.

'Let's have a meeting with Marakon after breakfast and formulate the details of our battle plan?' she offered.

'Indeed,' said Asaph clapping his hands together. 'We'll meet at dusk on the west side of the encampment, beside the forest, and there I'll brief you.'

His belly growled hungrily and with relief he watched the reluctant crowd leave to return to their duties. Leaper stayed at his side and showed them through the tents to the food hall. Velonorian accompanied Issa, chatting to her as they walked. Asaph only half-listened as the elf taught her the words for ice and snow in Elven.

'*Lin farna* means ice. You could say it means hard cold. *Els farna* means snow.'

'Soft cold?' Issa offered.

'You got it,' Velonorian laughed.

Asaph surveyed the encampment. The number of people and soldiers and tents was staggering. In the distance, he could see a long line of people, old and young, dressed smartly or in rags, queuing before several desks where Feylint Halanoi commanders recorded their names and professions.

'Scores come each day,' said Leaper nodding to the war-torn people. 'Some have such bad injuries you wonder how they made it this far.'

Asaph felt deeply sorry for them, especially when he picked out the Draxians amongst them. A people who'd already lost one homeland had now lost their second. 'We'll give them all a new land to go to,' he swore, clenching his jaw.

CHAPTER 27

The Way of Dragons

WITH Asaph's help, Issa heaved the dragon harness onto his enormous back just as the morning sun burst through the trees, its rays touching his golden scales, making them shine.

Asaph shoved the harness up with his shoulder blades and wriggled it into the place where it felt the most comfortable. It had taken them at least half an hour in the frigid dawn light to carry the harness into a clearing where he could change into a dragon without causing alarm.

She gathered the long dangling straps, the frozen ground crunching underneath her Dread Dragon boots—not even dragon skin could protect her from this cold. She looped the straps around his torso and tightened them.

'It's not uncomfortable, just unusual,' he said, still wriggling around. 'Hopefully I'll get used to it.'

'They said you would,' said Issa, eyeing the whole set up critically and fighting back the dread of actually getting into the thing. Ehka landed on the harness and began inspecting it thoroughly.

The sun fell fully on the glade, causing a cold mist to rise from the thawing forest floor. She raised her face and enjoyed the warm rays.

'Well, I guess we may as well get going. The others will be boarding the ships, and some may have already left,' said Asaph, looking up at the sky. Heavy snow clouds drifted in the north.

Issa took a deep breath and went to the main rope, then hesitated. Asaph looked at her quizzically.

'It's not that I'm afraid of flying…it's just that the white raven is warning me of something,' she said. Though the sense of foreboding had waned, it was still there, lurking. She didn't think it had anything to do with flying on Asaph's back, but the whole premonition had left her on edge.

'It was just a dream,' rumbled Asaph.

'Although, right this moment, getting on that ship with Marakon and the others seems like a great idea.' She forced a smile and pulled on a strap. 'Anyway, how can you trust this thing?'

'I trust their design. It's the same as I see in the Recollection, only more beautiful. It's better, if anything, and will be even betterer with you in it.' The dragon tried to smile but ended up simply displaying his enormous fangs.

Issa's eyes widened, and he stopped smiling.

'If you fall off, you can always turn into a raven,' he chuckled.

She gave him a withering look.

A heavy cloud passed in front of the sun and wispy flakes of snow began to fall. A chill wind blew, and she wrapped her thick cloak closer and did up more of the clasps. It was well made, a beautiful, deep royal blue and had soft, fluffy white trims and cuffs. Asaph had bought it for her in Port Nordastin with the gold Coronos had left to him. It wasn't cheap—the most she'd ever spent on clothing—but he'd insisted and now she was very grateful for it. She pulled on her matching gloves and flexed her hands for warmth.

Taking a deep breath, she awkwardly inched herself up the rope in the same manner she had seen Coronos do, by walking up the dragon's side. Sweating, she flopped into the seat, became entangled in a strap, and nearly fell out the other side. Flailing wildly she accidentally booted Ehka off his perch. The raven flew into the air squawking.

'Sorry!' she called.

'What's going on?' Asaph struggled to see behind him.

'N-n-n-nothing,' gasped Issa as she righted herself. Finally, she found where her feet should go and what she should hang on to. A gust of wind blew, and heavier snow cascaded down. She pulled up her hood over her hat and caught her breath.

'I'll bet it's even colder up there.' She looked up at the heavy grey clouds swiftly covering the deep blue sky.

'If you get cold, I can always breathe fire on you,' Asaph laughed.

'You're full of fun this morning,' Issa grumbled. 'Are you sure it's like spring in Yis? I might be able to thaw out once we get there.'

'Yes, it's beautiful, like nowhere else you have seen.' Asaph's voice was full of wonder. 'You'll meet the other dragons and won't want to leave—none of us ever do. But it's not Draxa, my *real* home; it's my dragon home I guess.

'At least five dragons will aid us in Draxa, but I pray to Feygriene there'll be more. To take Drax fully, we'll need all the help we can get.'

'It's a long way for the ships,' said Issa, thinking about the plans they had made with the others all day yesterday and deep into the night. Marakon would lead the knights, soldiers, Draxian exiles and Navadin to Drax. They would sail up the west coast straight to Draxa, during which time Asaph and the dragons would have secured safe landing spots. There was little element of surprise and it was frightening, as it always was going into battle, but it was happening, and nothing could stop the flow of events now.

Asaph stood, and the saddle lurched violently. Issa stifled a squeal and grabbed at the rails for balance, her heart pounding. The Draxians had shown her how to ride in it, and she hoped it would get easier like they had said.

Asaph stretched his head and tail, making himself even more enormous and terrifying. Just a flex of his muscles could break the straps and send her tumbling to the ground. He spread his wings and arched his back. *Goodness, these beasts are too big for Maioria!* thought Issa, watching as powerful muscles rippled over his shoulders.

'Asaph! Asaph!' A voice shouted.

'Hold on!' shouted another.

Issa turned to see Leaper and Velonorian running out of the woods towards them, followed by a horde of Draxians. They poured into the clearing and stopped short, dragon fear and awe spreading over their faces, then sending them to their knees.

'I tried to stop them,' said Leaper, spreading his hands. 'But they refused to board the ships until they had seen you for real.'

'Hail King Asaph, Dragon Lord and King of Drax!' said the tall, red-haired man rising to his feet.

'Hail King Asaph!' roared the others, getting up.

With the hail and cheer of his people, Asaph proudly beat his wings and leapt into the air. He swooped dangerously low over all of them, sending many to their knees again, before the cold wind lifted him up into the snow and sun.

Issa waved down, trying to look calm and composed as she clutched the lurching dragon seat. Velonorian and the others waved back until they were mere pinpricks in the trees.

Asaph headed due north, and it was as she had expected, freezing.

'Warmth,' she commanded and both the raven talisman in her belt and Illendri in its scabbard grew warm. Poor Ehka was certainly going to get cold, she thought as she watched the bird fly close. She pulled her scarf up over her nose and mouth and tried to loosen her death grip on the reins that weren't really reins as she couldn't command Asaph in that manner, but it gave her a feeling of control thinking of them as that.

She found the dragon seat remarkably comfortable. When Asaph flew straight, as he did now, flying was easy, almost boring when thinking she could be flying as a raven. All she had to do now was hang on—and even that she didn't have to do when he flew straight and steady.

Asaph rose higher and higher until he cleared the low snow clouds. Bright sunlight lit up a field of white clouds and the deep blue sky above them.

'Our ships are departing,' said Asaph.

Issa looked down through a gap in the clouds and spied three Frayonesse and two Atalanph ships leaving the port. Two remained in the dock, probably waiting for the cheering Draxians.

'How about some fun?' shouted Asaph over the frigid wind.

'What do you mean?' Issa shouted back, feeling less than enthusiastic as the cold plastered her eyes.

With a roaring laugh Asaph folded his wings close and dropped through the clouds. Issa's stomach somersaulted. She became aware of her own screaming when he slowed his descent just above the ships' swaying masts. She couldn't breathe to even shout at the foolish beast.

Soldiers and sailors screamed and fell to their knees. Was Asaph laughing? For once he didn't seem to feel guilty about spreading dragon fear. He spurted a joyful bout of flames into the air and circled merrily above them as they recovered. Some shook fists at him—Marakon and

Bokaard—but others broke into cheers and waves. Issa began to chuckle and waved back.

The great gusts of wind Asaph created helped to fill their sails. Eventually Marakon and Bokaard grinned and nodded. With a mighty roar that trembled her seat, Asaph lifted back up into the clouds and the ships were lost from view. The noise of the wind was too much for her to shout over, so she spoke with her mind in the Daluni way.

'I hope they make it there all right. Let's hope we don't miss them or they're attacked before they even get there.'

Asaph said, *'They have weather wizards for speed and cloaking, and Bokaard is one of the best captains they have. At least one ship will make it.'* She detected humour in Asaph's mind speak. *'Don't worry, if anything, we dragons will be there first. It'll take them a week to even reach the tip of Drax.'*

He was right but still Issa worried.

It was dusk by the time Asaph finally angled his wings down into the freezing cold clouds. When they dropped below them it was to emerge into huge fluffy snowflakes falling upon a mountainous land already covered in white. Craggy peaks cradled smooth white troughs and valleys that stretched on for miles. If there were trees, they had long been lost to the deep trenches of snow.

The Kingdom of Ice, thought Issa, noting how frigidly beautiful the white lands were. There was barely a breeze and the snow fell unhindered to rest peacefully on the land. The whole place was silent, reverent, frozen in time and space.

'This is a place of dragons?' asked Issa. It was so quiet and still, she didn't need to shout. 'I thought dragons liked hot places with lots of sun?'

Asaph didn't reply immediately. He dropped lower and glided effortlessly over a flat plane, the cracks in the ice glowing a luminous aqua. *Perhaps a frozen lake lies beneath them,* Issa thought.

'They came here long ago, when Feygriene first sent them forth from the sun, so the legend goes. This was a green, fertile land rich with crystal clear lakes and rivers, mountain flowers and long summers under a hot sun.' Issa frowned as Asaph spoke, trying to imagine green meadows and mountain flowers under the snow.

'When Baelthrom came eons ago, the North froze over, slowly at first as his evil was small, then more and more over time. Now the ice sheets reach to smother even northern Drax. No one ever thought the sea itself would freeze.

'In the Recollection, I have seen ancient dragons from long ago discovering and mapping out all the corners of Maioria in their minds. I have seen the southern pole, also encrusted in ice—a place so cold and dark not even dragons could live there.

'Dragons know—from deep memory of a time before they even came to Maioria—that a planet with frozen poles cannot breathe properly. Something in the ice I suppose, I don't know. I would have thought Elven or human wizards would know more, but they don't. They've forgotten because the memories and histories have been destroyed by Baelthrom.

'Planets live through the grace of the sun's energy. Through the poles, the sun sends a life energy into Maioria, and all the planets. It circulates through each and then returns to it. A symbiotic and intimate relationship between our sun, beloved Feygriene, and Maioria. This is dragon knowledge, for we are born of sun fire. Perhaps Feygriene foresaw the fall of Maioria, so she sent her dragons to come here, to help. I like to think so, anyway.'

Issa listened in fascination, trying to imagine Maioria and the sun as living sentient beings like she and Asaph, and the essential flow of life-force between them. It wasn't easy.

'If we destroy Baelthrom, will the ice melt?' she asked, meaning would things ever return to a harmonious, normal reality, one she had never known?

Asaph chuckled. 'I would have never believed it possible until I witnessed what happened at Yis.'

Issa remembered all that he had told her of the land being restored from a frozen desert to a beautiful spring sanctuary through the grace of Feygriene. Just as she was picturing it, they crested a mountain peak and a green oasis appeared below.

Issa inhaled sharply at the emerald land sparkling in a sea of white. Inlaid in the centre was a blue lake, and on its banks, a shining golden castle and temple. A powerful magical shield protected it.

'Beautiful, isn't it?' said Asaph. 'Only a living dragon, Dragon Rider or pure blood Draxian can see through the shield, so I guess you must truly be a Dragon Rider.' He glanced back at her and she grinned.

They descended through the shield and warmth engulfed them. She rolled back her shoulders to relieve the hunched position she'd adopted for the entire ride to keep herself warm.

Asaph alighted on the grassy shore and dipped his snout into the clear waters to drink. Ehka flopped down beside him. Issa drank from the canister at her side and took in the beautiful scenery.

It was the hairs on the back of her neck raising, and then fear that prickled her skin that alerted her. A gust of wind blew, and giant red wings swooped overhead making her yelp. She froze in dragon fear as the red dragon circled, said something to Asaph in mind-speak, then landed to his left.

The red dragon was smaller than Asaph, more slender in every way apart from its wings, which were longer. It looked elegant and built for speed. Both dragons dipped their heads and held a pose in respectful dragon greeting. Something passed between them again and Issa assumed they were talking mind to mind. She was not privy to the conversation despite being Daluni.

The red dragon turned its amber gaze onto Issa. 'Greetings, Raven Queen Dragon Rider,' said the dragon in a rumbling female voice.

'Meet Garna, Issa,' said Asaph.

'Greetings, Garna,' said Issa, her voice betraying the remnants of her dragon fear.

Another dragon descended fast towards them in tight circles. This one was green, and it shook the ground as it landed beside Garna, its dark eyes shining and black horns like a crown upon its head. The three dragons dipped their heads and communed.

'Issa, this is Pennarc,' said Asaph, gesturing.

The green dragon said nothing but eyed her with interest. Feelings of respect came from him. Issa managed to smile as the dragon fear waned.

'The others are sleeping or hunting for our kin or food,' said Asaph. Issa sighed in silent relief. She didn't fancy going through the dragon fear every time a dragon appeared.

'There are eighteen of us now, Asaph Dragon Lord,' said Garna. 'But six are still in deep recovery. We sense more but they are weak and far away...we do not have much hope. Once we were nearer a hundred, but that was long before Baelthrom came.'

'Eighteen,' echoed Asaph, his sapphire eyes looking far away. 'Eighteen must be enough.'

There was a thoughtful silence and Issa wondered why. They didn't seem to be speaking. She decided she didn't understand the way of dragons at all.

'Drax calls to us,' said Pennarc, lifting his mighty head of horns and looking to the South. 'The land will belong to dragons once again, it is as Feygriene wishes. When must we leave, Dragon Lord?'

Asaph took a long time to answer, as if he were trying to look into the future and discover what he must do. 'I will leave tomorrow at dusk. You and Garna gather those willing to fight and leave three suns from now.'

'Where is Great Morhork?' asked Garna, lifting her tail.

'I don't know,' said Asaph. 'Morhork follows his own guidance and is beholden to none. It's my fervent wish that he joins us, but I know how he feels about dragons getting involved in what he perceives as human affairs.'

Issa had not seen Morhork since Eiretonne had presented her with her sword. She still had trouble thinking of Domenon as the blue, wingless dragon.

'Morhork has always been his own master,' Pennarc agreed. 'Strong, powerful, free.'

As the dragons talked, Issa longed to stand up and stretch. She slipped out of her harness and used the rope to walk down Asaph's leg. It was easier than before, especially when he helped by angling his leg in a certain way, flattening himself.

She reached the ground sweating, and pulled off her hat, gloves, scarf and cloak. Her heart skipped a beat when she looked up at the three enormous dragons, one red, one green and one golden. From ground level, they towered above her, and a single dragon eye was bigger than her head.

She found herself stepping backwards until her back pressed against Asaph's huge chest. From there, she turned and busied herself undoing the dragon harness.

The dragons finished discussing their plans and began saying goodbye—a strange display of angling necks and nodding heads. She found everything about the beasts fascinating.

When they leapt into the air, it was with such grace that she held her breath. A shimmer surrounded Asaph, the Flow surged, and then the man was standing there holding the dragon seat she had been fighting with for the last quarter of an hour.

'Let's go to the castle. I can't wait to show you around,' he said. With one easy movement, he hefted the entire seat into the air and carried it alone a few paces towards the castle.

'It's so beautiful,' said Issa, staring at the smooth golden domes shining in the sunlight. 'Is it really gold?'

'You bet,' said Asaph, setting the dragon seat down with a grunt. 'You know how much dragons love the stuff.'

They walked into the courtyard, passing under the enormous arches and over the beautiful mosaic paving. She marvelled at the sprinkling fountain and followed Asaph through the great metal-scrolled oak doors and into a reception room. The floors and walls were covered in cherry wood panelling reaching to about his waist, and the high ceilings were supported by huge arched wooden beams.

Great windows everywhere let in plenty of light. The inner walls were decorated with beautifully painted scenes depicting dragons and humans— great moments from lifetimes lived thousands of years ago, captured forever in stunning colours.

Issa ran from room to room, hallway to hallway, letting her curiosity run wild in this fabulous, enormous palace. Asaph laughed as he followed. Finally, she paused and whirled to face him.

'As stunning as it is, the whole place is completely empty,' she said. 'There isn't even a chair to sit on.'

'Only the structure itself survived,' said Asaph, folding his arms and leaning on a wall. 'Come, I've stored firewood and food in the kitchen. Fish from the lake, mostly, and some rations I brought with me. The dragons have also helped bringing food and blankets. In one of the smaller rooms, I've almost made some semblance of a bed.'

He led her to the kitchen on the ground floor. Soon, he had the oven blazing and was cooking lunch, while a kettle hanging above it boiled water for tea.

As they ate, Asaph told her everything he had seen of this place in the Recollection, and the details of how it had risen from the lake. Though she'd heard it before, now she was here, his retelling was far more magical.

Atop the balcony overlooking the lake, Issa and Asaph sipped Frayon port from chipped cups and watched the sun sink into the white mountains.

The long rays turned the landscape purple and red. White birds with long legs and necks flocked to the side of the lake where tall reeds provided a safe roosting spot for the night. *Serene, protected, holy,* thought Issa.

As darkness fell, Asaph took her hand and led her inside to their room where a warm fire crackled in the hearth. She did not protest as he sat her down on the pile of rugs and blankets that made their bed.

As he slipped her tunic off her shoulders, they kissed. She wasn't hesitant when he laid her down—instead she was eager, excited, and free. Their passion rose when their marks touched. Power flooded through her body as he pressed firmly upon her. Again, the world turned into the magical energies of the Flow, lifting them both higher and higher. She felt the edges of her being blur and begin to meld with his in a way she could never describe or understand. It was as if their combined energy lifted them up into higher, purer realm of beauty and spirit.

As the waves of ecstasy gently subsided. She floated slowly down until she opened her eyes to find herself in his arms.

He smiled at her, a sheen of perspiration on his face and his hair dishevelled and red in the low firelight. She closed her eyes and hugged him close. The world of war and strife was far from this place, and this night, in the sanctity of Yis, Feygriene's Haven, she would dream only of peaceful things.

They watched the sun sink into the mountains again the next evening, only now they stood before the lake.

Issa was dressed warmly in her cloak and gloves and seated in her dragon seat atop Asaph's back. Both were subdued, pensive. Ahead lay victory or death—there could be nothing in between.

'A strong wind blows from the South. It will hamper our journey but at least it's a warmer wind,' rumbled Asaph.

'I wonder how far the others have got,' said Issa.

Asaph nodded and looked up at the darkening sky. They waited in silence until the first stars appeared, then, without ceremony, Asaph spread his wings, Issa gripped the rails and held her breath as the dragon ran and launched them into the air. The wind and rush of excitement made her gasp, then as the shock faded, grin with delight. They swooped over the lake and up the mountainside over the tiny golden temple. The mountain fell away, and a star-filled sky filled her vision.

When they cleared the magical shield, frozen wind blasted her face. She pulled her scarf over her nose and blinked the tears from her eyes. Glancing back she glimpsed a black speck following. *Poor Ehka must be freezing,* she thought. When he landed on the bar in front of her, she took hold of him and pulled him inside her cloak to thaw out. It would be warmer in Drax, though not by much.

As she thought of the ancient land of Dragon Lords, she found her hand resting on Illendri. There would be a battle, a terrible one, but it would not be like Venosia, they had a fraction of that army now. Would it be enough? *It must be enough.*

Would Cirosa be there? She chewed her lip, feeling the anger for what she had done to Asaph, to the priestesses, and to the entire Temple, rise. What if she still had a grip on Asaph? Too many questions… But Cirosa could be their downfall. She could not be allowed to harm him. She must be located and taken down first.

There were other worries besides Cirosa, and her palms grew sweaty. It was known that Baelthrom's right-hand man held Drax. *Hameka, you bastard! You murdered my friend, now you'll face justice.*

Issa tasted blood in her mouth and released her bite on her lip and her grip on Illendri. Many would die. The fear of battle wound her stomach tight. *It won't matter if we lose Drax, because I'll be dead, too.* The thought offered her some courage.

CHAPTER 28

Broken

'JOIN me or be *nothing.*'

Baelthrom's claws scraped the floor in front of Freydel's face. The wizard's cheek pressed into the cold stone of the dark chamber and black energy poured through the enormous iron ring suspended before him. The energy settled in his stomach and made him want to vomit. The walls of the chamber angled inwards and upwards, so far above he could not see where they ended.

Freydel inhaled cold damp air but he could not lift himself up. Not a single muscle would obey his command. The translocation had been violent, now all he could do was lie here before the terror of the world.

'I'll join Ayeth, the being who you once were,' rasped Freydel.

'That part of me is gone. Ayeth was weak, he should not have fallen to the ways of the Yurgha. His goddess *made* him weak. Now I have no ruler, and I cannot be ruled.'

'So you remember, then? All that occurred?' This was a surprise to Freydel. Did Baelthrom know *all* that had happened, including Lona's betrayal?

'The iron ring has shown me all, and memory has returned to me. I am now complete.' Baelthrom's voice was a rolling tide that echoed around the room. 'I am ready for the ultimate journey into the Dark Rift. You may serve me, or be torn apart in the transition. No being who has not imbibed the black drink will survive such a journey—at least in their current form. This planet and all its lifeforms are about to embark upon an incredible transformation.'

The wonder in Baelthrom's voice sickened Freydel further. Through the fog of black magic, a little feeling returned, and he weakly searched in his pocket for his orb. It wasn't there. The bottom of his world fell away.

Unwillingly, his eyes were drawn to the flaring black crystal Baelthrom slowly held up in his hand. 'Looking for this?' asked the Immortal Lord. Freydel's staff and his orb sizzled with rage as they were held by the very one he had fought against all his life. Tears filled his eyes and he could not breathe.

The orb should have destroyed anything that was not its Keeper. Was Baelthrom's power now so great he could withstand even the orbs? *And he is not truly alive!* The thought rattled in Freydel's tortured mind.

Baelthrom read his mind. 'Wrong. I have that which necessitates life— I am not one of my Maphraxies. Hmmm, it's clear you still do not know my plans, but then again, how could you decipher something built by a master?' The Immortal Lord walked towards the pedestal holding the three other orbs, his great lizard tail swinging, and set the black orb in one of the indents beside the others.

He turned back to Freydel and lifted a very human looking hand. Dark magic moved, surrounded the wizard, binding him and lifting him to his feet. His body was so weak he doubted he could stand unaided anyway.

'My Maphraxies, their souls I've gathered, for safekeeping, if you will. When we're all within the dark embrace of the rift, they will be returned to them. Changed, yes, but better, purer. They will know me as the One Light and no other.'

'Their souls are not yours to take,' Freydel dared to utter.

'Ignorance must be overcome, through force, if necessary,' said Baelthrom, his eyes glowering dark blue. 'Either you will serve me, or you will be nothing.'

The Under Flow began to build, a heavy cloying weight filling the room and pressing down upon him. Freydel swallowed and closed his eyes.

'Ayeth,' he screamed as searing pain exploded within every bone.

In another dimension, Lona asked, 'Where is your human?'

She stepped beside Ayeth onto the crystal balcony overlooking the forest. 'We have not seen him for many moons. Has he abandoned you?'

'His name is Freydel,' Ayeth reproached gently. 'I don't know, but I try not to give into the small mind of fear and worry. Their planet is undergoing many difficulties. Through the orb I search for him every hour, but I cannot reach him.'

He tried not to think about the human wizard who had come so suddenly into his life, and now had vanished. Instead, he wrapped his arms around Lona's slender frame. They looked to the East over the stunning landscape of waterfalls, rock pools and forests that were Aralansia. But it was to the sky their eyes were drawn—and it was an incredible sight to behold.

Three planets and a moon rolled imperceptibly before them. All felt the immense power of the alignment; the gravitational pull alone was enough to know something amazing and rare was taking place.

'Within a few days, they'll be in a perfect line,' said Ayeth, kissing Lona's head. 'Perhaps the energy of the planets is overpowering my own feeble attempts to find Freydel. But enough of that. You've been busy, too, so much so I've barely seen you for months. Tell me more about this human *you've* made contact with. A girl, yes? Yurgha technology truly is something to behold.'

Lona's cheeks blushed pale blue—a sign of anger or sadness, sometimes even embarrassment; Ayeth could never be sure which—and she tried to pull away but he held her closer.

She relented and after a moment said, 'Yes.' With a sigh, she rested her chin on his arms folded around her.

When she didn't say more, Ayeth said, 'The link between Aralansia and this Maioria is intriguing. But how did *you* do it? Why this girl? Does this child have special powers?'

'It's not like with your human,' said Lona. 'She's so small and innocent, you wouldn't think she could have so much power, so much…potential. But it's early days. I'd like you to meet her, but you might frighten her so we must wait until she is more used to me and our ways…our powers.'

'Is she not too young, hmm? And what is it you desire to teach her?' asked Ayeth, frowning at how nervous Lona seemed to be. She was wringing her hands and the blush on her cheeks had spread to her neck.

Aware of his scrutiny, Lona chuckled, wiggled out of his arms, and gazed at him with her penetrating black eyes that had the ability to mesmerise him. 'So many questions. Do you not trust me? Let it be a surprise. For now, let's not talk about our pets for they are more a hindrance than a help. We must think only upon the alignment; it won't happen again for near a million years. The Yurgha won't survive that long. I've done everything to prepare my race and our planet. The emancipation of the Yurgha and all of Yurgharon is upon us.'

Ayeth smiled. He could barely believe Lona would soon be healed, and the race of Yurgha would enter a bright future. 'You will soon be free of disease, of the sickness that plagues you, and of the Rorsken and Anukon who invade and destroy your lands. They won't be able to cope with the pure frequencies of the One Light that will shine upon Yurgharon once more, and they'll be forced to leave. And, who knows, perhaps they'll take a little light back to their planets; perhaps, one day, they too can be healed.'

'It would be better if they were annihilated completely,' Lona growled quietly, hatred passing across her face. She caught herself and the hatred was replaced with her usual smooth smile.

A large blue bird landed on the balcony rail beside them, making Lona jump. Quite unafraid, the bird cocked its head and watched them through dark eyes. It stretched its dark beak and ruffled its beautiful indigo feathers that captured the soft light of dusk.

'Stunning,' Ayeth marvelled. 'And what a marvellous omen.'

But Lona drew back, eyes wide, lips pursed. She did not like animals, least of all Aralansia's, but this reaction was stronger than usual and Ayeth noted it.

'Don't worry, this is a raven,' said Ayeth. 'They're friends and helpers of all Aralans. Blessed by the goddess, they bring luck and good fortune, and are among the most intelligent creatures on all Aralansia.'

'I find it…ugly,' gasped Lona. Ayeth was shocked to find her trembling. 'I mean, unsettling,' she corrected herself.

The bird appeared to sense this and stared at Lona all the more. Then, with a loud caw, it flew away. Pushing Ayeth's helping hands away, Lona gripped the balcony. Slowly she relaxed, and they watched the planets in the darkening sky.

When Lona is healed she'll rediscover her love of all creatures, Ayeth nodded to himself and lost himself in the beautiful scenery.

Freydel gasped yet the air brought him no life. The magic—the only thing that could feed him—was gone.

'Ayeth!' he cried out, but his voice was a rasp whipped away by the unrelenting wind tearing across the barren plains.

Without his orb, Freydel could not reach Ayeth. Ayeth, his grand master and beloved teacher from a different time, a faraway galaxy, even a different dimension, was lost to him forever.

Forever!

Freydel lay where he had fallen, thrown out from Baelthrom's Mountains of Maphrax like garbage. Down he'd rolled, his body smashing over rocks and rubble until every part of his body had been bloodied or bruised. The pain in his physical body was nothing compared to the rent in his soul. He wished the earth beneath him would swallow him up or that Baelthrom had destroyed him utterly rather than simply hurl him from the mountain.

Discarded waste, that's all I am!

'I am nothing,' he gasped. *I live only for magic, and now it's gone.*

Baelthrom had not killed him because removing his magic was a far worse death.

Oh clever, clever, clever, we could never out-best you.

Heavy boots marched on the ground not too far away. Maphraxie grunts – hundreds of them, fully armoured and carrying their black iron weapons – marched the winding road into the Mountains of Maphrax. Freydel was clearly visible in his prone position atop a jutting rock, but the Maphraxies weren't interested in him.

I am nothing.

If the light in his heart had gone out, did it matter whether he served the light or the darkness? He could return to Baelthrom and say, "Yes, I'll join you."

I would do it, only in the hope to be close to Ayeth. The realisation chilled him, and he swallowed against a dry throat. *I would join Baelthrom only in the futile belief I could reach Ayeth somewhere within him.*

He thought of Issa, of the Wizard's Circle, and of all the people fighting battles to win back their meagre lands. It was all so pointless. Nothing they did could stop them falling into the Dark Rift.

After all that he'd done, he knew he could not return to Issa. *She would think I'd abandoned her and joined Ayeth. Perhaps she would even believe I joined Baelthrom.* But would she be wrong? *No, I joined Ayeth willingly, heart and soul. The Raven Queen can only free those souls trapped here before the end. I thought it was more, but now I realise the truth. A noble quest, a noble goddess, but nothing can truly save Maioria.*

CHAPTER 29

Fall of Myrn

SEERS and Elven refugees flooded the boats under an electric night sky.

Lightning cracked against the failing shield covering Myrn, tongues of fire snaking all over it, trying to find entry. The shield flickered and fought in a battle it could not hope to win. All beneath it knew the might of Baelthrom was above them. For so long they had hidden but now his power was too great, and their end had come.

Naksu's boat couldn't get to the dock for all the boats piled with fleeing seers and elves. She was going in the opposite direction, she was going into Myrn. There hadn't even been a boatman waiting on the Western Isle to pick her up when she'd—rather miraculously—arrived through an electrical storm, the effects of which still crackled in her hair and made it stand up on end.

The boat jerked and crunched onto the pebbled shore some distance from the packed jetty. She jumped out as a wave of seers and elves ran towards the boat. The fear on their faces had been unseen on the tranquil Isles of Tirry, and a lump rose in her throat. Their fear was catching, quickening her pulse. She could give into it, under that terrible sky, under the terrible feel of the Under Flow surrounding them, ready to smother them, but she gripped her staff firmly and forced her feet forwards.

Scanning the people, not one of them was Iyena or the Trinity. *But they would never flee Myrn, not now, not in her final hour.* There were only two places they would be. She looked up at the sky, noting the cracking shield and the awful power beyond it. There were moments left, not hours, not even minutes. *I cannot reach Sheyengetha in time, so I shall try for the Star Portal, if it will let me find it.*

Naksu ran without looking up. She pelted along the quaint cobbled streets of Oray ignoring the dark grey of the houses which reflected the sky above, rather than their usual gleaming white. Her staff vibrated a warning. Red flared from above and was reflected in the fountain spurting in the centre; its stone dolphins still seemed joyous despite the destruction about to befall them. Naksu still did not look up.

Her legs ached, her breath came ragged and sweat trickled down her back. Onwards she ran, out of the village and up the path winding through the ancient forest of oak and chestnut. It was dark, almost like night, but the crystals along the path did not glow because it was not night and it should not be dark.

The shield shattered. Her soul cried out and an immense invisible force hurtled her forwards. Great winds gushed around her, and her staff flared white, protective, angry. The Under Flow heaved, and like a light being swallowed by darkness, the Flow fled.

A Dread Dragon screamed.

Naksu kept her eyes to the ground. Inch by inch she heaved herself onto her feet. There came another deafening scream and red fire blazed overhead. Hardly able to breathe, Naksu staggered up the hill. She could have looked back—always at this spot, beside the old chestnut and the sapling, she looked back, for Myrn was so beautiful with its white town of Oray, the rich green of the trees and the turquoise blue of the sea beyond. And that's how she always wanted to remember it.

Off the path and into the denser forest she plunged. Oddly, calm and silence descended, even now after the shield had shattered and the people beneath it left to their fate. Here, she could almost pretend there were no Dread Dragons in the sky…almost.

The ground trembled. A soft mist grew, reaching around her ankles. *Please let me find you,* Naksu pleaded, tears filling her eyes. *Not for my sake, but for yours and for all the others who need you.* The ground trembled, violently enough to make her stagger. The mist thickened defiantly. Ahead, a pale stone loomed out of the darkness, massive, stoic.

Naksu sobbed.

Beneath her feet the earth rumbled, then was still. The sky cleared, and stars twinkled. Through the rows of giant standing stones, she ran towards the sacred mound.

Before it she paused and thrust up her staff. The Flow filled it in halting, stuttering waves. Hand and staff high, she closed her eyes feeling the magical energy surround and fill her.

'Myrn is falling!' she cried. 'As in the past, so too now. Retreat into the mist, fall back beyond the veils, until a time will come when it is safe for you to emerge, should ever such a time come again.'

The Star Portal did not need to be told. Naksu felt she had only put into words what the portal itself was already doing. She was an assistant, nothing more.

The mist thickened. Everything became darker, as of night deepening. Silence became absolute as the world of mayhem and death moved further away.

With her mind, Naksu reached for Iyena and the Trinity. She could feel them out there, further beyond the veils and into the mists above and beyond Maioria. With her senses, she saw and felt them, standing as she was with staves and arms raised high, before a tree made of golden light. So bright it was she could barely look at it.

The staves of the Trinity flared, and everything was lost in white light. Naksu's staff responded. The power of the Trinity rushed towards her, knocking her from her feet. The Flow engulfed her, a raging sea which she had no hope of withstanding. Pulled out of body, her spirit rose with the Flow leaving her physical being somewhere far below.

Time passed. It could have been years, or mere moments as everything slowed and she floated in nothing but energy. She couldn't feel Myrn or her body, maybe they were simply too far away, but a certainty came upon her that the Trinity and Sheyengetha and the Sacred Mound still remained, that they were safe.

She smiled and let herself drift in the light. Was this the Ethereal Planes of which people spoke? It felt purer here, clean and safe. She wanted to stay here forever beyond the confines and ills of her physical body.

A voice called out for the light. It came from beneath her, where the darkness dwelled, capturing Naksu's attention. She didn't want to hear it, it marred the peace of this place. Again it came, pain-filled, terrified, and embodying utterly the world of suffering that existed far below.

Naksu knew that voice, and for all her wishes to remain here, she could not ignore it. She descended, following the pull of her attention, and the darkness engulfed her.

Pain, fear, darkness—and a voice crying out for the light within it. A voice she remembered.

Freydel,' she called. '*Freydel.*'

The light of a staff and an orb flared. The haggard face of an ageing wizard formed within it. He appeared to see her, his eyes widening with hope and desperation. Then both staff and orb shattered, and he was falling away from her. The Flow failed in his grasp as his physical body tumbled over red rocks and dirt. His robes ripped and tore until they were rags billowing around him. He rolled down and down the mountain until he stopped at the base, bruised, broken and bleeding. Life remained within him, but the Flow did not. In his hazel eyes Naksu saw something worse than death—the loss of power, a way of being that was one's entire life. If a wizard had no magic, he was a wizard no more.

Naksu's heart bled. She reached for Freydel, but instead felt herself rising away from him, unable to help. Ahead, the three peaks of Maphrax clawed for the Dark Rift above it and a terrible power flowed between them.

Her physical body pulled on her. The pull grew stronger and stronger and suddenly she was rushing through darkness and flickers of light. Solid earth formed beneath her, but the darkness and flickers of light remained. Howling wind lashed and tore at her. She pushed herself onto her knees, battling against the chaotic maelstrom trying to drag her in every direction.

A distorted voice wailed. 'Naksu, reach for us!'

'Iyena?' Naksu shouted. 'Where are you?'

She tried to gather her senses in the chaos. Uncontrollable magic flared and hissed. She spun around and around squinting against the flashing light, so bright in the black. There, far away, she glimpsed a still point of light. She ran towards it until she felt a dropping sensation, as if she had fallen off a ledge. The raging wind faded, and the flashing lights dimmed.

'Is she awake?' Dar's voice came from far away.

'Almost,' replied Iyena.

The women spoke, their voices coming closer—or was she moving towards them? Naksu blinked open her eyes. Thank the goddess the magical vortex had gone. All was still, silent, and doused in a strange pale mist.

Iyena's face came into view, her blue eyes clear and shining though deep creases lining her face.

'They came,' Naksu said, a sob catching in her throat.

'We know, my dear. Nothing could have stopped them.' There was calm resignation in Iyena's voice although her eyes sparkled. 'But you did it! You saved the Star Portal. You came just in time. The goddess truly is divine.'

Naksu frowned, not understanding. Iyena explained.

'We could not hold them both, so we chose to save Sheyengetha and Averen whose body and soul is within. It took all three of us to do it. We could not have moved the Star Portal as well, but we didn't need to in the end, because of you. Now both Sheyengetha and the Sacred Mound are safe, for a time.'

'It worked?' Naksu allowed herself to feel a small amount of joy. *But the rest is gone.* She didn't speak her thoughts out loud, but instead she said, 'Where are we now? I feel weak as a kitten.' Suli helped her to sit up and she squinted at the strange, pale grey mist.

'Beyond the world of Maioria, just. Within the veils between worlds, you could say, but we cannot remain here for long, our bodies can't take the higher frequencies of these places. Come, help me get her up.'

The three older women helped Naksu stand. She found she could take her own weight but only with support from Suli. 'Where can we go if Myrn is lost to us?'

Iyena held her staff before her. 'It's not over yet—not by a long shot. We must go now where we are needed most.'

CHAPTER 30

Prophetic Dreams

'WHAT is it?' Asaph asked from across the small campfire that lit up the cramped cave they huddled in.

Issa looked at him, noting his worried frown. Embarrassed, she wiped away the tears on her cheeks she had not felt fall.

'Oh, uh, nothing.'

But it wasn't nothing, there was a hole in her heart and she didn't know how to heal it. Her sister was gone. In the bitter few moments she'd had with her, she'd memorised every feature, every bruise and cut, every mannerism born of a frightened child inhabiting a young woman's pain-filled body.

She had gone from being an only child, to knowing she had a sister, to holding her bleeding, dying body in her arms in a matter of days. The soul just couldn't cope with that. How had she been ripped from her mother's womb by Lona? How had she made her grow so unnaturally fast? What despicable Yurgha technology had she used? Issa didn't want to fathom.

'I was thinking of my sister, she didn't even have a name. I promised Father I'd save her, and all I could do was hold her dying body in my arms.'

Asaph shuffled round and held her tight. She couldn't hold back the tears. He didn't say anything, there were no words to speak.

After a time, the tears stopped but the sorrow remained. She could turn it to anger, it would help her fight, but her sister was forever gone.

'We should try to sleep,' Asaph said softly, stroking her hair.

Issa nodded and lay down. He tucked her cloak over her then lay beside her, huddling close for warmth.

Issa watched the fire cast dancing shadows on the walls. They had landed northwest of Draxa, on a craggy mountain range just as the sun had begun to rise. Being so overcast, they did not actually see the sun, just a slow brightening of dawn. Tonight they would venture as close to the city as they dared and search for Marakon's fleet. She didn't think she would sleep but an emotionally exhausted slumber consumed her. In it she had four vivid, prophetic dreams.

The white raven swooped along the tree-hugged path.

Issa ran after it. 'Who are you? What do you want? Tell me!' She refused to be afraid of this bird, despite the horribly ominous feeling clenching her stomach.

The trees and pathway suddenly became familiar—the ancient oaks and chestnuts, the rich green grass, a lushness about the place that remained even in winter.

Myrn!

When she turned the corner, the sea would be visible and the white domed houses of Oray would be nestling in the cove below.

Cold fear swept through her as she crested the hill. The raven landed high on the tree and cawed. Red clouds rolled in to cover the sky, moving too fast to be natural. Strong winds blew, heavy with the sickly-sweet scent of death. Lightning torched the sky, thunder peeled and the Under Flow rolled around her.

She rounded the corner and looked down, stopping with a gasp that sunk her to her knees. Not one pretty, white-domed house remained—all were blackened rubble and ruin. Vast sections of ancient lush forest were flattened and smoking.

Deep scars ripped up the earth around Oray, and amongst everything, like patches of cleanliness in a defiled world, were the pale blue robes of fallen seers. The scarred earth threw her mind back to Little Kammy and she thought her heart would break.

In the distance, a Dread Dragon screamed. Another, closer, answered it.

Issa clutched her temples and clenched her eyes shut. The white raven cawed, again and again.

Red triangular eyes burst into life, bringing light to the darkness of her dream. A light she feared and hated.

'I'll join Ayeth, the being who you once were,' a strained, pain-filled voice rasped.

'Freydel?' Issa whispered, then drew back, not wanting to draw attention to herself.

She couldn't see him – there was nothing but darkness and those eyes smouldering to a dangerous, midnight blue.

Power flared, roaring and tearing through her, trying to rip her apart. She screamed as Freydel screamed. The world turned into raging energy, lightning searing through every fibre of her being, ravaging all that she was.

The raging pain lessened, the magic calmed.

She was falling, she hit the ground hard, her breath exploding from her lungs. Over and over she rolled, her physical body battering and breaking then rolling some more.

'Where is the light?' Freydel's soul called desperately. 'I am nothing!'

All became still. There was no magic, no voices, no eyes. She was alone.

The world lightened into grey mist. Ahead, a point of white flared, drawing her. The light was the halo of an ancient tree. *Sheyengetha, such beauty!* Its rich green canopy was draped in gentle mist, and four seers stood before it, too far away to see who. The mist thickened and turned to fog, engulfing all and she lost them from view.

Everything turned to billowing grey.

A hoof stamped, distant but closer than the tree had been. A snort and then a patch of smoke appeared, marring the endless grey. A dark form as big as a horse took shape.

Issa turned and fled.

Trees jostled around her. Not healthy trees with strong trunks and green leaves. These were withered and wilting, their drooping leaves mottled, their trunks flaccid and slumping. A strange gloom smothered the place and it was deathly silent.

A vague pathway wound ahead, and a black shape hung from a tree trunk. She walked forward in halting steps, and her stomach heaved. A young raven had been nailed to the tree and the rusty nail poked out of its chest.

'Who would do this?' Issa gasped. She turned away, hugging her chest.

Ahead, another dark shape hung from another wilting tree. Perforce, she had to go to it. It was another raven, an adult, dried blood on the nail sticking out of its chest. Dead and lifeless, eyes shut and its beak partially open. Issa lifted a trembling hand, then slowly let it back down. She couldn't bring herself to touch the bird, not even to pull the evil nail free.

'Who did this?' she shouted and looked up at the heavy sky. Her voice echoed eerily. When the echoes died away, a deeper silence descended. She swallowed and moved along the path, forcing her feet to walk faster.

Ahead were more dark shapes nailed to trees, ravens all of them, stiff and lifeless. Issa thought she might vomit.

A strangled caw came from ahead.

'Ehka?' she called, *or another raven in trouble?*

If she was quick, she might be able to save it. She launched into a run, trying not to see the dead ravens, and the living raven cawed again, louder. The trees clustered closer around the trail, bending over it as if to ensnare her in the trailing limbs. Dead ravens were nailed to every one of them. Her breath came in gasps and her legs were weak, but she forced herself onwards.

The white raven swooped across her path and cawed. With a yelp, she pulled up.

'I don't want to follow you,' she said, cold fear coiling around her.

A raven cawed from further away, its call familiar.

'Ehka!' Issa cried and ran.

She burst into a clearing. A screech escaped her throat as her eyes clamped upon the tall, grey-faced man. The loud, grating cawing of the white raven faded into the background and its frantic circling around her barely caught her attention.

All her senses focused upon the man before her, a man she longed to meet but on the tip of her sword, the one who had murdered Ely and destroyed Celene. Now he was here, all she could do was freeze, paralysed by fear. In one hand he gripped Ehka, the indigo sheen of his feathers unmistakable, in the other, he held a nail and hammer.

The bird struggled helplessly and screeched in pain as the man clenched his fist, crushing delicate feathers, then lifted the hammer.

Issa screamed and ran forwards, her hand reaching for her sword that wasn't there. Her fear forgotten she cared only for Ehka's life—but she was too far away. The man's hand descended in slow motion, yet too fast for her to stop it.

Agony exploded in her own chest. Issa screamed and fell onto a ground that melted beneath her, and she sank into a world of darkness and pain. Before the light faded, she glimpsed the white raven perched on a tree above the grey-haired man, head cocked as it watched her fall.

There was no slow growing of light, no pinprick in the blackness towards which she could move, there was just … nothingness, and then a blue light appeared. With the light came sound, a growing roar of pure light and energy that overwhelmed every sense, a noise so immense it was hard to define.

Raw energy, raw essence, filled her, over-powering and cleansing all that was darkness and corruption, all that should not be there—disharmony melted under the power of harmony.

Issa gulped and gawped at the light-sound. It was the essence of everything; nothing could be apart from it. She could do nothing in its presence but succumb and become one with it—so she did.

All the terror of the previous dreams vanished in the light-sound. The worries and concerns of just moments before were gone, petty compared to this purity. A knowing came upon her.

The blue moon is rising again, I must be ready.

A sense of self returned, and with it, a diminishing of power. She sighed in relief but also sadness at the lessening light which turned from indigo to pale blue and finally, to white.

She sensed space before her, enormous space. Before her, a circle formed, *not a circle, a planet!* An indigo blue planet orbiting the vastness of space. Beyond it turned another, larger yet pale peach in shade and beyond that, yet another planet turned. Between them shone a moon.

Memory, old and deep, resurfaced.

'The planets align, I have seen this. I remember,' she whispered to the light.

CHAPTER 31

The Keen Edge of Revenge

ASAPH stepped onto the snow and ice-covered ledge high up on the western-most mountain of the Grey Lords.

From his vantage point, he surveyed the range of mountains cutting across the tooth-shaped continent of Drax. A sky, heavy with snow clouds, crushed down upon all. Howling wind tugged on his hair and whipped his cloak around his body as thick snow flurries whirled before him and snowflakes stung his face where they kissed. It was bitterly cold, biting even through his wool-lined gloves.

The weather, the mountain, the snow…they all mirrored his dark, determined mood. He clenched a frozen fist and pressed it against his chin.

Far away to the West, between the flurries of snow, he glimpsed the ancient city. Tall, majestic towers rose up between the peaks, ringed by walls and roads that hugged the mountain sides. A formidable, impenetrable city that should not have fallen. He clenched his fist tighter.

'In all things, one must have a singular, powerful, driving objective,' Coronos' wise countenance echoed in his mind. If only his adopted father were beside him now, guiding him. His anger keened as he recalled Coronos speaking. *'So, if all else fails, you can remain focused on that singular driving force. When it's complete, you can walk away satisfied in your achievement. Reach for too many things, and you will surely fail. When clear intention, directed will, and pinpoint focus are enacted, all is made possible'*

Coronos' voice faded away leaving him with one clear objective.

'I will kill Vornus.' He spoke aloud, as if Coronos were right beside him.

'I may not take Drax, that's a mighty undertaking I dare to dream of, but I—one man—can surely end the life of another, a traitor, a murderer of thousands.' With all his heart, he imagined Coronos leaning on his staff beside him, chiding him gently for his keen and bloodthirsty revenge.

'Perhaps now you will agree with revenge, Father.'

He was so close now, he could barely contain himself. Even the Sword of Binding was impatient to be home, to taste the blood of the traitor.

Asaph lowered his arm and slowly relaxed his fist, allowing the blood to flow back into it. He let his fury go and turned his thoughts to planning—cold, calculated planning. Usually filled with fire and passion and the violence of the moment, Asaph forced himself to be like Coronos. Coronos would plan and refine, then plan some more.

Issa had already scryed for Marakon; his fleet was two days away from the shores of Draxa. All they had to do was remain undetected by Dread Dragon scouts for as long as possible. For all the horror of Issa's nightmare about Myrn, if it *was* true it meant Baelthrom's focus was not on Draxa—something in their favour, bitter as it was.

When the sky darkened and the snow fell heavier, Asaph realised just how long he had been standing here, facing west to where his heritage lay. Issa would be worried. He should return to her in the frozen gulley at the mountain's base.

He stepped back from the ledge and resumed his dragon form, feeling the frigid cold bite even through his thick flesh. He would not wait for Marakon to set foot on the shores of Drax—he *could* not. The pull of home was immense and one he could not withstand. He would return to the castle—*his* castle—the same way he had left it over a quarter of a century ago, through the winding secret tunnels. He would infiltrate and break it from within, just as Vornus had broken them from within.

Kill Vornus, take Draxa. And if he could not take his city back, he would destroy it utterly until nothing of it, or himself, or his enemy, remained. Just as Faelsun had done when he called the Eternal Wind and Fire, destroying himself and all things around him.

But Issa would insist on coming with him—and if it came to the end... He couldn't bear to think about her, his mind was resolute. Suppressing a roar, Asaph spread his wings wide and leapt off the mountain.

'I am going to Draxa now.'

Issa looked up at Asaph from the other side of the campfire. The seriousness in his eyes, the clenched fist at his side, the determined set of his jaw—this was a man not a boy standing before her; one set upon a deadly mission. She could say nothing to dissuade him, and she should not dare.

Fear feathered the hairs on the back of her neck. She was afraid of him in that moment and saw the power he could wield, *the power of a Dragon Lord King!* He was asking her to be brave, to be a warrior. Although he did not say she should stand at his side, he *knew* she would. It was either going to be victory or suicide, and nothing bridged the abyss between them.

'I'll not leave your side, and I will not die alone,' was all she said, her own jaw clenching in determination.

His stance relaxed a little and a shadow of worry passed across his face. He gave the slightest nod of his head.

He needed some assurance to not worry about her. She said, 'Besides, you need me with you. Should Cirosa be there…' She let it trail off, not wanting to spread fear or doubt. *Should Cirosa be there and have a hold on you, I'll…* She bit her lip, needing revenge.

But did he really mean to go this night? She opened her mouth to speak then shut it. It was obvious—of course they would leave now, this very moment as dusk fell and the air chilled to a deeper bitterness.

She let out a silent sigh. 'I'm ready.' She lifted herself from her crouch before the fire and left its welcome warmth.

Asaph took her hand, his eyes saying everything—that he wished she would stay and yet he did not want to be without her. With her other hand she laid a finger on his lips. He took that too in his hand and kissed her fully.

Ehka got to his feet from his cosy nest by the fire. Ruffling his feathers, he reluctantly looked up into the darkening sky.

'He's right,' said Issa as she helped Asaph throw snow on the fire. It sizzled and fought against the onslaught, then with a whining hiss, succumbed and went out.

'Right about what?' asked Asaph. 'I didn't hear anything.'

'He says we should go ahead first and scout out the area. In fact, I shall insist upon it as a condition.'

Asaph grinned at her, 'I knew you'd find something to insist upon.'

'I don't know what you mean,' Issa huffed, feeling her cheeks warm. 'I just like to have a say in stuff, that's all.'

'All right, but half an hour and no more. It will give me time to think,' said Asaph, stamping his feet to keep warm. 'But any longer, and I shall come breathing fire. I'll meet you on the beach where we discussed. We must move quickly; our presence may already have been detected.' He scanned the evergreen forest as if half-expecting a Life Seeker to burst out from the gloom.

'Half an hour,' agreed Issa. 'But what do we do about that?' She pointed to the dragon harness slowly covering with snow.

Asaph shrugged. 'We'll have to leave it here, I daren't leave it any nearer to Draxa. Anyway, there are no paths here, and look, we're surrounded by mountain and forest. No one will find it.'

Issa nodded, hoping they would live long enough to retrieve it. She looked up at the sky, taking a deep breath she touched her raven mark, felt the rush of the change come upon her and instinctively beat her wings. Ehka followed her into the air. She watched Asaph looking up at her until he was lost in the darkness below. Through falling snow, she cloaked their presence and headed west where the sky was a little lighter.

The enormous city of Draxa emerged through a snow cloud complete with three Dromoorai circling the towers.

Issa slowed, strengthening her cloaking magic and trying to ignore the fear chilling her blood further. Maphraxies marched the turrets and courtyards, and lined the inner and outer walls. There were hundreds of them, their black armour stark against the grey stone and white snow.

I'll bet the bastards are impervious to the cold, too, she thought.

She watched a unit march through the great iron gates, flanked by bigger, higher-ranked Maphraxies with swords and followed by a Dromoorai passing low above them. The sound of their boots thudded loudly on the ancient cobbles. The number of enemies dismayed her. Was this to be a hopeless, suicidal battle? It would certainly be the hardest.

Diredrull had not been easy but they'd had an enormous army.

For all the years that had passed, the castle remained mostly unchanged. She could see where sections of walls and towers had been rebuilt so they were not all uniform, although one still had no peak but had, instead, a ragged wall around it.

Though the castle's original structure was largely the same, she could not say that about the town. In the place where houses, taverns, and market stalls had once stood, were now erected the ugly, squat, square buildings of Maphraxie barracks. *And beneath them, a warren of crawling Dark Dwarf tunnels,* she thought. It was just as Diredrull had been.

She circled high, keeping her distance. Ehka circled even farther away. *And where are the houses beyond the city walls? Where are the farmsteads, the breweries, the grain houses, the sheep flocks and horse paddocks? Where are the fields of corn, oats and wheat? There is nothing, it's all been destroyed. This disgusting, cancerous army creates and rebuilds nothing, and they're not even alive!*

A particularly cold wind gusted, piercing through her feathers, making her shiver. She headed to the north-western edge of the city where the walls stacked high upon rock, creating an unforgiving drop of a thousand feet or more to the sea below.

Between the towering cliffs, she spied tiny shingled coves where Asaph would meet her and where Marakon would hopefully dock. She descended cautiously, scouting the place for enemies. She dared to land and release her raven form but kept her shield up.

It was the flame ring growing warm on her finger that alerted her to Asaph's presence, but she could not otherwise detect the arrival of the huge dragon and all she saw in the Flow was the faintest wobble in the energies.

'There are many enemies, it almost seems hopeless,' she said silently in the Daluni animal speak before he could change form and lose the ability to commune silently.

'It was always going to be this way,' the dragon's deep voice rumbled in her mind. *'If you look carefully along the cliff, you'll see the steps up. I'll go first but I won't be able to speak or use magic. Can you shield us both?'*

'I can, but it will make us easier to detect.'

'So be it. Through memory, and the Recollection if I must, I can guide us once we're inside.'

'What do we do then?'

'Kill Vornus,' said Asaph, a deadly tone to his voice.

'What if he isn't in there?'

'He is, I can smell him. After, we continue the killing through stealth and magic. Inside, it's vast, even bigger now the dark dwarves are here. I know hidden rooms that may still exist where we can hide and rest. If we get caught we'll hold out until Marakon comes. We must secure an entrance for him. He will not be able to open the door from the outside, only I or my kin can enter…until I break the code. For now we'll secure and protect the beach with magic and light a guiding beacon that only a human wizard can see.'

Issa did not feel good about any of this. She bent down to Ehka. *'Where we go you cannot easily follow. Find the seers; tell them what we're doing. Find Freydel, wherever he is. I saw him… he's out there somewhere. But we need them now more than ever, all of them.'*

Ehka nodded but did not immediately leave. He was scared, too.

Silently, she helped Asaph protect the beach with magic wards and beacons, praying every moment that no necromancer was near enough to feel their magic. When they were done, the beach shimmered in the Flow, visible to any wizard searching the fields of magic. Hopefully it was invisible to anybody who used the Under Flow. It was a risk Asaph was prepared to take. She had never seen him so cold, so driven. It frightened her.

When he released his dragon form she quickly shielded him with magic. It was a slow but manageable drain on her reserves. If they could find safe places to rest, she would hopefully cope. She followed Asaph up the steps, palm sweaty in her glove as she gripped Illendri. Already she wished she were far away from this place.

The steps ended at a blank piece of rock. If she stared hard she could just make out the fine outline of a door. She looked up the sheer drop of the cliff to the turrets thousands of feet above. It was a long way to go in tunnels of darkness filled with Maphraxies and all the horrors of their most hated and feared enemy. Perhaps this was foolish. There had to be another way!

'Look, we don't have to do it this way. It feels…reckless,' she said, then felt cowardly.

Asaph whispered back. 'I know how you feel but I've thought this through and through. Vornus is a coward, he'll flee at the first sign of battle, just like he's done before. I can't let him go again.'

'But we'll end up getting killed, too,' she blurted. She'd promised to stand by him, and she would, but… The look on Asaph's face told her he was not turning back.

She sighed. 'All right…'

'Ready?' Asaph asked.

Swallowing, she nodded.

Excitement, fear, adrenaline, fury—all these washed through Asaph as he placed his hands upon the stone door.

For all that he could not feel or use magic in his human form, he felt the enchantments on the stone door respond to him, as if welcoming him home. The door ground inwards, making him wince at the noise, then slid to the left.

Wind howled past them into the pitch-black entrance. He grabbed Issa's hand and pulled her inside.

'What about the sudden wind?' she whispered. 'It will alert anyone.'

Asaph shrugged. 'We can't help that. Can you break the door? Otherwise it will seal shut behind us.'

'I can try.' Issa placed her hand on Illendri and her other on the stone. A loud crack sounded as the door broke into two.

She grinned. 'The enchantment I couldn't break but the door can no longer close.'

Asaph nodded. 'It will do.'

He peered into the darkness. Slowly his keen dragon sight adjusted, and he could make out the faint steps leading up between damp, narrow stone walls. He closed his eyes, remembering hurtling down these steps in Coronos' arms. Had he known then as a babe that he would return this very same way? *How funny destiny is.*

The steps went up forever, and it was slow going as each footfall was carefully, silently placed. He recalled all his stealth training with the Kuapoh, now called the Navadin—they would be here with him soon.

A scratching noise came from ahead, then a loud sniffing noise followed by a growl. Asaph paused and motioned for Issa to stop.

'Death hound,' she mouthed silently, her face paling.

Asaph nodded and wondered how many. With his fingernails he scratched the wall lightly. More sniffing noises came and another low growl, then the sound of claws on stone padding closer. It caught scent of them and barked, picking up the pace.

Asaph lifted his sword. A black shape leapt in the darkness, its yelp cut off as Asaph's sword severed the beast in two. Another shape followed but was unable to dodge his sideswipe. With a whimper it rolled, and Asaph severed its throat.

They waited in the darkness, listening for more as the patter of black blood dripped off his sword and the gagging smell of the undead assailed their noses.

Silence.

They tiptoed up the steps until they came to a wooden door the hounds had been guarding.

'They're clearly not expecting us,' Asaph snickered.

Issa let out a held breath.

He pushed on the door. It didn't budge. He slammed his shoulder against it, breaking the simple hinge and lock and falling inside. Another rock hewn tunnel led ahead, and a faint glow of light came from somewhere around the corner. There would be some shallow rooms, mainly for storing ropes, oars, and all sorts of boating equipment, then more stairs and rooms. He *remembered* this place clearly, the memories so detailed they almost overlaid his sight.

'What is it?' Issa asked, peering ahead.

'It's nothing… I just remember here.' He swallowed. And what if he found it? What if he found her chamber? Would the memory come upon him again? Would he be forced to relieve her final moments? A torturous rape of the worst kind—mind, body and soul? Maybe he was not ready to find it.

'Find what?' Issa asked.

He looked at her, wondering how much he'd spoken aloud. 'My mother's chamber…I don't know if I want to find it.'

Voices came.

They dropped back into the previous tunnel.

The voices came closer and the light moved as someone walked in front of it.

'…the dogs sensed something, I felt them,' said a high-pitched, almost hissing voice.

Ignoring Issa pulling on his arm, Asaph leant forwards and peaked around the corner. The alabaster face of a necromancer swathed in black robes flashed into view. He fell back and turned to Issa.

Necromancer, he mouthed. Issa held her breath. Slowly, he dared to peer again as another voice spoke, deeper and gruffer.

'They're barking at ghosts again. They'd better have done their job and seen them off. Master Hameka will not waste any more guards on this exit, or "the arsehole of this place" as he calls it. I told you never to leave it.'

Beside the necromancer walked a squat, heavily armoured dwarf, his mace swinging at his side.

Asaph thought fast. Make quick work of the necromancer before it cast any spells. Issa could distract the dwarf long enough. She wouldn't use the Flow, it would alert everything to their presence.

'The ghosts here have solid substance and a malice unlike any other,' hissed the necromancer. 'The dogs are no match for them.'

Gripping his sword, Asaph held his breath and got ready to spring. The dwarf came around the corner first, his yellow eyes seeing clearly in the darkness as he lifted his mace. Asaph grabbed hold of the nearest thing, which happened to be the dwarf's beard, yanked and used it to leap over his head. He smashed the pommel of his sword into the face of the necromancer. It had barely raised its hands to cast its spell when its face crumpled into the pommel, watery blood spurted, and it fell, smoke billowing up around it. Before it even hit the floor, the necromancer was gone, its robes just an empty smoking pile on the stone.

He spun around to see Issa grimacing, sword embedded in the dwarf's exposed neck, and her boot on its shoulder as she wrenched it free. The dwarf fell, and Asaph caught him to stop him clattering on the floor. Quickly, he dragged the body down the steps into the darkness. They waited again, panting, listening for any noise.

So, this was how it was going to be, inching through the darkness, taking out the enemy one by one. If it took him a year to clear the place in this manner, he would do it.

Issa wiped the sweat from her brow, hot despite the frigid cold of the tunnel, and tried to relax her taut shoulders.

She didn't like hiding and stealth fighting at all, especially not underground and in enclosed spaces. She preferred her battles outside, even against an entire army. She became aware of an unusual, unnatural presence, and small hands pressing into her calf.

'Maggot?' she whispered.

Only his eyes glowed in the darkness and then his ugly face and protruding tooth materialised.

'You can't be here,' she said. 'It's dangerous.'

'That's why I came. Does Issy need Shadow Demon warriors? King has them ready for you.'

'Not yet, Maggot, but soon,' said Issa.

A strange emotion stole over her. The demons had betrayed her parents, her trust had been undermined and there were questions that needed answering. Would they betray her too in the end? *Never trust a demon*…And yet when she looked at the evil, innocent face of Maggot—a demon who had always been loyal, always her friend—how could she doubt them? *I guess I have to take them one at time, judge each on their own actions.* It didn't make life easy, but she would have to trust them for now.

'Can we trust him?' Asaph asked, echoing her thoughts as he peered down at the little demon. Maggot shrank from his gaze.

'He won't hurt you, Maggot.' Suddenly she had an idea and crouched down to bring her face closer to his. 'How do you feel about doing something courageous? It will be dangerous but…rewarding. There'll be maggots, hundreds.'

Maggot laid back his ears, clearly not keen on doing anything brave. Issa continued anyway.

'We're looking for a man, a changed man. He won't smell like us, though he'll look similar. You remember the black drink I told you about? You know the smell of Maphraxies? Well, he'll smell like them but look similar to us. Asaph, you tell him.'

'You think this is a good idea?' asked Asaph, and she nodded. He rolled back his shoulders and looked at the demon. 'I guess it's worth a try. His name is Vornus. He's tall like me, but slender and older. He has dark hair smoothed back.'

When Asaph had finished, Issa said, 'Come back to us when you find him. You don't need to do anything else.'

Maggot nodded reluctantly then faded, slithering into the shadows ahead.

'He'll be all right,' said Asaph, gripping her shoulder reassuringly. 'If anything happens he can disappear straight back to the Murk, unlike us.'

She gave a half smile. Letting out a breath, she followed after Asaph, inching slowly forwards through the tunnel towards the light ahead.

CHAPTER 32

Fighting Traitors

A single brazier lit up the hallway.

At the end, steps led up to the dark entrance of another corridor. Issa kept an eye on the Flow, continually looking for signs of danger. Cautiously, she followed Asaph as he sidled into the darker hallway. They paused as the sound of voices carried towards them, but they were distant and soon faded away.

Asaph rubbed his chin for a long moment before speaking. 'Up eventually leads to the main hall; we can't go that way. If I remember rightly, there should be a room with a trapdoor that leads down. We'll have to go down to use a quieter route. Come on, this way.'

They slowly made their way through almost pitch-black walkways, their hands trailing on walls or holding each other's. Issa tripped over some fallen masonry, barely stifling a yelp. Asaph helped her up.

'Just bruised,' Issa whispered, rubbing her leg.

As Asaph seemed to be able to see even in the darkest places, she let him lead her. Looking into the Flow helped a little, but she couldn't see details in the fields of magical energy.

A strange distant boom came, followed by another. Magic or weapons or something evil they could only guess at. On they went, ears pricked; often she wondered how long they had been down here, and how far away Marakon was. Mostly she wished she was out in the open air, even the frigid night would be better than down here.

Asaph paused suddenly, breaking her thoughts and making her hand drop to her sword. He visibly shivered.

'What is it?' Issa asked, alarmed.

'Can't you hear it? That awful *sound*.' He rubbed his eyes.

She strained to hear and caught a low, continuous hum. *Not a hum —
chanting,* she realised. The more she focused on it, the more her skin crawled.

'What is it?' she whispered.

Asaph took a deep breath. 'You remember the red robes? The New
Order priesthood? It's them, I'd recognise that noise anywhere.'

Issa shivered too, recalling Asaph's awful experience in the sacrificial
chambers beneath the Temple of Carvon. Was Cirosa here too? She chewed
her lip. 'Where's it coming from?

'Asaph!' she hissed when he moved off at a faster pace. He wasn't
seriously going to take them on, was he? But she already knew the answer.
Dear Zanufey, protect us! She touched the raven mark on her chest and hurried
after him.

He didn't seem to care if there was anyone up ahead, and even
quickened the pace. The eerie dull chanting grew louder and a distant light
appeared.

Asaph took a turn and came to a huge, sealed wooden door with thick
metal bars and a grate covering a tiny window. The chanting came from
beyond it.

'The dungeon,' Asaph mouthed.

'Luckily we're on this side,' whispered Issa, noting the heavy beam
across it locking it shut.

'They would have come in from the other side—this is always sealed
shut. I don't think it will budge without a lot of noise.' Asaph analysed the
beam then pressed his ear against the door.

'I don't think they're directly on the other side but further beyond. The
Recollection is dark here and I can't quite recall the layout ahead.' He
grabbed the beam ready to wrench it, then paused and looked at her.
'There's still a chance to get out. If you leave now and go back the way we
came, you might be safer on the beach. Once we go through here, there is
no going back. There'll be fighting and…noise. I can't be sure what the
sword will do either. We'll be heard for certain and hunted from then on. I
can keep us safe, for a time.'

Issa thought about turning around and going back alone through all those dark corridors. She couldn't do it. 'I promised to stay by your side, even in death.'

He nodded, a strange look in his eyes. 'You're the only person to ever say that to me.'

He turned back to the door, his muscles bunched, and he *heaved*. The beam groaned loudly, lifted an inch, then stuck. Asaph heaved again, and with one short, loud squeak the beam lifted free. He slammed the door with his shoulder and it grunted open, spilling faint light into the tunnel. The ritual chanting became louder, hopefully drowning out the noise they made. They slunk inside, Asaph set the beam down in a dark corner and quietly shut the door.

They crouched in the darkest corner of a cell with chest-high walls topped with bars welded to the ceiling. Adjoining it were more cells, in front of which was a walkway, then another row of cells. At the far end, a brazier illuminated a wider walkway. The stench of urine hung in the air.

The chanting stopped abruptly, and a horrifying screech cut through the air. Issa gasped and clamped her hands over her ears, Asaph reached an arm around her, hugging her close. When the screaming stopped she found herself shaking.

'Human sacrifice?' she whispered, not wanting to ask.

Asaph nodded, his face grim. 'We'll stop this tonight and forever.'

Two red-robed people stalked around the corner, their faces hidden in their hoods, their robes billowing. Issa and Asaph hunkered down, and she held her breath, wondering if the person just murdered had been inhabiting their cell.

Whimpering came from several other cells as the priests hunted their prey. Large iron keys clanged as they unlocked a cell on the opposite row, followed by terrified echoing screaming as they dragged someone out. Either they couldn't stand, or they were too small because Issa couldn't see them from her huddled position. She didn't want to see them.

'We have to go now!' she hissed when the priests had gone.

'No, it's too late, we have to plan it,' said Asaph. 'I've seen this, there could be hundreds of red robes. This isn't the only cell block, either—when they come again, we'll take them out and free the others.'

'But whoever they have now will be dead!' Issa felt panic rising as the hideous chanting began. The Under Flow moved thickly in that terrible chamber ahead. She couldn't bear to listen to another person being sacrificed.

Asaph silently took her hand and ran to the cell that had just been emptied. He drew his sword. Issa covered her ears as the chanting crescendoed. The Flow was so weak she doubted she could command it, whilst the Under Flow flowed like a black river beneath her. She stuffed her ears to cut out as much of the sound as possible.

When the screaming fell to gurgling, she drew her sword, cold fury building, and the fear gone from her heart.

Footsteps came, keys jangled, red robes swayed. Asaph lunged.

The first couldn't scream for the steel in his throat. Issa booted the other in the stomach, stopping her from yelling. The priestess fell, winded. Issa turned away as Asaph's sword descended, completing the job.

Slowly, she turned back to look, a terrible feeling settling in her stomach. The woman's face was tanned, her hair dark. *Could* she have killed her? She killed Maphraxies with relish but this was a human—well, she *looked* human. Apart from her black heart, she had been human once, a priestess like those she'd met in Celene.

Issa was shaken. Here was a side to the war she was not ready for; killing humans, even if they were traitors. *Could I kill Cirosa? She's not human now anyway.* The thought and feelings made her doubt herself. She'd *have* to kill Cirosa if the time came—to hesitate would cost her own life, or worse, Asaph's.

'Issa!' hissed Asaph, snapping her out of it. He was dragging the priest and priestess into the cell. He grabbed the iron keys from the priest's flaccid hand and began taking off the man's robes.

'Quickly, put on their robes. We've a very slim chance of pulling this off,' whispered Asaph.

Issa jumped into action and struggled to pull off the priestesses' robes. Her limp body was heavy and bleeding and the thought of donning them made her feel ill.

Asaph looked awkward in the robe, dishevelled and bulky in areas that barely concealed his armour and sword.

Issa adjusted hers as he padded to the nearest cell and unlocked it. The door swung open and Issa glimpsed two small, fair-haired children huddling together, faces smeared in dirt, eyes wide with terror. They sacrificed children? She shivered with anger. At this moment she *could* easily kill all the priests in the next room.

'We're waiting, brother,' a man's voice called impatiently from beyond.

Asaph quickly unlocked the final cell. Issa couldn't see the inhabitants clearly but there were children, and men and woman of all ages, dirty and ragged like beggars. They shivered and cowered and not one of them left their cells. None were able to fight. Issa pursed her lips.

Asaph cleared his throat and spoke loudly. 'This one's proving bothersome, brother.' He feigned a strained voice. 'Perhaps a little help?'

An exasperated sigh came, then the sound of footsteps. Issa brandished her sword, willing Illendri to calm its glow. It often responded to her excitement, but she could ill afford to use magic here. She was not a master swordsman, and without magic she felt like she was fighting with one hand tied behind her back. However, lately, the magic sometimes came instinctively, as second nature, and there was nothing she could do about that. *Thank the goddess the Flow is weak in here,* she thought. Given the fury in her heart for what they were doing to innocent people, the magic might take a will of its own.

She caught Asaph's glance, saw the fire in his eyes, and readied herself. She crouched down behind the wall as the priest appeared, trailed by another. They passed her cell and went straight to Asaph. As soon as the last priest had passed, she leapt out silently and stabbed her sword forward. It passed through his unarmored body with sickening ease and he made an awful murmuring sound before staggering and toppling. It all happened so fast and so silently, the first priest didn't notice. He turned around as his colleague thumped on the floor, then Asaph was upon him.

The priest made a strangled 'Yargh!' then slumped.

'Usep?' called another priest from beyond, followed by the sound of many feet.

'Do what you must!' Asaph said, not bothering to whisper.

Issa nodded and entered the Flow. It was weak and slow but Illendri was ready and her talisman began to glow.

Five priests and priestesses appeared, their eyes widening as they looked upon their fallen colleagues. Asaph ran at them all, growling. One moved close to Issa, and rather than use magic it seemed quicker to use her sword. She was certain Illendri made her aim faster and more accurate. The blade seemed to sing as it swished through the air, slicing through exposed flesh in a manner that made her feel like she was going to be sick.

The priest fell whilst Asaph was already on his second. Two priestesses turned to run.

'Stop them!' Asaph barked.

Issa leapt over the bodies but was too far behind to catch them. She held up her hands, Illendri knew what to do and the raven talisman flared. Bricks from the ceiling and walls exploded around the women, knocking one out cold and tripping the other. Asaph was fast upon them and made sure they did not stand again.

Issa gasped, her knees shaking as the dust settled. 'Is that all of them?'

'I doubt it, but I didn't see any flee the room. Perhaps we're safe, for a time.' Asaph wiped the blood from his sword on the robes of a fallen priestess.

Issa leant against the wall, trying not to vomit.

'Are you all right?' he asked.

Issa barely nodded. 'I've not killed people before.'

'They're *not* human,' Asaph growled.

Issa's looked beyond him to the blood-soaked altar and her breath caught in her throat. There was blood everywhere, still dripping from the sickening spouts and dropped cups. In the Flow it was worse. Magic roared around her, the Flow coming from her and the Under Flow coming from a black tear in the air, an exact replica of the dark rift, a black scar hanging in the energies above the altar and not visible to normal sight.

'Where are the bodies?' she heard herself ask in a voice far away. 'Have they really been taken by *them*?'

She didn't hear Asaph's answer for a deep groaning came from the black hole. *Light Eaters.*

'There's a black hole, can't you see it? We must close it.' She forced herself towards the rift. *How did one close it?*

She was almost under it now, and the strange groaning was growing louder. If she listened hard, she could hear the dark words spoken—like dark dwarven runes, or necromantic chants, only more distorted. She peered up into absolute blackness, the Under Flow swirled within, hunting for a way to enter the chamber as it had before, but now something prevented it.

I'm preventing it, she realised, *but how?* The raven talisman in her hand burned, the groaning and grating paused. Had it sensed her? It started anew, in earnest. The hairs rose on the back of her neck and her heart began to pound. Something was *watching* her!

What could she do? She raised Illendri and the talisman. Without any will of her own, the Flow moved forcefully through her. White light flared into the tear and something inhuman screamed. Air rushed upwards, the tear shuddered then vanished, along with the Under Flow.

Issa swayed, and Asaph grabbed her shoulders.

'I don't know what happened, but my sword has only just stopped shaking,' he said. 'Others will have heard or felt that, so we have to get moving.'

'What about the people?' Issa asked, hearing muffled sobbing.

Asaph's face pained. 'I don't know how to help them. Perhaps it's better they stay here until the castle is liberated, or...' he didn't speak the alternative.

Issa hurried back to the cells. She looked at the dirty faces of men, women and children. 'You're free, all of you, but this city is not. There's an army coming, the army of the Free Peoples will liberate you. Until then, the safest place for you is here. Try and stay alive for as long as you can—there *is* hope and freedom.'

Asaph dragged her away to the growing sound of metal boots pounding on hard stone.

They ran through a door into a brightly lit corridor, then through another door. They hurtled along the hall, those boots getting louder and louder. Asaph swung through another door and shut it. Moments later, the grunts of Maphraxies accompanied the boots. He leant against the door and peered through a crack in the old, warped wood.

They were in a dark room. Issa could only see for the sliver of light coming under the door and through the cracks. It felt enclosed, as if they were in a small space. She held her breath as boots pounded past towards the dungeon they had run from.

'Maphraxies,' Asaph mouthed to her, his face only half visible under the hood of his robe. It sounded like *hundreds* of them!

The pounding boots faded away but it wouldn't be long before they found the dead priests.

'Come on,' said Asaph, pulling his hood up and smoothing his robes.

'Come on, where?' asked Issa, a cold feeling coming over her.

'Now's our chance. You look the part.'

Before she could protest, he opened the door and stepped outside dragging her with him. Her heart pounding, she copied his stance, head bowed slightly to hide face and eyes, and hands tucked before him in the long sleeves of his robes. Despite the odd bit of bulking and the strange swing of his sword, he could pass as any other priest.

Maphraxies appeared ahead. They were enormous and seemed uglier and more deformed. Her heart pounded in her ears as they walked *towards* where they had just run from. Surely they should be *running* the other way? What on earth was Asaph doing?

The first two Maphraxies approached at a loping run. The stench of them, blood and the sweet smell of Sirin Derenax made her gag.

'Not that way. They dead,' said one, barely able to form the words. 'Go other way.'

Asaph mumbled in surprise and nodded as the beasts lumbered awkwardly past, followed by five more. Not one suspected them. *Thank the goddess they came out stupid,* Issa prayed.

Asaph turned and followed them. 'That's not all of them,' he said under his breath without looking at her or changing his pose. 'The others are back there hunting for us. Word will spread, our survival lies in these awful clothes. Soon the entire castle will be hunting for us. The Maphraxies are too stupid to tell, but I would not want to meet many necromancers, and certainly not Cirosa or Hameka.'

Issa shivered at the names.

They passed the room where they had hidden. It was filled with brooms and buckets and other random things usually kept in a store cupboard. She was sorely tempted to crawl back in and never come out.

With as much composure and calm as she could muster, she let Asaph lead her up the steps and into the wider walkways of the bowels of the castle. Her legs never could shake off that weak feeling though and it felt like seconds passed as hours.

Mostly they met Maphraxies who did nothing but pass them by. She kept her head low; it helped not to look at the enemy. They entered into an enormous hallway several yards wide and so long she couldn't see the end.

A high, arched ceiling reached over them and at points along the walls, sconces burned. An old, gold-trimmed, red carpet ran the entire length and was in dire need of repair. There were more holes than fabric and it had long lost its lustre, now looking more brown than red.

Issa's heart fluttered as she watched the hallway teeming with Maphraxies, dark dwarves, and the tall forms of necromancers. She kept her gaze low as Asaph walked forwards but when she glimpsed the red robes of a priest and priestess coming towards them, her blood ran cold. Before they neared, Asaph steered her into an arched exit with stairs leading up.

'Should you not be channelling the dark energy at this hour?' called out the priest. Asaph paused and peered over his shoulder, carefully keeping most of his face concealed.

'Indeed, brother, but we've had a…spillage.' He motioned to the blood-stains on his robes from the original wearer. Issa turned to reveal her own bloody patch.

'Ah,' smiled the priest, knowingly. 'A fighter. Well, it always ends messily when they are, but the blood is so much sweeter.'

A lustful, savage grin distorted the pretty priestess's face at his side. Issa clenched the pommel of her sword.

'Yes, it does, brother.' Asaph's voice was low and strained. 'We'll swiftly change and return to our duties.'

Without waiting for a response he turned and hurried up the stairs. The stairwell wound around and up for a long way, clearly missing a floor or two, before it exited out into another, much smaller hallway which was blessedly empty. Remaining in the doorway, they both leant back against the wall, breathing hard. Issa willed her nerves to calm.

'I almost lost it,' said Asaph, eyes closed, a sheen of sweat on his face. 'I almost pulled my sword on them.'

Issa squeezed his arm. 'We've made it this far. Now where?'

Asaph surveyed the hall, left and right, taking his time. 'It depends on where Vornus might be. I can't believe this place should have been my home. It's so uncanny, sometimes when the Recollection is clear, I feel like I know every part of this place.'

Cold hands press on Issa's shin and she looked down into Maggot's glowing eyes that were almost orange.

'I've found him, Issy, there are two other humans with him. They don't smell like you, they smell better.'

'Where, Maggot? Where are they?' Issa bent down to his height.

'High up, in the middle of this place. There are tall windows.'

'What about the thin, pale necromancers? Like humans but not?' Issa asked.

Maggot nodded. 'Some. They sensed me. I had to leave.'

'Thank you, Maggot. Now keep yourself safe whilst we try to get there.' Issa stood and looked at Asaph, hoping he had a plan. It was clear Vornus was not alone, even if they could get to him.

'I know where he is,' said Asaph. The determination on his face made her sigh. He wasn't going to turn around and go back, he wasn't going to give up at all. She just hoped he wasn't going to try to take them all on at once.

'I'm worried, Cirosa is there,' Issa admitted. 'She knows your weaknesses and she can take you down. I'll not let her, I'll use the full force of the Flow if I must, but you must be ready.'

Asaph smiled at her ruefully, a strange mix of guilt and determination on his face. 'In the end, we must do whatever we can to stay alive.'

Issa nodded. 'So be it.'

Calmly, he walked into the empty hallway and turned left. He went up more stairs and along more corridors. Issa was shocked to see daylight spilling through the tall, stained glass windows. Had so much time passed? It had stopped snowing, but the sky was filled with light-grey clouds.

The carpet up here may have been more ornate, but it was still worn and frayed. Wind howled through broken windows, the long walls were empty of tapestries or paintings and there was no furniture or furnishings of any nature.

'Once this place was warm and adorned with beauty,' Asaph said under his breath, sharing her thoughts.

He took the first doorway on the left and went up a narrow staircase to a smooth oak door embellished with iron scroll work. He turned the handle and pushed. It opened into a large, unfurnished room, where four carved pillars held up a high ceiling and light spilled in from a handful of arched windows with stained glass like the others.

He led her through another hallway and upstairs again to more rooms until Issa was completely lost. If she had to leave this place in a hurry, she'd be better off jumping out of a window and taking flight as a raven.

That thought made her think of Ehka. Where was he? Had he found Marakon? The bird had a knack of finding that man, so she didn't need to worry. Now she thought of it, their army might well arrive *before* they ever found Vornus and Asaph's plan would be ruined.

While he paused for thought in the medium-sized room with a hearth that had not been lit in decades, she walked to the next door.

'No, not that way,' said Asaph, taking her hand and frowning in thought. 'It's somewhere close, I can't quite reach the memory.'

Voices came beyond the door Issa was about to open. Asaph dragged her to the only place they could hide – the fireplace. She ducked under the mantlepiece with him.

'We can't hide here, they can see our legs!' she whispered.

He didn't reply and instead fumbled along the soot-covered wall. His hand found a chain, it clanged loudly, making them both freeze.

'...there's nothing up here.' A male, human voice said crossly. Issa thought she recognised it, but did not want to think Hameka stood only yards away from her.

'My senses are never wrong,' hissed another voice, low and crooning. Issa's skin crawled as the necromancer spoke. 'Something comes to us, something powerful. We should be wary.'

'It will be the glory of the Under Flow,' said the other voice. 'Starting a faction of the New Order here has brought us all greater powers. Nevertheless, I'll heed your warning. Gather your necromancers, tell them to search the castle. I'll alert the Maphraxies. It'll be those cursed Draxian ghosts again—this place is crawling with them, but soon we'll be rid of them for good.'

The voices faded away. Issa let go of her breath.

'We can't be too far away from Vornus now,' Asaph said. It was a small relief, she decided. Even she'd prefer to fight him than hide like this.

'Here it is!' He pulled on something metal and a loud grating sound scoured their ears. Issa winced then stared as the back of the hearth—a simple metal plate—screeched open to reveal a pitch-black tunnel behind.

'Quickly!' Asaph said as footsteps returned. She jumped inside, hitting her head on the low ceiling and stalling. He followed after her, hunted for another lever, pulled it, and the door screeched shut.

Crouching, they shuffled forwards into the black. Issa went through a hundred questions in her head, the main ones being had they left footprints in the soot on the ground and had the hidden door shut properly? She paused as a darker object moved in front of her. Maggot's eyes flashed.

'You can get there this way too,' the little demon said. From the sound of his voice, he was enjoying this adventure with her.

Again, Issa couldn't see anything as she shuffled forwards, and her back soon ached for being hunched over. She hated trailing one hand along the wall and the other hand in front of her, there could be spiders or scorpions in every nook, and she was certainly already covered in soot and dirt. She preferred to worry about what she was touching rather than think about what would happen when they emerged out of this passage.

When she paused again Asaph grabbed her hand, she wondered how he could find it in the darkness. 'Let me go first,' he said, squeezing it.

They moved quicker now he was in front, but still she dared to let her talisman glow the faintest blue, just enough to see her feet and give a little comfort. They walked for ages.

'It goes on forever!' she said, wondering how long they had been walking. When her breath came harder, she deduced they were moving upwards. It seemed to wind to the left too, but in the dark it was hard to be sure.

'There are several branches,' said Asaph. 'Luckily I don't have to keep hunting through the Recollection because Maggot is leading.' He chuckled.

Eventually the sound of distant voices came. When they grew in volume, Issa reluctantly doused the light of her talisman. Asaph paused at what appeared to be a dead end, but a breeze blew from somewhere. Human voices came but they were muffled. A chill ran down her back when she heard a woman speak; could it be Cirosa?

Asaph began searching for a lever. He found it and turned to her. 'Ready?'

'Not really.' Issa swallowed.

Asaph turned the handle anyway. The metal plate grated a little, then opened an inch, spilling light into the passageway. The voices became louder but were still muffled. He turned the handle more, and inch by inch the door squeaked open. He peered into the light for a long moment, then shuffled forwards.

'Maggot, stay safe,' she whispered to the demon. He nodded and faded into shadow. With one hand on her sword and all senses alert, Issa crawled forwards. She stood beside Asaph and rolled her shoulders back, stretching her back with a silent sigh.

They stood not in another hearth but in a tiny, ornate alcove. There was an empty pedestal in front of them where once a statue or ornament would have been placed. Drawn across it, and a foot or so in front of them, was a heavy, frayed, blue velvet curtain, although time had faded it to a mottled blue-grey. The light, seemingly bright in the tunnel, was actually dim. There were no steps down and it was quite a drop to the floor. She noted that the curtain barely reached all the way down.

Voices came from beyond the curtain, male and female, but at a distance, possibly even in the next room. She didn't want to leave here. Her heart pounded as Asaph reached for the curtain and peered through.

He turned back to her, his eyes wide and face serious. 'We're in the upper hallways of the castle. I can't see who is talking but I think it's them. Maphraxies guard the doors and there are two necromancers on alert, but they are far to the right. No one is facing in this direction.'

He turned back to peering. After several long moments, nothing had changed. Issa hoped he was formulating their next move out of here.

'The longer we stay here, the more likely we'll be detected,' Asaph whispered.

Issa nodded, then something pressed upon her mind, the pressure growing in intensity and quickly becoming painful as she resisted. 'Wait!' she grabbed his arm as he began to crouch and get off the alcove. He paused, and she let the vision come.

Her sight turned inwards and Ehka's familiar avian mind touched hers. Freezing wind ruffled her feathers, and the air was rich with the smell of pine forests and snow. She whispered aloud what she saw.

'Wind, snow… I'm flying. I see the castle, there are Dread Dragons. They have seen me but ignored me, I'm just a bird. Here, Ehka, we are here. Can you feel us?'

Ehka turned. The upper ramparts of the castle came into view and the vision faded. She took a moment to regain her senses. A loud caw came, then the sound of something tapping on a window. Asaph glanced around the curtain. 'He's found us!' he whispered.

'Kill that cursed raven!' Cirosa's unmistakable voice shouted.

Beyond the curtain came an explosion of activity. Issa caught her breath wondering what to do as Ehka continued to tap on the window and caw. Heavy boots clanged the floor and Maphraxies grunted. Issa felt the Under Flow move as the necromancers sprang into action.

'Ehka, go!' Issa shouted in Daluni.

'Issa, now,' hissed Asaph, making use of the raven's distraction as he crouched and made ready to let himself down from the alcove.

Just before their connection broke, a thought-form from Ehka came to Issa. She saw different races and many knights, Feylint Halanoi, Karalanths, elves, and dwarves. She quickly translated it, *'I did not come alone.'*

Asaph dropped to the ground and helped her down. He opened the curtain an inch and she glimpsed Maphraxies, necromancers and a pale haired woman running to the windows lining the hallway.

Cirosa was dressed in white. Her arms were folded, and a black crown held back her platinum hair. Her flesh was devoid of colour and warmth, and dark power emanated from her. Her powers have grown, Issa thought. Beyond her stalked a man, tall and slender, with slicked back black hair, though his features were Draxian.

A terrifying roar tore apart the world. Issa gasped and fell against the wall covering her ears. The air outside the window swirled with purple magic and an enormous, ice-blue dragon appeared. Its giant claws grabbed onto the castle walls as it landed in the midst of its enemies.

'Morhork!' Issa breathed in.

The wingless dragon, uncaring of the Dread Dragons descending upon it, raised his head and let out another deafening roar. The Flow sucked away from her in a torrent towards the dragon. Morhork lifted into the air with the magic and moved so fast he all but vanished.

CHAPTER 33

Dragons of Drax

ASAPH froze and yet his blood boiled.

There, pointing at the raven outside the window, stood Vornus at an angle, his hawk nose in profile. The Recollection opened, and his mother's memories of this man flickered through his mind.

Vornus had been a brave fighter, fearless of dragons even though he wasn't a Dragon Rider. He'd also been a deeply trusted and wise advisor—now he was a traitor. The memories were overwhelming, filled with the deep pain of betrayal. How could he do this to his own? How could he let his own people die? *What price immortality?* The man looked as pale and dead as the woman beside him.

As his eyes fell upon Cirosa, Asaph's blood chilled and cold sweat instantly trickled down his back. For a moment he felt her chains still upon him. She had changed him in some way, Issa was right; she'd weakened him, and her evil claws dug deep into him.

He dragged his eyes from her and looked back at Vornus, his hand tightening on the hilt of the Sword of Binding. In front of him stood his single purpose, his primary objective, a task to complete before he could take Drax. The time had come.

All those moments he had lain awake in the Unchartered Lands, listening to the wind in the trees and Coronos slumbering beside him, thinking of his revenge for all that had been taken from them, all that had been destroyed.

A tremor shook him, his body held him back, yet his emotions urged him forwards, to stride right into their midst, lift his sword and hew the man's head from his body. His other hand clenched the curtain and began to draw it back. He stepped his right foot forwards.

Dragon magic moved in such a vast quantity he could feel it in his human form. The air outside the window shimmered and darkened. Asaph did a double take and stared at the enormous blue dragon straddling the castle walls. What in Feygriene's name was Morhork doing here?

The dragon's golden eyes locked onto him. Could he see him even from there? A thousand thoughts and feelings flew through him. Had the dragon come here to hinder and ruin his plans? Or had he come here to help them? Did his arrival mean Marakon had arrived?

It didn't matter what he thought for events unfolded rapidly.

Maphraxies poured into the hallway from the left and right, and the magic wielders in the room called the Under Flow. The enemy either pressed against the window or ran to the balconies outside, hands raised and crackling with latent energy.

Only one person did not act like the others and it was to him Asaph looked. Vornus had stepped back from the window, an uncertain expression on his face. Moving swiftly but not running, he sidled away from the others and made his way along the hallway, past where Asaph and Issa were hiding.

Asaph only realised Issa was using all her strength to hold him back after the man had passed.

'Not yet, wait and follow him,' she whispered.

Asaph nodded, forcing himself to be calm.

With one glance back, Vornus whirled to the left into a doorway and disappeared.

'The coward is running away already!' Asaph grabbed Issa and dragged her after him. As they emerged from the curtain, he realised how filthy their red-robes were, covered in blood, tears and soot. They'd be hard pressed to fit in now, he thought, but it didn't seem to matter, everyone was focused on the enormous dragon outside the window.

The passageway was small and dark, lit by a single lantern, a servants' passage. Vornus had already disappeared along it. There were two doors at the end; one led into a store room and the other opened into a stairwell leading up. Asaph ran up them two at a time.

They exited into another hallway and Vornus's black cloak disappeared through the door at the other end of it.

Asaph hurtled after him. With sword raised he threw himself through the door, splintering it off its bolts and landing the other side into a large chamber—a chamber he desperately did not want to recognise. Vornus was kneeling as if praying before an altar made of black metal and stone, and a great mirror tarnished with dark splatters that looked like blood. Dried blood also crusted the altar.

Her dresser had been where the altar was now. Her bed had been *there*, atop the three stone steps, and her wardrobe on the far side. He swallowed, his body shaking; he could see it all as it once had been. This was his mother's chamber, and now it was filthy and desecrated! Rage.

'Vornus!' Asaph cried.

The man leapt up from the altar and almost stumbled over his robes, his eyes wild. He threw something, and the air sparkled. Sharp pain pierced Asaph's eyes and face. He smarted and blinked, blearily glimpsing Vornus running to a door on the other side of the room.

'Wood, Flames,' Issa commanded and threw up a palm.

Anything made of wood splintered and burst into flames, including the door Vornus was just opening. Asaph heard him cry out.

Issa reached up and held Asaph's face. A wave of coolness spread over him from her palms and the pain began to clear. Asaph nodded his thanks.

'They'll all have felt that,' said Issa, her voice oddly calm.

Vornus was trying to get through the flames that licked the doorway. The flames suddenly vanished and in the place of the flaming door, stood Cirosa. She raised a hand at Asaph. Something pierced his heart and he fell screaming.

'So, you saw your death on that sword, did you, Vornus?' laughed Cirosa. 'Look at him, he's pathetic! I don't know what you were worried about. The blade will be destroyed in the Dark Rift and you won't ever have to discover yourself at the end of it. No, my dear Vornus, as you can see, we write the prophecies now.'

Asaph could barely hear her through the agony breaking his body. He saw Issa raise her talisman and a wall of blue flames flared. Cirosa held her hands up and the flames paused in the middle of the room. There they held, between the two women, sizzling, until something gave, and it hurtled back to Issa throwing her against the wall.

'The Flow has no power here, foolish wench!' Cirosa hissed.

Asaph writhed on the floor, unable to help Issa who remained pinned to the wall.

Cirosa pulled out her knife and slowly advanced. 'Which one do you want, Vornus?' She grinned maliciously, lips blood-red against the bloodlessness of her face.

Vornus, seeing the hapless state of his foes, lost his cowardice. He drew his slender sword, a gleam of hateful revenge in his eyes.

'Recognise this room, do you, *prince*,' he sneered. 'This is where it happened. This is where Drax fell and your mother was utterly destroyed.'

Asaph groaned with the pain and pent-up, unreleasable rage.

Issa wanted nothing more than to slice Vornus's smirk right off his face.

Why have we come here? What a foolish plan! Issa kicked herself as she strained against the unseen force that held her. She tried to speak but her throat constricted and her breath came in painful gasps. She tried to feel the Flow or will Illendri and her talisman to respond, but they were a dead weight at her side.

The Under Flow overpowered all. It swirled around Cirosa as she advanced, slow and cat-like with her knife in hand, her blood-stone amulet glowing. The Under Flow grew. Black and red clouds filled the room, distorting reality, twisting time. It came from all around but mostly it seemed to be spilling out of the old mirror Vornus had been kneeling before, as well as from Cirosa's amulet. It was truly mesmerising, and Issa found herself staring at it in cold horror.

Cirosa spoke but Issa couldn't hear her voice. The priestess began to fade into the black clouds.

'Issa.'

A deep, airy voice called out from within the Under Flow. Her name echoed around her.

'Issa.' The voice called again, drawing her in, whispering dark promises, offering her power if she would just reach for it. Triangular red eyes flared in the centre of the Under Flow. Issa gasped as the rest of Baelthrom's form materialised.

'You and I, we are the same,' he said. 'We do not belong here, and we never have. Come to me, Issa.'

Blood pounded in Issa's head and the Under Flow began to bodily lift her, drawing her into it.

A shard of white light appeared before her in the sea of darkness. It pierced the Under Flow with its purity and drove back the clouds. The shard grew brighter forcing Issa to shield her eyes. Cirosa fell back against the wall, staring at the light.

The shard hummed, lengthened, and separated into four identical spears of light. One remained in the centre and the other three began revolving slowly around it. Cirosa raised her hands and the Under Flow surged around the light, seeking to break it.

'Reach for the light, Issa,' Iyena's strained voice spoke from far away.

Inch by inch, Issa lifted her hand, fighting against the black magic that bound her. Her fingers touched the closest shard and she inhaled sharply. It was solid and smooth like well-polished wood, *like a seer's staff!* She gripped it firmly and the light burst up her arm and over her body. She reached and grabbed Asaph's leg, and the light spread from her hand to cover him too, and he stopped writhing. They both moved upwards, air rushing through every fibre of her being.

The chamber, the Under Flow, Cirosa and Vornus vanished.

White light bathed them, and she looked up into the face of Iyena. The woman's face was upturned, utterly serene and her eyes were closed. The white shard she held was a seer's staff, and her pale blue robes shimmered with effervescence—her whole body was ethereal and made of light.

Dar, Suli and Naksu appeared behind Iyena holding the other shards of light that were their staves, their robes billowing in an unseen wind. They looked like angels; power, love and light holding them all in this space. Only Naksu wasn't standing but sitting cross-legged in the centre of them all. Unlike the others her eyes were open.

Asaph blinked and sat up, rubbing his chest. He stared at the seers in awe. 'Is this the Ethereal Planes?'

'Yes,' said Naksu. 'The Trinity are holding us here and I am directing them. We cannot hold us all for much longer, just long enough to break Baelthrom's grasp on you.'

The energy jolted and they fell.

Issa hit the floor of the chamber hard, knocking the air from her lungs. Asaph rolled beside her and they both sat up gasping. Before them remained the giant pillar of light held in place in the chamber by the four white shards. The chamber was otherwise empty.

'The dragon's come!' Naksu's disembodied voice echoed around them, filled with joy and hope. 'We'll protect this space until we can hold it no longer. Do what you must, Raven Queen, take back your destiny, Dawn Bringer.'

Something red and dragon-shaped shot past the window, and the roar of dragons tore through the castle; not one, but many. They were answered by the screams of many Dread Dragons.

Asaph jumped to his feet and pulled Issa up—he seemed strong, glowing almost. She felt strength and power fill her, as if those moments in the Ethereal Planes had replenished her body and soul. *Or perhaps it's the power of the seers.*

'They can only have gone this way,' Asaph growled and ran to the burnt and splintered door ahead of them, still holding her hand. 'I need you to do whatever you can with the Flow, there's no point hiding now. Fight and survive.'

They ran up the steps, adrenaline making her giddy. At the top Asaph booted open the door. Beyond it was an enormous flat platform with a Dread Dragon perched on the far end and Cirosa and Vornus running towards it. They had emerged onto the very top of the castle, a place clearly made for dragons to land.

Issa dared to glance down, and her knees went weak at the drop. They were very high up and a frigid wind whipped all around. Tall, snow-covered mountains ringed the skyline, hugged in places by white clouds. Snow gusted in flurries but when she looked to the sky she almost stumbled at the sight she never believed she would see.

Dozens of dragons soared; reds, greens, greys and all the colours in between. Chasing them were equal numbers of Dread Dragons, diving and roaring. Fire and smoke filled the air.

'Vornus!'

Asaph's howl captured her attention, and she whirled around. Asaph raised his sword and gripped it in two hands, the pommel flared blood-red. In the Flow, the entire sword was made of fire, and it was hungry.

Cirosa paused mounting the Dread Dragon and Vornus turned.

Issa grabbed her talisman and unsheathed Illendri. The Flow poured into her. She was fast, but somehow Cirosa was faster. From the priestess's hands black tendrils spewed. They hit the ground and flowed along it like moving shadows straight towards Asaph. They surged over his feet and up his legs.

Issa's talisman magic reached him a second later, indigo magic surrounding the tentacles. The blackness was already half way up his legs, holding him solid. He slashed with his sword but could not cut the bounds.

'Undo!' Issa screamed. Her magic lashed around the black tendrils, fighting to pull them apart.

Vornus unsheathed his sword and cautiously came towards them.

'You betrayed us!' Asaph growled, struggling to move, the veins bulging on his neck. 'If it weren't for you, Drax would never have fallen.'

'Look at you, you snivelling runt! You're just like your pathetic father! See above us, my little Prince, look. Do you think you can fight that?'

Issa glanced up. Through a patch of thinning cloud there appeared not blue sky but black, the edges of the dark rift starkly visible. It was enormous. The Flow trembled in her uncertain grasp, her confidence faltering.

'No, my forgotten Prince, you must embrace it, embrace the raw power.' Vornus sniggered.

Cirosa held up her other hand. Scores of black tentacles wound around Asaph, crushing him. He roared in pain, thrashing uselessly. Issa renewed her efforts but Cirosa's grip on him was steel. She tried to reach for more power, but the black magic grew stronger, forcing her to focus solely on keeping it back.

The energy shimmered around Asaph and she realised he was trying to change form—but Cirosa already knew this and was keeping him from doing so. Tendrils snaked around his sword arm, forcing him to lower it and he roared, enraged.

Vornus laughed, raised his sword, and ran at Asaph. Issa screamed. Releasing her focus on Cirosa's black magic, she turned the Flow on Vornus. An invisible fist knocked him to the ground as Asaph was lifted bodily into the air by the black tentacles.

Issa tried to reach him, to drag him back with the Flow, but failed.

Commanded by Cirosa, the Dread Dragon lifted its ugly head and snaked towards Asaph.

A gushing wind suddenly howled over them, sending Issa to her knees and flinging Vornus backwards just as he was getting up. The air shimmered, the Flow jerked violently, and a blue dragon lifted its head over the parapet just yards away from Cirosa.

Morhork's giant claws clutched the wall, stone cracking between them as he heaved himself partially on to the platform. Cirosa jerked on her dragon's reins, but her mount, focussed intently upon Asaph, responded too slowly.

In one smooth movement, Morhork whipped his head towards the priestess, opened his jaws and, with a clap, snapped them shut on her body. He shook his muzzle savagely. Blood sprayed, slapping Issa in the face, then he tossed Cirosa high into the air. She hurtled skyward over the parapet, her body not in one piece but two.

Issa bent over and retched.

Asaph lurched forwards, Cirosa's tentacles disappearing with each step. Vornus halted his advance and now fell back, eyes wide.

Forcing herself into composure, Issa regained her stomach, her control on the Flow, and her balance.

Morhork, despite his savagery, struggled to lift himself further onto the platform. He trembled all over, though she could see no mortal wound upon him. *Perhaps magical flight has exhausted him,* Issa thought.

Cirosa's Dread Dragon showed no such weaknesses. Seeing the demise of its master, it lifted its ugly horned head and roared. Issa staggered and covered her ears, Asaph and Vornus paused, then Vornus swirled his hands in the air.

Swiftly, Issa released the Flow. The air shimmered and crackled over Vornus, stopping him casting.

Morhork snapped at the black dragon, his jaws closing on thin air. The Dread Dragon slammed its horns into Morhork and the two dragons locked together, a mass of teeth and writhing muscle.

Issa commanded the Flow. Blue fire snaked from her palms, flaring brightly into the black dragon, sizzling on scales and searing its sides.

It barely noticed as it clawed at Morhork, its black talons dug deep into the softer scales beneath Morhork's front legs and blood trickled from the weary dragon.

Issa struggled to keep her eyes on the dragons and Asaph, and turn the Flow fast to her bidding.

Asaph lurched into a run. Vornus turned and ran straight at the edge as if to jump off. Issa glimpsed the familiar shimmer of one trying to transform.

'No you don't!' she hissed. Her magic lashed out and knocked him to the ground, giving Asaph the much-needed moments to reach him.

A roar of pain came from Morhork, the Dread Dragon's jaws had clamped onto the base of his neck.

'Fire, Spear,' Issa gasped, sweat rolling down her temples as she flicked her hands forward. White fire flew from them, spearing into the sides of the black dragon until its flesh began to smoke. The dragon snorted and loosened its grip.

Morhork wrenched himself free but the motion cost him his balance and his claws slipped off the parapet. In one final motion he snaked his head up and clamped over the Dread Dragon's front leg. The Dread Dragon howled and beat its wings, trying to lift away but the weight of an entire dragon on its limb was too great, and it tumbled over the edge, along with Morhork.

Issa ran to the parapet.

Asaph hurled himself at Vornus and tackled him to the ground.

He landed several punches on the slighter man, surprised to find solid muscle as Vornus twisted and writhed. He slipped, and a leather boot caught him square in the face, causing stars to dance in front of his eyes.

Asaph clung to the man, not letting him wriggle away whilst his senses returned. He got up on one knee, finding the man's wrist in his left hand as they got to their feet. Asaph lifted his sword as Vornus attacked with his blade. The Sword of Binding flared as it struck metal and sliced straight through Vornus's weapon. Metal screeched, and the hewn edge spun into the air and over the wall. Vornus growled and threw the useless hilt after it, then glared at the Sword of Binding.

'Recognise it, do you?' Asaph hissed, his hand becoming a vice crushing Vornus's wrist.

Vornus winced and flicked his free arm up. Something flashed in the air, Asaph saw the tiny dagger too late as he released Vornus's arm and flinched away. The movement may have spared his life for the blade missed his neck and embedded itself into his shoulder. Asaph was too enraged to feel any pain.

With a roar and lightning quick reflexes, Asaph lunged and sliced his sword up, tearing through Vornus's clothing. The man stepped backwards, a surprised look forming on his colourless features as dark red blood splattered the white snow beneath him. He swayed and fell to one knee with a gasp. Asaph took a predatory step closer, raising his sword slowly.

'My mother trusted you,' Asaph said, emotion breaking his voice, unwanted tears blurring his vision.

Vornus's breath became laboured as he sank into an awkward sitting position, blood quickly spreading around him. Anger pinched his face and he snarled, blood flecking his lips, and then frowned in confusion, fear even. Something battled within the man; perhaps there was a tiny essence of who he had been before Baelthrom touched him. Whatever it was left swiftly, and utter hatred darkened his eyes.

'Your mother was a whor—'

Vornus never finished his sentence. Asaph pirouetted, his sword held at the perfect height as time itself slowed down. In the last moment before his blade reached Vornus's throat, Asaph closed his eyes, he barely felt the blade connect, so sharp was the steel as it passed through flesh.

When he stopped moving his gaze was drawn to the frozen beauty of the mountains beyond the castle, the snow-covered peaks, the way the white tendrils of clouds lazily caressed their steep sides.

There was a thud behind him, followed by another. Asaph took a long, deep breath and let it go. The world shimmered as he did so, and the mountains, the air, perhaps even his ancestors, sighed with him.

'It is done, Coronos, Mother, Father.' He reached down, picked up a handful of snow and wiped the dark blood off his blade. Without looking directly at Vornus's headless body spilling dark blood over the white snow—the man whose actions had destroyed the lives of millions, enslaved thousands, and caused the downfall of an entire continent—Asaph sheathed his sword in finality and walked towards Issa.

Issa turned away from the parapet just before Morhork made the killing blow.

She couldn't watch the Dread Dragon's throat ripped out, nor the deep wounds the beast had inflicted on Morhork's chest.

Asaph strode towards her and she stumbled towards him. There was a strange expression on his face, one of victory yet deep sadness; she had never seen him look so raw. Behind him lay Vornus's beheaded body. Cirosa was dead, Vornus was dead, but she could not find any joy in that, just a weary relief.

They embraced, saying nothing, finding comfort. When they pulled apart, there was blood on her hands.

'You're bleeding!' she said, feeling him all over. He cried out when she touched his shoulder.

'Now you mention it, I appear to have a blade in me,' he said ruefully. 'Great Feygriene, it doesn't half smart now I've said that!'

She saw the metal sticking out of his shoulder, a tiny blade embedded to the hilt.

'Dear goddess, you'll bleed to death. Look, it's got to come out,' she insisted when he shied away.

She made him lie down on the snow and pooled healing magic in her left hand. With her right she gripped the hilt of the blade and closed her eyes. 'Thank the goddess the blade is small, nothing more than a flicking knife, but still long enough to pierce the heart.' It didn't bear thinking about what might have happened.

With a quick, smooth motion she pulled it free. Asaph groaned, his hot blood flowed fast, and she filled both hands with magic, at once stemming the flow and easing the pain. She used the knife to cut cloth from her hateful red robes and tied them around his arm and shoulder.

'I've stopped the bleeding, but only if you don't use your arm. Thankfully it's not your sword arm.'

'Morhork,' said Asaph, forgetting his injury.

She helped him up and they both went to the edge. Below was the smoking mess of the Dread Dragon, blood and gore splattered all over the walls and the snow. She followed the trail of huge bloody footprints and saw Morhork limping away up the narrow valley.

'He's wounded, we should go help him,' said Issa.

'No,' Asaph said. He looked far away, and the golden dragon flashed in his eyes. 'He's sending me thoughts…I can't read them easily in this form, but he's done, needs rest. He cannot fight anymore.'

A scream and a rush of wind made them whirl around. Barely getting away they ducked and rolled as a Dread Dragon swooped at them. Giant claws raked the stones of the parapet where they had just been standing, reminding them that the battle for Drax had only just begun.

Following hot on its tail was a red dragon which may have been Rust. It roared as it passed and dropped something large. With a great clang and spray of snow, their dragon harness rolled to a stop in front of them and gleamed in the light.

'I guess that's a message,' said Issa.

Asaph laughed and ran to it. 'We're being invited to the battle.'

'Great Goddess, look!' Issa said, stopping abruptly and pointing east.

Asaph gasped, and his eyes widened. 'By Feygriene's Fire!'

There, in the far distance, marching along the white, snow-covered road towards the castle, was a legion of soldiers.

CHAPTER 34

Dragon Legion

ISSA secured the final strap under Asaph's chest and heaved herself into the dragon seat.

Asaph kept his eyes turned skyward, watching the skies for Dread Dragons. There were many, but his dragons were keeping them busy, never allowing them to turn their attentions onto the humans below. If they weren't attacking them directly, they were taunting or chasing them

'Is Marakon here?' Issa asked excitedly. 'Can you see Ehka?'

'Even dragons cannot see that far,' said Asaph. 'But I have a sense that he is not. It was his plan to split off from the main fleet and come via our route. We must protect the landing point at all costs.'

Two Dread Dragons dropped towards them.

'Trouble comes.' He bristled.

Issa braced as Asaph's muscles bunched then he leapt into the air in a spray of snow.

Asaph beat his wings hard, seeking speed and lift as the already airborne black dragons swiftly approached.

A grey dragon shot through the rapidly closing space between them, and one of the Dread Dragons instinctively went for it. The other remained on Asaph's tail. He darted into the clouds, hoping Issa was hanging on tight. He certainly didn't feel comfortable having her on his back when they were being attacked and wondered what kind of training dragons and dragon riders underwent for this.

The grey dragon—a male he didn't know—spoke to him mind to mind. *'Use your magic, stronger together.'*

Asaph focused on the Flow. As a dragon, he didn't need to enter it, he was always within it, all he needed to do was focus on the waves of energy flowing through and around everything. Issa was already there, a blaze of indigo light.

'Ice,' she commanded.

He felt the air freeze around them and added his own power to the spell, strengthening it. The snow turned to shards of ice which dropped out of the sky onto the Dread Dragon, tearing through its wings. The dragon screamed, its flight slowing.

Asaph arched down and emerged through the clouds above the approaching army. All factions marched as one unit, Feylint Halanoi, Elves, Dwarves, Lans Himayans and Navadin—their bears roars lifting to meet the roar of dragons. His heart suddenly lurched with pride and awe; there, at the front, marched soldiers wearing the old armour of the fabled Dragon Legion. Golden helmets sported royal blue crests, tabards gleamed white with the head of a golden dragon, *a head that looks just like the dragon door.*

'Praise Feygriene, look, the Dragon Legion of old! They must have kept their armour and their colours, and now we've all returned to take back what was stolen from us.'

Asaph roared his pride as he passed overhead. The army, already overcoming dragon fear, paused their ordered marching, raised their weapons, and an almighty cheer rose up to greet him. Issa laughed, and Asaph roared again.

'Wait; the dragons,' said Issa. 'They're leaving!'

Asaph banked towards Draxa. The Dread Dragon with the torn wings had gained on him. His dragons were flying away from the city.

'No,' said Asaph. 'They're leading the Dread Dragons away. They're giving us a chance to take back our city. It's our job now.'

Asaph turned tight to face the dragon trailing him. He pooled the Flow and Issa joined him. Orange and indigo fire ignited his vision, and their combined magic, far greater than its parts, exploded into the Dread Dragon. Screams and the roar of the Dromoorai rider tore through the flames. Then they were flying through ash, scales, and smoking armour.

'Incinerated!' gasped Issa.

Asaph understood then the power of a dragon and its rider. Roaring their victory, he angled his wings towards the castle and flew to the city gates where hordes of Maphraxies now poured out.

The rush of their combined magic filled Issa with awe.

She could read his will and intention in the Flow as if she were reading his mind. All she had to do was combine her power to his and the two willingly conjoined and became something far more powerful. Had her parents, a powerful bard and seer, felt like this when they used magic together? She suspected they might have.

It reminded her of the orbs, the magic *wanted* to become one, like Illendri had wanted to become one. Water and earth combined, two forms of magic that should never have been separated. Magic strove for balance and harmony.

Combining magic with Asaph was not without its cost, she felt exhaustion nagging at her mind and body. Asaph must have felt similarly for he did not pursue another enemy dragon but instead flew high and to the West.

'Buying us a moment's rest,' he shouted over the rushing wind.

'Look, ships!' Issa shouted and pointed to the ocean beyond the craggy ridge west of Draxa. At least five of them could be seen. 'Marakon.' Butterflies swirled in her stomach. Ehka was somewhere out there too.

'They're not alone,' Asaph grumbled.

She squinted. Moments later she saw what he had seen, tiny gleaming boats moving uncannily fast.

'Histanatarns,' Issa said. 'Hundreds! We have to help Marakon.'

'We can only help them by keeping the Dromoorai away.' Asaph beat his wings harder, spying another Dread Dragon rising up to them from below. 'Just one Dread Dragon can take out the whole fleet. I doubt I can fight well in the air with this shoulder, my wings tire too soon.'

Issa thought fast but came up with nothing good. Drawing on the Flow she burst it out behind them as white fire but the Dromoorai was ready and deftly pulled his mount back, and her fire passed harmlessly under its wing, energy wasted. The red amulet on its chest flashed, entrapping her attention.

'*Raven Queen,*' a voice called inside her head. She tore her eyes away.

Another Dread Dragon came out of nowhere. It appeared suddenly above the peak they were passing and must have been lying in wait. Asaph jerked violently up. Issa saw the sky then the ground and thought she might be sick. The other dragon followed and then they collided. If the seat hadn't been enchanted to keep her in it, she would have been thrown from it.

Instead she was shaken left and right, the horrific maw of a Dread Dragon opened barely inches from her face, its red eyes seeing food. Issa screamed. Asaph rolled, and the ground came rushing towards them whilst both dragons clawed at each other as they fell.

The second Dread Dragon was right beneath them now.

Desperately she hunted the sky for the other dragons who could help but they had gone, taking as many of the Dromoorai away as they could.

'*Issa.*' Her name echoed from two amulets. The Flow weakened and disappeared, blackness swirled around her in the magical fields.

Asaph shuddered and jerked. She glimpsed his enormous jaws biting and wrenching into the shoulder of the other dragon whilst he beat his wings furiously, trying to keep them all airborne. He twisted, managed to free himself and lifted into the air. She felt him hunting for the Flow but unable to grasp it.

The second Dread Dragon came alongside them, truly enormous, its black metallic scales gleaming. So close was it, Issa trembled. Then the Dromoorai beast came into view. Its blazing eyes locked onto hers as the chains of the reins it held clanked and strained in its metal gauntlets. It lifted its claymore and struck savagely at her before she could pull Illendri free. The sword missed, sliced downwards and scoured the dragon harness instead.

Asaph turned his head and breathed fire at it, forcing it to drop back. The immense heat of his flames instantly made her sweat. The first Dread Dragon came alongside them again, on the other side. It closed to attack and Issa held Illendri ready. The claymore came down—awkwardly, or so she thought, and missed her by a good margin, striking the harness in a spray of black fire.

The harness jerked loose and Issa grabbed onto the rails realising what they were doing. *They don't want to kill me!* She stared at where the straps had been sliced and were now fraying on both sides. *Clever bastards!*

'They're attacking the harness, with magic too!' Issa shouted, rushing the words out. 'They're trying to separate us.'

'Or force us to land,' growled Asaph.

Dread Dragon fire forced him to bank sharply left. One of the straps snapped and the dragon seat lurched. Issa screamed and clung on.

'We can't land and take on two. Perhaps I can lead them away,' said Asaph.

'The harness won't last that long! Wait, let me fly, I can fly,' said Issa. But trying to think in the midst of battle was impossible.

'They'll snap you up in a moment, no!' Asaph flew harder but with each beat of his wings the remaining straps frayed a little more.

They were north of Draxa now and there was nothing but white and grey jagged peaks below.

'Asaph, it's going to break. When it happens, I'll fly. I'll be able to hide my fall with the talisman. I don't know what else to do!'

Asaph growled. 'So be it, I'll lead them away. You get to Marakon or Velonorian or even the seers, if you can. I'll come back for you.'

A Dread Dragon screamed above them and dropped out of the sky. It landed on Asaph's back, its enormous talons gripping on to the harness rails and shunting them down. The straps snapped. Issa fumbled with her own ties as the harness came completely free. The dragon wrenched it off Asaph's back with her inside.

Trying not to scream, she let go her grip and slipped through the rails. The talisman pulsed, and her raven mark burned. Wind rushed around her then through her feathers. Flapping, she righted herself and drew her wings close, darting towards the earth as fast as she dared.

When the ground was only a few yards away she slowed her descent and dared to look up. Still in the grip of the Dread Dragon was the dragon harness, but Asaph was free. Perhaps they hadn't noticed her fall, for both Dromoorai continued to harry him.

Fly, Asaph, fly fast. The Goddess protect you!' She sent her mind-speak out to him hoping to let him know she was safe.

A raven cawed in the distance. Between her and the looming walls of Draxa, flew Ehka. She cawed back, overjoyed. Lifting high over the castle she looked down. There lay Vornus's slain body and a pool of dark blood now frozen on the ice beneath him. She ruffled her feathers and looked ahead.

South west and at the edge of the city walls, the Feylint Halanoi had engaged the Maphraxie horde. East, Marakon's ships had just reached the inlet. Histanatarn boats swarmed them, preventing them from launching smaller rafts. Perhaps she could help them from a distance.

Issa spied an empty balcony jutting out from the castle with a partial view of the inlet. She landed and changed form.

'Water, hear me,' she commanded, touching Illendri and holding her other hand outstretched. Away from the enemy, the Flow came unhindered, but exhaustion weighed heavy on her. She needed to sleep.

The elemental responded eagerly, and she closed her eyes to listen to it. In her mind's eye she saw water lifting each Histanatarn boat into the air, higher and higher. Gargled screams came, but she did not need to open her eyes to look and risk losing her concentration.

'Higher!'

The screams intensified. Then she swung her hand to the left in a chopping motion and released her grip on Illendri. She opened her eyes to see every Histanatarn boat tumbling out of the sky to smash into the ocean. The archers on the ships swiftly hailed arrows into the sea.

Maggot appeared, making her jump. He crawled up onto the balustrade and sat beside her. Without saying anything, the demon lifted his beloved Jabber and hurled it. It flew fast as an arrow and passed right through the nearest Histanatarn climbing onto wreckage, causing it to fall and disappear beneath the surface. Jabber arced and shot back to its master. Maggot caught it deftly. With his tongue clenched between his lips, he concentrated and hurled it again.

She smiled then had an idea. 'Illendri,' she whispered to the orb, asking it to command earth and water once more.

She raised her hand and snow lifted from the ground then solidified into shards of sparkling ice. Marking a group of Histanatarns aboard a large piece of wreckage, she flicked her fingers and let the shards fly. With the Histanatarns in disarray, the unhindered sailors now lowered their rafts. She swept her eyes over them, thought she glimpsed a tall, dark-haired man, then lost him in the rush.

Issa scanned the steps and the walkways above and below. There were no Maphraxies or necromancers. *Yet!* They would be too focused on the army at the front gates, but Dread Dragons could see Marakon's ships. It was only a matter of time.

CHAPTER 35

The Perfect Shot

ISSA called her raven form to her as the first rafts ground on to the pebbles, and flew to land on the beach.

There, in the front boat, was a man with an eye-patch. She ran to Marakon.

'Well met, Raven Queen,' he bowed in a showy manner making her blush.

Bokaard jumped out of the boat beside him and gave Issa a hearty slap on the back. 'We never anticipated sea dogs,' the big man growled.

'Have you seen the Navadin?' Marakon, pressed eagerly.

Issa nodded. 'Indeed, they're with the Feylint Halanoi and attacking the front gates as we speak.'

'Then let's not delay. We'll storm Draxa immediately and meet them on the other side,' said the commander, his expert eye analysing the granite cliff and walls before him.

'We made it through the castle in disguise but there are many within. Maphraxies, death hounds, necromancers…It won't be easy,' said Issa.

'We'll hunt every one of them down,' growled Eiretonne, swinging his axe.

'Most will be engaged at the front. Our greatest advantage now is the element of surprise. Let's go,' said Marakon, motioning his soldiers forward.

Issa ran to the steps with him, then paused. 'I'm best out here. I've been in there and I can't say I want to fight in dark tunnels again. Asaph and

Velonorian need me, and probably my horse.'

'So be it, Raven Queen,' Marakon agreed. 'Look out for Jarlain, tell her we're here.' He squeezed her shoulder and ran on, his soldiers piling after him.

'Stay safe, missy,' Eiretonne called back with a wink.

Maggot, who had been hiding behind her boots the whole time, now spoke. 'Where to now, Issy?'

She bent down to speak to him. 'You remember Thiashar?'

He wrinkled up his nose.

'Thiashar is with Iyena,' she said. 'I need you to find Thiashar and stay with the seers.'

Maggot winced. 'They're too bright, the seers, their magic hurts.'

'I know, Maggot, but where I go you cannot come. I have to fight, on a horse. You won't be safe with me. Stay with Marakon until you find the seers.'

'Much danger, Issy. The one the Dragon Lord killed, he's not the dangerous one. The other human hunts only for you, I heard him talking. He has much power. You must stay away from him.'

Issa stared at Maggot, a shiver trickling down her spine. 'I know who he is, Maggot, Hameka, Baelthrom's chosen. I'll be careful.'

She glanced up at the cliff and the windows high up in the castle above, feeling as if eyes watched her every move, she swallowed. 'Go, Maggot. Stay in the shadows and with the soldiers for as long as you can, then stay with the seers. If anything happens, go back to the Murk and tell the King. We might need his help before this day is through.'

Ehka cawed above, so she lifted her arms and let the raven form become her. Maggot's upturned face shrank as she rose into the sky then turned east towards the front gate.

The battle had moved, thankfully in their favour. No longer were the Feylint Halanoi at the gates; they had spilled through the city walls into the ancient market square, filling every corner of the city and reaching even to the front gates of the castle itself.

Battle fury was thick in the air. She could sense it keenly in this form for it filled her with anxious excitement. Fighting outside, against the abominations that were Maphraxies, was what she longed to do. She soared over the outer courtyard where the battle raged thickest. Black and red blood splattered the snow all the way from the outer gates to inside the city walls where it turned into slippery dark mud.

The snow and ice made fighting difficult. Boots slipped on the frozen ground, sometimes in the soldier's favour, sometimes costing their lives. She spotted a gang of elves, golden helmets gleaming beneath the splatters of blood and mud. Velonorian stood amongst them. Thank the goddess the elf was alive.

Animal roars shook the air and she looked to where the Navadin fought. Two dark brown bears lay unmoving in the mud, black iron spears sticking cruelly out of necks and spines, their riders unmoving beside them. She lost sight of the fallen as other Navadin swarmed over them, savagely fighting back the enemy horde.

Another bear roared, lifted himself up, his rider hanging on somehow, and smashed its paws down upon a Maphraxie, crushing its skull. His rider stabbed her spear through the neck of another. *Jarlain.* Her keen avian senses recognised the way she moved and her smell even from this distance.

Issa lifted higher and turned back to where their army flooded into the city. Feylint Halanoi horsemen pressed forwards, trampling any enemy careless enough to get in their way. Further back, stretcher bearers exited the forward press of soldiers, working tirelessly to collect and carry the injured and dead. Far beyond at the tree line stood hastily erected tents, more soldiers readying themselves, and spare horses tethered.

A horse neighed and reared, his black coat freshly brushed and shining. *Duskar!* Issa cawed. Someone had even managed to get a saddle and bridle on him. *Velonorian,* she smiled inwardly.

She landed beside the horse, changed form and hugged his neck. He quivered and whinnied.

'You're full of pent up energy,' she said as she pulled herself into the saddle. 'I'll bet you can't wait to get into battle.'

'Do you need a weapon, my lady?' asked a young squire struggling under a burden of swords and spears. 'Maybe some metal armour, or another to accompany you?'

Issa smiled down at the freckled-faced boy. 'The dragon armour I wear will protect me better than any steel, and my own squire is waiting for me, in the thick of battle.' She winked.

The boy suddenly turned crimson and opened his mouth to speak but no words came out. Then, to her dismay, he kneeled and said, 'Yes, my Queen Issa. I–I didn't recognise you. Immediately, that is.'

Issa blushed. 'I'm not really a queen, I don't even have my own land.'

'A Queen of Ravens is still a queen,' said the boy quietly, awe in his eyes. 'More will follow you than any other in all the lands.'

The words hit deep, and she recognised the foresight in the boy's words.

'If you carry on reasoning like that, you'll make an excellent knight one day,' she said.

She wheeled Duskar around and he reared and neighed excitedly. Issa laughed at his power and eagerness, and he leapt towards battle, snow spraying up from his hooves.

The city gates loomed, and the first Maphraxies appeared. The closest did not see Illendri arc down across the back of its exposed neck, and they had already moved past it before she could see it fall. The next—a dark dwarf—disappeared under Duskar's hooves. A black axe swung, Duskar reared, Issa clung on. Hooves and Illendri struck out together. The Maphraxie flew backwards, taking down its comrade. On she pressed, not needing to tell Duskar where to go, together they fought in every direction.

For a moment, she was beside a bear, a deep wound in its shoulder made it limp and its rider bled from a gash to his forehead. The rider constantly wiped blood from his eyes. A Maphraxie advanced on them, another coming from behind. Issa whirled Duskar around trusting the Navadin to take the first. Her sword struck hard against the blade of a black axe. The shock should have shattered her sword or her arm, but Illendri didn't buckle or even notch. With the slightest command of the Flow, sparks flew, and the black axe cleaved into two.

The Maphraxie stared at its blade, shock an odd look on its deformed face. Issa brought her sword back and the Maphraxie fell, jerking. Dancing Duskar back around, she found the Navadin had gone and instead a group of mounted Feylint Halanoi fought beside her.

Screams and shouts, the clashing of metal against metal, the sound of magic sizzling and fire flaring, all was a melee of noise, light and fury. A thousand sounds, sights and smells, and to each one she reacted. There was only the battle, there was only now, and there was nothing else. She understood Marakon's need for it, the strange solace in chaos it brought.

'Until the body gets tired, until an arm moves a moment too slow, then is it over. All there is between life and death is a moment.' She found herself thinking upon his words as she stabbed and parried, moving with Duskar as he reared and struck.

Snow began to fall again, and tiredness gnawed at her mind and body. When had she last slept? Eaten? Would she sleep or eat again? More Maphraxies poured out of the castle, preceded by packs of death hounds. Their numbers never seemed to dwindle, where were they coming from? It was as if Baelthrom had a secret city underground where he kept all his foul beings. *That, or a portal to Maphrax!*

The thought made her pause—a pause that nearly cost her life. She booted the Maphraxie in the face, shoving it back. Duskar turned and trampled it. She took a deep breath, trying to ease the weariness. They were still in the outer courtyard. Had they made any progress in the last hour? *It can only have been inches!*

'Issa!' a voice cried out.

'Velonorian?' She scanned above the bristling sea of swords, axes and spears.

There, several yards away mounted on a white horse, was the elf amidst others. She turned Duskar towards him. Maphraxies and soldiers blocked her path and it took an age to fight through them. The battle swayed, and the enemy was pushed to the left—but not back though, Issa noted.

The frontline broke and suddenly she found herself beside the elves. Shaking with relief, Issa and Velonorian embraced atop their horses, grateful for the moment's rest.

'We cannot beat them in this manner,' said the elf, his flawless face serious.

'Where are they coming from? Something's not right,' Issa said, trying to catch her breath.

'No, it isn't. Beyond that wall, see where it's collapsed? There's a massive trapdoor. That's where they're coming from. Perhaps there's a portal below? It feels like there might be as the energy moves strangely there. I can close it if I can get a clear shot.'

'How? How can you close it?' Issa asked. Portals couldn't be closed by arrows and swords. Through the throng of enemies, she glimpsed an open gate in the snow and more Maphraxies piling out of it.

The elf grinned, reached into the quiver of arrows at his side, and withdrew one different from the rest. It was thick, made of sheet metal rather than wood. To its front was tied a pouch and its base was wrapped in rags. It looked far too heavy for an arrow.

'That'll never shoot! It probably can't even be aimed,' said Issa, frowning.

'That's true, but it can make short distances,' Velonorian explained, inspecting the arrow proudly. 'And it's not built for accuracy, but you know how they make flaming arrows? It's like that but with something I've been working on. Let's just say it's a special Elven alchemical recipe.' He winked. 'See here, you light the end and fire it quickly. When it hits anything it crumples, and the flames hit the pouch. When that happens, the ingredients along with the enchantments do something extra special.'

He spread his fingers wide, 'Boom! Like I said, I just need to get close enough.'

Issa stared at the endless stream of Maphraxies and felt cold. The Feylint Halanoi were flagging, their faces weary and blood-stained, and morale was dropping as fresh enemies hacked towards them. 'We have to try *something,* otherwise we'll not win this battle,' she murmured.

'We're ready.' The elf nearest Velonorian spoke over his shoulder.

'Help me get close,' Velonorian winked at her.

The elf secured his bow on his back, stood in his saddle, and jumped and heaved himself onto the building above. From there he ran across the squat Maphraxie roofs and up onto the castle walls. Black arrows whizzed past him and Issa's heart leapt into her throat.

She pulled a reluctant Duskar back as far away from the battle as she could and stood beside the relative protection of the wall. There, she entered the Flow. Velonorian was a bright yellow light leaping between patches of enemy black. She hurled the Flow at the black forms, and flames exploded both in her physical and magical vision. It was the arrows that were impossible to see in the Flow, so she formed a flaming shield around the elf as he somersaulted towards the collapsed wall.

Once there, he lay down and flattened himself against the stone until the enemy arrows abated, thinking him dead. He surveyed the scene beyond that she could not see, then readied his special arrow. The aim would be difficult and awkward from his prone position.

Issa held both the Flow at her command and her breath as the elf aimed and loosed his arrow. It wobbled madly in the air, then plummeted. Issa let go her breath and slumped her shoulders, it couldn't possibly work, they had failed!

An enormous flash and mighty boom filled her ears. She blinked, momentarily blinded, and then the ground shook so hard bits of rubble and dust fell onto her from the wall. The noise of battle fell into an uncanny silence. It was broken by a great cheer from the Feylint Halanoi as her vision returned. Thick clouds of smoke rose up where Velonorian had loosed his arrow.

The elf was already running back towards them, taking advantage of the surprise to get back to safety. He swung down the wall into his saddle, a huge grin on his face. 'Now, the battle is ours.'

Soldiers, morale renewed, pushed forwards eagerly, whilst the enemy, shaken and confused, fell back. The inches they had gained turned to feet and soon the inner part of the city was in view and within their grasp. Issa fought beside Velonorian and the other elves, occasionally scanning the skies for Asaph – but there were no dragons at all. Neither, thankfully, were there any Dread Dragon.

And what about the Trinity, Maggot and Marakon? Had they made it to the main halls? She tried not to worry if any of them were still alive.

Thunder cracked overhead, announcing the storm. Thick clouds boiled, red and muddy—not natural clouds at all, and the air turned thick and cloying. She imagined Drax becoming the wasteland that was Venosia and hated it.

Black lightning cracked up from the ground behind enemy lines, and she glimpsed necromancers standing in a circle. Smoke and shadows billowed, and a piercing sound cut through the air, like a horse screaming. *I know that sound!* A shiver ran down her spine and she felt giddy as the Under Flow thickened.

In the Flow she saw the shadow knights as clear as day – two Knights of Maphrax standing behind enemy lines – walking nightmares taking solid form. They lifted their hands and swords, and marched forwards.

Soldiers gasped then screamed their warning, fear etched into their brows. The Flow vanished as dark energy flooded from the shadow knights' palms. Where the dark magic hit, soldiers staggered and fell, weapons became heavy and clumsy, missing their targets, ordered thoughts scattered.

And the Shadow Knights walked onwards.

'Fall back!' Issa howled, but her voice was lost in the rush of the Under Flow.

White magic flared from above. It gushed like a waterfall over castle walls and ramparts towards the enemy. Maphraxies fell back from it, howling as it touched them. *Seer magic, white and pure!* Issa realised.

The shadow horses screamed, their black hooves smoking in the white magic. Magic flared and crackled as the Under Flow and the Flow connected, the two opposing energies too bright to look upon as they battled.

Black magic pooled beneath the shadow knights and still they walked onwards, Maphraxies parting to let them through. They reached the battle front and, in unison, swung their swords in the air. A wave of power surged from them. The unseen force battered into the Feylint Halanoi, hitting the front line so hard, soldiers hurtled into the air, their broken bodies flopping rag-doll like onto their friends below. Inner city walls shook and then were laid flat.

The wave hit Issa, nearly knocking her from the saddle. Duskar staggered, and the outer city walls collapsed, opening up the battle field for friend and foe alike.

'I can help them if I can just get a clear shot!' Velonorian shouted over the din, clutching his reins as his mount shied and whinnied. His eyes were wild with fiery excitement. 'Seer magic and one of my arrows…a powerful combination.'

Issa came to her senses and tried to comprehend what the young elf was suggesting, but before she could stop him, he'd turned his mount and was pressing forwards to the front line.

'Velonorian, wait! It's too dangerous. You don't know how powerful they are!' but he was out of range.

She looked at a Knight of Maphrax, desperately wondering what to do. It turned towards her, tendrils of smoke coming from its shadow face. Cold fear struck her heart and the Flow vanished from her grasp. She had no power before this beast.

Shaking, she tore her eyes away and nudged Duskar after Velonorian whose white mount was disappearing through a collapsed wall. Maphraxies jumped into her path, coming around the fallen masonry on her right. Raising Illendri, she struck at the first before it could lift its weapon. Duskar sidled right and kicked the second with a sickening crack.

Not waiting to see if it got up, Issa urged Duskar onwards. The horse stumbled as he picked his way through the rubble. Blood trickled from a cut on his shoulder and sweat soaked his flanks. The horse needed rest, but he was still eager to fight.

Velonorian and his white horse captured her attention as it reared amongst the bays and the chestnuts of the Feylint Halanoi. The elf hacked his sword down, but Issa couldn't see his enemy, every other moment he looked towards the Shadow Knights stalking unstoppably forwards. Courageous soldiers charged at them only to stop a yard away, faces stricken, raised weapons trembling but unable to strike.

Another soldier tried coming at the Knights from behind, but he, too, hit an invisible force. His face twisted in pain and turned deathly grey, even his red tabard drained of colour. His sword tumbled uselessly from his hand, then he fell too, the life leached out of him. Issa stared at his fallen body, disbelieving, his soul was gone! The decay didn't stop there, his body crumpled in on itself until it was nothing more than a pile of ash for the wind to pick up.

All around the Knights of Maphrax were piles of ash, the dust and bones of the fallen. More soldiers tried and every one of them fell, the colour and life drained out of their bodies.

Seer magic flared at the Shadow Knights' backs but failed to affect them. Issa struggled to draw breath.

Velonorian crouched beside a pile of rubble towards where the Knights of Maphrax walked. Ducking low, he prepared an arrow, one of the special ones, and there he waited.

Issa mind whirred, analysing the elf's hare-brained idea, seeing if it could work and deciding it couldn't. *Suicide! How could it possibly work?* If he stayed where he was, when the Shadow Knights passed, he'd be in range of their life draining magic. She had to stop him.

She urged Duskar on. Between her and Velonorian, a tight knot of Maphraxies and foot soldiers battled. She navigated round them only to be hampered by the piles of rubble. She looked to Velonorian; he was still a distance away. A Shadow Knight turned its eyes upon her, the air wavered and she felt the life draining from her even from this distance.

'Issa,' a voice whispered, quiet, yet cutting through the din.

She pulled Duskar back. Sharp pain stabbed in her mind making her gasp, the world rocked and became faint and immaterial. A mournful caw ripped through the sound of battle. White wings passed across her vision, and ice-cold fingers trailed down her spine. The white raven looked at her as it glided over the battlefield, then turned and disappeared.

The world ceased wobbling and rushed back towards her. Blood sprayed her face as a soldier fell beside her, his screams deafening. Duskar reared to take down the Maphraxie. Dazed, she could only hang on. Smoke filled her nostrils, making her choke. The enemy was everywhere, twisted Maphraxie faces roaring all around. Her eyes fell on Velonorian and time slowed.

The Shadow Knights had stepped past the wall he hid behind, and his drawn bow was already aimed. The Feylint Halanoi and Maphraxies wrestled beside him, then fell in front of him, blocking his view. She could almost hear his cursing from here. Controlling his mount like no human could, the elf climbed to stand deftly in his saddle, lifting above even the heads of the Feylint Halanoi horsemen.

His aim was clear, and he was close enough for his shot to be true. The angle was such that the Shadow Knights would not see the elf unless they turned right around. Issa held her breath as seer magic moved, and she entered the Flow. Reaching out, she touched the seer magic, guiding it, drawing it towards Velonorian and his target.

Velonorian loosed his arrow – he could not miss. Using the Flow, Issa bridged the gap between his arrow and the seer magic, forming a connection between the two, making it more powerful.

She didn't know why she turned then and looked out of the Flow, something caught her eye but only after something nudged her to look that way. She only caught a glimpse, but there, in a doorway to the right, one storey above the ground in a broken turret, stood a man. A man not dressed in metal armour but in dark leathers and a pristine cloak, a man with a pale grey face and smoothed back slate-coloured hair looking towards Velonorian. His hand was raised and the device he held fired, a little bout of orange and yellow flames to light up the grey and white picture. The dart was small, tiny in fact, she shouldn't have been able to see it, but she did, and she knew that its aim was also true.

Velonorian's arrow and the seer magic reached their destination, and her attention was caught in the deafening explosion. The scream of a shadow horse was cut off as white fire engulfed it. The Knights of Maphrax reared, black forms writhing in white fire and becoming more solid as the fire forced their shadows to become real. Their hooves pounded the ground making it shake, then molten red cracks snaked over the nearest horse's legs and up its fetlocks, splintering keratin and flesh. The front legs crumbled under it, followed by its chest and its head. The Shadow Knight resisted, clenching its fist and raising its sword, then it exploded in a spray of black rocks and smoke.

Seeing their victory, the Feylint Halanoi dared to run forwards to attack the still standing Shadow Knight. Behind it rushed a horde of Maphraxies and death hounds to meet them.

Issa's gaze dropped to the ground and rested on the pale hair and golden helmet of the man lying there. Against the grey of the wall, the press of friends and enemies, and the smoke and gore, he was a fallen flower, a splash of vibrant colour in an otherwise grey and dark world.

'Velonorian!' The scream tore itself from her throat. She leapt off Duskar and ran, clambering over the fallen walls and destroyed buildings. She didn't even look at the death hound that jumped at her, Illendri was already swinging. She felt its cold blood on her face but did not see the mortal wound she'd delivered. She saw only Velonorian, the angel laying still upon the ground.

She fell beside him, shoved his helmet off and lifted his torso. Vivid blood spurted from his lips—lips that were turning an awful shade of blue. His eyes fluttered open, his beautiful violet eyes she wished she'd been born with, and they were fading. He looked at her, his cursed adoration and loyalty brighter than ever.

'What a shot, my Queen,' he said, trying to laugh but gasping instead.

'The best!' she sobbed. She clutched at his armour, looking for the straps to undo it, and her fingers touched the horrible hole in the metal above his heart. 'Get it off, Velonorian. I can fix this,' she snarled.

He lifted a cold hand and took her fumbling ones. 'No, Lady Issa, the dart has passed right through, touching my heart with its poison. Also a perfect shot. Hah, what a weapon, strong enough to pierce even Elven metal – we have never heard of the like. Fight for me, my Queen, help my people take back their land.'

'I'll fight beside *you*.' Issa clenched her jaw.

'It is cold,' he said.

'No, Velonorian, no.' She took his hand and held it against her cheek. She would not let another die in her arms like her sister had, like her mother had.

The light in his eyes faded.

'No,' she screamed. Grabbing her talisman, she shouted the ancient words and slammed it against her chest. Her raven mark flared, and the Realm of the Dead engulfed her in a cold embrace.

Issa blinked in surprise at the flare of white that greeted her. The world was not grey for Velonorian was there in ethereal form, and an incredible pure light surrounded him. He was larger than in life, his body not armoured but dressed in swathes of light. He was beautiful, serene, an angel looking down at her.

She stared up at him and he smiled, his face so full of wisdom and understanding she felt like a child who understood nothing at all, nor the magnitude of what was occurring.

He reached down a hand and caressed her cheek smoothing away the tears. In his touch came understanding. She could not save him. She could not keep him here and it was not her right to do so. For one moment filled with longing, she wished she were going with him into the light.

'You must go on, you have not finished yet,' he said, his voice more melodious and harmonic than ever it had been in life. 'Zanufey is here. Free the magic, Issa, free Woetala and our people will be free.'

Velonorian began to glow, brighter and brighter until he was all light, and then he vanished, along with the Realm of the Dead. The battlefield came rushing back to her and the beauty and reverence of the spirit world was lost. Blood, dirt, clanging metal and the screams of the dying assaulted her.

She let Velonorian's body go, his face now as grey as the world around him. For all the peace and wisdom of the moments before, it was fury that descended upon Issa.

The white raven was for Velonorian and for the others. It wasn't for me! It should be for me! With a roar she jumped to her feet. Her raven form came quickly, and she flew high, scanning the turrets and hunting for Hameka. She would kill him like Asaph had killed Vornus.

'Issa.'

The voice shook the air and she stumbled in mid-flight. The dark rift above filled her vision, a black tear in the darkening sky that the grey clouds could no longer hide. She beat her wings harder, lifting higher into the air, and looked to the horizon. In the distance, barely visible, flew a golden dragon and two black ones beyond it. *There is hope!*

'Hameka!' she screamed with her mind.

Where was the worm hiding? Issa ordered the weak and unwilling Flow forwards. It flickered over the ground below, hunting for the one she had named. It flared upon a cross-section of walkways connecting the ramparts to the castle. She darted towards it, the spell already forming on her lips ready for when she landed.

A long mournful caw echoed across the mountains, and white wings glanced across her inner version. *But Velonorian is gone, so why do I still see the white raven?* She had no time to ponder, Hameka appeared, just where he had been moments before, his hand already raised with his strange device, from which a strange clicking sound came. *He must have cloaked himself!* she thought as Ehka shot towards him. The man lowered his arm, not taking his eyes off her, had he decided not to shoot her?

She didn't see this dart, perhaps her soul spared her. It ripped through her right shoulder, barely missing arteries, scraped several bones, then passed out the other side in a spray of black feathers. For a brief moment she felt relief, she would live through this, the wound was not mortal, and then she felt the trace of what had been on the dart just before the pain hit.

Not poison! Every cell in her body cried out and trembled, and her soul shrivelled. Her squawk turned into a cry as her raven form left her, forced from her through no will of her own. Icy cold radiated through her body and she tumbled out of the sky.

Not poison, something much worse. The white raven was always meant for me.

Issa hit the hard, snowy ground at the base of the castle well behind enemy lines. Her body convulsed. She had broken no bones in the fall, but her body would not respond, she was paralysed. It convulsed again.

Hameka leant over the rampart to look down at her, the barest smile touching his emotionless face.

'Issa,' the voice whispered, so close, it sounded like it was right next to her. Beyond it she heard the sounds of the Dark Rift, the contorted howls, the twisting metal, the strange words that made sense only to a lost mind.

The Sirin Derenax forced its way into her veins, rapidly spreading throughout her body, carried by her traitorous blood into her heart, her lungs, her brain. It was a small amount, the dart could not carry much, but it was enough. Her body convulsed again, and the freezing pain spread. She arched her back, a strangled scream clawing up her throat and out of her mouth.

Maphraxies crowded over her view. She surprised herself, fury found her even then. Illendri tightened her grip around it, and through its will, she smashed it up into one of their ugly faces, and watched its head disappear in a spray of black goblets. The Maphraxie beside it roared, lifted a huge iron boot and stamped down onto her sword arm. Ely's bracelet at first resisted the boot, then it shattered, followed by the bones of her wrist. More pain added to her agony and she screamed.

Illendri flared madly. *Protect the orb!* She was about to speak the spell but another Maphraxie pounded a fist into her face. Blood sprayed, this time her own.

The world shook and she felt a strange whooshing sensation. In the next instance she was looking down at her body from above. She saw herself utterly surrounded by Maphraxies with Hameka commanding them from above.

Her body was polluted, she could see blackness infecting every cell, pulsing in every vein. The wrist was broken, blood poured freely from it, and Ely's bracelet was shattered around her bloodied hand—not that it could heal this curse within her.

She looked up. The mountains were beautiful, patches of orange sunset broke through the clouds and touched their snow-covered peaks and valleys. She could go now, she could leave and never live through whatever might become of her and all that they would do to her.

In the distance a golden dragon roared, reaching for her.

She glanced down at her body. A symbol snaked upon the ground beneath her, luminous green upon the snow. Smoke billowed from it.

She felt a strong pull and suddenly she was rushing back towards her body. She fell into it hard, only to find herself plummeting further. Darkness and green smoke engulfed everything, then she slammed into something solid and it was agony that made her consciousness leave.

CHAPTER 36

Knights Falling

ASAPH slowed enough to let the first Dread Dragon get close.

Its fire singed the tip of his tail and in response he dropped dangerously close to the ragged edge of the mountain where one twitch of his wings could catch the rocks and send him catapulting.

The Dread Dragon closed in, its fearlessness and skill impressive. *Skill from when it was a Dragon Lord,* he thought, *and dead things don't feel fear.*

The next ridge loomed. He darted over it, the snout of the dragon behind him almost touching his tail. Asaph pretended to falter, clumsily losing his grip on the air. The Dread Dragon bore down on his rump, mouth open and roaring.

Asaph pulled in one wing, virtually closing it and turned violently right. The immense force on his open wing tore at his muscles, spraining them painfully. The wound in his shoulder ached and wind wailed around him.

There was a loud thump from behind and a crack that shook the mountain. Asaph glanced back to see the Dread Dragon sliding flaccidly down the mountain, its neck broken and its Dromoorai flailing on its back. The other Dread Dragon dropped back, watching its fallen comrade as it tumbled into the ravine.

One day, some explorer will find a Dromoorai encased in ice. Asaph found the thought amusing. He considered turning on the other dragon, he could take it on now the other was dead, but as he flew over the next ridge he faltered. On a wide snowy slope stood another Dromoorai beside its Dread Dragon and alongside them, a sight that sickened him. Laid out before them was the destroyed and gutted remains of a green dragon. Blood soaked the mountain for yards around the carcass and a blood river trickled over the edge.

Asaph roared. *Dromoorai feed upon their own kind!* But they were not his kind, he reminded himself. *I'll destroy every last one of them!*

Fury blotted out all reason as a dragon's rage was meant to do. He dropped out of the sky, intending to land upon the Dread Dragon's back, but the well-rested and well-fed dragon was quick. It lifted its bloody maw, roared and moved with lightning speed to attack. The two dragons smashed into each other.

The dragon's power and strength swiftly reminded Asaph he'd been fighting for more than a day. He hadn't slept, and he hadn't eaten. Quickly, his attacks turned into evasive manoeuvres, and all he could do was keep away from those massive snapping jaws. Its Dromoorai rider and the other Dread Dragon were closing in, too.

Blasting magic and fire, he drove it back and, rather than attack, he turned and leapt off the ridge. He dropped low and found a strong wind to lift him up. He sent his mind out, searching for other dragons to help him, but he found their minds far away and scattered. They did not respond, they were busy. How many had fallen like the green behind him? Was this to be the end of dragons? *No, it must not be!*

Asaph tried to use magic to fly faster, but it required an immense use of the Flow and he simply didn't have the strength.

A cry cut through the ethers, not the cry of a dragon, but a human. It took him a moment to realise he'd heard it in his head, in the Flow, not with his ears.

Dear Feygriene, Issa!

He turned back towards Draxa, forgetting the Dromoorai. The Grey Lords loomed, their sides so steep even snow had trouble clinging to them, leaving them a patchwork cloak of white and grey. As they passed beneath him, Draxa loomed in the shards of an orange sunset.

A dark beam of energy flooded from the ether directly onto the castle. He looked into the Flow and saw the Under Flow pouring from the sky, streaming from the dark rift. Baelthrom, it had to be. Beneath that unholy beam, white light pushed back. Even from this distance he could feel the two energies straining against each other, a battle between magic.

As he neared, he saw the white light came from within the castle and focused on its signature. The magic was wholly female, and it had no particular elemental feel, meaning it used earth, fire, water, and air in equal measure. Seer magic, he recognised it now, but there was no ether, there was no prime force. Issa was not a part of that magic, so where was she?

'Where are you? I can feel you!' he sent his thoughts out, sparing a glance behind to see the tireless Dread Dragons had not given up. *'Reach for me, Issa!'*

He heard her scream in his mind, the flame ring she wore burst into fire in the Flow, calling to him. An explosion rocked the air and the Flow shuddered violently. Asaph struggled to see what was happening. The Under Flow built in pressure, but the seer magic increased to match it, and both flared as the Flow strained, it was exhausting just to observe it.

Green light flashed, and he felt strange dark magic move—not black like the Under Flow, this was different, natural but touched by evil and not of Maioria. *Demon magic,* his dragon memories told him, it rippled swiftly outwards from its centre and then vanished, along with the flame ring and Issa. Asaph paused in the air, blinking. Where had she gone?

'Issa!'

Marakon hurtled after the fleeing priest, leaping up the stairs, uncaring if Eiretonne and Bokaard were right behind or if he had run ahead alone. Asaph had told him everything he needed to know about the New Order Priests. He didn't care that they might still be human – any blood drinker or murderer of children deserved to die.

The closed door halted the priest momentarily as he fumbled for the handle. Marakon leapt upon him, seeing the terror in the man's eyes as he brought his sword down. He shielded himself from empathy and remorse and ran the man through.

'I gave you mercy with a quick death,' he said between clenched teeth as the dead priest slid down the door. 'It's more than you deserve.'

He kicked the door open and paused. Bokaard slammed into his back then Eiretonne slammed into Bokaard. They all staggered into the room and stared.

The entire room was filled with a humming and thronging pillar of bright white light. The pillar rotated in both directions and figures stood within it, barely visible in the glare. The pillar extended up into the ceiling and seemingly beyond. Where it touched the ceiling, black light flared.

'I'm no magic wielder, but I *can* see this,' Marakon whispered, too awe-filled to break the silence.

'An epic struggle ensues,' said Eiretonne, gripping his axe before him and staring up at the black light.

The black and white light flared and crackled against each other. The black light grew, pushing the white light down, the white light flared and pushed it back. Again and again this happened.

'It's coming lower each time,' Marakon noted of the black light.

'Seer magic is strong, it will fight,' said Bokaard.

'The stories of old are true,' said Eiretonne. 'These *are* the end times.'

'Get the wizards,' commanded Marakon, stepping further into the room but keeping his distance from the pillar.

'They're exhausted, Marakon,' Eiretonne replied, who was his friend more than his soldier. 'Shelley can no longer stand and Haelgon sleeps whilst he's being carried. Luren? He can't stop shaking.'

'Get the wizards!' Marakon shouted, his eye locked onto that slowly descending black light.

All three wizards were brought into the room. Haelgon's eyes flickered open and he stared at the pillar, then the others did the same. All the wizards' eyes were luminous and otherworldly, and Marakon had trouble looking at them.

'The Trinity!' Haelgon gasped and got off his stretcher. The three wizards stood and stared at the pillar of light.

'You must help them,' said Marakon. 'Look at the black light. The Under Flow will break us all.'

As he stood before the pillar of light, Marakon knew his use here was over so he shuffled out of the room. Now it was up to the wizards. He considered hunting for enemy to kill when the unmistakable roar of a bear rattled the broken window.

He ran to it, smashed through the remaining glass with his armoured fist and peered out, trying to make out who was who in the war that raged outside. The entire city was a battlefield, everything was levelled, and bodies littered every bare patch of ground. Given the utter destruction, he wondered if the place was worth saving. His eyes lingered on a fallen brown bear, a terrible wound gaping in its side. He quickly scanned the field. There were other bear riders, alive and dead, but none of them were Jarlain.

It was to the black lightning and shadows materialising out of the ether that his gaze locked on. He held his breath as the two Knights of Maphrax formed. *Knights of Maphrax…My knights!*

Soldiers fell writhing before them, their eyes rolling back in their heads and their faces turning ashen. The shadow horses, once shining white steeds, were now beasts made of horns and ugliness. Their riders, once noble knights, now lost forever to the oblivion from which they were made.

Hally, Drenden, Konnen…The pain in his chest was physical. He clutched the windowsill, the world rocking violently, the sting of unsurmountable sorrow. There was no warning, just a flaring arrow wobbling wildly as it streaked from the rubble towards the knights, followed by a flash of light, then an explosion that blasted him back against the wall. Stunned, he rolled and crawled his way back to the window.

The light faded and a Knight of Maphrax turned to crumbling, smoking rubble. The emboldened Feylint Halanoi rushed forward cheering and Maphraxies ran to meet them. One knight still stood; still powerful. It lifted a smoking hand and with a simple movement, soldiers fell to the ground screaming for the death hounds to leap upon.

Velistor hummed on his back, making its presence known, reminding him of his duty. Sheathing his sword he reached up and pulled the spear free.

In the hallway behind him echoed the howls of Maphraxies and the yelping of death hounds. They were coming. He caught Eiretonne's gaze.

'Do what you need to do, we'll cover your back,' the dwarf said, then turned and ran. 'Bokaard! Maphraxies! Let's go!'

Marakon gave a grim smile and looked back to the last knight of his cursed legion. The Knight of Maphrax raised its arms and swept its sword wide, the movement hurling soldiers high into the air.

Hefting Velistor onto his shoulder and stepping away from the window, Marakon prayed to Zanufey to make his aim straight. Bracing himself, he ran, a scream tearing from his lips. He reached the window and hurled the spear with all his weight. It was a long way between him and the Knight of Maphrax, impossibly far.

Staggering against the window frame he could barely watch the spear fly. It wobbled under the forces, shooting over the heads of Maphraxies, then straightened, keen on its target. Marakon stared, his mouth hanging open as it thudded straight into the last Knight of Maphrax.

There was a brief pause and then an explosion shook the world. Rock and shadow flew into the air, and Marakon squinted through the smoke. Cheering erupted from the Feylint Halanoi, and Marakon sagged against the wall, laughing. 'It is done,' he sighed.

'The wizards are here, beloved Iyena,' said Dar, joy in her voice.

'Then the transition can begin, blessed Dar,' said Iyena, hearing and feeling the other seer's thoughts and words as her own. They were the Trinity, and now they had become one.

'No sadness, my bright ones,' said Suli.

The three seers allowed the light to fill their bodies completely, they would not be needing them beyond the mortal planes, and assigned themselves to their last task—to hold the pure light for as long as they could. There was no sadness, only joy, the promise of freedom, and the satisfied knowledge of a task finally completed.

Only Naksu, who was outside of the Trinity, emanated immense sadness. 'Is there no other way? I can bring you back. For a short time, I can be the portal to Maioria. If you go, the Age of Seers will have ended.'

'Do not weep, beloved Naksu,' Iyena's beautiful voice caressed her, angelic in its tone. 'This is as we have foreseen. Now the time has come. The seers upon Maioria have outgrown their purpose and now reach for that which is higher. They will, in time, become something far greater than we ever were. Do not be sad to let go of those things you have outgrown. Maioria is moving upwards, so all things must follow her too, but first we must all rid ourselves of the darkness.'

Wizard magic suddenly moved into the light, surrounding them in effervescent silvers, purples, yellows and greens—a beautiful rainbow swirling into their white pillar. The seers sighed, a sound filled with absolute relief and absolute joy. Naksu could feel a little of what they experienced—

something broken combining, a missing part found, completion of the ultimate, and in its wholeness, greater power forming.

'Our magic is whole once more,' breathed the Trinity. 'Feel it, Naksu, feel the combining of our power, it is wondrous.'

The power grew exponentially as the two magics combined, faster and faster. The black energy above them trembled and was shoved back. It resisted and then the light exploded.

Naksu felt power move through every particle of her body, rushing around and through her. The Under Flow disappeared. There was nothing but the light, within her and without, rushing and flaring and exhilarating.

The beautiful light and all the power it contained, faded. The seers were gone, and all the light and power she had felt dissipated. They had given their lives to push back Baelthrom one last time. Naksu's senses returned and her physical body became heavy and dense as a deep exhaustion she had never really known dragged her down.

Strong arms caught her. She blinked in the darkness, barely seeing the dark empty room where the Trinity had once been. Her eyes travelled over the purple robes of the one who held her and into the luminous eyes of the Atalanph wizard. Knowledge, power and understanding united them in a moment. As their eyes met, she felt again a touch of what had been shared in the pillar, seer and wizard magic made one.

The man smiled. She knew his name but couldn't recall it. She knew him better from the divine feel of his energy signature that she had touched only briefly in the pillar of light.

He smiled, he felt it too, and in that smile, all the sorrow and loss of the Trinity, and of her friends, left her. She was not alone. She would never be alone. She lifted her hand, noting how white it was, and he caught it in his large dark hand and brought it to his lips.

CHAPTER 37

The Darkness Within

MAGGOT cowered as another ear-breaking scream burst from Issa.

She arched her back and clawed the air with her good hand. She had tried to use both but her broken arm was tied down, along with her legs and shoulders to restrain her against her own convulsions. The veins bulged on her neck, not the usual delicious human blue, but black.

Maggot covered his ears and whimpered. 'What's happening to Issy?'

'Yes, what's wrong with it?' Wekurd scowled at the ugly, writhing human.

King Gedrock stared down at her, frowning. 'Why did you bring her here, Maggot?'

'Zorock told me to!' Maggot tugged on his ears. Nobody fully believed him but Zorock *had* told him to.

In the darkness of the human castle when the black light fell from the sky, the Demon God had come to him in a flash of light. His terrible green face and mighty black horns made even Maggot's blood run cold with fear and reverence.

'Take her to the Murk,' he'd commanded. 'The race of demons depends on her survival.'

Maggot repeated again what Zorock had told him. Convincing King was not easy, convincing himself that the demon gods spoke to him was hard enough.

Gedrock rolled back his shoulders, muscles rippling in the dim green crystal light. He opened his wings and then closed them again as he considered the enormity of Maggot's words.

'Why the gods speak to the smallest demon in the Rock, I'll never understand,' huffed Wekurd, coming to stand beside King.

Issa let out another pain-filled howl, making the raven beside her squawk madly as well.

'Shut it up,' Wekurd hissed, snapping his fangs together threateningly at the bird.

'He wants us to help her,' Maggot wailed over the noise, clamping his claws over and squashing his pointed ears. 'He wants us to stop her pain.'

Issa's scream subsided.

'Demon magic is not good for humans,' Gedrock said quietly. 'It changes them. This one is being changed enough already, it would kill her.'

Maggot crawled over to where the large demons stood and peered at Issa. She looked so sick with her skin so white and veins pulsing black. Her broken wrist was a blackened mess of blood and bruises. It had taken them quite an effort to release her grip from the sword she had held. It stood in the corner now, leaning against the wall, the blinding orb covered over with a bloody rag.

'We should get rid of her now before the whole of the Murk falls again, my King,' urged Wekurd, standing as defiant as an old demon could in front of his most commanding king. 'I'll do it, if you prefer. Now, whilst she's weak, it can be done quickly.'

'No!' King barked. 'Wekurd, you have seen the tear in our skies— distant, faint, but there. Every demon can see it; we are no fools. If it's as large and close as Maggot says it is on Maioria, then it will be coming here soon after that planet is gone.

'I've seen things in the crystal I wish I'd never seen. I cannot undo the visions, and I should not ignore the warnings.' Maggot glanced at the green crystal beside the giant stone throne as King spoke. 'You saw our days were numbered even before we fought Karhlusus. In this girl, rests our future, even now in this state. I've seen a time that has not happened yet, so I know she will live in some form or another.

'Not far from now we'll stand on a red and barren plane under skies that aren't our own. Demon blood will flow, lots of it, but we will not be destroyed. The alternative vision is…is our end complete.'

Wekurd stared hard at the ground, his eyes narrowing and the tip of his tail curling and uncurling around the base of his staff. 'I do not like this, I do not,' he muttered shaking his head. Gedrock turned from him and glared at Maggot.

'Maggot, fix her hand,' he ordered. 'Get Dung if you need help. Fix it in the demon manner with demon magic and we'll see how she copes. There is no other choice.'

King stalked off, his tail swishing and his shoulders hunched. He wasn't pleased – Zorock's message did not sit well with him. Wekurd followed the king leaving Maggot alone beside Issa.

'Issy?' he squeezed her arm.

She moaned and fluttered her eyelids but did not open them. Using demon magic, he set to work on her shattered wrist.

Issa's soul evacuated her poisoned body.

It couldn't easily inhabit something tainted by a substance meant to remove and enslave it. From afar she watched her body fighting and trying to rid itself of the plague spreading through every cell. It was not a battle that could be won.

The Under Flow moved all around her, not taunting, not attacking, *waiting*. For some reason she no longer feared it. But it was the newfound lack of fear that made her afraid—afraid of herself.

'Issa,' the voice called from close beside her. 'Issa. How do you like my gifts?'

Issa opened and closed her spirit hands, feeling the Under Flow move around them. There was power there, much power, she only had to reach out to use it.

'No,' she said.

'Have you seen what's in the Dark Rift? Great things, great understandings, great beings.' Baelthrom's voice came from everywhere.

'No,' she whispered.

Despite the darkness all around and within, there was the light, there was herself, she had not lost that, *yet*. There was also clarity in this disembodied state and she understood a little of what the Under Flow was. It was simply a type of power, the light turned in on itself and made into its opposite. That was how it existed, because of the light.

'Just because a thing exists doesn't make it natural; it doesn't mean it *should* exist.' Her voice was calm and well-reasoned. She pulled away from the darkness and Baelthrom's voice, and focused on the light within.

She thought about Asaph and an image formed before her. A golden dragon flying, desperate to get to the burning city ahead. She saw his thoughts and they were filled with her.

'Asaph, I'm alive, my love. I'll come back. Wait for me.'

A blast of white light blinded her, *seer magic.* Immediately the Trinity and Naksu appeared in the image engulfed in a pillar of white light. The Trinity were giving their souls to the light, becoming one with it, and Naksu grounded them.

Each seer represents the elements, Issa realised. Knowledge came easily to her in this space and she found she understood things she couldn't possibly have worked out before.

Iyena is the strongest element; air. Dar is fire. Suli is water, and Naksu is the earth that grounds them. I will not see the Trinity again; this is the end of the seers.

The realisation made her ponder. It wasn't sadness as such, just a deep brooding. *Go into the light, my sisters.*

Wizard magic flared into the white pillar and the purity of the power touched even her in this suspended state. *A power made whole, two broken factions united, a prophecy fulfilled.* She witnessed Haelgon embrace Naksu and all was made right. Something new was being created in the ashes of the seers and wizards, something far more powerful.

The image faded. Just thinking of a person would draw her to them or them to her, she was neither bound by time or space, nor hindered by a physical body. Was this what the soul did when the body died? They say the soul remains for three days after death to comfort loved ones, was this what was happening?

She saw Marakon running over a field of the slain, his face covered in mud and blood. He caught in his arms an equally bloodied warrior woman with a spear; beside her, a great bear limped. But they could not embrace for long for a battle raged around them.

The battle for Drax goes on without me. Where is Freydel? An image of a red, ravaged plane appeared. Travelling fast over it, the image slowed to settle upon a stooped old man dressed in ragged robes.

Freydel? He looks so old, it cannot be. Where is his staff? The old man clung to a gnarled piece of wood that held no magic. His aura was dull and not the vibrant colours of a Master Wizard. She watched him crawl into a cave and huddle his knees to his chest, eyes staring out fearfully.

His magic has left him, he's broken. But he did not choose darkness to get his power back, there is his honour. For a noble soul, there is always redemption.

Her vision lifted and travelled some distance before slowing upon another figure. A plump old woman walked carrying a heavy sack slung over her shoulder. She clung to her walking stick and used it to stumble along the rugged mountain pass, whilst a heavily burdened donkey snorted beside her, struggling under the bags tied to it.

Edarna? Issa felt joy.

'Come on, Miss Burdens,' the witch wheezed to the donkey. 'We're all tired, but if Naksu can do it, then so can I!' She paused at the top of the hill gasping for breath. A cat meowed long and loud and jumped down from a rock. The blue cat purred and looked directly up at Issa from where she watched.

Edarna snorted. 'Now Mr Dubbins, don't be ridiculous, Issa is NOT here. She's busy fighting and doing warrior things—all those things I told you she would do. Hah! Now we must do our part and clean up the smaller messes. War is no place for an old lady.'

She sighed, wrapped her green cloak around her, and sat down on a rock. She pulled out her monocle and squinted into the distance. Through the gaps in the mountains, red earth was revealed, and in the distance the sky darkened with muddy clouds.

'There it is, folks, there's Maphrax. Somewhere in there is a broken wizard. Now, Mr Dubbins, you tell me as soon as you sniff that wizard stench.'

Edarna heaved herself up and continued her waddling down the road towards Maphrax.

Issa smiled, the simple strength of Edarna again making her wonder.

The image faded, and she drifted easily. There was no pain here, there was only serenity and clarity. She did not want to return to her body, not ever.

A beautiful sound of tinkling bells came from above. It was like nothing she had ever heard on Maioria, and it grew louder, the music filling her soul and becoming part of her. She joyfully lifted up towards it.

'No, Issa,' a melodic voice spoke and her upward rising halted. Murlonius appeared, tall and elegant, swathed in shimmering robes.

'You're here? You can see me?' she asked, then noticed the terrible sadness on his face.

'Yes, I too wait for the light, but I cannot leave, I cannot leave her here. You can't leave either; you must face him. Each of us must complete our tasks. The end is close now. I care nothing for the outcome any longer. I long only to sleep.'

Issa stared longingly at the warm light above that beckoned her, the music coming from within it, calling to her. *But what about Asaph?* The light and music faded a little.

'No, you're right, I can't leave him,' she said, feeling weary and sad.

Murlonius vanished, along with the light and music. Immense physical pain dragged her back into body, her right hand felt like it was both on fire and encased in ice at the same time. Her whole body spasmed with pain, icy fire burning within every particle. She longed to leave her body again, just to be rid of the pain.

She tried to open her eyes, struggling to know where her lids were. Darkness, a green glow, then Maggot's huge yellow eyes with long slitted pupils appeared.

'Maggot,' she gasped, relieved to not be alone. 'The pain!'

'Maggot,' she whispered his name over and again. 'I'm falling.'

'No, Issy, your hand is healing. It's the Dark Rift poison causing the pain.'

She tried to flex her right hand and screamed as the pain stabbed deep. She looked at her hand, it was whole and no longer a crushed, mangled mess but it was dark and had a green sheen to it. For a moment it morphed into a demon hand, slender but dark grey with long, sharp demon claws. Was she hallucinating? She blinked, and her hand returned to normal, albeit dark and green glowing.

'We had to, Issy, your hand would have killed you, so we had to use demon magic. The ring you wear, it's green demon crystal, it saved your hand from being destroyed completely. Without the ring, our magic would have killed you, too.'

Belledyn's ring, who'd have ever guessed! Issa tried to laugh but a moaning sigh came out. 'Thank you, Maggot,' she managed before a nauseating wave of pain flooded over her.

Her soul retreated, Maggot and the room vanished, and the Dark Rift gaped open before her. Fear slithered through her and she steeled herself against it. The black drink moved within, and she detested the plague inside, but there was strength to it, it gave her power, determination, and a certain bloody-mindedness.

'I defy you!' she shouted at the Dark Rift and embraced her raven form. She launched herself at it and the tear in the sky swallowed her.

Within it, a whole universe unfolded. Entire planets moved amongst great plumes of cosmic gases, dark reds, blues, greens and blacks—a heavy place of slow but powerful energy. A planet loomed, and a gaseous cloud formed beside it. The cloud was conscious. It reached out an enormous hand to grasp the planet in long, spindly, gaseous fingers and the planet turned ashen. Great cracks snaked across its surface and then it shattered into dust in the cloud's hand. The dust swirled and was then sucked into the gaseous being.

Light Eaters!

In the distance, other planets and more Light Eaters moved. She didn't feel fear, but she did feel a loathing hatred and desire to end this.

'Issa,' Baelthrom whispered.

She looked for the owner of the voice but there were only planets and Light Eaters in this enormous space.

'Don't you recognise me, Issa? I don't need that cumbersome physical form anymore.'

Cosmic shadows clustered into a giant cloud. A Light Eater rose before her. Fear brushed her soul, but it was anger she felt.

'I feel your fury, it belongs here,' Baelthrom sighed wistfully.

'Nothing belongs here,' Issa said. 'Maioria is not yours to eat.'

Laughter came, not mocking, only amused. 'It's far too late. If Maioria does not fall into the rift, it will be shattered by all else that does. Come to me and I will give you the power to move planets.'

'I don't want it!' Issa screamed.

Her energy flared as light and Baelthrom sucked it towards him and devoured it hungrily. He sighed and grew larger.

Shaken, Issa struggled to control energy, her emotions. *It's the Black*

Drink, it gives me rage. My rage feeds Baelthrom.

Weakened, Issa drew back, and Baelthrom followed, eager for more. She would not give it to him.

'It will be as I have seen,' she said, her voice low. 'We will stand against you on that unhallowed earth you call Maphrax, and we'll drive you from it, or we'll lie down forever with our ancestors, but you shall not have our souls—not now or ever. I'll give everything that I am to see this come to pass so that all others can live.'

'So be it, Raven Queen. Either way, *you* are mine.'

'There is a dragon outside, my King.'

Wekurd tore his eyes off the enormous golden dragon gleaming with a greenish hue beneath the full moon of Zorock to look at the Shadow Demon king on his throne. 'A dragon has not been seen in the Murk for five hundred thousand years. Not since…'

'Not since Firestrike,' Gedrock finished for him.

Gedrock got up and stalked through the door onto the balcony and stared down at the dragon. Maggot followed, flapping up and down excitedly. The dragon looked up and lifted its head, rising so high, it came halfway up Carmedrak Rock. Sapphire blue eyes narrowed as it looked at Gedrock.

'Where is she?' the dragon commanded rather than asked.

Gedrock stared at the beast for a long moment, then beckoned. 'Come and get her. Please take her away, she's too much trouble.'

Asaph gripped his sword but did not unsheathe it as he walked into Carmedrak Rock.

Demons watched from the shadows and hissed at him as he passed, but when he looked at them, they fell back and huddled against the walls, reminding him that they too were nervous. Sweat covered his face though it was cold and clammy here, and fear nibbled at his heart, demon fear. Unlike Issa, he had no good relationship with these cursed beings. *But if it weren't for them, she would not be alive.*

A gnarled, stooped, old demon with a staff appeared in a dark doorway.

'This way,' he hissed, his yellow eyes gleaming.

Without saying more, he led Asaph up and up until he was breathless and soaked in sweat.

The demon paused beside a room. 'We have saved her, but there have been some...*changes*. Nothing can be done about the black magic that consumes her.'

Thoughts spun through Asaph's mind. 'I must see her.'

He pushed past the demon into the room and gasped.

Beside a green crystal lay Issa, her face deathly pale, her hand oddly green. He gasped again when it turned dark grey and became a demon claw, then returned to normal.

She moaned, and he dropped down beside her. Grabbing her good hand, he brought it to his cheek and kissed it. She opened her eyes, dark clouds moved in her corneas and then cleared to reveal luminous turquoise.

'Asaph,' she breathed and gave a faint smile. 'You came.' Her face contorted in pain and she cried out. He pulled her against his chest and held her.

'It's inside me, Asaph,' she gasped. 'Hameka's dart, it had Sirin Derenax, not much, but enough. I can *feel* the Dark Rift, it calls to me, it's within me, I'm falling to it.'

He stroked her hair, swallowing his fear, trying to be strong for her. What could he do, how could he help her? He felt ill. 'No, not yet, we can fight it. There's time, not much, but there is time.'

He held her as she drifted off to sleep, then curled up beside her under the watchful eyes of Ehka and Maggot. The little demon kept his distance, but Asaph was touched that he would not leave her side.

When Asaph awoke, Issa was looking at him. She smiled and lifted her good hand to touch his cheek. He kissed it. She seemed stronger.

'You must come back with me,' he said. 'The Murk will make you weaker, not stronger. You need to come back to Maioria.'

A look of longing passed across her features and she frowned. 'Not yet, I can't make the journey, travelling between realms will tear me apart, but you must go. Gather the armies, take them to Maphrax. Forget all other battles, let all be lost if it must. I've seen the alignment, there's so little time. We'll face him on the planes before the Mountains of Maphrax.

Many will die, but we must do this.'

The effort of speech wore her out and she closed her eyes.

Asaph pursed his lips, he didn't want to do this alone. He didn't want to leave her here. He watched her for a long time as she drifted back to sleep – at least the pain could not touch her there. He caught his breath as her veins pulsed black and ugly, and then paled back to faint green. He dared not think he might lose her.

Setting her hand down gently over her chest, he stood and turned to Maggot.

'I leave her in your care, Maggot. Do not leave her side,' he commanded the little demon.

'Yes, Dragon Lord,' said Maggot, struggling to meet his hard gaze.

Asaph softened his tone; this loyal demon had never left Issa from the start. 'I know you will stay with her, Maggot, you have most unusual qualities.' He walked towards the door and paused. 'Be ready. Soon, you and all your kin will fight alongside us on Maioria's soil. It will be for your own freedom too.'

He forced himself to walk out of the room and leave Issa, and headed down the dark stairs to Gedrock's throne room. He'd get the king to rally the demons, then he'd return to Maioria and rally the dragons. Issa was right, they had little time.

'You killed my mother and therefore my sister.'

Issa stood before King Gedrock seated on his throne. She was not recovered, and never would be, but enough days had passed where she could now stand. She placed her hands on her hips, feeling both weak from her wounds and yet strong from the black drink. Fearless—fearless enough to face the King of Demons.

The black drink gives me immortal strength—a strength I neither wish for, nor enjoy. I will endure and use it, until I can be rid of it.

Maggot clutched her calf and Ehka perched on her shoulder. Gedrock's eyes glowered at her, but she did not care, she demanded answers.

'Not directly,' Gedrock growled. 'Things were different between demons and humans then. To be enslaved by a human is the greatest insult to a demon. All humans who conjure demons and ensnare them deserve to be killed by that which they enslave. Your mother, and her mother before her whose ring you wear, knew the risks and deserved all that unfolded.'

'You betrayed them,' Issa growled.

Gedrock stood to his full, towering height and raised his wings menacingly. 'Demons are beholden to none, especially not humans. Deceit is survival, honour is worthless to us, a weakling's attribute,' he scoffed.

Issa rolled back her shoulders and looked at the green crystal. She was letting her pain and sorrow for her sister and mother cloud her judgement. *Demons are what demons are.* They acted in accordance to their nature. She could not blame them, and she could not fight them for being what they were—it was a double-edged sword, to trust a demon. *It was Lona who truly killed my sister in the end. I need these beings as allies, no matter how distasteful they might be.*

She turned away, unsatisfied, with her need for revenge unfulfilled. Her sorrow at the way the world was, at how things had unfolded, unsalvageable.

Gedrock relaxed and reseated himself. She could feel him watching her.

'The Dark Rift grows within you,' he said. 'An ocean of rage, never seen before in a human.'

Truth spoken by a demon! Issa shut her eyes. The rage swirled within her and it would boil up if she didn't control it. She could let it consume her, the hatred and desire for revenge against all that had befallen her, against those who had done this to her. The power of the Dark Rift was ever there, exhausting, all-consuming, but it was Maggot's pressing hands that calmed her.

'I only have to bear it for a little while,' she whispered. 'The end is coming.' She didn't know if she meant her end or the end of her enemies.

Gedrock nodded. 'We demons are ready. When Velistor opens the portals, then can we come. Do not waste time, Raven Queen, we grow restless. If the Dark Rift consumes you fully before then, I'll kill you myself.'

Issa nodded, strangely grateful for his merciful words. 'You have become a demon with mercy, King Gedrock. Please see to it that you make it swift and painless.'

Gedrock held her gaze then gave a slight nod of his head.

Issa stood before the Star Portal.

She didn't think she would find it from within the Murk, not in her condition, but it came to her as before. Ehka perched on her shoulder and Maggot hovered beside her as she stood before the sacred mound. It was dark but not a fearsome dark, rather one of permanent twilight, the peace and stillness found at the closing of the day.

Tiny white and blue flowers dotted the grass over the mound, hinting at spring, and thick, billowing mist marked the boundaries through which she could not see. This place was a small patch of Maioria moved into the higher realms to protect it. *And all that might be left of the planet once this battle is over…*She pushed the thought away, she would not think of defeat here in this sacred place.

I should just walk in and get this over with. Asaph's waiting for me. Marakon and the Knights of the Raven, the Navadin, the wizards, and what remains of the seers— they're all waiting for me on the borders of Maphrax, waiting for the final battle. And I'm waiting for the dark moon to rise.

But for all the urgency, Issa stood gazing at the sacred mound, its pitch-black entrance framed by ancient monoliths and the standing stones surrounding it as silent guards.

What if she could no longer enter? A fear like no other paused her first step, caught the breath in her throat, ate at her soul. The black drink coursed through her veins; she had become that which she hated most. What if Zanufey had abandoned her? She stayed poised, staring at her deepest fears and the guardian stones turning into her accusers.

Ehka croaked, making her jump, and flew off her shoulder straight into the entrance. The spell broke, her fear shattered, she let out the breath she'd been holding and laughed. Maggot looked up at her questioningly. Issa shook her head, shrugged, and followed Ehka.

Intense cold seeped into her bones and then a warm wind greeted her. She breathed deeply of the dusty desert air before opening her eyes, allowing the relief to wash over her. She could enter; she was not barred.

The night sky and blue sand stretched out before her, and ahead stood the dark, sparkling trilithon. She walked slowly towards it, her Dread Dragon boots sinking into the sand. A feeling stole over her that this was the last time she would ever come here. She should be sad, but she wasn't. *If I fall or rise, at least there will be change, release, anything but this unending war.* She was ready to go into the Dark Rift herself, to make the ultimate sacrifice in the attempt to save Maioria, she realised that now. *I can make peace with that, and I must do it before the Dark Rift within consumes me.*

The air between the stones shimmered, and out stepped a tall, majestic woman robed in the stars. Issa's eyes lingered on the huge black hole now engulfing the goddess's torso. There was no surprise, just the monumentality of the task before her.

Issa bowed her head, overwhelmed. 'I feared that I could not enter and you would not come.'

'Fear does many things to a being, Maion'artheria.' Zanufey's soft voice was filled with wisdom and compassion.

Issa nodded, then dared to speak the truth, the facts. 'The darkness is within me now, I feel it growing. I can see from within the Dark Rift. It's become a part of me... I'll not be able to withstand it for long.'

Zanufey spoke softly, 'How can you heal that which you don't understand? How can you remedy a malady you have never felt?'

Enlightenment touched Issa's mind and for the briefest moment she felt the pure light of the One Source shining down upon her, so awe-inspiring and encompassing she caught her breath, and tears filled her eyes.

Issa whispered. 'On the edge of Oblivion I stand. I see the light disappearing far above me and the end of all lights. Within the rift, there is no love, there is only disharmony, only darkness. All things light and whole, it shatters and consumes.'

'Then you must be the light unto the darkness, Maion'artheria,' said Zanufey. 'Be the last light in a falling world.'

Unstoppable tears blurred Issa's vision as they fell. Zanufey cupped her cheek, her cool hand stilling the torrent of emotions that welled within. She wanted to cry for all the lost, all the darkness, and all the evil growing within her – it was a torrent only Zanufey could soothe.

'I could try to save Ayeth,' Issa whispered. 'Now I can reach him in the rift, now I can hear Baelthrom inside my head. Maybe I *can* reach Ayeth like Freydel did. The light has left Baelthrom, but it is still within Ayeth.'

'There can be no hope of saving one so far gone,' said Zanufey. 'The mercy is in ending it. It is hardest for those still connected to the light to watch others disconnect and fall into darkness.'

'Is there no hope for the damned?' Issa whispered.

'Always there is hope. Why else did Ayeth let himself fall trying to save Lona? If enough beings return to the light with memories of how they were before they fell, the fallen can be reborn anew. In that way, nothing is ever lost. Nothing is ever outside of the One Light.'

Issa sniffed and wiped her eyes. 'But we must not lose ourselves, Maioria and all her people…I have to try.'

'I am with you, Maion'artheria, always.'

CHAPTER 38

Gates of Oblivion

'ARE you all right?' asked Asaph.

Issa stared up at him, noting the frown creasing his brow.

'You fell asleep again and were moaning and tugging your clothes,' he said.

The darkness passed, her clenched guts relaxed, and air filled her lungs, bringing her back to life. Baelthrom's image faded but the blackness within her did not.

She didn't say anything, she didn't want to speak aloud about the poison within her, and instead embraced him. He rubbed her arms and she pressed her face against his hard chest, finding solace in the strong beat of his heart.

The din of the officers' tent descended upon her as the darkness passed. She'd fallen asleep on the chair but thankfully no one other than Asaph had noticed. She often fell asleep suddenly, without warning, even in the saddle, and the Dark Rift would open and swallow her up. She'd returned to Asaph from the Murk two days ago and re-joined the legions marching to Maphrax.

'You don't have to be here with the soldiers,' Asaph said softly. 'You've done enough, and you are not... *well.* The war will continue with or without you.'

She glanced at the view partially revealed through the tent flaps. Red sand and rock, no grass or trees or rivers to be seen for hundreds of miles, and in the distance, the three black peaks of Maphrax.

Military commanders clustered around a table full of maps and diagrams, voicing their thoughts and concerns, some almost shouting to be heard. King Navarr was taking the lead, dressed in full armour apart from a helmet, he leant on the table. Though most bent to his authority, everyone was tired, and tempers were frayed, the march here had been long and arduous. Dread Dragons harried them the entire journey, murdering scores of soldiers then flying off before they could be taken down. Such attacks came at random, especially in the night, and it wore them down.

Watching the officers quietly from beyond, stood Naksu, Haelgon and Luren. Even Marakon had stepped back from the heated table, the look on his face mirroring her own feelings; they could plan all they wanted but war had a mind of its own.

When it came to it, a strategy was useful, but this battle they were about to fight would not follow any rules, they could not plan it all. Little they did now, in this flimsy tent before the gates of the enemy, could possibly change what was going to happen in the next few days. War was chaos, and this would be chaos defined.

Her eyes were drawn to the black mass in the sky, partially visible through the gap in the tent. She could feel its draw on her physical body now, not just her mind and soul. They could all feel it drawing them in. If she stared for too long she felt herself lifting towards it. She shut her eyes and focused on another power growing, another power calling to her. She focused on the rising dark moon. She was sure it helped slow the immortal changes she was going through, helped slow the death of her physical body.

In a day or two, the dark moon would rise. Then was her chance, then was her strength. It was the only thing that could give her the power she needed to face Baelthrom.

'Come, let's get away from here,' said Asaph, interrupting her thoughts.

He took hold of her hand and led her outside. Duskar snorted, he was tethered beside the tent with a few other horses. She stroked his nose. In the valley below, partially obscured by a line of jutting rocks, she saw the giant rumps of two dragons, a red and a green, sleeping. *Even the dragons will not be enough,* she thought and tried not to imagine their race being utterly destroyed.

With their eyes to the skies, Asaph and Issa walked hand in hand along the dusty path. Perhaps this had been a main road once, thought Issa, imagining the land that had been Tusarza covered with green grass and meadow flowers. Was that a dried river bed down there? Could it flow again? She sighed.

They came to a rocky alcove that faced east, away from Maphrax and out of sight of the black scar in the sky. Asaph sat on a flat rock and she perched next to him, neither of them speaking. They watched the dark red clouds billow above.

After a time, she turned to Asaph and kissed him. He cupped her face when she drew away and pulled her close. They kissed again, and their passion ignited. Fiercely, wildly, they pulled off each other's clothes, both fearful it would be their last. Issa let the magic take her, giving herself fully into it as Asaph's yellow and orange fire consumed her.

She gasped, feeling once more the purity of wholeness when they combined. For one beautiful moment the black drink within her was gone, as if he had the power to purify her. She wanted her innocence back, and Asaph could give it to her.

She trembled as he trembled beneath her, for now she was free. She clung to the feeling. 'Never let me go,' she gasped.

'I cannot even if I try,' he whispered.

Issa gripped Duskar's mane.

They cantered up the side of the ravine to the cliff above. Illendri was warm in its scabbard at her side; the orb sensed its sisters in the distance and wanted to return to them.

The air was heavy and charged, and her head had pounded with a dull ache ever since they'd stepped into the cursed land. Something to do with the red thunder clouds pressing down on them, something to do with the tear in the sky she and everyone else tried every minute of every hour not to look at.

For now, she looked down, down into a wide ravine where their armies marched. The boots of the soldiers pounded rhythmically, their pennants trailing like ribbons, their freshly polished armour glinting.

At the front rode the Knights of the Raven headed by Marakon. As if sensing her eyes upon him, the half-elf commander looked up from his bay mount. He would not take a white mount, not since his previous one had ascended. Their eyes met, and he saluted her. She smiled and saluted back, the gesture feeling awkward.

The Knights of the Raven's ranks had grown to reach nearly a thousand. They were the best of the Feylint Halanoi, well-seasoned though not jaded or injured, and ready to fight Maioria's last battle and pay with their lives. Pride swelled within as she appreciated their pristine tabards, squared shoulders and determined expressions.

Hundreds of Navadin followed the Knights, led by a proud woman holding her spear high. Even from here Issa could hear the bears' growls, their massive bulks lumbering behind the horses. She'd never have thought she'd see the beasts of the forest fighting alongside humans.

Following the bear riders marched Draxians, their blue tufted helmets vivid against the red and grey desert. They were far fewer in number, but their ranks grew every day as more Draxian exiles joined them.

Behind them, in far greater numbers, marched the Feylint Halanoi, their tabards a blaze of red and gold, and then she stared at another sight she never thought she'd see. A thousand-strong Saurians walked without armour, holding their brightly feathered spears and turning their quick, furtive faces this way and that, ready to leap upon the enemy at any moment. They did not march, and she sensed such orderly undertakings did not come naturally to the lizard folk, and neither did being surrounded by so many humans. She suspected, worried even, that what she gazed upon was the entirety of the Saurian race. *An entire race ready to die for their beloved Maioria.*

Her eyes travelled to the elves who followed them, dressed in their ornate golden helmets and armour. *'Save our people,'* the pain stabbed deep as she remembered Velonorian's final words. She took a deep breath. *I will do all that I can, brave Velonorian.*

She turned her gaze from the elves and looked at the Karalanths walking behind them. At the front she was sure she could see Rhul'ynth, and maybe that was Cusap'anth beside her. Was Grast'anth with them? She had not seen her old sword master for a long time. *Dear Zanufey, I hope we meet again when this bloody battle is over.*

Her eyes travelled over the armies of Atalanph and then Davono, noting their distinctive tabards and fearsome looks. Picking up the rear with their war drums marched the barbarians of Lans Himay, who wore no helmets or metal armour. These tall, heavily muscled warriors, were swathed in fur and leathers and armed with any blade or blunt weapon they preferred—and lots of them.

She trailed her eyes back and forth over the thousands of soldiers; so many armies combined into one force and from this day forth they would fight as one. They were a vast army to her eyes, seemingly unstoppable, but how could any army defeat a rift in the sky? She swallowed hard.

Wizards marched amongst them, she even spotted the purple robes of one of the Circle, but it wasn't Freydel. He was not here when his people needed him the most. She no longer felt anger towards the wizard, to the teacher who had abandoned her. Instead, she saw the old broken man cowering in a cave.

She lifted her gaze to the top of the ravine where two red dragons perched, on lookout duty. Rust and Garna were tasked with guarding the ravine as they marched through it. This road—the only passable route to Maphrax—was ripe for an ambush. More dragons circled the skies.

'The Dread Dragons have retreated,' said Asaph, bringing Ironclad alongside her.

His mount tossed her head, sensing what was to come. Asaph stared hard towards Maphrax. The three ugly peaks reared less than two miles away, and they were enormous, dominating the landscape. Issa refused to be intimidated by them. *They will fall, they will fall,* she said to herself, over and again.

'For days, the cursed Dromoorai have harried us, trying to wear us down, but they have not stopped us.' Asaph gave a hard grin.

Butterflies fluttered in her stomach as Issa considered the monumental events taking place, of what was expected of her, expected of them all. It seemed impossible. Seemed.

'Let's join the others, companionship and camaraderie are the things we need most right now,' Asaph said. He must have noted her pensive expression for he reached over and squeezed her arm.

She smiled, allowing the tension to ease, then jumped when a roar came from directly above, making their horses whinny and rear. Issa gripped Duskar's mane and tried to calm him as Ironclad bucked and Asaph cursed. The ground shook as a young green dragon landed several yards away. The dragon was smaller than the others but still enormous at this distance. It opened and closed its mouth and seemed to be grinning – if dragons *could* grin.

There was something on its back and Issa gasped. 'Can it be…Is that a…?'

'A dragon harness? Yes,' Asaph finished for her as he grappled with sword and rein.

An intoxicating laugh boomed, and a man stood up on the dragon's back, gripping the harness. His shoulder-length white hair was kept out of his face with a headband. His thick beard came to his chest and his face was wrinkled yet his body was well muscled. He looked to be at least sixty years old, and she could definitely add ten or twenty years to that for the longer-lived Draxians. He wore a very beaten Draxian helmet, ragged Dragon Legion tabard and leather jerkin, and leather trousers.

He pulled off his helmet and whirled it around his head. 'I got one, look!' he shouted.

'Goodness me, a Dragon Rider of old!' Issa said incredulously.

She managed to calm Duskar enough to get him to walk forward. Asaph forced Ironclad closer by shouting at her and jerking his body. The horse stepped slowly, determined not to be ruled.

'You managed to convince her?' Asaph said to the man when they neared, indicating the dragon and gawping.

'Over Draxa, you two made it look like so much fun,' said the female dragon, answering the question for the man on her back. 'A Dragon Lord and a Dragon Rider hold their own inspiration, though most pure bloods might not agree. But anyway, I can always take a dip in the sea should I tire of his company.' The dragon gave a smoky snort.

Asaph laughed and looked from the dragon back to the man. 'You're a Dragon Rider, one of the original?'

The man nodded, grinning from ear to ear. 'I was barely a man when Coronos led the Dragon Legion just before he retired. I never thought I would fly again, but ahhh, the majesty, the wonder! When Drax is rebuilt, we'll live the glory days of old once more.'

The man's joy was catching, and Issa dared to imagine Drax restored to its former glory, of even Tusarza beautiful once more.

'Now one dragon has accepted a rider, others will too,' Asaph said, his eyes sparkling. 'You, Sir, are the First Dragon Rider! The responsibility rests upon you to guard the army and liaise between man and dragon. This, I command you, as your prince.'

'It will be done, Sire, and you command me not as my Prince but as my King! Yeeaaah!' he yelled, lifting up. The dragon beat her wings, gusting air and sand around them, roared, and rose fast into the air where it joined the others.

Garna and Rust, having witnessed the whole spectacle on the opposite side of the ravine, roared and lifted to join their sister.

Asaph laughed and looked at Issa, his face alight. With a whoop he kicked Ironclad into a gallop down the hill and back to the marching army.

Issa chuckled. She was just urging Duskar after him when something made her pause. Fear, an icy finger down her spine, the movement of the Under Flow to which she was now so attuned.

'Issa,' a voice called, all other sounds stilling to silence. She turned Duskar around looking for the owner of the voice, it sounded so close.

There, on the closest part of the opposite ravine where the red dragons had perched, a black cloud swirled and took shape. Issa suddenly felt alone, vulnerable. A pounding began in her head.

Baelthrom appeared in the same manner as he had ages ago when she'd stood in the burnt-out ruins of her house and knew nothing of the horrors plaguing the world—smoke and darkness turning to form. His lizard legs bulged with muscle and his eyes blazed red. Seconds passed as hours as she stared at her emerging enemy, fighting the fear that threatened to overwhelm her.

Ehka landed on her shoulder. Her guardian glared at Baelthrom.

'Raven Queen,' Baelthrom said and gave a low chuckle. 'You can't stand against the power of the cosmos. The might of the Dark Rift and all within it cannot be withstood.'

'There are other powers rising—ones over which you have no control,' Issa growled.

'The Dark Rift grows within you, making you stronger, my gift to you. How else do you think you could survive the fall into Oblivion? You *will* survive, and then you'll come to me. You will have to.'

'No,' she shook her head. 'It won't happen as you plan. The will of the people, their power, is stronger than you think. If any of us survive—here or in there—we'll find you and we *will* destroy you.' Rage boiled, almost overpowering her. She trembled, trying to hold it in rather than unleash all her power into the bastard right now. It would be a waste and he could best her easily. She needed the dark moon, and she needed it soon.

'As you wish, Raven Queen. See you on the other side.' Baelthrom's form turned to swirling smoke and vanished.

Issa let out her breath, feeling suddenly faint. She gripped her saddle for a long moment.

'Issy?' a small voice spoke. Maggot flapped in the air before her. 'Danger.'

She straightened. She scanned the area where Baelthrom had been, but he was gone. 'Yes, there was, but it's gone now.'

Worry, fear of failure—she clenched her right fist, the one she now kept gloved to hide its demonic appearance. At least it was strong and fully healed, she thought, maybe even stronger. It was a small price to pay compared to Velonorian. *No, do not think of those fallen, think of those saved.*

She turned from her reverie and looked at the little demon. 'Get the demons, Maggot. The time has come.'

Edarna heaved herself along the craggy path huffing, panting and sweating.

The old donkey snorted and strained alongside her, and the blue cat padded ahead unburdened, a permanent smile on his face, or, rather, a smirk, so Edarna thought.

'These legs ain't what they used to be, Mr Dubbins.' She paused and pulled out a hanky to wipe the sweat from her face.

'Oh my, Mr Dubbins, look at that.' Her mouth went dry.

Down in the valley and far into the distance, so far they were just pinpricks, thousands of soldiers gathered before the black peaks of Maphrax.

'No, that's no place for an old woman. Best left to the younger folk, those wars and *things.*'

She didn't like war or battles much either. Sure, she'd enjoyed creating Issa's armour, and enjoyed a well-muscled man just like the next, but the whole fighting bit? She'd rather do without it.

'It's just not me,' she sighed. 'I was never a battle witch. I make my potions and work my powers far from the front line.'

Her eyes travelled further, resting on the horde of Maphraxies amassing at the mountains' base. Dread Dragons circled above them, their screams faint but audible. A cold shiver shook her body and a heavy feeling settled in her heart.

'Pray to the Great Goddess the armies of the Free Peoples are enough, Goddess bless them. We can only do what we can do, Mr Dubbins.'

Mr Dubbins meowed, his whiskers flicking as he looked to the Mountains of Maphrax.

Edarna turned away from the battlefield and focused her attention, and her monocle, on the task at hand. 'Ah, there's the trail again,' she said, noticing a barely visible footprint. 'And look, man-sized, long and skinny, just like wizardy feet. I can almost smell him; we must be close.' She rubbed her hands together with a grin.

Freydel rocked back and forth on his haunches, his hands clasping his head. He was only vaguely aware of the moaning coming from his lips. He was beyond hungry, but a ravenous thirst consumed him. The last trickle of his canister had run dry yesterday morning, or perhaps it was the day before, but he refused to look for water, not when before now he would just have caused it to spurt from the ground.

No, he would not look for water when it had always been at his command! Now his one love had left him, he would rather die than be without his power. He sat on his haunches because the hard ground hurt his bony hips, and his spine ached when he lay down. There was no point laying down anyway, sleep never came.

He lived in a hapless world devoid of magic, devoid of anything worth living for. Time may have stopped for all he cared. So he sat, on his haunches in the narrow cave, his own moaning keeping him company as he waited for death, waited for release.

'Now stop that!'

Thwack!

Pain smarted his eyes as something small and pokey struck him on the back of his head. Another hallucination come to taunt him! Wouldn't even his mind leave him alone? Cursed consciousness, when would it end? He moaned all the louder.

Thwack.

'Yeow!' he howled as the stick struck again.

'Stop it! Or Wandy gets cross!'

Freydel stopped rocking and peaked through his fingers at the hallucination—this time it wasn't a giant frog but a plump old woman. She couldn't be real, could she? What did it matter if she was?

'Leave me alone, curse you!' he wailed, glaring at the awful woman whom he vaguely recognised but whose name completely escaped him.

The wicked woman brandished her stick menacingly. Freydel slowly put "Wandy" and the wand she held, together. 'Get away from me, foul witch, can't you see I'm busy?'

'Nobody ever got busy dying,' she scowled, unimpressed.

'I'm already dead, I just have to get out of this cursed body!' he screamed, although his parched throat and emaciated body ensured his voice held no commanding authority. Even he realised he sounded like a wheezing old man.

'Now you listen to me, you wizard, there's more to life than wizardy things. There's magic in all things if you dare to look for it. The magic has left you, any fool with half an ability can see that, but when one door closes—'

'Another one slams in your face. Now leave me alone!' he howled.

'Nope!' she scowled and crossed her arms under her large bosom. 'You drink this potion I have, and you'll start seeing sense in no time. There are people out there asking where you are, they need you and you owe it to them to return.'

She rummaged around in a large pouch tied at her waist and pulled out a thin blue glass vial. She waved it in front of his face. Inside, an insidious grey liquid sloshed. He thought he was going to vomit.

'You've got barely a day left in you, now drink it.' She pulled the cork and shoved it towards him.

'No, let me die here alone!' he wailed. Only one day to freedom? Oh happy days! He was so close…The moaning came again, this time with anticipation.

Thwack.

'Ow!'

Something invisible took hold of his hand, it made him clench his fingers around the bottle and slowly forced it to his lips. He tried to resist but he was so weak a child could have pushed him over. His own body had betrayed him, curse it and curse the goddess for making it!

His lips were forced open, the bottle tilted and liquid burst into his mouth. He refused to swallow but unseen fingers pinched his nose. Now he couldn't breathe—he refused to breathe. His throat betrayed him with a gasp, and he spluttered as the foul liquid sloshed down, feeling like his nose and ears were ingesting it also.

He breathed liquid and air then keeled over retching. Nothing came out, though he wished it would. His desperate, traitorous body clung to whatever had been delivered down his throat. It tasted like mud—no! Excrement—demon excrement. It was ghastly!

The horrendous, maddening dehydration began to fade. The pounding in his head turned to a slow soothing whooshing and the world softened into colourful hues all around him.

'Ahhhh,' he sighed as overwhelming relief washed over him.

Edarna grinned and nodded her head. Without speaking she settled herself beside the wizard and took out her last sandwich. Carefully she set half aside for the wizard for when the potion had worn off. Giving him anything else at this moment would cause all sorts of nasty eruptions from all sorts of orifices. Well, that's what had happened to her anyway.

The wizard giggled. 'I see fairies.' He lifted a bony finger and pointed at the ceiling. 'Blue and greens, they float and laugh.'

Edarna smiled at the old man suddenly turned into a child. Perhaps the wizard might just live. Perhaps the wizard might just put aside wizardy things and learn some of the other magicks of the world.

Mr Dubbins watched the wizard then turned to Edarna and purred loudly. She grinned at the cat over a mouthful of food, and he winked a large golden eye.

CHAPTER 39

Oblivion's Reach

ISSA made her way down the winding path to the bottom of the ravine.

Asaph cantered a hundred yards ahead, and a hundred yards beyond him marched the tail end of the army. The air suddenly rippled and shimmered between her and Asaph, as if someone had dropped a pebble into a pond. It was so subtle, not even Ehka sensed it as he flew the distance between them. There was no rush of either the Under Flow or the Flow, and no prickling feeling on the back of her neck as the black vortex opened up before her.

Duskar reared to a halt before the swirling black. Issa pulled her sword free. The dull throb of her constant headache now turned into thunder. Time slowed, and her limbs became heavy as an immense weariness weighed down her sword arm.

The Under Flow hit her full force in the chest, straining ribs, and shuddering through her pounding heart. Duskar staggered beneath her.

Issa raised her hand to command magic, but the Under Flow rose to do her bidding. She gasped, horrified as black magic gathered at her fingertips, so strongly she couldn't even feel the Flow. There was no time to choose, so she whipped her hand and the energy blasting her rebounded back to where it had come from.

The heavy feeling abated and Duskar recovered.

Lona appeared in the vortex, her eyes vicious and scowling, and behind her clustered at least twenty of her race. Most of the Yurgha were bald but some had black hair tied up in elaborate styles. They all wore the same strange shimmering black robes, made neither of cloth nor leather.

Lona lifted her hands. In one, she gripped a black orb. Issa stared at it. It was just the same as Freydel's Orb of Death. Black and blue lightning flared from it, towards her.

'Shield,' Issa commanded.

Again the Under Flow responded, leaching power back to her, away from Lona. It shimmered around her protectively. Lightning snaked over it as she held back Lona's power. It crackled and hissed, the shield strained, sweat soon trickled down her temples and she began to feel sick. *It's the Under Flow,* she thought, her body rebelling against the unnatural forces she unwillingly commanded.

Lona roared and dropped her hands, the lightning vanished. 'So, the fool has given you the power of the Dark Rift. This, then, must be done the old way.'

In her other hand, Lona raised a thin black rod—it looked like a wand but made of crystal or stone, not wood—then turned and motioned her people forwards. The black-eyed Yurgha started walking towards Issa, their faces hard and expressionless as they stepped out of the vortex onto solid ground.

Issa pulled Duskar back, she could not take on twenty. The black stick hurtled towards her, she didn't even see Lona throw it. She ducked but it hit her shoulder. Agony ripped through her body, her jaw slammed shut biting her tongue and drawing blood. She fell from Duskar and hit the ground hard.

The horse bared his teeth, flattened his ears and pranced between her and the Yurgha. Suddenly the horse was lifted bodily and slammed against the cliff face.

'Duskar!' Issa screamed, as the horse slid to the ground.

The stick that had caused her so much pain lifted in the air and struck her again. She convulsed and screamed, unable to do anything but endure it. She glimpsed Duskar struggling to his feet, sides heaving, nose to the ground.

The Yurgha advanced slowly and a cruel smile cracked Lona's face. Through the agony, Issa fumbled for the Flow or the Under Flow, she no longer cared which.

'Block her!' Lona shouted.

Just as she touched the magic it vanished. The stick lifted in the air, Issa tried to roll away, her entire body shaking as if she had been hit by lightning. The terror of that pain was uncontrollable, if she could run away from this fight, she would, but her body had been turned into useless jelly.

Lona made a strange movement with her hand. Her fingers danced in the air, and the Yurgha beside her did the same. The vortex surged forwards swallowing Issa and enveloping them all in walls of swirling black.

Lona advanced, lifting the black orb and stick, her eyes predatory.

There was a shudder, a vibration in the ether that made Lona pause and the Yurgha look around them. It came again. The air rippled and swayed, making nothing appear to be quite solid.

'What was that?' Lona hissed to the man beside her who wore his black hair just on the back of his mostly bald head, tied into a small but elaborate top knot. His eyes were black and as cruel as Lona's.

'Something comes,' he growled, looking back into the vortex—then his eyes widened in fear.

Issa heard and felt nothing, not even in the Flow, but all the Yurgha fell to the ground as if the earth had been pulled from under them. A golden rope snaked out of the black and lassoed the man around the neck. He screamed and grabbed at it but the rope tightened, yanked back and beheaded him in a spray of white blood. His head and body fell into the black vortex.

Issa gagged.

'Anukon!' howled a female Yurgha.

Another golden rope darted out of the bulging black walls of the vortex, lassoing the female who had screamed in warning. The other Yurgha leapt to her aid and then they were all battling against a force Issa could not see. She rolled on to her stomach and scrabbled to her knees, her body shaking so much there was no way she could stand.

She watched as the Yurgha screamed and fought and died in front of her, their alien howls piercing her ears – a sound she would never forget.

A Yurgha dropped right in front of her, felled by a strange alien being that shimmered as it appeared on top of him and stabbed down with a glittering blue shard. The Yurgha screamed and writhed and then vanished. The being stood and turned to Issa. It was bigger than a Yurgha and humanoid in form but hairless, and a little like a Histanatarn. However, this beast was powerful and heavy with muscle. Its skin was green, becoming pale peach on its chest and stomach. Dark green spots flecked in an orderly fashion over its hairless face and head. Its nose was wide and flat, and its mouth long and turned down. Its ears were large and pointed and its eyes small and yellow-orange.

Issa caught her breath. It opened an impossibly large mouth to reveal a blue tongue and rows of tiny, dark, pointed teeth. It roared and started towards her.

Issa crawled weakly away, crab-like. The black stick that had tormented Issa now turned upon this creature. It battered the Anukon on the head, sending it to its knees with a roar.

'Die, Anukon!' Lona screamed, and the Under Flow burst from her orb into the creature. It howled, convulsed, went silent, and then exploded, showering everything in pale green gore. The smell was something else. Issa vomited.

The vortex wavered erratically and the walls that had imprisoned Issa now began to flicker and fade. Another Anukon leapt close, but it didn't see her trying to crawl away and whipped its lasso to snare another Yurgha. Chaotic energy exploded and the whole vortex shuddered and shrank.

She had to get away before the Anukon came for her as well. Issa crawled onto her feet, hunting for a way out, but the vortex walls still surrounded her.

Lona screamed suddenly and ran towards Issa, panic vivid in her black eyes. In her desperate haste, the Yurgha dropped her orb and agony wand. A lasso whipped up and Lona fell, her arms out-stretched. The look of absolute terror on her face made Issa lurch towards her.

She caught Lona's pale, delicate hands, a wave of conflicting emotions assaulting her. An Anukon lunged, blue shard raised.

'No,' Issa screamed as the shard descended.

She felt Lona jerk, her hands clench and release. Her black eyes opened wide and stared at Issa as a pearly white liquid fell like tears from them and from the corners of her mouth. Lona gasped, her eyes glazing over as she was viciously yanked from Issa's grasp and back into the vortex.

Five Anukon appeared before Issa and roared. The black orb rolled towards her, capturing their attention, and they scrambled for it. One fell in the struggle, impeding the others, and a fight broke out between them.

Another pulled free and lunged for the orb.

'No!' Issa screamed and lunged for it as well, sprawling on the ground in the process.

The Anukon got to it first and with a roar of victory grabbed the orb. A look of surprise formed on its face, then it twisted in pain and jerked violently. The veins in its neck turned black and it screamed as its skin burst into flames, the orb tumbling from its grasp.

The vortex trembled violently; there were no Yurgha to manage or sustain it. Air rushed into it, sucking on Issa as she got to her knees. She fell back to the ground as tornado-like forces tore at everything. The vortex heaved, then folded into itself and vanished.

Issa lay on the red dirt gasping, her cheek pressed into the ground. She looked up, there was nothing, no Yurgha, no Anukon, no bodies or blood of any sort. She sucked in the heavy air, wishing it would give her sustenance. In the next moment, Asaph and Ehka were by her side.

'Are you all right?' Asaph helped her to sit. 'What happened, did you fall? Another vision?'

'No.' Issa almost laughed at the thought. 'Didn't you see anything? Something much more…much worse—Lona came, in the vortex. There were many Yurgha and then the Anukon attacked them. Hah! Maioria is being attacked by far more than Baelthrom and the Dark Rift.'

She suddenly remembered Duskar and staggered to her feet, using Asaph for balance. The horse had trotted over, his ears back and his head drooping. He seemed unharmed apart from the grazes on his side. *Thank the goddess,* she thought, and hugged his neck.

As she drank water from her canister, she told Asaph what had happened. Some of her strength returned but she longed to lie down and rest. Duskar could do with it too.

'The Yurgha are always fighting the Anukon and the Rorsken, so Freydel said,' she finished. 'That was how they fell in the first place. I…I tried to save her, I don't know why. I saw her terror, like my sister's, like any other being afraid. But I could not.' She felt confused.

'That bitch just tried to kill you!' Asaph growled. 'I hope she died painfully. Pray to Feygriene, they don't return. The last thing we need right now is more enemies attacking us.'

She nodded and was about to climb into her saddle when she froze, her gaze falling onto the black orb lying innocently on the ground.

Asaph stared at it too. 'What the...? That thing is evil.'

Issa walked slowly towards it. 'It *is* evil, I suppose.' For a long moment she looked at it remembering how it had destroyed the Anukon. She crouched down beside it and slowly reached forward her gloved right hand, the strange demon magic in her hand tingled.

'Don't touch—' Asaph spoke too late. She touched the orb. It became hot and energy flared from it over her hand, not painful but sharp, like pins and needles. It was testing her just as the other orbs in her care had done, and then it accepted her. *Is it the black drink running in my veins?* But she could not know why it hadn't destroyed her.

Illendri did not respond to the orb at all, not like it did when in the presence of its true sisters. Slowly, Issa stood lifting the orb. 'It killed the Anukon because they're enemies of the Yurgha, and perhaps because Lona was not dead at that moment. I suppose she's gone now. We're not enemies of the Yurgha, though they try to make us so. This holds Yurgharon power, I assume it uses the Under Flow.'

'Throw it into the Abyss before it destroys you,' Asaph growled.

'I'll get rid of it, but not into the Abyss where it can be used by something worse than demons,' said Issa, pondering on what to do. 'It must be destroyed, but for now I must keep it away from those who would use it to do harm. It *will* destroy me in time, just as Freydel's orb has destroyed him. I won't keep it long, but I feel that this thing has an as yet unforeseen purpose.'

'I don't like it at all,' Asaph shook his head but said no more as he helped her into the saddle.

They took an easy canter to catch up with the others, and all Issa could see in her mind was Lona's face, her terror, her fading eyes. *The woman murdered my sister, destroyed my mother and tried to kill me several times. She corrupted Ayeth and caused the fall of Aralansia.*

Issa *did* hate her and it was a burning hatred, yet in the woman's last moments she had felt pity. *The Dark Rift might be within me, but it has yet to destroy my humanity.* She clung to that, even if being human was painful. How long would it take before the black drink consumed her completely? How long before she could no longer fight it? If there had been any more poison on that dart, the change would have happened already. She would not think about that, there was still time to do what she had to do before the end.

I'll be dead before the black drink takes me, she promised herself.

Issa stared at the monstrosity that were the mountains of Maphrax. The three peaks of black rock she'd seen in visions and nightmares made the breath catch in her throat. They towered above an otherwise flat plane, bridging the gap between the barren land and endless stormy sky.

Between them and the mountain stood hordes upon hordes of Maphraxies, more than she had ever seen, an insurmountable number.

'Do not be put off by their numbers,' Marakon said gruffly by her side.

'Whatever our numbers, our soldiers are worth two to every one of them,' spat Bokaard, who stood the other side of the commander.

She glanced over her shoulder and saw legion upon legion of their own glorious army, helmets gleaming gold and silver, pennants trailing above them. Her heart swelled, how could they fail?

Her raven mark tingled. She closed her eyes and felt for the dark moon. She imagined it rising, huge and dominant over the mountains, casting its blue light over the barren land and banishing the unnatural storms plaguing this place.

Thunder peeled, making her jump and forcing her eyes open. Black light burst down through the clouds hurling straight into the central mountain.

'What's this, more trickery? Better get on with it,' growled Eiretonne, indicating the impending battle. The dwarf looked rather awkward atop a huge chestnut stallion. He had his axe already drawn.

Dark energy moved, and the Flow became erratic. Issa gripped Illendri in a sweaty palm, licked her lips and prepared to use it in an instant. She glanced up, Asaph flew above them with five other dragons, all keeping their eyes on the huge forms of the Dromoorai perched on the mountainside of Maphrax. The Dromoorai had not yet been given their orders, otherwise they'd be attacking, and somewhere, deep within his lair, Baelthrom watched and orchestrated this whole evil scene.

Soldiers shifted nervously as the air became charged with unbearable anticipation and fear. Issa forced her breath to come slow and deep.

Light flared and the Under Flow surged towards them, faster than she could track. It smacked against their magic shields, shattering them. Horses reared and bucked, soldiers fell or were hurled into the air. The Under Flow engulfed them, confusing minds, making horses bolt, spreading terror into every living heart. Their entire ordered front line scattered into disarray.

A piercing horn sounded, followed by a roar and the shaking of ground as the Maphraxies advanced.

Perhaps it was the black orb at her side or the black drink within, but Issa regained her senses before the others. She struggled to control Duskar but he whinnied and shied, and her mind could not reach him.

'No, no, no,' she gasped, whirling around to see the Maphraxies and their Foltoy and death hounds pounding towards the floundering army. They struggled in the Under Flow, whereas she did not. *I must break the spell!*

Issa leapt off Duskar and forced her shaking legs to run towards the enemy horde. She tried not to look at their howling faces, their swinging black iron maces, and paused somewhere between the two armies. Unsheathing Illendri, she let the Flow fill her body, and with a scream, plunged her sword down into the earth.

The Flow burst out of her body, through her hands and into her sword, joining with Illendri's power as it streamed into the earth. The immense force threatened to drag her with it, and she pulled herself back, fighting to withstand the unleashed power of Illendri.

The ground heaved and became like liquid around her blade. It rippled outwards from her in a wave, the ripple growing in size as it rolled towards the enemy with increasing speed. Issa stared open-mouthed as the enormous wave smashed into the Maphraxie front line, hurling them into the air. The lesser waves that followed it knocked those still standing to their knees.

'Maioria fights back!' she gasped and pulled Illendri from the ground.

A roaring cheer split the air behind her, and she joined them. Duskar came to her and she remounted him and turned back to her position beside Marakon. The armies of the Free Peoples quickly ordered back into line, their faces alight with renewed confidence.

'A neat trick,' said the commander. Then, without waiting for a response, he roared, 'Soldiers, charge!'

The horses needed no telling, and they leapt towards the floundering enemy. Issa gripped hold of Duskar, excitement rushing through her. The gap between them and the enemy closed before the Maphraxies had managed to form a defensive line. Metal clapped against metal like thunder as they hurtled through them before being forced to slow, at which point the world turned into chaos.

A Maphraxie loomed before her. Duskar rose and cut it down. Another swung a battle axe, and she fell to the left, dodging it. Righting herself, she slashed down into its face. She never saw it fall for Duskar turned to another. Seconds later, a Feylint Halanoi spear took it in the throat. For a moment she saw nothing but a sea of ugly howling faces and black weapons shaking, then, knights pressed in around her and she was behind a line of comrades.

Duskar stumbled over a body. There was a clash of steel and iron barely a foot from her head and smoke filled the air. Something sprayed in her eyes; black or red blood, although she couldn't be sure, but it stung, and she struggled to see.

A hand grabbed her leg with a crushing grip. She kicked and stabbed her sword, seeing the Maphraxie fall through the blur. Regaining clear vision, she parried a descending club, the bludgeoning force shuddering her entire body. Her right hand strengthened its grip on Illendri and she struck back, releasing the Flow. The club severed into two, and the Maphraxie blinked at its broken weapon, then a spear tip exploded through its shoulder.

The battle heaved forwards and back. Sometimes she faced Maphraxies, other times she couldn't see them for the press of knights before her. In the brief lull behind a line of knights, a roar from above caught her attention. The golden dragon dove and breathed fire upon the enemy. A red dragon followed and clawed the ground, filling his talons with Maphraxies. It crushed them and hurled their mangled bodies onto the enemy below.

Three Dromoorai darted in and chased them away, and Issa lost sight of Asaph and the red. Energy shook the ground, and she looked to Maphrax. In the Flow, black magic poured from the sky into the mountains. Cold fear trickled down her spine. What was the bastard up to? *I should be fighting him, the head of the beast, not out here fighting his hordes.*

Another power made itself known and she suddenly felt light-headed. *Two powers are rising, the dark moon and that of Maphrax.* A wave of energy tingled through her body and she gripped Duskar's mane. *I cannot fight in battle and command the Flow. The dark moon is rising.*

She hunted for a way to get out of the melee. To the West, the press of soldiers thinned, and she spied a bare patch of ground beside some rocks. She urged Duskar towards it.

It took an age to get through the press of spears and soldiers. Even as she made the inches to the bare ground, she felt the moon's power increasing in ever greater waves. Her raven mark burned, the talisman flared, and shimmering indigo magic suddenly swamped her vision. She could no longer see Duskar beneath her for the indigo light filling the Flow. It grew and grew within her until she felt as if her body would burst into light too, pushing back the Under Flow, pushing back the darkness that infected her.

Stopping Duskar, she gripped the talisman finding it helped to channel the overwhelming magic. In the Flow, an enormous black vortex appeared over the battlefield. She blinked to look into the physical, and it was there too! Soldiers and Maphraxies fell back from it, forgetting their fight between each other.

'The demons are waiting, Issy,' said Maggot, the shadows moving beside her. 'King says they need a portal.'

She looked into Maggot's yellow eyes, all that had materialised in front of her. 'Tell Marakon now, Maggot. He has the spear that will open up a portal, and I can't reach him from here. Don't be scared, he won't hurt you.'

Another surge of power came from the blue moon and her reality expanded. Her body began to feel distant as she felt herself rising, becoming detached from all that was happening around her.

The power receded, and reality came back to her in a rush. Maggot was no longer there.

The black vortex had doubled in size, larger than she had ever seen it. It jerked and shuddered, and a roaring scream erupted from within, making her heart leap into her throat.

Anukon poured out of the vortex, running on long powerful legs straight at the soldiers and Maphraxies. They wielded staves made out of shining metal and another weapon Issa could only describe as three hooks.

Taller than Maphraxies and as intelligent as humans, the Anukon quickly turned the battle into chaotic hell. Their staves discharged flickering orange power into whatever they hit, and soldiers screamed and fell. They slashed their hooks creating horrific wounds, spraying living and dead blood wherever they passed.

Scores of Anukon swiftly turned into hundreds as they poured out of the vortex and attacked everything.

Issa turned Duskar away and galloped to a foothill. There, she swung out of the saddle and looked at him.

'This battle is not for you, make your own way, boy, but stay safe. I'll come find you like I always do.' She patted the horse, but he remained by her side.

She scanned the soldiers for Marakon, but it was impossible to tell anyone apart. She prayed Maggot would make it safely to the commander in the centre of the battle.

The soldiers closest to the vortex and witnesses of the carnage inflicted by the new enemy, tried to flee. The Maphraxies, less prone to fear, pressed forwards only to fall in great numbers. At this rate, Maioria would not fall to the Maphraxies, but to the Anukon.

A burst of white light flared behind Feylint Halanoi lines and knights and soldiers surrounded it, facing outwards to protect it from attack. She glimpsed a knight holding a shaft of light. *Marakon and Velistor!* She thought. He struck the spear into the ground and a massive green symbol flared. It covered at least four yards of ground beneath the soldiers' feet, spewing billows of thick green smoke that engulfed anyone near.

Another roar tore over the battle. Out of the green smoke poured demons, grey and brown, large and small, some flying, others running on four or two legs.

Soldiers now fled from the demons and the whole scene became even more chaotic. Some demons paused and turned to follow the fleeing prey, the human fear enticing them and confusing their instincts.

Issa held her breath. *Show no fear. Don't run from demons!*

Marakon started shouting, she couldn't hear what he said but he managed to calm the soldiers and capture the demons' attention. With his spear he directed them north. Checking themselves, the demons sighted the Maphraxies and the soldiers fell back to let them through. Roaring demonic battle cries, they flooded into the fight.

Issa let go of her breath.

The ground trembled and she looked to Maphrax. A twisting tornado of black light swirled down through the clouds and made contact with the central mountain tip. Lightning flared, magic crackled, power built. Baelthrom was drawing upon the Under Flow. When she closed her eyes she could feel it flowing to him.

Everything began to slow down.

She looked back at the melee that was the battlefield. Soldiers screamed and fought, demons exploded into ash or simply vanished with their opponents. Anukon took down swathes of Maphraxies and soldiers with one sweep of their power-filled staves.

Death and blood assaulted her vision, and yet she found herself becoming detached from it and her emotions—detached so she might become something else, something more, a vessel through which power greater than herself could move.

She became keenly aware of Maioria's pulse beating beneath her feet; the heartbeat of her beloved planet was still strong. Maioria wanted to live, she wanted them to live, and she did not want to descend into darkness.

Another pulse beat.

Issa felt as if she were lifting up with a gentle energy. She raised her arms, feeling light and ethereal as blue light swirled in the sky, and she smiled and breathed out.

Indigo beams burst across the tops of the craggy hills to the east, and a great wind picked up. The tip of the dark moon appeared, and moonlight flared into the muddy storm clouds. Light flickered, and the red clouds began to fragment and dissipate. As they vanished, the Dark Rift was revealed in all its horrifying glory, and the black power pouring from it into Maphrax was starkly visible. There was nothing in the rift, no stars, no lights, nothing but the deepest black.

Issa tore her eyes away and held her arms up to the rising blue orb. Its light soaked her, banishing the darkness until she could no longer feel the Dark Rift inside of her. It rose, enormous over hills, and just the presence of such a large object so close to Maioria was enough to break the inexorable pull of the Dark Rift. Here was the lull point; Maioria held static between two incredible forces.

'This is how we destroy the Dark Rift!' she shouted aloud. 'Nothing can withstand the purity of Zanufey's moon, all that remains of beautiful

Aralansia. In its light let all evil be cleansed from this land!'

She lifted the raven talisman high above her head and the light of the moon filled it until it flared with light. Images formed in her mind, the talisman and the spear, and she understood what she had to do.

'To Velistor, now,' she commanded.

The light beamed out from the talisman straight over the battleground, and in a silent blinding flash it connected with Velistor.

Marakon could not hold the spear and let it go. The spear flew towards her over the heads of the Maphraxies and Anukon, over the top of the alien vortex, and straight into her outstretched hand.

Guided by the will of a power greater than herself, Issa slotted the spear into the hole at the base of the talisman and held it up. She was aware of the eyes of the entire battlefield watching her.

The power of the moon flooded into the raven and spear.

'The Staff of the Gate,' Issa whispered.

Everything fell away into flaring indigo light. There was no battlefield, no skies filled with dragons, no roars of men and demons – nothing but the light and the power that consumed her. The energy flooded from the blue moon, through her staff, through her body, and into Maioria. Power, magic, life energy.

She felt the Dark Rift respond. The Under Flow surged from Maphrax and grew within her. A crack of thunder split the air and felt like it split the ground beneath her feet. She felt herself tearing in two, the agony of the opposing energies within her made her scream.

The indigo light stuttered, and black light engulfed her. Her world flickered between black and indigo magic, and the physical world. In the brief glimpses between the veils of magic and the material world, she witnessed the black light surging down from the Dark Rift into Maphrax suddenly refract and explode towards the sky—not back to the Dark Rift, but towards Zanufey's moon.

Issa gasped, suddenly understanding the intention of the Under Flow. The Mountains of Maphrax were a giant conduit of energy and now they directed and amplified the will of the Dark Rift itself.

'It wants to destroy the moon!' she howled.

In a matter of moments, the black light covered thousands of leagues. Issa stared at the moon and lowered her hands, the Flow and the Under

Flow becoming oddly stable and of equal strength within her. Then she witnessed the unbelievable. Cracks began to snake across the moon's surface, and a deafening howling noise vibrated the air so loud and piercing it sounded as if the cosmos itself was screaming.

The energy refracting from Maphrax doubled and the blue moon visibly trembled in the sky. With a moaning cry as if in pain, the dark moon shattered. Issa felt her soul and body tearing in two. Like a glass smashing on the ground, the pieces of the blue moon scattered across the sky.

In her mind she saw the Star Portal shatter into fragments of light. A thousand souls wailed in despair, a harrowing sound that rent at her soul. *The guardians of the portals!* Issa gasped from the agonising pain in her chest, and tears smarted her eyes. *It cannot be, it cannot be, I cannot believe it!* but her eyes and feelings were not lying. The raven talisman and spear flared erratically and shook. She cried out as they burned in her hands, turned molten orange and exploded into nothing.

The power of the moon within her surged outwards, magical energy exploding within her, tearing her apart just like the moon had been scattered. The moon's magic gushed out of her as if a magical artery had been cut.

It is over.

Vast physical forces began to unleash across Maioria. A howling tornado picked up and the ground shook violently sending Issa to her knees. The fragments of the moon flowed like a river of rocks across the sky towards the Dark Rift, gaining momentum as they neared. She watched all that had given her power shatter apart and the pieces of it hurtle into Oblivion.

Zanufey, where are you? She cried out in her mind, but for the first time, there was silence.

CHAPTER 40

Into Darkness

THE black poison within Issa spared her from despair and hopelessness. Instead, it fed her rage.

She allowed the now ever present dark energy of the Under Flow to fill her, for the first time willingly drawing upon it and embracing it instead of fighting it. *We're near the end anyway,* she thought, *and for me it is over.*

In seething anger, she turned her gaze upon the peaks of Maphrax, called her raven form and flew straight to the peak of the central mountain, heedless of the Dromoorai guarding it. They did not see her, a tiny raven, whilst their eyes watched the battle below. Now and then, one would launch from its platform and join the battle, and another would return to rest.

One looked right at her, or at least she thought it did, and her heart pounded, but then it turned back to the scenes below. *They think the battle is over, they think they've won. They have, but they will not live to see the inside of the Dark Rift!*

Issa circled the black energy pouring into Maphrax, feeling the darkness within her responding to it, growing stronger and feeding her rage. Looking down, she could see it flooded through a crater in the peak several yards wide. Into the narrow gap between the energy and the walls, Issa dropped. She pulled her wings closer to avoid hitting the wall or being sucked into the black light, and descended a long way until the darkness was nearly complete. At the end, a light grew.

A light which became four distinct balls of light. *The orbs!* The four remaining orbs now lay just ahead of her. Illendri flared into life, calling to her sisters, and the sudden light of the Flow reminded Issa of purity, of peace, and it calmed her raging hatred.

She emerged into a vast chamber. Beneath her, the great iron ring she had witnessed in nightmares burst with red and black light. Garbled voices came from within it, chattering, overlaying the deeper sound of something moaning. The ear-bending noise of metal twisting and grating upon itself made her wince.

Beyond the ring and beside the floating orbs, stood Baelthrom.

Issa released her raven form before landing. She came to a running stop the other side of the ring, threw up her hands, and released the Under Flow straight into Baelthrom. It coursed through her like once the dark moon's energy had—how she wished the dark moon's power filled her now. Every waking hour she had thought about this moment, and now her power was not here. *No, I'll not think about the shattered moon in our skies. I'll not feel fear. There's only do…there's only die.* All that mattered was that she destroyed this abomination with everything she had, even if it cost her her own life.

Her immense grasp upon the Under Flow ensured she denied Baelthrom its full power. He fought back, seeking for a way to wrench it from her whilst also shielding himself from it. She gripped it harder, feeling sweat prickle her face. Through the flaring dark fire that poured from her hands, she realised Baelthrom was not in his usual form and was no longer solid. His eyes still blazed red, but not from behind metal – from within swathes of billowing energy. *He's becoming a Light Eater!* As they hung before him, the orbs looked like planets upon which he would feed.

'I knew you would come to me in the end, Raven Queen,' his low voice echoed round the chamber, almost soothing.

He did not come towards her, he could not, she realised, no more than she could go to him. The energy they battled to control kept them apart.

'You *will* go into the Dark Rift, but Maioria will not follow,' she said between clenched teeth.

Illendri lifted itself from her scabbard.

'No, Illendri,' she gasped, sweat trickling down her back as she struggled to maintain concentration. She couldn't drop her hands to grab it because that would relinquish her hold on the Under Flow. The sword lifted up and the wire basket holding the orb snapped open. The blade clattered to the floor and Illendri floated towards her sisters.

The Under Flow lurched towards Baelthrom. Issa roared and reached for the orbs with the power she commanded. Slowly, they inched towards her, away from Baelthrom. A tiny green symbol flashed in her peripheral vision and then small hands squeezed her calf.

'Not now, Maggot!' she gasped. These energies would destroy him utterly if he got too close.

'Not yet,' Baelthrom breathed.

Issa didn't know what he meant but the strain in his voice gave her confidence that she might be winning. She jerked on the Under Flow and the whole pillar of dark light spasmed. She had power, lots of it, enough to stand against Baelthrom!

A voice called out, tiny and strained. For a moment Issa looked out from the darkness of the Under Flow she held and glimpsed a world of beautiful swirling light in white and pastel hues. A familiar consciousness reached out from the orbs and touched her mind.

'Yisufalni!' Issa called out, tears filling her eyes. The Ancient was alive! Could she help her? Not while she was in the Under Flow...

The black magic lurched, this time towards Baelthrom. Issa gasped, the blood pounding in her head, her heart thundering in her chest as if she were sprinting. *I'll not let go, I won't! I'll be destroyed by this power rather than enslaved by it.*

Baelthrom's might increased. The dark energy vibrated alarmingly between them, his power pressing upon her harder. *'Save the orbs!'* Issa screamed.

'Call him, Issa, call him now when you still have the power of Illendri!' Yisufalni's disembodied voice echoed around her. 'While I'm here, Murlonius can find us.'

The fields of light vanished, and Issa swooned in the dark. Magical wind whipped around her and she grappled frantically to retain her grip, no longer trying to attack but to shield.

'Murlonius, Murlonius, Murlonius!' Issa shouted, her words consumed by the maelstrom.

Moments passed like hours, then a being surrounded in pale purple light stepped beside her. Murlonius moved fearlessly forward and lifted back his hood, his perfect face beatific in the dark, an angel descended from the light. He said nothing and did nothing to help Issa. How could he when he could not even touch the Under Flow, much less command it?

Baelthrom tried to force the Under Flow to attack the Ancient, but Issa turned the Under Flow away and shielded Murlonius.

'The time has come,' Murlonius said, his voice low, beautifully melodic and calming. There was a strange look on his face, one of acceptance and complete knowing.

'These powers will not be corrupted by evil,' he said, almost lovingly. He raised his six-fingered hands towards the orbs and his whole being turned into light.

The Flow moved through Issa, and for a few seconds she held both it and the Under Flow. She couldn't describe the feeling—no one had ever used both, no one had ever stood in the darkness and the light. She couldn't breathe and yet the purest air filled her lungs and she cried at the agonising darkness and the wondrous light. She understood completely both harmony and chaos, how the energies of the cosmos worked and what happened when they began to corrupt and fragment.

The orbs flared white, spun fast on their axis, then burst towards Murlonius. When they touched him, light exploded, flooding through and all around him. Light flickered and flashed as Murlonius's body became an ethereal pure energy, then he and the light surged into the ground.

In the fields of magic, Issa watched in awe as it descended deep into the earth, moving fast and faster until it reached Maioria's core. Once it touched there, an immense flash of white light burst forth, and Murlonius, the orbs, and Yisufalni's spirit vanished.

In that light Issa glimpsed Doon bathed in white moonlight, and a strangely calm silent scene unfolded when all around flared chaotic magic. The light trickled over his majestic antlers, over his powerful body and onto the prone figure of Woetala laying on a stone plinth before him. The woman stirred. Doon inclined his head towards Issa then looked up, lifted his arms high and called to the elements. The image disappeared along with the Flow and the light.

Issa blinked into darkness. The Under Flow was absolute and she felt herself falling.

'Now, Hameka,' Baelthrom spoke, his voice unstrained.

In the corner of the room, a grey-faced man stepped forward. She hadn't noticed him before, had he been watching the whole time? He raised his weapon, Issa tried to move only to find the Under Flow she had commanded now trapped and held her.

Maggot leapt into the air towards the man.

'No, Maggot!' she screamed, but the little demon flew so fast he filled the space between her and Hameka in an instant. Time slowed, time in which she could do nothing.

The dart exploded through Maggot's back in a spray of black demon blood. The demon squeaked and dropped to the ground, flopping like a rag doll. The whole world trembled, Ehka screamed from above and flew at Hameka, and the Under Flow lost its grip on her a little.

Another dart flew towards her. She moved to dodge it, then saw it wasn't a dart at all, it was Jabber but there was no Maggot to catch it. Tears blurred her vision; the world had changed. Surrendering, Issa relinquished the last of her grip on the Under Flow and instead reached and caught the demons' beloved weapon. She looked down at it, her tears splashing over the strange weapon, and Jabber hummed in her hand as if agreeing with her desolation. She looked at the blood smearing her hand. Blood that covered Jabber—*red* blood, human blood.

Issa stared from Maggot's still form, his crumpled wings and tongue hanging out of his mouth, to the grey-man who had killed him. The man who gurgled, and had blood dribbling from his mouth, who didn't even lift a hand to beat back Ehka. Instead he sunk to his knees, red blood spurting from the base of his neck from the wound Jabber had made, then he fell forwards onto his face.

She sensed fury as Baelthrom's power surrounded and held her. All the while it had been growing, and now it filled the chamber. The room began to vibrate and then shake. Cracks snaked over the walls and floor as the entire chamber began to disintegrate. Bricks and masonry rose in the air and drew towards the black pillar as everything was sucked into the rift magic. But all she saw, all she cared about, was the demon on the floor.

Over the crumbling swirling ground, Issa ran to Maggot. She grabbed his cold body and held him to her chest. His eyes were fast closing. She howled a noise she had never made and screamed with every fibre of her being, 'A'farion, A'farion, A'farion.'

The Under Flow vanished, and before utter silence descended, she heard the fading roar of Baelthrom.

Maggot was as solid in the Realm of the Dead as he was in the world of the living, but his eyes had closed fully. He was gone. In her hands his body began to disintegrate and turn to ash.

'No, no, no!' Issa screamed, tears streaming from her eyes.

Ahead, ghostly figures turned towards her, attracted by her cries. Issa didn't care about them and focussed all of her remaining power on her connection to Maggot. She could feel the faint thread of his life line and she followed it. Unlike all the other beings she had felt, his led down, not up.

The enormous form of a green demon appeared before her, black horns reaching high, face scowling in rage. It swiped a clawed hand; long black claws which flashed and knocked her back so hard the ghost world trembled.

'Zorock,' she gasped, clutching her bruised and bleeding cheek. Her vision was filled with the demon god's terrifying face, squat nose and long black fangs roaring. In his hand he cupped a tiny light. He stepped back, his long tail swishing, the rage lessening in his face, and then vanished. 'Not your domain, Raven Queen,' a demonic voice echoed around her.

Grey mist swirled, and a multitude of ghosts walked and floated towards her, more than she had ever seen here. Their forms were thin and tall and swathed in rag robes that moved in a non-existent wind. Perhaps it was the black drink that no longer made her afraid of them, but still, her hand went to her sword, to where Illendri should have been, but was not.

Her eyes passed over the approaching multitude, a sea of ghosts surrounding her. Their faces were sometimes visible, drawn and weary, and other times they were just a blur of grey in a colourless world—not menacing but *waiting*. What were they waiting for? *They wait for release, for freedom.*

A thought came to her, and she spoke. 'You're trapped in limbo, and the whole world from which you came is falling into Oblivion.' Her voice sounded loud and echoey. The words were her own, but they came from a higher, wiser part of herself.

'You'll fall into Oblivion too, all will fall, both living and dead, unless you fight, unless you choose the light with your actions, with your will.'

'Who are you, come to disturb us?' the voice came from many places and no one ghost in particular. 'We neither rise nor fall, there is only here.'

Ehka squawked and landed on her shoulder where he surveyed the gathered dead.

A gasp rose up from the ghost and the air tingled.

'I am the Raven Queen,' said Issa. It came out quietly, but the words held power.

The ghosts murmured. 'The Raven Queen has come to set us free.' Hope filled the voices of the dead.

'You can be free, but you must fight,' Issa said, louder. 'Darkness shrouds the place that was once your home. There is no longer passage from this place to the One Light, it is engulfed by the Dark Rift. If you choose freedom, you must return to the world of the living and help them fight. There you will find the light that will set you free.'

A moaning sigh escaped the crowd and weariness hung heavy in the air. 'We cannot return; we are trapped here. Some have waited for thousands of years.'

Issa rolled back her shoulders. 'That is no longer so, for the end of all endings is upon us. Now you only have to reach for the light, should you wish it, and your freedom, and a new world will be found.'

Issa held her arms wide and spoke with the commanding Voice. 'Ravens of Zanufey, come to me.' The call echoed far and wide, searching for ravens on the four corners of Maioria.

The first raven appeared quickly and was followed by two more. Issa smiled, and in moments, the sky was filled with them. They circled her in an orderly fashion, flying so close to each other it was a wonder they didn't crash.

'Ravens hear me! As you did in life, now do so again in death. Carry the souls of the dead to the world of the living where all of you fight for the light. This is the last battle and our last chance to be free of the darkness smothering our world.'

The ravens cawed and circled faster and faster until all she could make out was a fast spinning pillar made of black birds and shining beaks. They rose and then dove into the ground creating a shimmering pool of raven magic. When they had gone, the dead had gone with them, too.

'It is done,' said Issa. Ehka croaked in response. She let the ever-present draw of Maioria pull her gently back, her spirit filled with a sense of fulfilment and completion regardless of what awaited her in the Realm of the Living.

The aliens flooded out of the vortex in the centre of the battlefield. Asaph swooped low to hail them with fire and grab them into his talons, but his flames flared harmlessly off an impenetrable shield and his claws scoured off something hard in a spray of sparks. He couldn't even get close.

Roaring in frustration, he turned and sprayed fire onto the Maphraxies, grabbed a handful and hurled their crushed bodies onto the horde below. A Dread Dragon dropped fast from above, forcing Asaph to turn sharply and arc high into the air.

Now this new invader was here, should he even be trying to kill the Maphraxies? he wondered. They'd help to hinder the aliens' efforts; whatever it was they were trying to achieve.

Keeping distance between himself and the trailing Dromoorai, he analysed the shield. It fizzled with light and didn't look solid, but neither was it made of magic for he couldn't see it in the Flow. It appeared to be formed out of something physical, a technology he had not seen before. He hoped the Feylint Halanoi could attack this new enemy from the ground for there was nothing he could do in the air.

He circled back to the West where he had last seen Issa, ever keeping a watchful eye for her. Duskar pranced back and forth at the westernmost edge of the battle, but where was Issa? With growing panic, Asaph hunted back and forth. Perhaps she was in the sky?

He turned north and glimpsed two black specks flying towards the column of black magic pouring into Maphrax. Issa and Ehka, he had no doubt.

No, Issa!

Asaph beat his wings hard after her. *You're not going in there alone! I'll follow you all the way into the Dark Rift if I must.*

Seeing his approach, Dromoorai urged their mounts into the air to intercept him. Ignoring them, he reached the mountain peak and found he couldn't follow where she went. The gap between the black magic and the side of the mountain was too small for him to fit. He circled it several times, the Dromoorai getting closer, but there was no way in. He turned and hunted the mountain for another entrance, moving fast to keep the Dromoorai at bay, until his wings ached, and his mind spun from circling the mountain. The Dread Dragons were closing in.

The Flow vibrated, slight, yet rippling for miles and miles. Beyond the mountain, a cloud of black birds appeared. *Ravens! Issa must have called them,* he thought.

Before he could move out of the way, thousands of ravens surrounded him. They cawed and squawked and darted towards the battlefield, paying him and the Dromoorai no attention. The air turned deathly cold as they passed and he shivered as he caught a glimpse of shadows between the birds. Raven magic? he wondered. No, there was more to this—the smell of death and cold fingers touched his heart. *Ghosts.*

The ravens reached the battlefield and the shadows between them took shape. Grey wraiths floated down onto the enemy, and howls of terror rang out from the Feylint Halanoi. Many turned and fled, but the ghosts did not attack them, instead they attacked the Anukon aliens.

Magic surged beneath him and black light exploded from the mountain peak, engulfing him. The immense force of the Under Flow forced him upwards, choked his lungs, and burned his eyes. He tumbled and spun helplessly in the magic, unable to fly, unable to use the Flow.

Suddenly he was no longer being pushed but *sucked* upwards. Grating noises echoed all around and a terrible moaning filled his mind. It reminded him of Keteth's madness, seeping into and infecting his brain. He thrashed and beat his wings, trying to find wind, trying to find a way out of the darkness., but not even a dragon could fight the pure, dark energy of the rift.

Issa closed her eyes as the Under Flow surrounded her and the ghost world vanished. The darkness gripped hold of her with a vengeance, and her body was ripped upwards into the maelstrom. There was a sickening joy in that black energy that she tried to resist. It was returning to the Dark Rift, and she along with it. There was no point fighting it, it was too powerful, and she had no remaining will to survive.

Now the orbs were gone, in the growing power of the Dark Rift energy she felt a forgotten orb awaken. Lona's orb, in the pouch on her belt, grew heavy and warm. Issa smiled grimly, *another power giving itself to me, although I do not want it.* She tried to ignore it.

Triangular red eyes burned above, and below, a field of pure white light moved.

'Touch me one last time,' she called to the pure light, reaching down to it. A fragment of the Flow responded and touched her for a moment, powerful and pure, relaying information to her. She sighed. She could still feel it, she had not lost herself completely yet. Maioria could break free, there was still hope.

Fight, Maioria, fight for the light. Issa let go of a long, slow breath and watched the light disappearing far beneath her as the Dark Rift drew her away. *How beautiful it is, a shining diamond in this black sea of chaos. Remember me, Maioria.*

Had Baelthrom heard or felt Maioria fighting back, sensed the hope? Would he halt this vortex into the Dark Rift and return to fight? *He must not!* If he could not feel the Flow, he could not know what was occurring below them. *I will go with him and distract him. I'll make sure he goes into the Dark Rift.*

She spread her arms, closed her eyes, and surrendered. The chattering, the grating metal, the deep moaning grew until they were deafening. Her soul and body trembled as unseen powers pulled on her in all directions. *The Light Eaters; they see my light and also the darkness within.*

When the upward motion slowed, she opened her eyes. Black and red cosmic clouds rose in grotesque pillars around planets of varying light. Some of the planets were black orbs floating listlessly; empty husks, the life force gone from them and places where fallen beings walked. Others were brighter but dwindling as the Light Eaters fed upon them.

Baelthrom loomed enormous before her, his body black, grey and red clouds like the other Light Eaters. *His true form revealed*, Issa thought. Another gaseous Light Eater appeared beside him and then another, their faces black pits into which the light poured.

'I accept your gift,' she said. She didn't feel fear, the black drink within her prevented it. She looked at her hands and saw black veins pulsing. *Consume me, my dark poison, I am yours.* For all the time she held Baelthrom's attention, it bought Maioria time. *A lot can happen in a moment.* She thought of Maggot, but even sorrow was a distant thing, a peculiar emotion that had no hold on her.

She looked down and saw that her body, held in the dark magic, was no longer solid but made of light flecked through with spreading black. Her light grew and then dimmed, becoming dimmer with each passing moment. She thought of Asaph, saw his blue eyes and warm smile. There were moments of sadness as the light dwindled, but these, too, faded.

Baelthrom's giant hand reached towards her and she felt her spirit and all physical energies being drawn out. She closed her eyes and allowed in the cold, the dark, and the emptiness. Her body weakened, her mind grew foggy and her soul surrendered.

Warmth tingled her back, irritating her and the darkness she embraced. She denied it at first, how could there be any warmth or comfort in this place? It made her angry and she pushed it away, but it grew and grew and the drain of her essence into Baelthrom stopped.

Let me die! she cursed and opened her eyes. Before her, floating in the air, hung Lona's orb. Free of its pouch, it had lifted itself up and now pulsed darkly. White lightning struck within it, cracking through its impenetrable black.

Behind her, a brilliant light flared, striking back the darkness. It hurt her eyes and her mind, and she screamed as the darkness within screamed. How she hated the light!

'Let me die, I've done all that I can and can do no more. I give my life so that others might live!' Issa sobbed, she did not want to be reminded of the light. She tried to look away, to move into the darkness, but the light held her.

'No,' a voice said from within it, deep, soothing, yet utterly commanding. 'Embrace the light. You *are* the light; it's yours, it was always yours. Look at me, I am the light.'

A face formed within the light, burnished gold, large slanted eyes, beautiful. Memory sparked.

'Ayeth?' Issa breathed.

He smiled, benevolent yet filled with sorrow. In his hand of light, he held another black orb, just like Freydel's and Lona's floating before her. That was why Lona's orb responded, she realised; the two orbs were drawing together.

She looked beyond Ayeth and gasped at the stunning cosmos revealed. In perfect alignment planets of blue, green and amber turned in fields of beautiful light and cosmic gasses. Was this how the One Light saw? It *is* the One Light, she realised, beauty and perfection.

Ayeth whispered a word, the sadness on his face heart-wrenching, and Lona's orb flew straight to his. Black light flashed as the two orbs collided and Ayeth's hands shone with white light so bright Issa had to look away. When she looked back, the orbs were gone, along with the darkness that bled from them.

Ayeth held her gaze and reached his hands of light towards her. She gasped as they reached straight through her body and soul, pushing back the darkness therein. The hands continued through her, towards Baelthrom's mass, and a terrible wrenching filled her as the forces of light and darkness battled to control her essence. She looked from the worlds of light beyond Ayeth to the ruined worlds consumed in the Dark Rift, and felt herself as the centre point between the darkness and the light. *I stand between them, the darkness and the light, they are both within me!*

Ayeth's hands reached the darkness and Baelthrom shrieked. His gaseous face contorted, his mouth opening in a howl. He pulled back but Ayeth followed and she felt the two sides of the same being battling as if it were happening within her own body. Cosmic winds raged through her but Ayeth drew her to him, through him, pulling her away from Baelthrom and towards the light. She felt herself become a part of him, his feelings a part of her own.

'I sacrificed myself for you,' she realised. 'So that this might be possible?'

'Without you and the power of Zanufey within you, I could never reach myself, I could never reach Baelthrom,' he whispered, his voice strained. His power wavered. It took all of his strength to hold onto Baelthrom. 'The final sacrifice must be my own. Now you must reach for the light, I cannot hold us both for long.'

Issa convulsed as Ayeth released her. She felt her mind and body tear from his as the darkness was drawn out of her.

'Ayeth!' she shouted and stared helplessly as he hurtled into Baelthrom's gaseous form. A deafening howl, like a mighty wind, tore through everything, and the darkness and the Light Eaters and the Dark Rift rushed away. Her world turned into fields of flashing and vibrating pure energy.

'Issa!' a distant voice called across the prismatic planes far beyond the Ethereal Realm.

'Asaph?' she called back, her voice loud and strange as it echoed through the planes of energy. 'I chose the light!' she cried, feeling again the joy and freedom that had once been hers. At her will, light surrounded her, too bright to bear looking at, and sound accompanied the light, a tinkling, ringing sound so beautiful she could not describe it with human words. The radiant splendour made her gasp – she couldn't breathe for the beauty of it.

Her senses adjusted, and in the light, she saw faces smiling—the golden face of Feygriene, the antlered head of Doon and the awakening face of Woetala. Beyond them all stood Zanufey, and beyond her stood many other guardians whom she did not know. But it was on Zanufey her eyes rested.

The Night Goddess lifted back her hood and her eyes blazed indigo light. It flooded into Issa, burning away the remaining darkness and releasing her. She felt herself becoming one with these beings as they became one with each other, and more knowledge flooded her mind.

Such incredible sights! She saw worlds of light orbiting blazing suns, millions of them stretching into distance. Her viewpoint focused on a particular darker area, and she saw thousands of solar systems spinning around the Dark Rift, the darkness blighting not just Maioria but the entire cosmos. She saw the people of those planets, many of whom looked like those of Maioria and Aralansia, with some having races somewhat similar, and some far different—but all fought against the darkness infecting their world.

The beings coming out of the Dark Rift took on different forms, too. On Maioria, she knew them as Maphraxies but on other planets they appeared differently: some were huge beasts with horns and teeth; others were tiny, like flies with deadly poisons or stings, but most had no form and appeared just as shadows or smoke—dark wraiths that possessed any beings of light they touched.

'The un-light takes many forms,' a voice said, Zanufey's voice that was also her own voice, answering her own thoughts.

Issa understood intrinsically that the battle had never been just for Maioria and her soul, but for all. Maioria was the battleground, but the war was the entire cosmos. *And it is an ancient war.*

Issa's consciousness expanded and lifted away from the darkness, moving higher and higher until she saw that it was small in comparison to the radiant light flowing between the solar systems. There were many patches of darkness, but they were mere specks in comparison.

'What is beyond the darkness?' an eternal voice asked.

Issa knew the answer and her soul cried with joy. 'There is light; there is infinite light beyond the darkness! We cannot fail, I see that now, but we can always choose.'

'Then choose wisely,' said the eternal voice. 'Choose love, and then choose freedom.'

Issa couldn't hold on to her singular point of consciousness as she understood it. Her being and her observation expanded until it was all light and sound and intention, and the One Light engulfed her.

It was a subtle change that directed her consciousness and focused her attention. Beings passing through her body of light. Aralans - and they were also a part of her.

In this place of radiant light and sound there wasn't really a clear distinction between this and that, or what was her and what was not. She was a portal to the light and of the light, and the beings were moving through her at her guidance.

'I am Zanufey, and the Guardians of the Portals are moving through me,' a thought or a voice echoed around her, the voice of her higher self, the voice of Zanufey. 'Finally free after eons in the darkness. They're going home to the One Light and I know you understand fully that I have always been a part of you, within you, beside you, all ways.'

'And Ayeth?' Issa thought aloud.

'Gone into the darkness to be the light unto it. Nothing can heal Baelthrom, other than himself. That is the way of all healing.'

Issa, sighed, wisdom and understanding setting her free. *Only the self can heal the self.* 'The darkness exists because freedom exists, but it does not have to be chosen.' She smiled. In this place there was nothing but divine perfection and there was nothing but the light eternal.

CHAPTER 41

The New World

ASAPH flew in darkness.

If there were mountains in front of him he would crash into them without ever having seen them. Perhaps he hurtled towards an ocean, or a forest where his body would smash apart on the ground. There was no Flow to see into, there was no keen dragon sense of wind or tide or anything at all, just a swirling mass of black, ravenous energy surging around him.

He turned his mind and his senses to Issa. Knowing that she suffered this tormented darkness gave him the only reason to go on. Things moved in the darkness and distorted voices reminded him he was not alone.

An enormous black and red cloud mushroomed before him. *Light Eater!* He knew what they were and dipped his wings, trying to fly lower, but a Light Eater bloomed there too.

'Issa!' he roared, but could feel nothing, not even the flame ring.

Sharp rays of light cut through the darkness, blinding him, and he rolled in the air uncontrollably. He sensed horrendous darkness battling against the eternal light and incredible cosmic forces ripped through him, tearing at his wings, shuddering his heart, scattering his mind.

'Come into the light, Dawn Bringer,' a beautiful voice called to him, cutting through the din.

Feygriene! He didn't need to move for the light reached out to him. He couldn't see for the sudden brightness and the wondrous pure energy that engulfed him. All that he was melted into that powerful light.

Time passed, but it was not linear time. Change had occurred, he corrected himself, for his consciousness had returned to him, or rather, reduced itself into something he could manage, something he could define and comprehend.

Before him, Issa floated on a field of light swathed in robes of indigo; but it wasn't Issa, it was Zanufey—and yet it was also Issa for her hood was pushed back and the face was the same as his beloved's.

Asaph dipped his head in reverence. The light of the Night Goddess could no longer destroy his physical eyes; not here in this place of pure light.

'Let's go home, Dawn Bringer,' said Issa.

'Yes, my Goddess,' Asaph replied.

The light spiralled down taking them with it, and the incredible ringing noise lowered in pitch. Everything slowed and became denser, heavier. The light refracted into physical objects and a cool wind blew, carrying the scent of the sea and something else his delicate nostrils could detect. *Spring.*

The ocean formed as an impeccably calm blue-grey sea, and an endless horizon reached out before him. Above it, a ribbon of blazing orange burst between the blanket of clouds. The setting sun reached out to him, caressed his body and filled his heart with awe and reverence.

But what he cared about most was that which he held in his arms.

'Issa,' he whispered, stroking her cheek. She stirred and opened her eyes, and they blazed luminous white, like the eyes of Zanufey.

'Asaph?' she whispered.

Tears filled his eyes. 'I thought I'd lost you forever,' he said. He pulled her against his chest and sobbed for joy and sadness and exhaustion.

When the tears subsided, he looked down at her. Her eyes blazed less fiercely, and she wiped her own tears away.

'You came,' she said.

He nodded. 'It was my destiny.'

She laughed. 'Tell me what happened.'

Asaph took a deep breath. 'The ravens came, and with them, legions of ghosts. There was terror amongst the Feylint Halanoi but the ghosts did not attack them, instead they attacked the Anukon. I couldn't see too well, I was too far away and heading for you. Then Baelthrom's magic and the power of the Dark Rift took hold of me and dragged me into it. I would have gone anyway, to find you, even if I lost myself.'

He smiled at her and she stroked his cheek. 'You came for me in the Dark Rift.'

He nodded. 'I tried to find you, but there was only darkness and Light Eaters. Then Feygriene guided me.' He paused remembering the awe he'd felt.

Issa's breath caught in her throat and she pointed at the sky. 'Look, Asaph, look!'

The blanket of clouds had broken apart and beyond them twinkled thousands of stars.

'It's gone,' he gasped. 'The Dark Rift has gone!'

They stared up at the stars—far more than he had ever seen before.

Issa sighed. 'Maioria's free, praise the Goddess. The Dark Rift has gone from here, but I guess such a thing will always exist for those who choose the long and lonely path away from the light.'

'Maioria is free,' Asaph echoed, considering her words. 'Do you think you're ready to tell me what happened?'

Issa took a deep breath and nodded. 'It won't be easy explaining it all, the human language is so limited, but I'll try.'

She looked into the distance, and Asaph didn't say a word as she spoke and began to relive the events once more. 'I knew I had to go into the Dark Rift. I knew I had to go with Baelthrom, to keep him distracted long enough while Maioria reached for the light. I couldn't tell you, but I had chosen to give myself to him and the Dark Rift so that all others had a chance to reach for the light. When the moon exploded, I...I knew it was time. It was a slim chance with little time, but it was worth taking.

'You see, there were the orbs, and there was Yisufalni—she still lived but trapped within the Orb of Life—but that's another story—and then Murlonius came. Well, he and Yisufalni combined the orbs, and that healed Maioria's broken magic and set it free. That, in turn—and I think I've got this right—allowed Woetala to awaken and set her free. Oh, and before that Baelthrom's magic grew beyond anything...Ugh, I'm explaining it all wrong, there's just so much! All right, let's start with when I entered Maphrax...'

Asaph pieced it together as Issa fumbled her way through events. He could tell she held some things back when she paused to swallow and tears filled her eyes. He didn't want her to lose momentum though, so he listened until she came to a long, thoughtful pause.

'Ayeth came?' Asaph said.

'Yes, but he could not have had I not gone into the Dark Rift. Only there could he reach me. Only there could he reach Baelthrom. I feel it has something to do with the alignment of planets I kept seeing, something to do with the creation of the Dark Rift in Ayeth's time, and its destruction in our time.'

'But in the end,' Asaph spoke slowly as he reasoned it through, 'this would not have been possible had Freydel *not* reached Ayeth.'

Issa thought about his words, her face shining with awe. 'Spirit really *does* guide us.'

'So it was up to Ayeth,' Asaph said. 'He could have chosen differently in that moment, but he chose to reach for you, having seen what will become of himself, us, and his whole race.'

Issa nodded. 'In a way, yes. Only he could heal Baelthrom, or at least stop him. You see, only the self can heal the self and no other. There was this deep sorrow in his eyes. I guess it was for Lona, I guess he realised what she was, what she had become, and that he could not help her.' Issa trailed off quietly.

'I think you're going to have to go over this again some time,' Asaph said.

'I think we have time,' she giggled. 'I should write it down, so much knowledge was given to me, a great gift to our people and planet that must not be lost or forgotten. Hmm, do you feel different? I feel rather…*odd*. Better, but better than I've ever been.'

Now that she mentioned it, he did feel odd. 'Yes, I do, I feel *stronger*. More complete in some way.' He couldn't quite describe the feeling of wholeness and contentment that filled every part of him.

'And look, everything looks more alive, I can feel the life-force in even the rocks.' Issa pointed to the sand; it had a beautiful pale shimmer all over it. The rocks had a soft aura too, even the ocean shimmered faintly with blue light.

'The magic is whole,' said Issa, 'and it pulses within all things.'

Something flashed in the sea just beyond the shore. It flashed again, and he saw it clearly – purple and silver fins that were soon joined by many more.

'Oh, my!' he said, rising to his feet.

'Wykiry!' said Issa, jumping onto her own.

The Wykiry lifted their smooth, shining heads out of the water, and then the rest of their long, aquatic bodies appeared as they moved into the shallows.

'Look, Asaph, they're changing!' Issa squeaked.

Their bodies began to shimmer and morph as they emerged from the ocean. Long caudal fins shortened into arms and legs, round snouts shrank to become delicate noses, and recognisably human eyes and mouths formed.

With each step, on graceful, trembling legs, the Wykiry became humanoid. Their skin remained shimmery, like fish scales, and their hands and feet were webbed but they were as tall as humans, just more slender and fine-boned, like elves with large, round, golden eyes. They stared at their limbs and flexed their fingers and hands, as in awe of their changes as their onlookers were.

Issa and Asaph looked at each other, then back at the Wykiry.

'Your curse has lifted, you are free,' Issa whispered, only half-believing the transformation that had just taken place.

The nearest, a tall, masculine-looking Wykiry smiled, then touched his cheeks as if feeling his smile for the first time. He wrapped long fingers around his throat and in halting, difficult words, spoke. 'Welcome home, Raven Queen and Dawn Bringer. In our visions we knew you would return, but you have been gone longer than you think, and much has changed.'

The other Wykiry nodded and smiled. They moved awkwardly, uneasy in their land form despite their obvious fluid grace.

'We went into the Dark Rift. I had to…' began Issa. 'Yes, much has happened, I can barely come to terms with it myself. I need time to…to think it through and remember. Asaph came for me. When the pure light receded we found ourselves here. Where is here? How long have we been gone? What happened?'

'There will be plenty of time, Raven Queen,' the Wykiry continued, speaking slowly. 'It will be hard to explain with our voices as they are right now, but I shall try. Feel for the images I'm sending you; it will be easier.

The Dark Rift came down to us, we thought it was the end, then there came this incredible light, a beautiful powerful energy, a purifying cosmic wind that swept through Maioria. It came from above and from below, closing all vortexes. How much time passed when the light came to us, we cannot say.

'After the light, the ravens came to us and told us what had happened. They said that the Anukon could not withstand the light and retreated or died, and the Maphraxies fell under it and disintegrated. The demons fled back through their portal to the Murk. Even the humans and dwarves compromised in their choices fell fast to sickness and death. How long this took, we do not know, it maybe moments, maybe days.'

Issa blinked back tears as he spoke, seeing everything clearly in her mind. She saw dark dwarves and red-robed priests collapsing and choking as the light cleansed them. She watched the demons fleeing and the Anukon howling and clawing the air as their flesh peeled from their faces. She forced herself to look away, to look into the light which was only nourishing to her.

'Only those true races of Maioria could withstand it,' the Wykiry continued. 'The light made us strong, all of us—all wounds it healed, all rage it soothed. Then the black vortex lifted up into the rift and the Mountains of Maphrax vanished. The ravens said that Woetala has awoken now that the life-magic is made whole again, and Maioria grows strong now her guardians have awoken.

'As for how long you've been gone, well, it has been many days since the black light left and the pure light healed all. However, you must understand that in that time, new lands have arisen, right before our eyes. Old lands have gone, and some lands remain, but there were no earthquakes, no tsunamis, no devastation … there was only change. We do not know why or how, but Maioria is not the same as before. It's as if she's been born anew, arisen.' The Wykiry tired of speaking and paused.

Issa struggled to believe they were talking literally, and yet in her mind she saw lands emerging out of mists, rising up through the oceans, and other lands fading away, much like the Elven Land of Mists faded away when she'd left it.

Seeing her expression and the other Wykiry's weariness, a smaller female Wykiry stepped forwards. She also placed a hand on her throat as if it somehow helped her speak, and struggled with the words.

'I will speak, for he tires. We cannot say how long because when the Light of the One Source came, all darkness receded, and a deep sleep swept over all Maioria. Even the fish, even the coral, slept—but we all dreamed the same dream and it confirmed what the ravens had told us. Here is that dream.'

In Issa's mind she witnessed what the Wykiry and all Maioria had dreamed as she spoke.

'The evil energy of Maphrax, which we have long seen in our visions, lifted into the Dark Rift as six orbs of light fell down to the earth. When they struck, Maioria's life-magic burst alive and became whole. We saw Woetala arising from her endless sleep.'

'Before I was taken into the Dark Rift, I saw Doon, and Woetala awakening before him,' Issa said quietly, remembering when Doon acknowledged her.

The female Wykiry smiled. 'The light of Maioria spread through us, nourishing us, healing us of all wounds. You can feel it even now. We are strong and whole, like never before.'

'Yes, the darkness within me is gone,' Issa said, tears filling her eyes. She could feel no trace of the black drink or the hating rage it brought. She looked at her right hand and saw it was no longer grey and demonic but smooth-skinned. There were no traces of the fine scars about the wrist, and her skin shimmered the faintest blue, like the Wykiry's skin shimmered. She looked at Asaph and noticed he had more of a yellow glow around him. Was she able to see aura's clearer now? *Maioria is not the same as before!*

The Wykiry male spoke again, the wonder in his eyes mirroring her own. 'In our shared dream we saw the vast armies of menfolk and Maphraxies fall to their knees in darkness. Then came the pure light. It came from the sky, beyond the Dark Rift. In moments it engulfed the rift and Maioria. In that light, all things were revealed, laid bare, made true.

'When we awoke from that deep sleep and dream, Maioria was anew. This place we are now is west of what was Maphrax and east of Frayon. Our brothers and sisters tell us Atalanph, Drax and Frayon remain, but changed. And vast new lands and oceans…'

The Wykiry trailed off and lowered his eyes. Warmth and yellow light came from behind Issa and Asaph, spilling over them like honey. They turned to see a portal of golden light open, and within it, two beings walked.

Surrounding the light was a forest that Issa hadn't noticed before. Ancient oaks and sycamores with rich green leaves and birds singing in their branches. Bluebells and buttercups blanketed the forest floor and deer stepped gently between the bushes. It was as if the forest had sprung up in response to the light.

The first figure took on defined edges; a woman in shimmering white robes, long bronze curls cascading over her tanned shoulders, and her eyes blazing forest green. In her hands she held a golden bow, and beside her walked the beasts of the forest, deer, foxes, even a bear. The other figure towered to her right, the golden light spilling over Doon's antlers and broad shoulders.

At the edge of the forest they paused and beckoned. Issa and Asaph looked at each other then walked hesitantly towards them.

'That which was broken has now been made whole,' Woetala's voice was strong and vibrated powerfully through Issa. 'Now Maioria can heal. You have served her most honourably, Chosen of Zanufey and Chosen of Feygriene.' She nodded to Issa then Asaph in turn. 'For as you have come to understand, nothing exists in isolation and we—all the beings of the higher and lower realms—had to stand against darkness smothering us. We all had to choose.

'We made our choices and here we stand, in the light eternal. Those beings from Aralansia have returned to the light they so long worked for, finally freed of their tireless commission to help other planets and beings afflicted by the Dark Rift.

'Those who did not choose the light could no longer remain on Maioria's ascending planes. They have gone into the rift and other such places where they can live out their choices and the consequences of those choices. In the worlds of light, free will is always honoured.'

'Zanufey is gone?' Issa's voice sounded weak compared to the resonance of the goddess's. She feared to ask the question and was deeply saddened that Aralansia could not be saved, in the end.

Love and compassion emanated from Woetala. 'When the last of Aralansia was destroyed, its guardian Zanufey could no longer hold her presence here. She has returned to the One Light, but a part of her lives within you, for you and she are one. In time, you will relearn how to connect with the higher part of you, the part of you that *is* Zanufey. Indeed, you and

I and all of Maioria are one. We are *all* one in the higher realms—this you have seen.'

Issa nodded, tears filling her eyes as she remembered the wondrous light and fields of creation in which there was no this or that, just pure light, sound and intention.

'So, what do we do now?' Asaph shrugged.

Issa couldn't help herself and laughed. Woetala and Doon smiled.

'There is a new, wondrous world to explore, to protect, and to nourish,' Woetala said. 'You are reconnecting to what you really are – pure spirit, love and joy as it was in the old times. You, and all the beings of Maioria, are awakening to a new way of being, the old way of being that has so long been forgotten, so long been lost to you.

'No longer blocked by the Dark Rift, the pure light of the One can reach Maioria and her beings again, and so you will find many things have changed for the better. Age happens much more slowly, and some will not age at all. A few may even grow younger.

'There will be seasons, but they will not be so extreme, and neither will it be cold at the poles or sweltering in the arid deserts. Maioria has become a far gentler place and all lands share an agreeable climate.

'As it was in the past, so shall it be again, for it is the nature of things to return to that which they once were. You and Asaph in particular are relearning to be that which you are destined to be—Guardians. For that is what this is all about.'

'But how can we be Guardians? The magic is gone, I cannot feel it,' said Issa, feeling ashamed. 'I don't even have a talisman or an orb.' She hadn't tried properly, she was too afraid to, but despite the magic and life-force in everything, she could feel the Flow just wasn't there anymore.

Woetala nodded. 'Do not worry for the things that have passed, they are as toys – out-grown, out-lived. That which you call the Flow was only a fragment of the pure magic that now flows through all Maioria. You shall be guided but not told. Search for this magic with others. Together, learn its ways, and you will do incredible things.'

Woetala's smiled deepened. 'Now listen, another awakens…'

Woetala and Doon began to fade and the golden tunnel of light retreated back into the forest revealing a pathway. Along the pathway flew a large black bird.

'Ehka?' Issa whispered. She hadn't dared hope he might have survived the destruction of Maphrax.

Ehka cawed and landed on her shoulder. She pressed her cheek into him closing her eyes. 'I feared for you, so much. I could not bring myself to think you were dead.' He ruffled her hair with his beak.

'Look Issa, Sheyengetha!' said Asaph.

Now the light was gone she saw the soft glow of a blue trunk at the far end of the path. She stared at its beautiful canopy of rich green leaves standing taller than all the trees around it. Issa held her breath as the trunk glowed brighter, then a figure emerged out of it. Her hand went to her mouth as she stared at the tall man walking gracefully towards them. Ehka squawked and flew to him. The man laughed and held his arm up for the bird to land on.

'Averen!' Issa cried out. Tears fell down her cheeks and she ran to the elf.

He smiled and embraced her with his free arm. Asaph embraced them both in a bear hug and they all laughed.

'Easy now, I'm a little weak,' said the elf.

She looked up at him. His hair, once copper, gleamed white as did his eyes. He held her gaze and direct cognition passed between them, surprising them both. She saw the light reaching him and setting him free, but his soul and the soul of Sheyengetha had become melded in some way—a part of Sheyengetha lived within him, and a part of him lived within Sheyengetha.

'So it *is* true,' whispered Averen, his eyes wide. 'Telepathy returns to us, even between human and elf.'

Issa didn't know what to say, the elf was right. Everything the Wykiry had said to her she had received in her mind already, and with Asaph too. It had come so naturally she hadn't realised it had been different before, communication relying only on words. The Wykiry didn't need to speak, but they had wanted to use their voices for the first time in so long.

'It's really true,' said Asaph, his eyes widening. 'It's the same as when I speak with my dragon mind, I can *see* what you are saying.'

Issa looked at Averen. 'And I can *see* that you're no longer a High Wizard. You are beyond even a Master.' Even the terms sounded silly and pretentious now. 'You have knowledge of Tree Lore; I can *feel* it within you. This is something you must teach us.'

'That is right. I feel there are few things we'll be able to hide from each other, and perhaps that is a good thing. Sheyengetha and I have returned to bring the trees back to Maioria. That is my new purpose. New lands need new trees,' he laughed. 'And we must begin right away. Ah look, there they are, my brothers and sisters have returned to the land. They will bring life to new oceans.' He walked towards the Wykiry and made a graceful, sweeping bow.

The Wykiry spread their arms wide. 'Elf friend,' said the male, and in Issa's heart she felt the Wykiry's joy. 'There's one last thing we forgot to mention: to start anew, all menfolk have travelled to Drax to await the return of the Dawn Bringer and Raven Queen. The seers amongst them have foreseen it.'

Asaph laughed nervously.

'Then we should go there right away,' said Averen smoothing his pale green robes, and Issa realised his clothing was woven entirely of leaves. The elf clapped his hands together and smiled, bursting with energy and keen to get going.

CHAPTER 42

Reborn

ASAPH angled his wings and descended through the thick white clouds.

Issa watched the plane of green grass loom up to meet them. The golden dragon landed and set her and Averen gently down before resuming his human form.

She looked to the ruins of Draxa some distance ahead. The sky was only just brightening with the oncoming dawn, but she could make out some of the still-standing turrets in the low light.

'Knowing my home is still here holds some comfort,' Asaph said. He looked behind him at the enormous mountain range. 'There are the Grey Lords—but *all* the snow has melted.'

Issa looked back. Indeed, there wasn't even any ice or snow in the upper crevices.

'Spring fast approaches,' said Averen, smiling. 'I can feel the seeds laying expectant in the earth, the trees are eager to grow.'

'How long *have* we been sleeping?' asked Issa, shaking her head.

'It's been a long, long winter,' said Averen. 'Let's get to Draxa!' He started walking briskly along the path.

Issa and Asaph grinned at each other, then hurried after him. What would they find? Issa wondered as she hurried to keep pace with Averen's long stride. *Our friends will be there,* she hoped. Rhul'ynth, Naksu and Edarna. And some friends would not. She tried to think about only those she would see.

The dawn light grew, and with it the sounds of voices and human activity. They reached the top of a hill and paused to stare open-mouthed at the hive of activity going on below.

Where once a great battle had been fought, now was alive with reconstruction. Temporary wooden scaffolds surrounded and filled the city of Draxa, and people busily worked, even before dawn, to rebuild the fallen city. Pennants streamed in the breeze, the bright colours that had adorned the army now adorned the castle walls. Hammers rang on anvils, nails thumped into wood, people called for assistance and announced new supplies. Even a couple of dragons worked, moving giant stones, carrying great logs and setting them down wherever they were needed. Everybody was busy doing something.

Issa looked at Asaph and his expression matched her own. A neigh rang out from somewhere and people suddenly ran and fell out of the way of a black horse charging. The horse hurtled through the crowd dragging along a man only just managing to retain his desperate grip on to the rope around its neck.

'Duskar!' Issa squealed and ran to stop the horse. She followed it with 'Marakon!' when she realised it was the half-elf attached to the end of the rope.

'Well met, Raven Queen,' Marakon gasped and struggled to his feet. He bent over to catch his breath then straightened to catch her rough embrace.

'And Jarlain and Bokaard…and Eiretonne?' she asked.

'Don't worry, they're all here. We're all here,' he nodded then shook his head. 'Although, I'm seriously thinking about retiring now, that battle was…'

The sun burst over the horizon casting them all in golden light. Workers paused and closed their eyes, smiling as the much-needed warmth spread over the thawing landscape.

'The Dawn Bringer comes!' shouted someone, spotting them.

'The Raven Queen returns!' shouted another, and people turned to point at them.

If she'd thought the city was busy now, it was soon thronging with people, elves, dwarves, Karalanths, Draxians and dragons. The time for talking vanished as friends and onlookers surrounded them. Rhul'ynth gripped her shoulder, then Eiretonne hugged her. Naksu was suddenly before her, smiling, with Haelgon's arm over her shoulders, then Bokaard was slapping her on the back. Everyone embraced, everyone cried. Everyone was here.

Asaph was beset upon by five men she had only spoken to a handful of times. 'My Loyal Men,' she heard him say and grin from ear to ear.

Leaper was first—she recognised his tied back, long fair hair, but Asaph's Loyal Men were swiftly followed by hundreds of Draxians.

'Our King returns!' they shouted. 'The Dawn Bringer comes.' They cheered and laughed and many cried. Tears soon ran down Asaph's face too.

'We've been busy reconstructing the place,' Eiretonne winked at Issa when the crowd settled.

'I can see,' she said, still in awe of the activity going on here.

'Come and look,' said Marakon.

The crowd parted and they walked towards Draxa. Lining the road leading to the old, destroyed front gate were scores of new, unfinished statues, and dwarven stonemasons stood on ladders chiselling away at the smooth lumps of white-grey stone. Some of the statues already had faces and, now she was closer, she could see a couple of them were finished.

Marakon followed her gaze. 'It was decided that those who fought for Drax, and for all Maioria, should not be forgotten. They have become known as the Guardians of Draxa.'

The half-elf commander turned to Asaph and spoke hurriedly. 'We hope you don't mind us taking the initiative. However, it *was* an overwhelming, unanimous decision of the people, of the Draxian people. We knew you would return to us; we just didn't know when. We hoped it would be complete to welcome you…'

'It's perfect,' said Asaph, his eyes alight, as he walked towards the statues. 'This is not my city, nor my kingdom, it is ours and it belongs to everyone.'

Issa followed him. The statues were incredible with the tiniest detail, flick of hair, lift of robe in the wind, attended to and captured in stone. The dwarf working on the nearest one paused his polishing and pulled away the rest of the sheet to let them marvel.

'Beautiful,' said Issa.

A deep smile of pride spread across the dwarf's face.

Issa looked harder at the statue, at the bow and notched arrow held at his side, at his long hair and almond eyes looking far into the distance. Deep pain struck her heart making her gasp.

'Velonorian.' Tears blurred her vision. He looked so perfect, his eyes full of life and eagerness, as he had been in life.

If only you could see the new world now, my beautiful guardian. She reached up and stroked his foot, the only part she could reach from the ground. *Your people are free, Woetala has awoken. I did what you asked, what I promised.*

'We thought he should be first; the first Guardian, my Queen. Don't you like it?' asked the dwarf stonemason, his voice uncertain after her reaction.

'No, I mean, yes, it's perfect. I just wish he were here,' she whispered.

The dwarf's eyes sparkled. 'Aye, many have gone to the light… We haven't started on them yet, but the Trinity will be placed in the new gardens as a wondrous fountain such as you have never seen.'

'Yes, that would be a most fitting memorial,' said Issa, wiping back the tears. Then she shook her head. 'No, let it not be a memorial, but a celebration of life, of freedom. For that is what they lived and died for, so we could be free.'

'Yes, indeed,' said Asaph softly.

'As you wish, my Queen. No stone is beyond the skill of a dwarven stonemason,' the dwarf winked.

Issa looked at the statue opposite Velonorian on the other side of the road and the world stopped turning.

The dwarf, seeing her shock, coughed nervously. 'Well, the other statue…it's a little unconventional, and maybe you and King Asaph, Dragon Lord Dawn Bringer would like to rearrange them, a-hem. Their placements are not set in stone, so to speak…'

The dwarf's voice faded away as she stepped towards the other statue. Uncontrollable emotions rolled through her. This one was small, so small, it was the only completely finished one. There, at the start of the road to Drax, standing defiantly on his short stubby legs, his wings spread wide, unruly fang protruding over his lip, was Maggot. His stone image was perfect in every way as if someone had frozen him in time. There was even Jabber in his out-stretched hands as he fearlessly took on anyone who dared to invade the city of Drax. There was nothing she could think or say—she could only cry.

Thiashar appeared and buzzed softly around him. The green fairy light nestled at his feet and did not move.

Issa eventually became aware of Asaph's arms around her, and the voice who had brought her back from her sorrow.

'Issa,' the voice said softly again, weak but recognisable.

She lifted her face from Asaph's chest and he released her, his face a mask of pain too. Beside him, Marakon suffered his own grief as Jarlain wrapped her arms about him, tears on her cheeks, but it was none of them who had spoken.

'Freydel?' Issa wiped her eyes.

Her friends stepped aside. There, leaning on a simple wooden staff, stood Freydel. He had a stoop and grey covered his beard and hair, but his eyes were alive and they were filled with peace. He walked towards her, aided heavily by his staff, everything passing between in the gaze that they held. She embraced her old tutor. He had returned to them.

'I saw you broken and alone,' she whispered. 'Just as I have been broken and alone. Ayeth came for me, Freydel. Through me he reached Baelthrom.'

'I know,' he said gently. 'In the last moments, he reached for me also. He gifted me a vision to ease my soul before he said goodbye.'

'Everything you did was true,' Issa nodded. 'The magic is not gone, Freydel. It has been reborn anew. Together we will learn its ways.'

'Found him naked and gibbering in a cave, I did,' said a familiar voice.

Edarna stepped from behind Freydel. Issa laughed and hugged the beaming witch.

'Praise the goddess you did,' said Issa.

A great wind gusted around them and a trembling in her stomach made her look up. On wings the colour of blue ice, flew Morhork, and she did a double take at the dragon harness on his back. There was dragon fear, but not the gut-wrenching, heart-stopping fear of old. At least her legs did not give way.

Issa stared at the dragon as it landed. Morhork's paw was no longer black, and his wings were clearly not magic holograms, but living flesh and blood.

'All things have been healed,' said Issa, coming to a stop before him.

Morhork blinked his golden eyes and dipped his head reverently. 'By the grace of Feygriene, I have earned back my wings.'

There was something different about him, a gentleness that hadn't been there before, and could that even be compassion in his eyes? Issa could but wonder as the dragon lay down and not one, but three beings stepped out of the dragon harness, two Saurians and an old man.

Issa gasped. 'Father!' She ran to help the blindfolded man as Ekem and Ata assisted him down the dragon's leg.

'My Issalena,' the old man laughed, stretching out his hands to find her.

She grabbed hold of them and kissed them. In her father's arms, all the sadness of the world vanished. For a long time, they held each other, saying nothing, feeling everything.

'Oh, Father,' Issa said, trying to hold back the tears that would not stop falling. 'Your daughter, my sister is gone. I tried to save, I tried to reach her, but I could not hold on to her. She was the third Raven Queen. Father, I did not know.'

'Shhh,' Thanon said, stroking her hair and rocking her as if she were a child. 'I saw them both, they came to me to say goodbye. Eritara told me to tell you not to cry, for where they have gone there is nothing but joy and light.'

Issa tried to be strong and wiped away the tears her mother asked her not to shed.

'Blessed Woetala set her spirit free,' said her father. 'Our beloved goddess has awoken and now all is set right, all is made whole. Eritara and my baby's spirit are free, so you must not cry for them.'

'I will try,' Issa swallowed hard.

'She said something more, something very specific. She said your grandmother, Belledyn, managed to negotiate a small gift—a settling of unresolved issues, so she put it—and that you needn't grieve anymore. She said you would know this gift when it happened, and you will know joy again.'

Issa looked up at her father, but his expression was mostly hidden behind his blindfold.

'In all these years I've been without her, now I can find joy in her passing,' he whispered.

Issa nodded, allowing a little joyous lightness in. She wiped her cheeks and composed herself as she turned to Ekem and Ata, trying to be the Raven Queen they knew her to be.

'You fought most nobly, and it gladdens me greatly to see your race still with us,' said Issa, feeling it from the bottom of her heart.

The Saurians dipped their heads respectfully. 'As did you humans. We're honoured to have fought beside you for the good of all. We come with a message from great Hallanstaryx. A pact has been sealed between us in the shared blood we shed in battle. The Saurians are ready to begin new relations with your race on better, equal terms.

'Our numbers are few, but the Oracle has seen our future, and for the first time in millennia it is a prosperous one. She knew you would bring the war to us and in you she saw the end of endings—but there was the smallest chance of surviving. Should we survive, a new world unlike anything else before it would unfold. Her visions have not been wrong.'

Issa remembered everything the snake queen had said to her which was then echoed by Woetala. *The end of endings. It's cryptic, as goddesses are wont to be, but does she mean we will not die?* It was too much to grasp, too much to believe. She shook her head.

'Then let us enjoy a world unlike any before it,' Issa smiled, not knowing what else to say.

'That would please our Oracle very much,' said Ata. 'We hope you will visit us. Our lands appear to be flourishing in ways we had not foreseen. It is already quite beautiful.'

'I promise I will come one day soon,' said Issa.

The Saurians turned and bowed to Morhork before they climbed up the dragon's back into the harness.

'I never thought you'd wear one of those,' said Issa.

Morhork snorted and scowled, showing a little of his old self. 'It was a last resort. Dragons and Saurians are making alliances, and the seat needs modifying for them.'

Issa chuckled and Asaph rubbed his chin to hide his smile. Morhork turned and leapt into the air, beating his new, powerful wings.

'What is it, Wekurd?'

Gedrock tore his eyes away from his shimmering hands and arms that he held in front of his face. His skin had changed, becoming lighter and shimmering like silver. All of the Shadow Demons and Grazens' skin had changed, though the Grazen had become more bronze in tone. They had done nothing to cause it and could do nothing to stop it.

Gedrock felt less rage too. He wondered, worrisomely, if it were his age; but then why would he be stronger and faster than before? The changes had started when the terrible light blasted them on the surface of Maioria. The changes were deeply worrying.

'You'd better come and look, Sire,' Wekurd said, a strange tone in his voice. He gripped his staff and his eyes blinked continuously.

'What's happened now, Zorock blind it?' cursed Gedrock.

Wekurd continued. 'A new demon has been dug up, unlike any we've seen before. It's only small, but…'

Gedrock huffed and pulled himself away from the green crystal. Wekurd led him down into the lowest tunnels where the new demon had been dug out. Demon workers stepped back to let him pass. Their eyes were lowered and this worried Gedrock some more.

He stared down at the fresh little thing squirming and gurgling in the mud. One of the diggers hurled muddy water on it, making it laugh and squirm all the more. When the water stopped, the demon wailed and screamed.

Gedrock's eyes blazed as he looked at the demon's shimmering skin unlike any demon he had seen before. 'Zorock curse us to the Pit, it's blue! No demon is blue! We have been damned by Carmedrak himself!'

'As blue as that moon we saw,' nodded Wekurd, saying things Gedrock really did not want to hear.

Gedrock stared closely at the squirming demon, noting many things about it he did not want to see.

Reluctantly he reached for it and picked it up. The little demon giggled at him, his gold eyes wide. Without saying anything, Gedrock whirled away and stalked back to the green crystal.

'My King, what do we do?' Wekurd asked, hurrying after him. It was worrying when his advisor asked him what should be done.

'To the crystal, Wekurd, where we'll demand audience with the Raven Queen.'

He had been worrying about speaking to her since the painful light had forced them to flee the battlefield. Demons did not worry, they never worried. Something very strange was happening to them.

On a snowy, secluded outlook west of Drax, Issa stood with Asaph and Ehka watching the first sunset of the new world sinking into the horizon.

It was cold, but the wind had dropped and the air was fresh and pure. Asaph stood behind her with his arms wrapped around her shoulders.

'You're right, the sun is definitely bigger than before,' Issa agreed. It was whiter too, at least when it was high in the sky. At this moment, it was a glorious blaze of oranges, pinks, and even purples.

'Just look at that,' said Asaph, marvelling at the beauty. 'It's nice to get away from the city. It's only been a day and I can't stand the sound of another hammer. Don't get me wrong, I love being home, and this beautiful country, but there's just so much to do, and there's rubble everywhere! I'm so glad Coronos left those infinity stones, I just hope I don't spend them all at once.'

Issa giggled. 'You could rebuild every city on Maioria with just one of them. And don't worry, Freydel and Navarr are most wise and will always give you sound guidance. Anyway, I sense a world of great abundance and imagine no one going without. How could they in this beautiful new world?'

'Then let us make it so,' said Asaph seriously, kissing the top of her head.

'But,' she added firmly, 'if Drax is to be our home, I want another one somewhere hot! Spring may be coming in the new world and all, but…I insist!'

'Yes, my Queen,' Asaph laughed. After a moment he sighed. 'But it's, hmm, it's just that I…Do you remember when it was just you and me and Coronos? When we sat around the campfire with only our swords and our cloaks and the night sky above? I miss that—the freedom. I could never be a king sat inside on his throne.'

'I want freedom too,' Issa agreed. *Choose freedom.* The voice echoed in her head. 'And I do remember it well; they're moments and memories I'll cherish forever but you're never prying me away from my bath again, and I'll only ever sleep outside if it's on a proper bed.' Issa spoke firmly, making sure she was understood clearly.

'Yes, my Queen,' said Asaph, squeezing her tighter.

'But,' she added, 'there *is* a whole world out there to explore. Imagine if we found a place like Celene. We could build our own house together.' With a pang of emotion, she remembered all that she had envisioned and longed for so long ago when she had made Celene her short-lived home.

She smoothed back an errant hair, and as she did so the demon crystal in her grandmother's ring flashed. She inspected it and it flashed again and was followed by Gedrock's voice in her head making her jump. He sounded oddly…*worried.*

'Raven Queen, great changes are occurring.'

'What is it?' asked Asaph as she pulled away and stared at her ring.

'It's the demons, it's Gedrock. I can *hear* him.' She closed her eyes and saw the green crystal shard and Gedrock's huge eyes beyond it. He looked different, his skin was lighter and shimmering and he looked younger, his features softer.

She replied aloud, 'Yes, there's so much happening, and much has changed.'

'No, there is something very strange happening here, you need to see it,' Gedrock growled, a deep frown creasing his brow into rolls of flesh.

'What do you mean?' Issa asked.

Gedrock lifted up a small, squirming, ugly demon with skin the colour of indigo, the colour of the dark moon. It opened its golden eyes and wailed.

Issa stared then gasped and stared some more, her heart pounding in her ears. Could it really be? Its features were unmistakable; its ears, its pot-belly, its one protruding tooth…Everything was the same, everything except that it was blue!

"You will know joy again," her father's voice echoed in her mind.

Barely able to breath, Issa said, 'Maggot?'

The blue demon instantly stopped wriggling. It blinked and opened its eyes wider as it saw her face in the crystal. Grinning from ear to ear, and in that unforgettable voice, he squealed, 'Issy!'

CHAPTER 43

Becoming Guardians

ASAPH let out a satisfied sigh as he lay down beside Issa.

Their small bedroom was one of the few remaining clean and whole chambers located high up in Castle Draxa. She was already asleep, so he restrained his desire to kiss and cuddle her.

Every inhabitable room and corner of the castle was filled with people from all over Maioria come to build the first city of the new world. With this many people, the entire castle, city and beyond would be rebuilt within a month, and for most of them it was a labour of love and being done without monetary payment.

He did not intend such labour to go unrewarded—far from it. All would receive something for their hard work and there was plenty of land available to give.

He nestled deeper under the cover thinking over how he would rebuild this magnificent country when a golden light grew. He stared at the light as it hovered beyond the bed. It filled him with warmth, and something more—love and contentment. The presence became a being with thought and conscience, and a face formed in the light.

'Feygriene,' Asaph said, dropping his gaze as she shone a brighter beautiful light.

'Dawn Bringer,' her harmonious voice echoed around him.

'I feel a contentment I've never known before,' he said. 'I'm home, after so long, and I feel I have fulfilled my purpose.'

The face made of golden light smiled and joy filled his heart. 'You will rest, for a time, and then your spirit will seek something new to accomplish. You would do well to think about your future journey and what you would like to do.'

Asaph nodded. He needed rest—maybe for an eternity—but his adventurous spirit would not stay still for too long. 'I will, my goddess, what is it you would like me to do?'

Laughter tinkled all around him and he smiled, feeling a little foolish.

Feygriene said, 'It's time for you to choose. After all, you have ever been in charge of your own destiny. Even the One Source of All can only guide.'

'Then I shall think on it, my goddess,' he said and bowed his head reverently.

The light began to recede, and he had a second thought. 'No, beloved Feygriene, I already know that which I desire most.' The golden light returned, and Asaph continued, 'I would like to bring the Dragon Lords back. No, I *must* bring them back. Man and dragon can find peace and harmony in each other. We can grow and learn together.'

'You have learnt so much, Asaph Dawn Bringer, and grown wise in your experiences. You have all the power within you to regenerate the Dragon Lords upon Maioria. Speak it and it shall be so.'

Asaph relaxed, relieved, then realised the light was waiting for him to say something. 'Oh, um, well, I had given it some thought, but I've not fully worked it out. So, uh, how about something like this? Twelve born with a mark, uh, a mark of the sun? Yes, let it be the sun, let it be you, beloved Feygriene. Those with the mark shall feel a need to come to me. When they do, I'll instil within them the knowledge of the Dragon Lords that I alone hold, somehow. I'm not sure how this will happen. From them, other Dragon Lords will arise.'

'So be it, Asaph Dawn Bringer, First of the Dragon Lords,' said Feygriene. 'May the sword be with you. Always.'

A new sense of purpose filled Asaph as he lay back down in the fading light.

'Maion'artheria,' a soft voice whispered, rousing Issa from her deep and peaceful sleep.

She opened her eyes. Asaph slept soundly beside her, his hand warm on her shoulder. It was very dark, and it must be late for not even embers burned in the hearth.

Beautiful white and golden light fell from—or rather through—the stone ceiling. It glimmered gently and wavered like ribbons, a golden borealis filling the room. It touched her cheek, bringing warmth.

'Maion'artheria,' the voice repeated, closer, inside the room.

'My Goddess,' whispered Issa as feelings of love and peace rolled over her.

Figures appeared in the ribbons of light dancing at the end of the bed, too bright to see any distinct features. Issa sensed that she should go to them. She swung her legs out of bed and walked into the light.

Warm, shimmering fields of light and sound energy surrounded her.

She realised the subtly different shades of light each had consciousness, and each shade was a being, yet all the shades made up the one being. The sound was music, like bells but much softer, like nothing else she had ever heard. The harmony was so rapturously resplendent, no instrument or voice on Maioria could possibly recreate it. She wanted to cry with joy just listening to it, and she wished she could capture a piece, so she could take it to Asaph to hear it.

It feels like home, she realised, *real home.* This beautiful place of belonging and contentment had existed, and would exist, for all eternity and she cried for the wonder of returning to it.

The figures of light were now too numerous to count. They did not speak but they were sending her feelings of joy and gratitude. Issa understood that they were grateful to her for helping them to come home, though she did not quite understand why.

A figure stepped closer, its light lessening and its form condensing until it was the same height as Issa and she could look upon it without squinting. She sensed the being did this for her benefit. A face formed, one of a perfect smooth chin and lips. *Zanufey,* Issa realised.

Beautiful indigo eyes beheld her, and for a moment Issa was reminded of her mother, and then she was reminded of herself. The face was hers, but in its perfected form. Light suddenly flared from her eyes, so pure, Issa fell back with a gasp. Intelligence, benevolence, and rapture – she felt all at once. *It is the One Light of the Source of All!* she realised what she looked into.

Gentle power flowed into Issa. Lifting her hands, she saw her skin glowed indigo blue, *like it did when I was a child!*

'I feel you within me,' Issa whispered, trying to wrap words around the purity she was feeling.

The light calmed, and she looked again upon Zanufey. The goddess reached a hand forward and caressed Issa's cheek. 'The light has always been within you. You and I are one, and now the physical body is purer, the spirit can connect more.'

'Who are the others?' Issa nodded to the figures, and instant cognition gave her the answers.

'Aralans,' she whispered.

Zanufey smiled. 'They are the Aralans you set free from the mortal planes. When the last Star Portal of Aralansia was destroyed, they became trapped. You became the last gate, the last portal home.'

'I am a portal?' Issa frowned.

'All human beings are portals, gateways in themselves. How else do you think spirit takes physical form?'

Issa took a sharp breath. 'Ayeth...' The understanding of what had occurred between Baelthrom and Ayeth within the Dark Rift struck her.

Zanufey nodded. 'Yes, in those last moments, Ayeth was able to reach his fallen self through you. You are the gateway between two worlds, and you always have been. Baelthrom knew the danger you possessed to unravel his plans so innocently.'

'Did I save Ayeth?' It was too hopeful to ask. She longed to save the kind, intelligent and powerful being.

'No being can save another, only they can save themselves,' said Zanufey. 'But we may assist. Without you, Ayeth could not have reached his Baelthrom self in Maioria. Without the destruction of the last remnants of Aralansia, the dark moon, it could not be done either. Without just one of us travelling through the physical planes of time and space, all the remaining Aralans would have been trapped in time since the cataclysm. You were that noble spirit.'

Issa felt faint at the monumentality of all that had occurred. Memories of everything she had decided to do before her current lifetime came through in overwhelming waves. Thoughts, feelings, ideas, too grand for her small physical self to comprehend.

'But why did I not know? Why didn't I remember?' Issa asked.

'You did know, your soul has always known, but it is the physical being who forgets,' said Zanufey gently. 'All beings coming to Maioria since Baelthrom arrived can no longer retain their conscious connection to spirit—it is there but forgotten, hidden behind a veil. You always knew you would forget why you came and all that you were before, and perhaps that is a good thing, otherwise, things may not have gone this way.

'There are many timelines and many outcomes. Nothing is predetermined in the way you might think it. Always look to the spirit for guidance for it is that which guides the incarnate, though the incarnate always has—'

'Free will choice,' Issa finished. 'To forget yourself, and then to remember…It's like being given a gift, the greatest gift, knowing who you are.'

Zanufey nodded. 'In assisting others, the self is helping itself. You of Aralansia might also have become trapped in the Lower Realms, had you failed.'

Issa swallowed and imagined being stuck here with Baelthrom. Death was better. 'It's just not how I imagined things might have gone. In the Dark Rift and beyond, I saw that it wasn't just Maioria, the darkness affected other worlds and realms far beyond here.'

'Yes, all beings of light were called to assist, and that was what you witnessed,' said Zanufey. 'Maioria is the centre point where the final outcome was decided.'

'And Ayeth? Where is he now?' asked Issa quietly.

'He has gone to the Lower Realms where he can begin a long healing process. He must heal the part of him that became Baelthrom, and to do that he must descend to where his vibration matches that of a place to incarnate. If one chooses other than the light, then seeks to return to the light, this is how it happens.'

'It's a brave soul who chooses other than the light,' Issa shook her head in awe. How brave were those warriors who dared to go into the darkness? 'Can he be helped?' she added.

'Always there is help and guidance for a soul asking for it,' Zanufey smiled.

Issa sighed, feeling relieved. 'None of us are ever lost.'

'No, but we can *choose* to be,' said Zanufey. 'Now comes the time for you and your current race, and all Maioria to heal. The dark energy has been cleansed from her planes, and old lands have gone whilst even older lands from eons ago have arisen as Maioria ascends to her pure form.

'Now is a time for rebuilding and learning about the purer magic that pulses through your world. Use the power of your precreative force to create things anew and teach others the gift. Write down all that you have seen and witnessed. Become the scribe, the historian, and teach it. Think it, write it, speak it, be it. When you feel you have done all that you can do, we will speak again.'

'What happens after I have written it down?' Issa asked. If she had an assignment, as she saw it, she was keen to know about it this minute.

Zanufey laughed—a sound like the low notes of a harp. 'In the realms of physical matter, there are always beings and planets requiring assistance. Think on this if you wish: if you were to save a world so fallen its magic had gone completely, how would you help it?'

Issa frowned and rubbed her chin. 'Hmm, it's not so easy when you say it like that. Hmm, perhaps, it sounds silly, but perhaps I'd give them a relic, like the raven talisman or maybe a sword with special powers—like Velistor, Staff of the Gate. Yes, that's it! I'd give them something with the power to open the gates to higher dimensions, where help may come through as needed.' Issa laughed nervously, it sounded foolish saying it out loud, but how did one save a falling planet?

Zanufey smiled. 'Thinking on how to help is the first step, you're fast becoming a noble Guardian and Way Shower. When you're ready, there are many beings who need such help, but for now, healing the self is most important.'

Issa yawned, the higher frequencies of the light were swiftly tiring her, and the light began to fade along with the figures within it. Issa closed her eyes just to hear the resplendent music one last time before it faded away completely.

Rather than the empty, lonely feeling she experienced whenever Zanufey left, she was filled with energy and joy, and something else, a keen desire to help those worlds Zanufey spoke of. *Not yet, I must heal myself and help Maioria and her people first.* There was a whole new world out there to explore, and fantastic new magics to discover.

Chewing her lip, Issa held up her hands. Did she dare try? What if she felt nothing? *What harm can trying do?* Someone had to be the first... She reached for the Flow. There was nothing, nothing responded, it wasn't there...

She let go and was about to drop her hands, and then she felt *something*. She realised she had always found the Flow in her head, but she felt this *something* deep within her chest, above her heart and in the middle of her body. It was where she felt joy and excitement.

She focused on that feeling and brought it forth—it felt like tiny bubbles flowing from her chest into her fingers. Letting her breath go, she pushed it out. Sparkling light burst out of her palms and into the chamber swiftly filling it. It bounced and refracted off everything, humming and thronging so loudly every object in the room vibrated with increasing frequency. A half-drunk wine bottle from the previous evening jostled off the cabinet and smashed on the floor, followed by the two glasses, the windows rattled and the floor rumbled.

Ehka, who had been roosting in the rafters, left his perch and squawked madly as he flew around the room.

Asaph bolted upright in bed, clutched the sheets and stared wildly at the dancing light and the bird dodging it.

Issa laughed hysterically at the shock on his face as the power continued to flood from her fingers. With quite an effort she let go of the power coursing through her and jumped onto the bed.

'It's back. It's back!' she squealed.

Asaph started to laugh as she jumped around him. 'The light save us,' he sighed. 'Why do I feel the adventure has only just begun?'

An new Epic begins…

FARSEEKER

JOANNA STARR

ALSO BY ARAYA EVERMORE

The Goddess Prophecies series:

Goddess Awakening ~ A Prequel

When darkness falls, a heroine will rise.
The Dread Dragons came with the dawn. On dark wings of death they slaughtered every seer and turned their sacred lands to ruin…

Night Goddess ~ Book 1

A world plunging into darkness. An exiled Dragon Lord struggling with his destiny. A young woman terrified of an ancient prophecy she has set in motion.
He came through the Dark Rift hunting for those who had escaped his wrath. Unchecked, his evil spread. Now, the world hangs on a knife-edge and all seems destined to fall. But when the dark moon rises, a goddess awakens, and nothing can stop the prophecy unfolding…

The Fall of Celene ~ Book 2

Impossible Odds, Terrifying Powers
"My name is Issa and I am hunted. I hold a power that I neither understand nor can barely control…"
The battle for Maioria has begun. Issa faces a deadly enemy as the Immortal Lord's attention turns fully in her direction. Nothing will stand in Baelthrom's way—he must destroy this new power that grows with the rising dark moon…

Storm Holt ~ Book 3

Would you sell your soul to save the world?

The Storm Holt... The ultimate Wizard's Reckoning, where all who enter must face their greatest demons. No woman has entered and survived since the Ancients split the magic apart eons ago. Plagued by demons and visions of a strange white spear, Issa must take the Reckoning to find her answers and fight for her soul to prove her worth to the most powerful magic wielders upon Maioria...

Demon Spear ~ Book 4

Demons. Death. Deliverance.

All these Issa must face as darkness strikes into the heart of their last stronghold. Greater demons are rising from the Pit, Carvon is brutally attacked, and a horrifying murder forces Issa and her companions to flee. But despite the devastating loss, she must keep her oath to the Shadow Demons and alone reclaim the spear that can save them all...

Dragons of the Dawn Bringer ~ Book 5

An Exiled King. A Broken Dream. A Sword Forged for Forever.

Issa can trust no one. Her closest allies betray her and nobody is as they seem. When a Dromoorai captures her and a black vortex to another dimension rips into her room, she realises the attacks will never stop and there is far worse than Baelthrom reaching for her out of the Dark Rift...

War of the Raven Queen ~ Book 6

"Be the light unto the darkness…Be the last light in a falling world."
They had both been chosen: he to save another race; she to save her own from what he had become. Now, both must enter Oblivion and therein decide the fate of all…

BOOKS BY JOANNA STARR

Farseeker

Enlightened. Enslaved. Erased.
Earth, 50,000 years ago before the magic vanished. Invaded by aliens posing as gods, advanced civilisations crumbled. Now, these powerful off-worlders war for control of the planet, and the people who remain no longer remember what they once were. Seduced then enslaved, humanity has fallen…

Free Starter Library

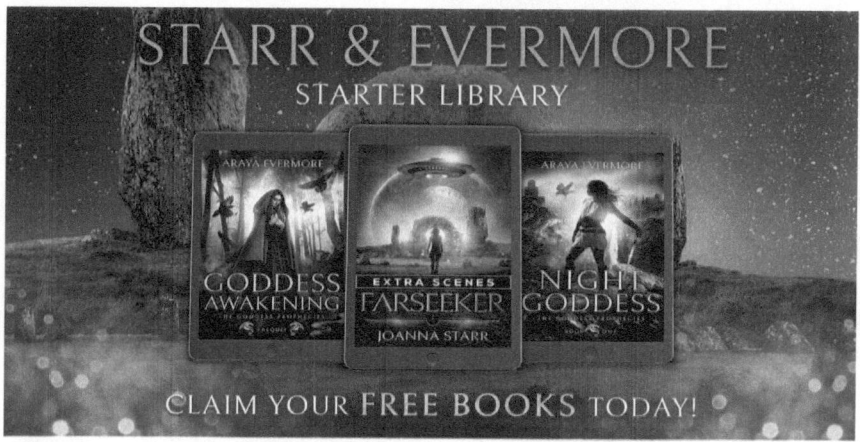

Join the mailing list and get your FREE Starr & Evermore Starter Library available only to subscribers. You'll discover Issa's origin story in my prequel, *Goddess Awakening*, which is not available anywhere else. You'll also get a taster of my latest *Farseeker* series with extra scenes not included in the main story.

To receive this epic free gift, please go to my website below. As a subscriber, you'll also be the first to hear about my latest novels, and lots more exclusive content.

www.joannastarr.com

About the Author

Araya Evermore is the pen name of Joanna Starr - a half-elf and author of the best-selling epic fantasy series, *The Goddess Prophecies*.

Joanna has been exploring other worlds and writing fantasy stories ever since she came to Planet Earth. Finding herself struggling in a world in which she didn't quite fit, escaping into fantasy novels gave her the magic and wonder she craved. Despite majoring in Philosophy & Religion, then Computer Science, she left her career in The City to return to her first love; writing Epic Fantasy.

Originally from the West Country, she's been travelling the world since 2011, and has been on the road so long she no longer comes from any place in particular. So far, she's resided in the Caribbean, United States, Canada, Australia, New Zealand, Spain, Andorra and Malta. Despite loving the mountains, she's actually a sea-based creature and currently resides by the ocean in Ireland.

Aside from writing and working, she spends time talking to trees, swimming with fish, gaming, and playing with swords.

Connect with Joanna online:
www.joannastarr.com
author@joannastarr.com

Enjoyed this book? You can make a big difference...

If you love fantasy books and would like to bring this series to the attention of other fantasy readers, the best thing you can do to reach them is to leave a review.

If you've enjoyed this book I would be very grateful if you could spend just a minute leaving a review, (it can be as long or as short as you like) on the book's Amazon page.

A heartfelt Thank You in advance.